THE LOVE OF A LIFETIME

From the moment Elizabeth Nugent arrives to live on Richard Wilde's family's farm in Shropshire, he is in love with her. And as they grow up, it seems like nothing can keep them apart. But as the Second World War rages, Richard is sent to fight in the jungles of Burma, leaving Elizabeth to deal with a terrible secret that could destroy his family. Despite the distance between them, Richard and Elizabeth's love remains constant through war, tragedy and betrayal. But once the fighting is over, will the secrets and lies that Elizabeth has been hiding keep them apart for ever?

THE LOVE OF A LIFETIME

THE LOVE OF A LIFETIME

by

Mary Fitzgerald

Magna Large Print Books
Long Preston, North Yorkshire,
BD23 4ND, England.

British Library Cataloguing in Publication Data.

Fitzgerald, Mary
The love of a lifetime.

A catalogue record of this book is
available from the British Library

ISBN   978-0-7505-3918-0

First published in Great Britain in 2013 by Arrow Books

Copyright © Mary Fitzgerald 2011

Cover illustration © Lee Avison by arrangement with
Arcangel Images

Mary Fitzgerald has asserted her right under the Copyright, Designs
and Patents Act, 1988 to be identified as the author of this work

Published in Large Print 2014 by arrangement with
Random House Group Ltd.

Magna Large Print is an imprint of Library Magna Books Ltd.

Printed and bound in Great Britain by
T.J. (International) Ltd., Cornwall, PL28 8RW

Chapter One

I've just come from the doctor's surgery where my death sentence has been read out. The intervening time between judgement and last breath might be longer than the judicial three weeks that a murderer used to get, but I know that there is no chance of an appeal.

'You've had a good innings, Mr Wilde,' said the doctor, folding up the letter from the hospital and putting it away in its small, brown envelope.

'I know,' I growled. Of course I know. I'm old and sick. And I'd been the one insistent that he tell me the truth. But I didn't want to hear it. Who would?

'We can arrange help for you. At home or perhaps...' He paused. 'You might consider residential care?'

I didn't waste any time on that. 'No.' I got up from the uncomfortable plastic chair and headed for the door. 'Good afternoon, doctor.'

Sitting in the back of the taxi on the way home while the winter rain rattled against the windscreen, I thought about the short time that I have left. How to use it, how to fill the two or three months before I become hopelessly dependent and have to be hospitalised.

My first thought was to get away. I could return to India. Live out my last days in a country I have loved almost better than my own.

9

To die in India wouldn't be so bad. It would be a quiet death. Without fuss. And after, my body could lie on a wooden bier, garlanded in pale blue smoke as a simple fire crackled beneath. Perhaps my soul would fly away across some holy river to a new life. No bother or commotion; I would be merely another old man who had lived beyond his allotted time.

It's tempting.

But I know it cannot be. I have one last duty to perform, a duty that through reticence and cowardice I have baulked from fulfilling. I have to explain what happened. Tell all the dreadful secrets that have festered in my heart and in my head for so many years. They've lessened me, I know that, when I could have been so different.

But, fair play, those secrets were not mine to tell. I kept them for the family. For our respectability, even when the best of us, and the worst, had gone. And soon I'll be gone too and the Wildes of Manor Farm will become a fading memory and I can't allow that. Not without telling how things were and how they should never have been.

I have more paper than this blue writing pad. On the table in front of me is a pile of unused desk diaries, gifts from a feed company I ceased to patronise years ago. They'll do; a wealth of unused pages ready for me to fill. What does it matter if I scribble over the dates? I can fill them with my memories.

Outside, the rain has changed to snow, muffling all sound, and I am alone in my kitchen in the early twilight. My kitchen; this dear room where once, long ago, I fell in love with a girl in a ragged

10

blue dress.

I was born in the snowy week before Christmas in the year of 1905, the youngest child of three. Marian, who was then eleven, always said that particular Christmas was the most memorable of her life. She never went so far as to say that her witness of my birth put her off childbearing, but maybe it was so. Albert Baker hinted more than once, always jokingly, that she'd been turned against men by her brothers and one in particular. I assumed that he meant me.

I sometimes wondered about the gap between Marian and us boys but I found out later that there had been three other babies who'd died. At first I only knew about the twins, but then, from family gossip, I heard about another one. It seems that a baby boy, who was baptised Philip, had been born the year before my sister, but lived for only a week. Granny whispered that he'd been sickly from the second he drew his first shallow breath and that it was a blessing that he'd been taken. Mother never said anything about him but she did talk about the twins, Maude and Leticia, who had lived into their third year. Diphtheria took them quite suddenly, one after the other on a February weekend when the doctor was busy with the dying babies in the slums by the abattoir. Their little clothes had been burnt and their rag dollies too, in case of germs, so there was nothing left to say that they'd been alive, except for the photograph of two solemn-looking little girls which Mother kept in a silver frame adorned with a black velvet bow on her dressing table.

My father was a farmer. The best in the district we always believed, and probably rightly so, for our milk and our cattle were the most sought after at the local market. Mother and Father worked hard, he in the fields and she in the dairy. Manor Farm butter and cheeses had a good reputation and Mother was always determined to keep it.

In the early days they had little help, only Herbert Lowe, an old soldier who had been on the farm before Father had taken the tenancy, and Eddie Hyde, who was about fifteen years old when I was born. He lived with us because his mother was in the asylum and hadn't been able to care for him since he'd been a baby. To Mother's surprise, Father had taken him on straight from the orphanage, on his thirteenth birthday. Who his father was no bugger knew, certainly not Eddie, because even if his mother had ever known she wouldn't have been able to tell him.

'He's strong and will work hard,' Father had said and Mother had agreed, although I don't think she liked Eddie much. Whenever people asked about him she would merely shake her head and talk about his poor mother.

'Some men can be that wicked,' she would say, 'taking advantage of a simple soul like Agnes Hyde.'

On the day I was born, Father had bought a new horse. It was a gelding, a big raw-boned creature, ugly as sin, but a gentleman in his way. Father had bought him cheap from the Major, our local aristocrat, after the latter had been yet again embarrassed at cards and short of the readies. My father had no time for the Major. In Father's opinion, and in that of most of the village, the man was a wastrel and a disgrace to the family name.

But the horse, Peter, was a good 'un. In later years, as a teenager, I rode him often and didn't have a moment's trouble, and I was never the brave one with horses. Not like our Billy. He would get up on anything.

'See the horsey!' two-year-old Billy had roared when Father brought the gelding into the yard and Mother, heavily pregnant with me, had carried him out to see the newest purchase.

'Stroke nose!' was the next demand but, reaching forward, Mother slipped on the icy cobbles and fell.

What a to-do. Mother had broken her leg and gone into labour and, according to Marian, Billy had screamed the place down because he'd bumped his head.

Father sent to the village for Dr Guthrie and Granny, but the snow had turned heavy and was sweeping through the valley and it took the doctor more than two hours to reach our farm. By that time, I'd arrived, assisted into the world by Father and Marian, so apart from putting a splint on Mother's leg old Guthrie didn't have much to do and cleared off home as soon as he was able. Granny sent word saying that she'd leave it till the morning when it would be daylight and perhaps a thaw would have set in.

The thaw didn't set in for another five days and it took that long for Granny to move her bones a mile up the road to visit her new grandson. That, of course, was Christmas Day and she wasn't going to miss her gift. I don't think much love was lost between Mother and Granny, who was Father's mother.

'I had to drag you out of Mother when you were born,' said Marian, her mouth curling in disgust, 'and you were all covered in blood and slime. It was horrible.'

'Tell us, tell us more,' Billy and I would plead, inquisitive and repulsed at the same time the way schoolboys always are when talking about sex things. But she would never say, and even though I witnessed many calvings and farrowings and even helped my dog to deliver her pups when I was a lad of about twelve, I could never think of a woman, particularly Mother, having parts like that.

The next morning Father trudged through the snow to the village to tell Granny about my arrival and Mother's accident but she wouldn't come and help.

'The eldest Parry girl needs a job,' she'd said. 'She'll do as a farm servant for a few months until Mary Constance can get about properly again.'

'You were a puny thing, long and weedy, a real runt, with an ugly red face and even uglier red hairs,' Marian continued. 'The doctor said you'd better be named pretty quick in case you died, so when Father went to tell Granny he brought the vicar back with him as well as Mabel Parry.

'Mother lifted you out of the crib and stared at you. "He's to be called Richard," she said, which surprised Father, because there hadn't been a Richard in the family before. "After my younger brother,", she added, "the one that died in the war. He had red hair.'"

'Well,' Father had said, 'I'm glad some bugger we know had red hair, because there's never been any on my side. All dark, we are. Mother will take a fit when she sees him.'

'I dare say,' said Mother, 'but she'd take a fit if the cat had kittens.'

'Richard,' repeated Father, 'Richard Wilde. Not bad, I reckon.'

The end of the story about my birth was quite sad. Although I was supposed to be weakly and likely to die, I thrived, and Mother recovered from the birth and the broken leg very well, although she did walk with a slight limp when the weather was cold. But Mabel Parry was got in the family way within a year of being at the farm and was sent away in disgrace. The father wasn't known, at least she wouldn't say, and Father had to pay her mother some money, because it had happened while she was living here. Poor Mabel died giving birth, but the baby survived, a little girl, Jane, who was in the class below me at school. I remember her well.

Chapter Two

This old place hasn't changed much over the years. Improved, certainly, for it had been standing longer than two centuries when Father took over and must have needed renovation, which he did, after a fashion. Billy was keen to keep it well maintained, and when he was in charge made sure that the buildings were always in tip-top shape. I did my share in later years, putting in more bathrooms and central heating. But the land has mostly gone now, only a few dozen acres left, the home field and the remains of Mother's orchard.

In Father's time, our farm extended to over three hundred and fifty acres of Shropshire border land and Billy bought up the Major's bit of the estate, which extended the acreage by another fifty or so. The Major's land was actually the best on the farm. It wasn't clay like ours and always drained well. Billy grew vegetables there, potatoes, cabbages and the like, and they sold well. The Major's cottage, Gate House Lodge, was left vacant for years but later on let out and it brought in a decent rent.

Our house nestles into the lee of the hill and is sheltered from all but the worst gales which sometimes blow in. Five miles away is Wales and when you climb to the top of our hill and look west you can see the craggy shapes of the Cambrian range. In the winter those mountain tops glitter with ice and snow and hint of a magic land, strange to ordinary people like us. In summer, they loom, purple and shimmering, out of a clear sky, and the feeling is intensified. I always loved looking at them and imagining what lay beyond. But I've been to Wales many times and the people are just like us. Well, nearly like us.

The river runs through our valley, blue, fast-running water which tumbles out of the Welsh mountains and winds itself through the flatter, calmer lands towards the Midlands. At the bottom of our farm, the fields border the river and we have bright green water meadows which are the best grazing land around. In the summer, the cows used to stand under the willows flicking their tails and contentedly chewing their cud. I always thought that was why our cattle grew sleek and gave out such wonderful milk. We used to swim in the river.

A mile below us is the village. At its most populated, during the twenties when the mine was sunk, it only had a population of about four hundred, and when the pit closed people moved away. They're coming back now. People from the town who want a bit of peace and the chance to live in a fat green valley where they can wake up to the sound of birds singing in the May trees and walk out into the fresh morning air to breathe in the heady scent of blossom and young wheat.

Father had taken over the tenancy of the farm in 1892 when he was a young man of twenty-two. Previously he had worked as a farm labourer but when the tenant of Manor Farm died without a son to follow on, Father applied to Sir John Cleeton, the Major's father, for the tenancy. No one thought he would get it, but Sir John had a lot of time for him, and gave him the chance.

Mother used to tell us about the day she went with Father to the Hall. They had been shown into the big library and sat on leather chairs in front of a broad wooden desk. Mother particularly noticed the hundreds of books and the ladder that ran on brass rails around the room. 'It was for reaching the books,' she said, shaking her head and smiling. 'I never saw anything like it.'

'I'm sure you won't let me down, Wilde,' Sir

John had said as he handed Father the tenancy agreement.

Father took a deep breath before standing up and shaking Sir John's hand firmly. 'You can trust me, sir,' he'd said. It was a big step but he was up to it and the farm was never out of profit for all the years he ran it.

In 1913, just before the First World War, Sir John died and the estate was broken up. The widow offered Father first refusal and he was determined to buy. With a letter of recommendation from Lady Cleeton, he went to the bank to arrange a loan to buy the farm outright. We were sitting at the kitchen table when Father came home. Mother stood up and went to greet him.

'Well, Thomas,' she said, laying her hand on his arm and looking into his face, 'am I cooking in my own kitchen?'

I had never seen Mother and Father display their affection before. He wasn't the demonstrative sort and she, although loving with us children, didn't fawn and kiss as some women did. Looking back, I think their marriage must have had some rocky times in the early years because Mother had come from more refined stock than Father and his and Granny's lack of gentility must have been hard to bear. She kept the house and dairy as well as or better than any farmer's wife in the district but maybe she yearned for a more educated husband. I don't know. I don't know why she made the choice to leave her own father's comfortable rectory to marry Father all those years before I was born. I do know she couldn't have had a straighter, more loyal man than Father.

But on the day he bought the farm, he put his hands about her waist and twirled her round as easily as if she had been one of Marian's dollies before planting a kiss on her lips. 'We're on our own land, Mary Constance,' he said, the words choking in his throat and tears coming into his brown eyes. 'Our farm, our home.'

We children sat big-eyed at that. Marian got up and kissed Father on the cheek, which was a surprise because she was normally reticent in that way. Lately she had been walking out with Albert Baker and perhaps that was what made her act differently, or maybe it was simply the excitement of the occasion. Billy and I did nothing but I listened intently. I knew it was an important occasion and I stared at Father and Mother and now Marian all joined in an embrace. Suddenly, Father broke away and looked down at us, his two sons.

'Listen to me, William, and you too, Richard. Manor Farm is now Wilde land and that's the way it's going to stay. When I'm dead and gone, you must keep the place always.' He looked seriously at our Billy. 'Are you listening, William?'

Billy nodded. His mouth was full of bread and blackcurrant jam, which Mother had put out for our tea. He had eaten steadily throughout the entire excitement of Father's announcement.

'Yes, Father,' he mumbled.

'Good. This is Wilde land for ever.' He walked to the window and stared out on to the yard. Mother went to stand beside him and for a moment I swear I saw his shoulders shake. When he turned back his eyes were damp.

'Sit down, Thomas,' said Mother, all bustling

now and businesslike. 'Let me get you a cup of tea to celebrate.'

Father fished out his large handkerchief and blew his nose. 'Thank you, Mary Constance. That would go down a treat.' And he looked round the kitchen with a proprietorial air and when his gaze came back to me, he gave me a kind smile.

'It's very good news, Richard. Did you understand that?'

'Yes, Father,' I whispered.

We had an exciting few days after that because it seemed that every field and every hedge took on a new significance. It was something, I can tell you, for ordinary people like us, to join the landowning class. People in the village talked and said things about Father's getting above his station, but he ignored them and Mother said they were jealous.

Those were hard times that followed, and anxious ones, but in a way the war helped. Prices were good and we were able to make profits on milk and beef and vegetables that we couldn't have managed before. That set us up and afterwards, for the next few years, we did well.

As I said, the village is a mile from the house along the top road. It was small in those early days with grey stone cottages lining the one main street. Down one end was a cattle yard and abattoir but that closed in the twenties and then we used the one in the town, five miles away. In the middle of the village is the old stone church which we attended most Sundays. It's Anglican, which Mother liked for its lack of mithering.

'Not godly enough for true believers,' Granny

would snort, preferring the Free Church in the next village, where the services were less formalised but the worshippers busybodies to a man. Nobody got away with the slightest indiscretion in her church. Everything was looked down upon, from the merest medicinal brandy to the worst case of sexual indiscretion. Poor Mabel Parry was called before the deacons in front of the entire church membership and made to confess her crime. When she died in childbirth, being not much more than a child herself, they wouldn't even let her be buried in their scrubby churchyard.

'She was nothing more than a trollop,' said Granny with a dismissive shrug of her shoulders when Mother complained that it was cruel putting Mabel in a pauper's grave.

Father said nothing, but according to Marian it was after that that he started attending St Winifred's.

The village had a pub too, the Golden Lion. It's still there today, but you'd hardly recognise it as the same place. When I was a lad, it had sawdust on the floor and spittoons in every corner and as for drinks, well, if you didn't like beer, gin or whisky there was no point in your going in. There were two bars, the saloon and the snug, which the older men claimed as their territory. The few women who went into the pub never ventured into that part. They were considered common anyway because respectable women stayed away. All that changed, of course, after the Great War, and even if ladies like Mother kept away the younger ones began to go in, if accompanied by their young men.

Now the Golden Lion is a fancy place, with carpets and cushioned window seats and no sign of the spittoons. The young couple who run it do meals and have built a hotel annex on the old allotment gardens behind. I went a few weeks ago with Andrew Jones and drank a double whisky that went down a treat on a cold December day. He's a nice lad, that Jones fellow.

Father wasn't a drinker but went to the Golden Lion occasionally to conduct business. Quite a bit of buying and selling went on in there and Father, being abstemious, did well. He was good at bargaining, calm and determined.

As young men, Billy and I spent a lot of time in the pub, mostly at the weekends, because by then it had taken over from the church as the centre of village activity. I remember once drinking ten pints and being sick at every bend of the road on the way home. Billy was not a drinker like me. He could nurse a lemonade shandy for two hours without getting to the bottom of the glass.

The school was at the other end of the village, close to the fields where they were sinking the new mine shaft. We had a seam of coal in our district, but somehow it didn't seem to have the over-powering effect on the community that it had in other areas. Many of the miners worked the land as smallholders or farm labourers, going straight from morning milking into the cage that would take them underground. Father wasn't one of the men working at two jobs. He said it took all his time to do one properly.

'I hate school,' Billy used to say every morning as

he sat at the breakfast table.

Mother would sigh and shake her head whilst ladling porridge into the blue-striped bowls. 'You're going, my lad, and that's an end to it.' She would never let him get away with skiving off, even though he was more use on the farm than he ever was at school.

'I'm not learning nothing useful for a farmer,' he'd grumble, but he did. Top of the class at mental arithmetic he was, clever at those figuring sums, where you had to work out how many bushels of wheat you could get out of twenty pounds of money. In later years he would always drive a hard bargain at the market, working out in his head the best deal he could make, and when it came to shaking hands on the contract everyone knew that Billy Wilde had come off best.

He was no good at the other subjects, though. His reading and spelling were poor and I saw him break his slate more than once rather than show his work. Old Cutts, the schoolmaster, would get out his strap and Billy would get a leathering. Those slates cost a fair penny in those days.

'I'll teach you, Wilde,' Cutts used to say, and he'd belt our Billy on the backside in front of the whole class. It made me wince to see it and many was the time I felt like running out of the classroom and back down the lane to Mother, but I was a nervous boy and too frightened to get out of my place. Billy never seemed to care much. He'd look up at me from where he was leaning over the high stool and give a little wink, and afterwards all he'd do was knuckle his eyes quickly and walk jauntily back to his seat. The other children would stare round-eyed at him, specially the girls.

When I started at school Billy was two years ahead, but I soon caught up. I liked the lessons, and best of all Marian was an apprentice teacher then so she kept an eye on me and made sure that the bigger children weren't rough. She left the next year, though, when she married Albert Baker. They lived in the town and Albert worked for his father, the apothecary. In later years, after his father died, Albert had as many as three shops and became a very warm man. Marian was quite the lady in those days.

Our house and the barns were built of the old pinky-red Cheshire brick that always looked so fine and smart. When you got up close, however, you could see that the brick was crumbly and had to be repaired with lumps of mortar at regular intervals.

'This bugger will fall about our ears one of these fine days,' Father would say as he stood on the wooden ladder slapping a mixture of mortar and sand on the walls of the house. He was good with his hands generally, could make anything from wood and could even do a bit of black-smithing if necessary, but he made a hell of a mess of the house. Billy got in a proper bricklayer later and had the whole place repointed. It looks grand now and the council have listed it.

The roofs are blue slate topped with fancy red ridge tiles. As a boy I loved to watch the rain slip across those slates, leaving them bright and glistening. Then I'd get a telling off for daydreaming.

'For goodness' sake, Richard,' Mother would

shout, rushing out to get the washing off the line. 'Don't stand there all gormless, help me.' Mother was rarely sharp with me. Billy said I was her pet, and maybe it was true. But if I was her pet, I certainly wasn't Father's.

As well as the brick shippon and the hay barn, we had pigsties and kennels. They were generally in poor shape and mended with whatever material could be found around the yard. But if the pigsty and the kennel had tin roofs and gaps in the walls, we had good stables. These were home for Father's shire horses and he always took care with them and made sure that they were free from draughts and well cleaned out.

Our shires were grand. Old Diamond was a prizewinner and I saw Father cry when he died. The horse had a knotted intestine and Father had to shoot him. The old horse's colt, also called Diamond, grew up to be our Billy's favourite.

We never had the vet in those early days; it was only later, when the farm was doing well, that Father paid to have all the stock properly looked after. Sammy Philips, called Sammy the Oaks after his smallholding on the other side of the village, was a sort of self-trained vet who we used before the real vets came into the town.

He was a small man with bandy legs and a bright shock of curly fair hair. Father called him out for a difficult calving or trouble with the horses and he never minded getting out of bed on the worst of nights. As far as I know he was a good animal doctor but I do know that he drank and was often found in the ditch close to the Golden Lion. Sober, though, you couldn't ask for better or more reliable help.

The other thing about Sammy was that he could always find something you wanted. The right implement, the particular breed of cow, or chicken; even the occasional temporary labourer to help with haymaking or harvest. Sammy had it all at his fingertips and would get up on his old cob and go and make the deal. He couldn't read a line of writing or tell one number from another when it was put on paper, but word of mouth he was right good and made himself a bob or two. He never did you down neither and that was why he prospered. These days people have forgotten what it means to act as an agent. They're looking out for themselves and bugger you.

Even in later years when the animals became more valuable and Father was keen on the proper vet, Sammy still remained a friend and would be round the house often on a Sunday evening for a bite to eat and a bit of company. He hadn't got a wife and his old mother was as deaf as a brick and spent most of her time sitting on the rocker and gazing at the fire. I remember most fondly those Sunday evenings, sitting round the kitchen table while Father cut big slices of cold roast beef and Mother dished up fried vegetables and home-made pickles.

'Nice bit of meat this, missus,' Sammy would say, nodding whilst he chewed contentedly and looked round our cosy, oil-lit kitchen.

'Another slice, Sammy?' Father would ask, knife and fork poised above the big rib joint, but the man always refused. He knew his manners. Besides, on the dresser Mother would have put an apple pie and a jug of our cream for afters and he had to leave room for that. He and Father would smoke their pipes for a while after supper and talk about the animals. Those evenings he was always sober and would thank Mother most kindly before leaving. I dare say he would call in at the pub on the way home, but that was his business.

When Father was ill, before he died, a knock came on the door. It was Sammy, sober. 'Hear the master is poorly, missus,' he said to Mother.

'He's not himself, I'll say that,' Mother said.

'Well, I thought I'd call to see if I could do something.'

So it was Sammy who got Father on to the commode and kept him clean down below. It was he who shaved him every day, not Billy nor me although we were thirteen and eleven and could have helped with the nursing, I suppose, but Mother wouldn't let us. She was concerned, I think, about Father's dignity.

I'm getting ahead of myself now. I'll come back to Father's death later on. But now I'm tired and will put this aside for the evening. God willing, I'll be spared to continue it tomorrow.

Chapter Three

It's been two weeks since I wrote those last notes. Suddenly, in the night, I came over with a bad chill and was taken into hospital as it went to my lungs. And then, when I was better, what a business. They wanted to take me to an old people's home. Old people's dump! Never, never, *never!* I fought that and I'm home again, with the nurse coming in every now and then and some girl from the council bringing my grub and cleaning the place.

I've moved into the parlour now and use the downstairs bathroom so there isn't much for her to do. She's not a bad young woman, all told. Turns out that she's a granddaughter of one of the Major's by-blows. She told me that her great-granny and the Major were married and divorced. Ha! I laughed at that. That's what she thinks. He was never married to any of the village girls.

But, fair play, this girl, Sharon, has just brought me a cup of tea and a biscuit and made sure that the warm shawl is round my shoulders. This is one of Mother's shawls that I found in the big wardrobe in the main bedroom. Quite a few of Mother's clothes are still there: I could never bear to get rid of them.

I like wearing the shawl. It is comforting and has a faint smell of Mother's favourite scent, Attar of Roses. Mother always kept a little bottle of that perfume on her dressing table.

Sharon brought her son, Thomas, with her today. He's about seven or eight, I think.

'I hope you don't mind, Mr Wilde,' she said, 'but it's half term and there's no one to look after him.'

I'm not used to children, never had any of my own – well, none that I brought up – but this one is a kindly little chap and understands that I'm not to be disturbed. Sharon keeps him with her

28

in the kitchen and now, as I look out of the window, he is in the garden, kicking a football.

We played football when we were boys. I wasn't much cop, but Billy was good. He played for the school team and after he left school he joined the village team. The year our village won the Shropshire Cup, Billy was the captain. I went with him to the final against Market Drayton. What a day that was. Up at five thirty and a quick scamper to the village where we joined all the others, players and supporters, at the station. It took a couple of hours on the train and we enjoyed much jollity and some drinking. The members of the team stayed sober, but I, I'm ashamed to say, at age seventeen led the drinkers and Sammy Philips and I were taken into custody by the constable at the station at Market Drayton and missed the match. I was sorry not to see it, for Billy kicked two goals and was hoisted on the shoulders of the rest of the team. Sammy and I were released to re-join the others to go home, and after we got off the train at our station and were walking back to the farm Billy gave me a proper cuffing, he was that angry. He didn't tell Mother, though, and I told her that I had fallen when she wanted to know why I had a bruised face. I dare say I deserved it, but he didn't need to put stones in his fists to belt me.

We played lots of games. Football in the winter and cricket in the summer. Those were the formal games we learned at school. But that was at school. At home, after we'd done our chores, we were off into the fields to play at all sorts.

Birds' nesting was one of our favourite activities. These days you can't do it and rightly, I suppose,

29

but then we knew no better and climbed all over the hillside looking for nests. We had a rule amongst us lads that you didn't take all the eggs, but if you hadn't got a certain one and you needed it to complete your collection, well, who was looking? We were cruel little buggers in those days. Buzzards nested on the cliffs near the top of the mountain and that was a whole day's trip out for the eggs, but by God it was worth it on Monday morning when you could bring one of those bluish-white beauties out of your jacket pocket and show off in front of your mates.

'Look,' you'd say, 'look at the blotches,' pointing out the brown spots. 'Proves it's a buzzard.' There were always some lads who'd think you'd brought in one of your mother's own duck eggs.

Many years later, when I was on leave from the army, I went to the Lake District on a climbing holiday. I met a man who took me up to see an eagle's nest. I can't find the words properly to tell of the excitement I felt that day. It was breathtaking and frightening when the great birds screamed around us as we climbed up to their nest. It was on a ledge and I had a right struggle to find footholds to get close enough. Then I saw the eggs, two of them lying in the middle of a great collection of sticks and bracken with a warm heather lining. A baby could have lain down comfortably in that bed. Strange, considering how I'd been as a boy, I had no desire then to take one. It seemed too cruel, especially in a world that was full of cruelty. Afterwards, I hoped that our visit hadn't upset the eagles too much. I hoped that at least one of the eggs hatched and that the youngster made it into the world.

But back to games. In the autumn we collected chestnuts for conkers. Our Billy was the school champion at conkers. He used to bake them in the kitchen range and then soak them in vinegar. Father would allow him a length of good twine and give advice as to the best place to pierce the nut so that it wouldn't split. My conkers nearly always split before I'd got the knot tied, and even the ones that didn't broke on the first game at school. But Billy's didn't and he was fearless at holding out his conker for an opponent's hit. His hand never shook, and when it was his turn he would bring the conker down so hard that one hit would send bits of nut flying in all directions.

'Keep the bloody thing steady,' he would growl to his quaking victims, and I saw bigger boys than Billy crying when a piece of nut had flown into their face and scratched them. Some of the little lads ran away rather than challenge my brother. They said he hit their hands deliberately. I don't know. He liked to win, our Billy, and you had to stand up to him otherwise he took you for a sissy.

I wonder if young Thomas out there plays conkers? I expect not. These days, children have television and computers. I would like to have a go on a computer. I was always a good reader and knew my typing. They taught that to some of us in the army before the war started proper. I'm told that you can find anything on a computer, and do anything. I used to be good at lettering: Mother taught me before I ever went to school.

Mother knew her letters, better than Father. She would write out all the bills and read any com-

31

munications that came to the house. It wasn't that Father was stupid; no, my father understood everything well enough, but his reading wasn't as good as Mother's and his lettering was poor. They had their separate ways and that was good. Mother loved Mr Dickens and Mr Trollope whereas Father's favourite was the shire horse stud book, which he would pore over each evening by the light of the kitchen lamp. I can see his finger now, the nail broken and encrusted with dirt no matter how well he washed before supper, tracing along the diagram of blood lines until he came, with satisfaction, to the name of Diamond, our shire. After Father died, Billy added more Manor Farm names to that book and that was a proud legacy.

I loved to read – too much, I think, for a farm boy because there was always so much to do that was more important. But Mother never stopped me, only Father and Billy.

Billy hated reading; he hated being in the house really, all he loved was outside. 'Come on, our Dick,' he would say after tea and after we'd done our jobs around the house and farm. His jobs were bigger than mine, for although from the time I was about ten I was taller than he was, he was always stronger. He was built like Father, stocky and solid with huge shoulders and arms. They had the same dark brown hair and brown eyes, although Father's had flecks of green in them and Billy's were dark and muddy, like boot buttons. I had the red hair and blue eyes. My eyes were like Mother's, but she was more blonde than red. My red hair was a real nuisance when I was at school;

I got teased about it all the time. I don't know why – looking back it seems a foolish thing to be teased about the colour of your hair. Ha! Imagine how a black boy would have been treated in our village. They'd have made his life hell.

Anyway, I used to bring in logs and coal and help Mother with the hens. Billy cleaned out the pigsties and often helped Father with the milking, specially when Herbert Lowe was having 'gyp' with his leg and couldn't come to work. But on spring and summer evenings after tea, Billy would grab me and hurry me out of the house.

'Stir your stumps, carrot head, let's get up the mountain.' And off we'd go, across the fields and up through the gorse on to Windy Hill. One of the local legends was that Cromwell had halted his troops there during the Civil War and his cannons had been bogged down in a rainstorm. You could find the tracks of their wheels if you looked hard enough. We searched that hillside and although once I found an old coin we never saw those tracks. I have that coin still, green with age and not a complete circle, in the little wooden Chinese box I bought from a pedlar.

In later years, after Elizabeth had come to live with us, she would come up the mountain as well, running across the scrubby grass on the top, letting the wind pull her glossy hair from its ribbons so that it trailed out behind. She was a bonny sight and even Billy would look up from his search for cart tracks to watch her.

'You'll never find them, those old tracks,' she would say, throwing herself down on the grass to catch her breath.

'I will.' Billy was stubborn and determined.

Elizabeth laughed and put her head on one side, eyebrows raised. 'I didn't think you liked history. That's Dick's department, not yours. Why d'you bother?'

'Because,' said Billy, walking on towards another patch of gorse, 'if they came up here they must have brought money with them and might have buried it somewhere. That's treasure trove, and after the king has had his share the rest would be mine. Father told me that and I'm going to find it.'

I loved to run and walk through the rocks and heather but I loathed the caves which penetrated the side of the hill. Dark, echoing holes under ledges of rock that I hated to go in. Even Billy was wary of them, never venturing much further than the entrance although he was keen to dare me and some of the other boys to go inside.

Fred Darlington, who was my friend, once took him up on the dare. Taking off his jacket, he bent double and squeezed under the ledge. He quickly disappeared from sight but we could hear him whistling. The whistling got fainter as he went further into the cave and we stood outside, eyes round and ready to run if the ogre Billy said lived in there came howling out, angry at being disturbed.

'All right?' said Fred, emerging minutes later, his hair wet and a big rip on the shoulder of his shirt.

'Yes. Well done,' said Billy, giving grudging praise. 'I go in every day.' That was a lie, but I never told the others. I never told anyone either what Fred told me. It seems that he had only

34

gone a bit into the cave and stood behind a piece of rock. He had whistled quieter and quieter to make it sound as if he was going away.

'Your Billy is a pain in the arse,' he said. 'I just thought I'd show him.'

I chuckled at that, but gave him a bit of a wrestle too because I had to be loyal to my brother. But I never told. Fred stayed my friend for years, even when he came back to the village as the police sergeant.

Nell, my dog in later years, when I came back from the army, used to chase rabbits into those caves. Once she got stuck down a hole, held fast by something that caught round her leg when she tried to wriggle free. Her screams made me brave and I went into the cave then. I wish I hadn't, because of what I found there. Whether it was worth getting my dog out for what I learned, I don't know, now. But she was a good little animal and didn't deserve to be left, so although I walked home on that bleak winter afternoon with a sickened heart, at least I had my dog running happily beside me.

If Windy Hill was the scene of most of our summer activities, it was also a place of entertainment in the winter. You must remember that we didn't have the TV or even a wireless then, and Billy thought that quiet home activities like reading or drawing, which I was quite good at too, were boring.

'Oh, come on,' he would cry when I'd settled down for a good read in the big chair by the kitchen range on a Saturday afternoon, 'come on, let's play.'

35

Out we would go, bundled up in woollen hats and scarves. Us boys had the idea that only sissies wore gloves but by God, some winters I would have given anything for something to cover my knuckles. I used to get terrible chilblains. We wore wellington boots winter and summer around the farmyard and when we played in the fields and on the mountain. The rest of the time it was ordinary leather boots, worn for school and best. I never owned a pair of shoes until I was in my late twenties and bought some with my saved up army pay. The sergeants' mess in Meerut had something of a dress code and proper shoes were a necessity.

Sledding was one of our winter sports. Father made us a sled out of scrap wood and iron and, fair play to him, it was one of the best in the village. It was about six foot by three with sanded runners and raised sides to grab hold of. He'd even made a sort of movable tiller on the bar where the rope went through, so that the lad in front could steer it. Billy always sat in front if we went together. He couldn't abide being driven. It was the same later on with cars. He wouldn't sit in a car unless he was driving.

We didn't have that many really snowy days, perhaps a week or two each winter, but we dragged that old sled up the hill and launched ourselves off on the flimsiest covering of snow. Lots of village boys came on to the hill for the sledding, some with only a dustbin lid to career down on, but much fun was had by all. I saw some accidents, though. Some bugger always had a bloody nose or the odd cut and one year, I suppose I'd have been about nine or ten, a bit older than young Thomas

36

out there, Fred Darlington's brother Georgie was killed on the hillside. He was older than Fred, nearly fifteen, but simple in his mind. Mrs Darlington kept him at home with her most of the time because he couldn't go to school, and when I went round to their house he was always on the floor by her feet, playing with a toy train that his father had made for him.

'Hello, Georgie,' I used to say. Mother said that I must be nice to him because he couldn't help how he was and that it would be a kindness to Mrs Darlington.

'Train,' he would say, or 'Good boy' or something silly like that and push his fingers into his snotty nose and then lick them. Mrs Darlington never shouted at him but only wiped his face and gave him a kiss. She sometimes let him out to play and Fred was supposed to look after him, which he did pretty well most of the time.

This day, I had put my foot into a rabbit hole and twisted my ankle. Fred volunteered to help me home and our Billy said he would have one more go and then come and join us. I suppose he shouldn't have taken Georgie with him on the sled because the lad didn't properly understand about holding on to the sides, and if Fred had known what our Billy was up to he wouldn't have let it happen. But he was looking after me, not Georgie, on this occasion. I expect he thought Georgie was trailing along behind as he usually did. We were halfway down the hill when Billy came whizzing past us, yelling with excitement, with Georgie behind him. Georgie was screaming too, but with fright, I think. Suddenly he flew off the sled and tumbled through the air before landing with a thump on one of the rocks beside us.

He didn't move again after that, and when Fred and I bent over him his eyes were closed and his head all floppy on his neck. The other lads gathered round and Billy too when he had dragged his sled back up to where we were.

'He's not breathing!' Fred cried, and stood up quickly. 'I'd better go and get my mother.' His father was a guard on the railway and was never at home during the day.

Billy pushed him aside and kneeling in the snow put his ear to poor Georgie's chest. 'He's dead,' he said with a finality and authority which we all accepted, and Fred burst into tears. The other boys were scared and started to sneak off home, leaving only the three of us and the body of simple Georgie in the darkening afternoon.

'Right,' said Billy, unemotional but taking charge. 'You, Fred, help our Dick back to the house and I'll bring your Georgie.'

It's hard to believe now, but my eleven-year-old brother hoisted the dead body of poor Georgie on to his shoulders and carried him nearly all the way back to our yard. Father saw us coming from the shippon and ran to meet us.

'Oh, the poor lad,' he said, taking Georgie into his arms and carrying him into the carriage shed where he laid him on the floor of the little wagon. He sent Billy inside to tell Mother while he harnessed up the gelding.

'Oh dear,' said Mother sadly when she saw the dead boy. She had brought out a blanket to lay over the body and I saw her wipe the snot off his face and gently smooth his hair back from his forehead before covering him up. Then she helped Fred up on to the wagon beside Father so that the Darlington boys could be taken home.

We children didn't go to the funeral, and neither did Mother, out of respect for the Darlingtons' feelings. Being chapel, they were strict about women and funerals, but she did all the food for the funeral tea, cooking one of our own hams and pressing a tongue. Fred was quiet for a few months after that. I think he felt guilty about not taking proper care of Georgie, but once when I was at his house his mother said that God had taken the boy to heaven because he couldn't live happily on earth, and after that Fred said he felt better.

Our Billy was the hero of the village for carrying the body such a long way and in the snow. Father was that proud of him, and took many compliments at the market. My ankle healed up quickly. Mother treated it with hot and cold poultices and tied it up with a tight bandage. I got a couple of days off school and was able to read in peace without being dragged out into the cold. But for weeks afterwards I wondered about Billy taking poor Georgie with him. It was strange, specially as I knew that our Billy hated being around anyone crippled, either in body or in mind. 'They should be put down,' he'd say. 'It's the kindest thing. After all, you wouldn't keep an animal like that.'

Chapter Four

The first snowdrops have pushed up beneath the fruit trees and have made a real show these last few days. I asked Sharon to pick a few and she brought them in stuffed untidily into a sherry glass. She has no idea. No matter, they smell of cold fresh air and their green-and-white petals look well against the oak partitions of my desk.

I have been to the hospital for a check-up which is a total waste of time because I'm not going to get better, but it seems to make the doctors more comfortable if they see me. When I came home, the girl was still here and brought me a bowl of soup and some bread and butter. 'Thank you,' I said, politer with her now than I was when they first made her come to the house.

'That's OK,' she said. 'I'll just bring you a cup of tea and then I'll be on my way. There's more soup in the fridge. All you do is heat it up for your supper.'

I drank my soup; it was very good, and home-made, which surprised me. The girl – Sharon – doesn't look capable of proper cooking but there I go again, leaping to conclusions.

'I'm taking Thomas to the rescue centre when he comes out of school,' she said when she brought my tea. 'I'm getting him a dog. It'll be a bit of company for us.'

I nodded. A dog is company and I wish my old

Nell was still alive to sit by my feet. We always had dogs and cats about the house and farm. Mother didn't mind them coming inside in the evenings, to sit by the range in the kitchen, although Granny said she was foolish. She was of the firm belief that animals should be kept outside. Pets were for townsfolk.

Our dogs were of the working kind, although over the years some of them became pets as well. We always kept two at a time, cattle dogs, they were, who would work the herd with as much efficiency as any sheepdog worked a flock. I remember one of them, Ben, who understood the working of the farm better than any of the casual labourers we had over the years. Every morning, when Billy and I came downstairs, Ben would be waiting by the back door.

'Fetch them on, lad,' Billy would say, and while we were putting on our boots and having a pee, old Ben would chase off across the fields, jumping over gates and wriggling through hedges until he had reached the milking herd. Carefully, never barking or upsetting them, he would round them up and have them waiting by the first gate for Billy and me to open it. He would then bring them all the way to the milking parlour as we walked in front and behind, opening and closing gates. The funny thing was that he used to disappear for the rest of the day, rabbiting on the hill, I think, until about half past three in the afternoon when he would turn up again for the afternoon milking. He was a grand dog, that.

His half-brother, Fleck, was as useless as Ben was good. He never got the hang of rounding up the cattle and was a damn nuisance, either stupidly chasing the milkers or sitting gormless, gazing around, sniffing the air for rabbits in a way that infuriated Father and Billy. But he was an excellent house dog and could play ball. You could throw a ball as far as you like and Fleck would tear off to fetch it and bring it back. Billy was nasty with him and used to throw it into the big pond or into a bed of nettles, but Fleck didn't mind. He'd always retrieve it and bring it back to your feet. Father had to get another dog for the cattle, though.

The cats stayed in the barns mostly, except one big tortoiseshell who was Mother's favourite and was allowed in the house. One of my chores was to put out milk and scraps of meat for the barn cats because Father said that they had worked for it. They kept the vermin away and he believed that a labourer was worthy of his hire. Father was like that, a fair man who always paid for what he got, but he hated slackers and spongers. Any tramp who came to the house and asked for a bite to eat or a cup of tea would always get a meal but they would have to do a job for it. 'Nowt for nowt,' said Father.

I remember once playing with Billy in the hay loft of the big barn when one of those travelling men was below us, chopping wood to pay for his supper. I suppose I would have been about six or seven at the time and I'd seen him earlier when he'd asked Father for work. A young woman had come with him, a ragged sort of girl with her hair tied up in dirty ribbons and bare legs stuffed into gumboots. It was slating with rain, but they

42

didn't seem to care, simply pulling closer the old sacks they wore over their shoulders.

'You can go in the barn and split up logs,' said Father sternly. 'Your lady friend can ask my wife if there's any washing or cleaning to be done.'

Billy and I had crept up into the hay loft when the man had his back to us, piling the split logs into a barrow. We played a silly game, silently lying with our faces over the edge and pushing bits of straw down on to the traveller's head. Once or twice he looked up, but he never saw us.

After a while, the ragged girl came in and pinched the tramp on the arm. I saw him laugh and put out a hand to grab hold of her but, giggling, she twisted away and leant against the back wall of the barn.

'Open your mouth,' she said, still laughing in a silly way, and as he threw down the axe and moved towards her she put her hand into the pocket of her dirty dress. To my surprise, when she withdrew her hand she was holding a wedge of cheese.

'Clever girl,' the man said, and pulled her towards him as she lifted her fingers and put the cheese straight into his mouth.

'She's pinched that cheese,' muttered Billy angrily, but I was more interested in what happened next.

'Look,' I whispered, as the couple went into one of the stalls and lay on the dusty floor. 'What are they doing?'

'Mucky stuff,' growled my brother and we watched, astounded, as the couple pulled their clothes aside and mated as casually as any of the animals about the farm.

I think we must have made a noise for suddenly the girl opened her eyes and looked over the tramp's rough shoulder.

'Oh!' she squealed. 'There's lads up there,' and the man stopped his groaning and turned his head.

'You young buggers!' he shouted, leaping up and grabbing at his trousers, which were loosened and hanging about his knees. 'Watching like that. You're not right in the head!'

I stayed up in the loft but my brother wasn't having an insult from some casual worker. 'I'll tell my father,' he yelled, disappearing through the trap door and climbing down the ladder. 'He'll see that you don't get paid.'

The girl had got up too and was standing beside the man when Billy faced him. Her dress was undone and gaping at the front and she didn't seem to care that her breasts were showing. I stared. I'd never seen a woman even partially undressed and I don't think our Billy had either.

'You stole that cheese from my mother's pantry,' said Billy. 'I'm going to tell. And I'm going to tell Father what you were doing just now.'

I was kneeling up now in the loft, frightened by the row but not able to take my eyes off the ragged couple standing nonchalantly in front of my brother.

'Will you indeed,' said the girl, and parting her wet lips she bent down and laughed into our Billy's face. 'Tell your father,' she said, 'that for half a crown I'll do the same for him.'

Billy went as red as a beetroot then and lifted his fist ready to give the girl a punch, but the man

44

grabbed his arm and held him so firmly that no matter how he struggled he couldn't get away.

'You shouldn't be on our farm,' he shouted at the laughing girl, still trying to pull his arm free, and I could see tears of rage and frustration in his eyes. 'You're a dirty common slut.'

Suddenly the girl stopped laughing. 'Common slut, am I?' she spat. 'Well then, this is what common sluts do,' and lifting her hand she slapped my brother hard across the mouth.

I was on my feet and going to the ladder. I had to help him, but I was too late, as ever. The man had dropped Billy's arm and grabbed the girl. 'Come on,' he said, now looking quite alarmed, 'let's get out of here.'

I watched them run out of the barn and across the yard. 'Did you see her titties?' I said, still too astonished to wonder if my brother was badly hurt.

'Shut up!' he hissed, and wiping the tears from his face ran too, out of the barn. I thought he'd gone to tell Father but I don't think he ever did.

We never saw them again, nor did Billy ever talk about it. And somehow I had enough sense not to bring up the subject, but I thought of it often in later years and wondered.

Those days I'm writing about were long ago now but are as clear in my mind as my trip to the hospital today. Over eighty years ago it was, before the Great War, when I was a lad with Mother and Father and our Billy and Marian. And then Elizabeth came to live with us, when I was coming up twelve, I think.

Looking back over what I've written, I realise

our Marian doesn't seem to come much into the story and that's a shame because she was always there, even after she got married to Albert Baker. I think she preferred our house to their flat above the shop in the town. She was with Mother a lot.

My life was spent with Billy. We were that close, almost like twins, although he was my elder and better in most things about the farm. There was only one time when I remember getting the better of him, apart from reading and writing, that is, but that didn't count because Billy said those were sissy things. The day I remember was in the late spring when I would have been about ten years old. We had a big old laburnum tree in the back garden and Mother loved its yellow flowers. Father said he couldn't abide it because the seeds were poisonous and he was frightened that the beasts might get into the garden and eat them. But Mother thought it a pretty thing and would often walk in the garden and stand under the canopy of blossom. Well, this day she wasn't feeling too good and had taken to her bed for the afternoon. Marian had come over to look after her and, while she was waiting for the kettle to boil, she stood by the back door looking at the garden.

'I'll pick some flowers for her, when I've got a minute,' she said. 'Or perhaps you lads could do it.'

Billy laughed. 'Picking flowers is girls' work. I'm going to help Father in the shippon.'

'I'll get them,' I said. I never minded picking flowers. It didn't seem sissy to me.

Roses were just coming out, the early yellow ones, and some tulips in the bed by the wall, but

I knew what Mother would like most. I was up the laburnum tree, pulling the strips of flowers off a branch, when Father and Billy came round from the yard.

'What are you doing up there, Richard?' said Father sternly.

'He's picking flowers, the big sissy,' our Billy said as he pulled a face at me and did a little play of curtsying and being a girl.

I felt really bad then and climbed down the tree with my bunch of flowers. Father had no time for silly activities and he hated that old tree.

'They're for Mother, while she's badly,' I muttered. I've no doubt that my face was redder than my hair just then. Certainly Billy was pissing himself laughing behind Father's back. But I was taken aback by Father's reaction, for I always found it hard to please him and expected a row.

'You're a good thoughtful boy, Richard,' was all he said, and he went into the house to get a jug for the blossoms. Our Billy scowled and when we took them upstairs to show Mother he tried to say that it was him who'd climbed up the tree. But Marian knew better, because she'd been watching out of the window, and she told him not to be such a little liar. Anyway, everyone knew that Billy was scared of heights. I was the one who could climb.

Mother gave me a big kiss. She gave one to Billy too, but mine was better.

She was ill a lot that year. I never knew what was the matter with her; I wonder now if she was expecting another baby and lost it. It could have been but I think she was also upset about the war, which had started the August before. Some of the older lads in the village had gone to France and we had heard that young Jack Kendrick, the vicar's son, had been wounded in action. I saw him once in the vicarage garden.

'Hello,' he called when I was hurrying to catch up with Billy on our way to school.

'Come on,' yelled Billy over his shoulder, 'we'll be late,' but I lingered, intrigued by the bandage round the young man's head and the crutch that he was using to bash down the privet hedge so that we could see each other better.

'Hello,' I said.

'You on your way to school?' he asked and I nodded, one eye on our Billy's departing back.

'Old Cutts still in charge?' He laughed and started to cough, making an unpleasant racking noise just like the old men who sat on the wall by the church smoking their pipes. It seemed strange to hear that sound coming out of a person who wasn't that many years older than me.

'Yes,' I said and then I added, 'He'll give me the strap if I'm late.'

'Better go then. Don't want to get you in trouble.'

But I still hung on. 'You're a soldier, aren't you?' I said. He wasn't in uniform but wearing a pair of corduroy shooting breeches and a flannel shirt. I liked his face; it was open and friendly with hazel eyes that twinkled even though I could see nothing funny in our conversation.

'I am, at least I am when I'm over there.'

'Does that hurt?' I nodded towards the bandage on his head. A little bloodstain showed through the white gauze above one of his ears and I could

48

see a bald patch where his hair had been shaved away.

'No, not much. I was lucky; most of the shrapnel missed me.'

My eyes rounded at that and I would have stayed there talking about the fighting but Billy came running back down the lane and grabbed me.

'Hurry up, idiot!' he commanded, pulling at my jacket, and with a reluctant little wave to my new friend I ran after him.

'Goodbyee,' Jack called and I laughed out loud at the sound of it as I sped towards the toll of the school bell.

He went back after sick leave and was killed within three days. Mother went to the vicar to tell him how sorry she was. Mrs Kendrick had died when Jack was born, so the vicar had no one now and was brought low. Even his religion didn't seem to help. Mother was quiet and thoughtful when she came back from the vicarage and it was after that that she got poorly. But she was better in the autumn and back on her feet again by Christmas.

That year we had a visit from Mother's brother, John, who was a soldier like her younger brother, Richard, my namesake, but had survived the Boer War and then been posted to India. He told some tales so exciting and wonderful that even Billy would sit and listen for hours. Father would smoke his pipe and ask a few questions now and then, particularly about the animals they had out there, and became especially interested when Uncle John told us about a tiger hunt that he had been on. Mother was proud of him because he was an officer. He had been raised from the ranks and was now a captain.

'I'll never get any higher,' he said, but was cheerful about it, telling us that it would be too expensive to be a major or a colonel. They had to keep horses and grand houses and entertain, even in India. As it was, Uncle John lived in a bungalow that had a veranda all round and kept two native servants. He slept under mosquito netting and searched under the bed every day for snakes. We gasped in a sort of thrilled horror at that and I wonder if it was those tales that made up my mind to join the army later on. To a certain extent, my experiences in India were like his. He fought a few battles against warring tribesmen, as I did too and thought myself a grand, brave fellow. But later on I encountered the Japs, who damn near killed me.

On Christmas morning, he opened a big chest and brought out presents for us all. Billy and I both had curved daggers with fancy handles. I still have mine, but Billy lost his the following summer. 'Bloody useless on a farm,' he said scornfully when we were up in our bedroom, 'unless you wanted to kill someone.'

Father was given a pair of little pistols, in a polished box.

'This is too generous, brother John,' he said, examining them with delight and squinting down the sights.

Uncle John shook his head. 'No it isn't, Thomas. I've no family, except you and Mary Constance and the children, and it gives me pleasure to hand these things on.' At the time I didn't understand that sentiment but I suppose it's something that comes with age. It'll give me pleasure too when the time comes. That box with the duelling pistols is in the drawer beside my right leg. Perhaps another Thomas would appreciate it.

Mother and Marian had sandalwood boxes and coloured silk shawls with long fringes and exotic patterns of birds and flowers. I never saw Marian wear hers, but Mother went to the next church social with her turquoise shawl arranged over her grey dress and looked lovely. Granny said it was showing off, but Father said he was proud of her and that shut Granny up.

Uncle John went back to India in the early spring and we never saw him again. He stayed on there after coming out of the army and when I went out I was posted to the very same station and visited the church where he was buried, to see his grave. I got a surprise then. Apparently, he'd married a native girl when he was in his sixties and they'd had a son. Their names were on the gravestone too, *beloved husband of Aisha and father of Richard.* So another Richard Wilde existed, but I never found him. I'll bet he didn't have red hair.

That summer we went on holiday to Llandudno. We'd been on lots of day trips before, to New Brighton and sometimes to Rhyl, but this summer Father thought that Mother needed a proper break and paid for two weeks at a boarding house on the West Shore. Father only came for the first week, saying that he couldn't spare the time away from the farm, but Mother, Billy and I stayed on and Marian and Albert Baker came to stay in the same place.

In my memory that was the best holiday I ever

51

had. The weather was perfect and although we were into the third year of the Great War, people seemed to be quite cheerful around the town. Marian's Albert almost joined up at a recruiting rally we went to on the promenade, but Marian persuaded him that he was in a reserved occupation, as an apothecary, and that he mustn't go. He did go later that year. I think he was too ashamed to be safely at home when so many lads were being killed. He joined up as a stretcher bearer, having some knowledge of medicines and first aid, and served in a field hospital throughout.

Our Billy wanted to join up. He was nearly thirteen then and told me in bed one night at the boarding house that he was going to lie about his age and join the Royal Welch Fusiliers, our local regiment. I said he'd never get away with it, but he was determined. He did try, but the sergeant knew he was only a lad and sent him away. It almost spoiled his holiday and he was angry for days afterwards. I never told Mother what he'd tried to do even though she asked me what was making him so miserable.

He cheered up though when we went on to the beach. Our Billy loved swimming. Mother didn't go into the sea but Marian had a suit with a knee-length skirt and a frilly hat to cover her hair and she went to the edge of the water, holding Albert's hand, squealing like a pig. She never went in further than her knees but scampered back to sit beside Mother and shout instructions to us boys. Albert couldn't swim but he walked in all the way, doing a pretend breaststroke with his arms until he was nearly out of his depth. Once he forgot that he was still wearing his boater and a big wave came in and knocked it off his head. How we laughed as it floated away.

Billy was a good swimmer; he taught himself in the river at home and although he had no proper style he could get through the water safely, with a lot of snorting and splashing. I could swim too, but I was less daring and wouldn't go out as far. I preferred to stay away from Billy anyway because he loved to dive down and grab your legs and pull you under. One day some boys from Liverpool were in the sea too and we got to playing with them. Billy did his diving trick to one of them, and later the boy's father had a word with Mother. Billy got a telling off.

We also went on trips on Mr White's charabanc, a motor bus with a removable canvas cover in case of rain. It held about fourteen people and Mr White took us first to Anglesey, which I thought was a bit boring, simply more beaches and tea at a café at Rhosneigr. Mother and Marian enjoyed it, although Albert spent his time reading a newspaper and smoking countless cigarettes. Billy grumbled all the way and I couldn't blame him; we felt trapped. But on the next trip we went to Snowdon, and I found heaven.

We stopped at a pretty lake at the foot of the great mountain and everyone got out. Two lady schoolteachers from London were on the trip and they told me the Welsh name of the mountain and all the other peaks around. Then they let me come with them a little way up the hillside and said that they had hired a guide and were going all the way up the following day. Before we went back, one of them told Mother that if I would like to come with them on the morrow, they would be glad of my company and would take good care of me.

'He's a little young,' said Mother, 'and not as strong as some.' She nodded significantly towards our Billy, who was skimming pebbles into the lake and showing off, but the ladies could see that he wasn't in the least interested.

'Oh, please, Mother,' I begged. It seemed such an important moment. Mother pondered for a minute or two and then looked to Marian to see what she thought.

'Let him go, Mother,' said Marian with a smile. 'It'll get him away from you know who for a day.' She meant Billy, of course, and not kindly. They never got on particularly well.

Mother sighed. 'Very well, then, and thank you, miss. He'll be a good boy; I can assure you of that.'

Oh, I was. The best and happiest boy in the whole world. From the top of Snowdon I could see for miles, to the east way across the other mountain tops into mid-Wales, and when I turned and looked the other way the whole stretch of the North Wales coast lay before me and the flat round Isle of Anglesey floated like a green jewel in a shimmering sea. My heart was full. When we got back to Llandudno the sun was sinking into the west and I was late for the evening meal at the boarding house. Mother asked me if I'd enjoyed myself, but I couldn't really speak. I was still so overwhelmed by the experience.

Our Billy dismissed the climbing with scorn,

saying he'd done something better. I didn't believe him. I thought he was only trying to get one over me, but he told me that night in bed that he had taken a girl he'd met on the beach under the pier and kissed her.

The next day he pointed out the girl as she walked with a crowd of other lasses on the promenade. She was a brassy-looking thing, swinging along with her noisy gang. She had come on a trip to Llandudno with some of her friends from a munitions factory in Liverpool.

'She's older than you,' I said, shocked despite myself.

'Only a couple of years,' said Billy, 'that doesn't matter.' He waved to her but she ignored him.

He didn't mention her again and I was glad but I know he saw her again because that night he climbed out of the boarding house window after we'd gone to bed. I was asleep when he came back but the next morning when I asked him he told me I dreamed it. I know I didn't.

But something else happened that last week which took everything else out of our minds. We had one day left of our holiday and the weather had gone windy and the sea was rougher than it had been the whole time we'd been there. Mother said that we couldn't go swimming any more because it was too dangerous, but we begged and pleaded for one more paddle.

'All right, then,' she said, 'but it's against my better judgement. Make sure you only paddle.' She turned to our Billy. 'Do you hear me, William?'

'Yes, Mother,' he said, as nice as pie.

Of course, when we got down to the water's

edge he didn't only paddle. He splashed and jumped into and out of the waves so that his knickerbockers were wet up to the waist and even his hair was plastered to his forehead. I stood by the edge, allowing the trickles of water to run through my toes and suck them into the sand as the tide ran back to sea. We were moving with the water round the bay and ignored Mother's cries to stay close to her. She was busy trying to keep hold of her hat, for the wind had really got up and rain was beginning to patter. Not many people were on the beach.

We had reached the pier where the water was deeper and swirling about and I had to hold on to one of the wooden support posts so that I wouldn't lose my footing. How the next thing happened, I'm still not sure. I think it was a big wave that simply rolled in and tipped me up, off my feet, pushing my head under the water. Before I could even shout, it had swept me away from the post and out, away from the pier into the bay, where I was way beyond my depth.

'Help!' I yelled, nose and mouth full of sea-water, desperately trying to remember how to swim. I truly thought I was going to drown. No, I can't say that scenes from my short life passed through my mind, but I do remember being dreadfully frightened. It seemed that the harder I tried to swim to the shore, the farther I was being pulled out. Of course the tide was on the ebb and we shouldn't have been in the water at all. Then, just when I was sinking again beneath the angry waves, a hand grabbed at my collar and pulled my head up. It was our Billy.

'Chin up, carrot head,' he gasped and struck out for the shore, pulling me behind him. How we made it I'll never know. Put it down to Providence, or to Billy's great strength and ability; whatever it was, all I know is that my brother dragged me out of the sea that day and saved my life.

What a fuss there was then, Mother crying and people running down from the promenade to help us up the steps. Billy was cheered as a hero and a little piece even appeared about him in the *Daily Post. Brave Schoolboy Saves Brother from Drowning.* It was on the same page as the story about the girl being murdered. One of the girls who'd come on the trip from the Liverpool factory, it was. She'd been found dead on the Great Orme. Father cut out the bit about Billy and kept it in his wallet. He showed it to everyone.

Fair play to Billy, he never boasted about it. I got a bit of extra teasing, name calling and such, but I didn't mind. You see, the way he could be when we were lads, and whatever happened between us in later years, made no difference. He was my brother and I loved him.

He loved me too. I know that.

Chapter Five

I found Sharon looking as though she'd been weeping this morning when I came into the kitchen. She'd arrived early and had made me a bit of breakfast before getting on with the washing.

'What's the matter?' I asked.

'Nothing that would interest you, Mr Wilde.' She was short with me and I probably deserved it because it isn't nice to go interfering in another body's business. But I was curious, because I've got used to her and young Thomas when she brings him, and these days I can't do with upset.

'I might be interested,' I said. 'Try me.'

She poured us a cup of tea then and told me that she was going to have to leave the flat where she and Thomas were living. It was a friend's place, she said, and the friend wanted it back. They would have to go into bed and breakfast until the council could find them housing.

'What about the lad's father? Can't he help?' I'd never asked about him before. You never know these days, people don't get married like they used to. She shook her head. She didn't want anything to do with him. Neither, it appeared, with her parents. From the little she said, they seem to have been a bad lot. They lived in that big estate in the town and I've heard stories about what goes on there.

'I want something better for Thomas, and for me.'

She got up then and went into my parlour to tidy up while I ate my breakfast. She does have a look of the Major in a way. A sort of fine-boned face with a straight aristocratic nose. He was the younger son of Sir John Cleeton and I heard that he gave his mother and father endless grief. Always in trouble he was, what with gambling and drinking, let alone women. His elder brother had gone into the church, which was unusual even in those days. You would have thought he'd stay at home to look after the estate, but he had a vocation and took his religion seriously. Father told us that he'd crossed over and gone to Rome. For years I thought that meant that he was living in Rome, the city, but then I discovered that he had become a Catholic. He went into one of those strict monasteries where he died, still quite a young man.

That was why after Sir John died Lady Cleeton broke up the estate. She already knew that the Major wouldn't look after it. The Hall was sold and used as a school for a while, but when it burnt down the ruins were left abandoned. Many's the time Billy and I played in those ruins, jumping from the tumbled walls and exploring the remains of the cellars. How we weren't killed, I don't know, for it was a dangerous old place, full of broken bricks and glass and twisted bits of metal. I did cut my leg badly once, falling down the cellar steps, but when I ran home to have Mother wash and bind up the injury I kept quiet about where the accident happened. We'd been told often enough to stay away from the place and Father would have made sure I didn't forget again.

An estate of houses has been built on that land now. It makes me laugh to think that for years only one family and their servants lived on the same amount of land that now houses three hundred people.

The Major joined the army and served for many years in India. As a boy I knew nothing about his service career, but later when I was serving on the North West Frontier I came across people who had known him and spoke highly of his courage. In our village, though, he was considered something of a joke and was never accorded the respect that his station in life should have demanded.

I suppose he lived off his pension and the money he was left from the estate, but he was always broke and trying to borrow from his neighbours. Father wouldn't lend him a penny.

'Lazy good for nothing,' I heard Father say one afternoon after the Major had been round wanting 'a private word with your papa'.

When I brought Father from the yard and showed him where the Major was waiting, in the garden by the laburnum tree, he groaned and said in a low voice, 'Next time he comes to the house, tell him I'm out. Do you hear me, Richard?'

I nodded and would have hung around to hear what was being discussed but Father sent me away. I went reluctantly back towards the house, but when Father wasn't looking I dived down behind the dog kennels that were built on beside the back wall and peeped round.

'I'd be most grateful if you could see your way clear to advancing me five pounds until Lady Day, Mr Wilde, sir,' said the Major in his clipped voice. He had to bend slightly forward to talk to Father, being so tall and straight with his military bearing.

'No.' Father didn't bother with genteel excuses.

'Three pounds then. It would be a kindness most appreciated.'

'No,' Father said again. 'I don't lend money. I buy and sell and give to charity when I've got a bit extra. But I don't lend so I'll wish you a good

60

afternoon, Major Cleeton.'

I waited for an angry reply but none came. Instead, you'd have thought Father had given him a hundred pounds, the polite way that the Major took his leave. 'Thank you for your time, sir,' was all he said as he doffed his soft brown hat and turned smartly away.

I came casually round the corner, pretending that I'd been on the other side of the house, and that was when I heard Father saying about the Major being a good for nothing.

'He seems very polite,' I said innocently.

Father snorted and looked at me as though I'd said something insulting to him. 'I've no time for him, nor any of his sort. You stay away from the gentry, Richard. They'll do you no good.'

When I was growing up, the Major lived alone in the Gate House Lodge, which was all that was left of the Great Hall. I used to see him sometimes on my way home from school, or when we went fishing in the lake that had been part of the grounds. He might have been a wastrel, as Father said, but he was always polite and lifted his hat to old and young alike. When I was a little boy, Mother would hold my hand tightly if we met him in the lane. Why, I don't know, because he never did anything but pass the time of day with her and bow when we moved on. Her cheeks would be red afterwards like they were when she was boiling the clothes in the copper.

Once, he gave me a book. I found it on the ground outside the lodge and thought it must be his. No one else used that lane, except him and us. It was a back way from our farm to the village.

Anyway, I picked it up and somewhat daring, for I was only about eight or nine at the time, I knocked at his door and waited with trepidation for him to answer. He took his time, and when he opened the door I could see straight away that he was drunk.

'Ah,' he said, swaying, 'Master Wilde, I believe. And what can I do for you, sir?'

I held the book up; it was a copy of *David Copperfield*, a story which at that time I didn't know. I think Mother had read it; she liked Mr Dickens. Anyway, I took a deep breath and said, 'I found this in the lane, Major Cleeton. I thought it might be yours.'

'Did you, young sir?' was all he said, taking the book from me. 'Well, come inside for a moment and we'll consider the possibility.' He stepped back and held the door wider.

That was a facer. As I've said, I was a nervous boy and certainly not used to conversation with the gentry, but I was curious to see inside the Lodge so, throwing caution to the wind, stepped inside.

I had a surprise. Father was always scornful of the Major and his poor farming methods. He had fifty acres of the old parkland on which he fattened a few bullocks, poor stock really and only kept, according to Father, to keep the grass down. They never fetched much at market and would be taken by the butchers from the poorer part of the town, where the customers weren't so fussy. It was a cheap way of farming, and not for the likes of us. So I expected the inside of the Lodge to be cheap and poor also.

Well, it wasn't. In the room where he led me, the walls were lined with fine polished furniture and fancy foreign rugs covered the floor. We had one of these rugs on the floor in our hall. It had been Mother's wedding present from her parents. I'd thought that a poor gift, seeing as it was slightly ragged in one corner, but Mother said it was worth a bit of money and that she had always loved it. It was a reminder of her own home. The Major had several of those rugs, different sizes and overlapping, in places. Floor-to-ceiling bookcases were on either side of the window, stuffed with books of various bindings and obviously well read. The covers of some were tattered and others half protruded from the shelf as though they had been pulled out for a look and then hastily pushed back. A winged leather chair stood by the fireplace with a table beside it on which a pile of books and a half full decanter and glass jostled for space. I was invited to sit on a leather stool while the Major sank into his chair and examined the book.

'*David Copperfield*. Wonderful!' He opened the book, read the title page and riffled through the pages, an unsteady smile on his thin face. 'Yes, Master Wilde, this is indeed one of my books. There.' He turned back to the frontispiece where an intricately designed book plate had been pasted in. 'There, see, my name, Edward Cleeton. My proof of ownership.' He smiled at me and lifted the decanter. 'A drink, Master Wilde?' My face must have shown my amazement, for he nodded his head and set the decanter down again. 'No, perhaps not. But,' he frowned as he looked thoughtfully around the room, 'I must show my appreciation for your kindness.'

I wriggled on the stool, anxious now to get away, for even though nothing had happened untoward, I was mindful of Mother and Father's caution when having dealings with the Major. 'I have to go now, sir,' I whispered. 'Mother will have tea on the table and worry for me not being home.'

He said nothing for a moment, still gazing round the room and frowning, then suddenly he slapped the book down on his knee and I jumped off the stool in fright.

'The very thing,' he roared, and getting up he staggered over to where I was standing, now close to the door. 'Please accept this book, Master Wilde, as a small gift for your thoughtfulness.'

Barely stopping to say thank you, I hurried out to the garden. 'My compliments to your father,' the Major called after me, 'and to your most charming mama.'

Mother pretended to be annoyed when I told her about the encounter and showed her the book and Father warned me not to go near the Major again. 'Not that he's a bad man, Richard, but he's not our class and we shouldn't mix.' I think Mother wanted to say something about that, but she didn't. She did ask me later to repeat the bit about 'your most charming mama'.

That memory of the Major is still strong today, with Sharon about the house, taking a duster to the books on my shelves even now, as I write. I suppose I could get up and find that same volume and show it to her. But I want to continue my story and that would be a distraction. That's the trouble with writing these remembrances: my mind keeps wandering off the subject.

The Major died in that cold winter after the Great War. Mother was one of the few people in the village who went to see to him when he was ailing and that caused a row, I can tell you.

My father had died a couple of years previously and Mother and Billy were running the farm. Billy was only in his teens but very much the man about the house and tried hard to rule us just the same as Father, so he was angry when Mother proposed visiting the Major.

'He's no bloody use,' I heard Billy say, when Mother came out of the house with a basket of eggs and cheese to take to the Gate House. 'You should stay away from him.'

'I'll see no soul left alone to die,' she said defiantly, ignoring his opinion as no one else would dare to. 'Richard can come with me as my chaperon, if that's what's worrying you!' That was the winter that Elizabeth had gone back to Liverpool for a few weeks. Her father had got in touch and wanted to see her. Otherwise she would have gone with Mother.

Billy turned away then and went back to greasing the seed drill. Herbert Lowe was listening from the stable and Billy was embarrassed. 'I want the bull's stall cleaned before the day's out,' he growled at old Herbert. 'Should have been done yesterday.'

'Aye, boss,' said Herbert. He had easily transferred his allegiance to Billy when Father died. The fact that our Billy was at least fifty years younger than him made no difference.

I went with Mother to the Gate House. It was

December and extremely cold with a raw wind blowing off the mountain. I would have preferred to stay by the kitchen range with my book, having a few unexpected days off school. I was coming up thirteen then and was at the grammar, but so many had come down with the influenza that it had been decided to close the school until after Christmas. Billy wasn't impressed. He had left school three years before, even though he hadn't reached his thirteenth birthday. Some people are required to grow up quickly.

When we got to the Gate House, it had begun to snow. Only little flakes that swirled about in the wind, but it was bitter and the sky was heavy and dark.

'Major!' called Mother, rapping at the door as we stood in the porch. 'Major, it's Mary Wilde. Can I come in?'

We got no answer and I noticed that she was biting her lip when she looked at me. 'He's gone out,' I said. 'Let's go home.'

Mother shook her head. 'I don't think he can have gone out. According to Elinor Lowe, in the village, he's not able to leave his bed. She came up to do a bit of cleaning for him.' She knocked again and then turned the handle and cautiously pushed open the door. 'Major Cleeton! Hello!'

It was cold inside the house. The room where I'd sat when he gave me the book was dark, no lamps lit, and the fire had gone out, leaving a small heap of sour grey ash in the grate. Mother clucked her tongue and, pushing aside a pile of books on the polished table, put down her basket. She bustled through to the next room. It was a kitchen, with a

66

range and a scrubbed deal table and a dresser loaded with pretty cups and plates. A fire was still flickering weakly in the range, and someone had left a few logs in a big basket beside it, ready for replenishment.

Mother ran a finger over the dresser and clucked again. 'Elinor Lowe wouldn't know a cleaning rag if it jumped up and bit her,' she hissed and marched out of the kitchen. Before I could stop her, for I was certain Billy would be angry if he knew what she was doing, she had turned back towards the little hall and was climbing the stairs.

A smell came from the top of the house, a smell I recognised. It was the horrible odour of sickness, like the one that had pervaded our house in those dreadful days when Father had been so ill.

'Mother!' I called, thinking that it would be better for her to stay downstairs. 'Mother!' But she took no notice and carried on. I can remember now how I dragged my feet on those stairs as I followed her up.

The Major lay on a sort of camp bed in a bare room. The bedclothes were tumbled and untidy and a cup on the little table beside him had fallen over, so whatever liquid had been in it had dripped on to the floor. He was awake and staring at us, his eyes dark and his cheeks bright pink with fever. I thought he looked mad and backed away towards the door, but Mother was made of sterner stuff. She leant over him and smoothed the grizzled hair away from his forehead. His thin face moved up to look at her and the eyes softened.

She looked over her shoulder. 'Richard,' she said quickly, 'run to the village and bring back Dr

Guthrie. Tell him that the Major is very ill and needs him at the Gate House, and,' here she moved over to me and said for my ears only, 'if he says anything about payment, tell him that Mrs Wilde from Manor Farm has made the request and will see him right.' She looked up into my eyes, for I had grown taller than her by then. 'Make sure you say that.'

I hesitated, both reluctant to leave her and, truth be told, not keen on the run to the village on that cold afternoon, but she nodded firmly at me and there was no way I could refuse. As I walked slowly down the stairs, I heard her speak again but knew it was not to me. 'Oh, my dear,' she was saying, her voice breaking, 'how have you come to this?'

I brought Dr Guthrie back to the Gate House and we reluctantly climbed the stairs together. The bed was neater now and the Major lay against plumped-up pillows with a damp flannel over his brow. Mother had lit all the lamps downstairs and made a fire in the sitting room. She had brought a lamp upstairs and her trim figure in her blue dress and black shawl was illuminated as she sat on a chair beside the bed, spooning some liquid, I don't know what, into the Major's slack mouth. Every now and then she would wipe the dribble away with a clean handkerchief and encourage him to swallow. It put me in mind of how she'd been with Father. The sort of kindness and courage that you wouldn't find nowadays.

Dr Guthrie was pessimistic after examining the patient. 'He'll not do,' he said gloomily in his Scottish accent, which had remained with him all the years he'd lived in our marcher village. 'Too many years of drink and neglect can't fight the influenza.'

'You can do something, surely?' said Mother, standing up and staring at him with that look of scorn that most people recognised. My mother didn't take to givers-up.

Dr Guthrie shook his head. 'I've no treatment, lassie, other than nursing. This illness has nae cure.' He took out his stethoscope and, pulling aside the Major's soiled nightshirt, listened to his chest. While we waited for his opinion, Mother paced up and down, her long skirts swishing angrily against the oak floorboards.

'It's in his lungs now. Best let him be,' was the doctor's verdict, given with a shrug of the shoulders as he packed away the stethoscope into his bag.

Mother took his arm. 'Something for the fever, surely,' she begged, 'and for the pain.'

I was surprised at her eagerness and passion, although I shouldn't have been. Mother was well known in the district for espousing causes that others wouldn't. I've known her go into the poorest houses in the village to help with illegitimate births, where other folks turned away. But the Major wasn't exactly a poor person. Disregarded, yes, I supposed by the likes of Father and our Billy, but still someone of consequence who shouldn't need a farmer's wife pleading his cause.

Dr Guthrie sighed and opened his bag again. He brought out a small blue bottle with a cork stopper. 'Give him a few drops of this, if you can get it down. It'll ease his passing,' he said, and

69

picking up his hat he left the room.

'Damn him!' said Mother fiercely but quietly, and turned back towards the Major. She uncorked the bottle and poured a little of the clear liquid into a spoon. 'Take this,' she said softly. 'It will help.'

I watched as he struggled to swallow and saw a little flicker of hope spark his tired eyes. He hadn't entirely given up.

On the other hand, I had. 'Mother,' I said, knowing instinctively that I should take her home now. 'Mother. It's getting dark. We must go back to the farm.'

'Yes, we must.' Her voice echoed in the still room and resounded bleakly off the bare walls. She was leaning over the bed, refolding the cloth on the Major's forehead and fastening the buttons on his nightshirt. It was intimate, too intimate for me, and I turned away. I couldn't bear to watch her touch another man. I wondered what Granny would say if she heard what Mother had done, but knew already that I wouldn't be the one to tell her.

'Richard.' Mother spoke again. 'Richard, love, go home now and tell your brother that I will be a little while yet.'

'But...' I wanted to argue, knowing that it would be me who would get a tongue lashing from our Billy, but she turned round and gave me such a look of determination that I knew I had no choice.

'I'll be along later,' she repeated, and picked up the cup again. When I left the room she was holding the Major's head to her breast and spooning more liquid into his mouth. I could hear her making those gentle little crooning noises she did

with the newborn calves when she was per-
suading them to drink milk from the bucket.

She came home the next morning and said that
the Major had died in the early hours. The fever
had broken and he'd spoken a little and quite
sensibly before lapsing into a coma. She never
said what, though.

Our Billy was furious with her for weeks after
and with me for letting her stay, but she took no
notice. 'It would take a bigger man than you,
William Wilde,' she told him one teatime when
he had another go, 'to stop me doing what I think
is right.'

Chapter Six

I've been on a little trip into Wales. It's the first
time I've been out of the house for months, except
for going to the hospital and I don't count that.
No, this was a proper day out. Sharon took me.

She has a car, an old and battered one, but it
goes and I was quite comfortable on the journey.
She packed the back seat with cushions and
pillows and put a thick blanket over me. Thomas
sat on the front seat beside her. I gather that it is
now illegal for small children to sit in the front, but
there was no help for it. I had to sit in the back.

It is the first week in March and the weather,
although blustery, is quite warm. Daffodils are
coming up in the garden, only a few, but their
brave yellow flowers are a tonic to look at. On St

71

David's day, Sharon put a bowl of them on the desk beside me.

'I like them,' she said. 'They make you think that good times are coming.'

I don't know what she meant, but they certainly are cheerful-looking things and if they make her happy then who am I to quibble over her silly remarks. She has moved into the house now. It seemed the only sensible thing to do after she was put out of her flat and had nowhere to go. Eddie Hyde's grandson, I think his name is Jason, moved my bed down here into Mother's little parlour weeks ago and I spend most of my days in this room overlooking the garden. I can use the downstairs cloakroom which has a shower and I used to make my own meals in the kitchen. Sharon does that now.

She and Thomas had the choice of the bed-rooms and she tells me that Thomas picked the little room above the front door. I liked that room always. Eddie Hyde had been put in there when he first arrived at our house, so it was never available for me, but I did think about moving in when he joined up in 1914. Billy persuaded me to stay in with him. He said he liked to talk at night after we had gone up. I think he was afraid of the dark and didn't want to sleep on his own. He got over that later when he moved into the main bedroom. Maybe the memory of Father and Mother in there was comforting.

Later, of course, that little room over the front door was Elizabeth's and that holds precious memories for me too.

Sharon has chosen the room that was Mother

and Father's. I told her that I should have been born in that bed but came too fast, so opened my eyes to the world in the parlour. She laughed and shook her head. 'Couldn't wait to get at your books, was that it?' Silly, ignorant girl. I don't know why I like her.

Anyway, the other day she suggested a drive into the country. 'Maybe we'll see some new lambs. Thomas will like that. It'll do you good, too. Get some colour into your cheeks.'

I laughed. It would take more than a few hours out of the house to bring me back to health, but I agreed to the trip and am glad I did.

'Where would you like to go?' she said as we went out of the gate.

I thought for a moment and then ventured a suggestion. 'Do you know how to get to Rhaeadr? To the waterfall?'

She shook her head but carried on driving. 'I'll ask at the garage. I need petrol.'

So we set off, along the main road and then turning into smaller roads, winding our way through the hills. Thomas saw his lambs. Plenty of them, jumping around in the meadows and gathering in little gangs like naughty schoolchildren.

I remembered coming along this road as a lad, sitting in the back of the float with Peter the gelding speeding along at a smart trot. We were going with Mother and Father into Wales to buy a bull.

That would have been in the first year of the Great War when the prices were still high, but that didn't matter to Father. He was particular about the quality of our bulls. We had neighbours who would keep the odd bull calf and raise it to service the herd. These were what they called scrub bulls and no good they were too. It led to the herd being interbred and getting progressively weaker and more useless. It was a cheap method of farming and that was never Father's way. We used to have the best that we could afford.

'I've been this way before,' I said, looking out of the window at the fields and mountains, 'but a long time ago and never in a car.'

'Did you walk?' Thomas turned round in his seat and stared inquisitively at me. He is a nice little chap, with bright red hair and big blue eyes. He has a gentle innocence about him that I haven't noticed much in the other local children. When I was still getting about, I used to be a little afraid of them.

'Did you walk, Mr Wilde?' he said again.

'No, I went in the carriage,' I said. 'We didn't have a car in those days so we used to go out in a horse and carriage.' His eyes stared at me, disbelieving, I expect. These children nowadays know nothing of a world without motor transport. Cars have been around for eighty years and more. But, fair play, he's only a little lad, so how could he possibly imagine how it was. I smiled at him and thought that when we got home I'd get out some of the old photographs. I know I have some of the horses and I think I remember one of Peter harnessed to the milk wagon.

It was a Sunday, the day we went into Wales all those years ago. Father had met the farmer, Mr Pugh, at market on the Monday previous and they had fallen into discussing stock. Mr Pugh was looking for some good dairy cattle and he had heard of Father's name. Manor Farm was famous in its small way.

'I've got a couple of right good shorthorn milkers,' said Father. 'I'm changing to Friesians and getting rid of all the others, so we could come to some understanding there.'

'Ooh!' We learned later that Mr Pugh started all his conversations with 'Ooh'. 'Friesians? That's modern, I'd say. Well, well, Mr Wilde, very modern.' He shook his head and looked at Father as though he had announced that we were getting our milk from camels or something outrageous like that. The Friesian cattle were actually getting quite popular then amongst dairy men because of the large quantities of milk they produced, but Father was the first farmer in the district to go over entirely. They weren't cheap, mind.

Mr Pugh took off his cap and scratched the sparse grey hairs that covered his old head. He had a funny eye, which had muddled colours and never moved. I think now that it must have been blind but nobody ever mentioned it except our Billy, who used to call him 'old cod eye' behind his back. I think I've said before that Billy didn't like anyone, man or beast, who was defective or disabled. He said it made him sick.

'Ooh, we swear by our shorthorns for milk. Make lovely butter and cheese. Mrs Pugh will tell you that any day.' He thought for a moment and then added, 'Welsh blacks for beef, though.' He came to the house that evening and the deal was done. The deal included a possible cheap price for a young shorthorn bull that Mr Pugh was keen to sell. At that time, Father still favoured them over the Friesians, especially for beef calves, although later we had a fine Friesian bull that served the herd well for years. Two days later, Mr Pugh and his lad came for the beasts, driving into the yard in a small donkey cart. The lad had been brought so that he could drive the cows all the way home. It would take him all day but that was how it was done then.

We often drove the cattle to market, Father and Herbert and even Billy and I when we got older, getting a day off school. One would walk in front, with a bale of hay to tempt the lead cow, and the rest of us, armed with switches cut from the hedge, would follow on, pushing the herd ahead of us towards the town and the cattle pens. It was a job, I can tell you, to make sure that our cows didn't stray up the wrong roads or into people's gardens. But what a brave sight they were in the centre of the town with the small amount of traffic coming to a halt and people turning to watch. It was also wonderful sport. On those days I was proud to be a farmer's son.

And now, here I was back on the summer road to Wales, remembering a day from seventy years ago. The Pughs' farm was a few miles before Pistyll Rhaeadr, the highest waterfall in Wales, and Father agreed that we could make a diversion to see it. 'I believe it's a wonderful sight,' said Mother, and so it was. Even on that hot day at the end of a hot month, it leapt, full and sparkling, down the steep hillside, gushing freezing water into the little river below. I recited the rhyme we had learned in school:

Pistyll Rhaeadr and Wrexham steeple,
Snowdon's mountain without its people,
Overton yew trees, St Winifred's Wells,
Llangollen Bridge and Gresford bells.

These were the seven wonders of Wales, according to Mr Cutts, who had drilled them into us. I think he liked it because he had been born in Gresford. Mother loved that poem and made me repeat it a couple of times and then said we must go sometime and see the other wonders.

'Yes, well,' said Father, helping Mother back into the trap and clicking to Peter, 'that's for another occasion. Now we must get on.'

Mother had packed some bread and cheese, and a couple of bottles of pop. 'We'll stop somewhere nice for a bite,' she said, but we made good time and even though we had stopped at the waterfall for about half an hour we were at the Pughs' farm well before dinnertime.

It was a pretty place, an old stone-and-slate farmhouse, surrounded by ancient barns and set in the lee of a green hill, and it was just as well that we hadn't eaten, for Mrs Pugh had laid on a feast of heroic proportions. We were led into a dim low-ceilinged dining room and sat round an old and marked mahogany table. A huge platter carried a couple of their own chickens roasted to a pale gold succulence and she served them with quantities of vegetables and gravy, prepared to such perfection that I can truly say her cooking rivalled Mother's. We tucked in with relish and even the sound of Mr Pugh 'ooh'ing and 'well, well'ing before and after everything that was said

77

didn't put us off.

The Pughs had a granddaughter, whose name I can't remember now, living with them. Her mother was in service in one of the big houses in Cheshire, so she stayed with the old couple. Nothing was said about the father. The girl was about the same age as me, a little fat girl with yellow ringlets and creamy pink cheeks. She was very quiet and when she did speak it was to her grandmother and in Welsh. I didn't think she had any English. Mother said something to her in Welsh, only a little remark, the few words Mother knew, and the girl smiled but didn't reply.

After home-picked raspberries and cream, Father and Mr Pugh went to examine the bull. Mother helped Mrs Pugh with the clearing up, although the old lady kept protesting and saying that Mother should go into the parlour and have a rest. 'I'd rather help you,' Mother said. 'I don't agree with too much resting.'

We children went outside to play, Billy leading the way as usual and me trailing behind. The girl followed us and watched as Billy and I ran about the yard, kicking the football that Billy had brought with him. I pushed the ball towards her and she shyly put out her little booted foot and kicked it back. We three played happily for a while but then Billy got bored and went off in search of Father. He wanted to see the bull.

I've remembered the girl's name now. It was Kate Ann. I wonder whatever happened to her? She and I played on with the ball until she beckoned to me and I went with her to one of the barns. It was dark and cool inside and I wondered what she wanted me to do. She pointed into one of the stalls and I saw a cardboard box full of sheepdog puppies. They were about four weeks old, warm and smooth with wagging tails that felt like little slippery eels. I fell on to my knees in front of the box and put my hands in amongst them. They loved that and squeaked and tumbled over each other, licking me and giving little play bites. Kate Ann sat down beside me in the straw as we stroked and cuddled the puppies and laughed at their antics.

Suddenly, our Billy appeared at the barn door looking bored and bad-tempered. 'What have you got here?' he demanded, his voice rough and impatient as he bent over to look at the pups.

Kate Ann looked worried and, putting the puppy she'd been holding back in the box, she draped her arm over the litter in a protective way. But Billy wasn't going to be put off. 'Let's have a look, then,' he said, and pushed her arm aside so that he could delve in and grab a couple of the little dogs. He wasn't too gentle about it either and he must have pinched one of them because it let out a terrified squeal.

'Oh!' exclaimed Kate Ann, her plump face scarlet and tears starting in her eyes. 'Bad boy!' and lifting her hand she fetched our Billy such a good smack across his face that a spurt of blood shot out of his nose. I was startled. She seemed just a gentle little thing but she was really angry, so angry indeed that she had remembered some English words.

Well, if I thought she was angry it was nothing to what our Billy was like. His eyes narrowed and

79

that old still look came over his face but I could
see that he was shaking with rage. He threw the
pups down into the box and put up a cautious
hand to his nose. Normally, nobody ever dared
lay a finger on Billy. He was the boss at school
and in the village and I couldn't remember the
last time he'd been in a fight. The other boys were
too scared of him, but this girl seemed fearless. I
wanted to tell her to run, but couldn't speak
because it had all happened so quickly. It was
when he saw the blood on his fingers that he
launched himself at her, belting out an enormous
blow which landed at the side of her head. They
rolled about in the straw, smacking and hitting,
he pulling her hair, and at one point I saw her
sink her teeth into his arm. I was frightened then.
I knew he wouldn't stop until he'd really hurt
her, but I didn't know what to do. I hated fighting
and it was in desperation that I intervened and
tried to pull them apart but they easily shook me
off and I don't know what might have happened
if Mother hadn't come into the barn.

'William!' she shouted, white with anger. She
grabbed hold of his collar, and although he was as
tall as her she hauled him to his feet. The fight
stopped then. Kate Ann wriggled away and stood
beside me, panting, while Mother, still holding on
to Billy's shirt, gave him the fiercest slap across the
head that I have ever seen. He gasped in pain and
for a moment I thought he would start on her because his temper was so roused and he even lifted
a curled fist in her direction. I held my breath.
Nothing like this had ever happened before.

'Don't you dare, William Wilde,' Mother said,

her voice cold and steely. It was probably only seconds, but it seemed an age while I waited, terrified, to see what he would do. He gave in.

'We were only playing,' he said, pretending to laugh and shaking away from Mother's hold. 'Nothing to make a fuss about. She isn't hurt.'

I turned my head to look at Kate Ann. It was true, she didn't seem hurt. Maybe I have been exaggerating the ferocity of the fight, but Mother wasn't satisfied. 'I'm ashamed of you,' she said, looking at Billy as though he were a piece of dirt. 'Get out of my sight.'

When he walked out of the barn, I went with him. I thought that Mother would want to stay with Kate Ann and try to make things right with her and I couldn't let my brother go off on his own. It wouldn't have been loyal.

'She's just a stupid girl,' he said scornfully, but surreptitiously rubbing his ear where Mother's slap had left it red and swollen.

'You shouldn't have hit her, really,' I said. 'She was only taking care of her puppies.' I said this cautiously for I was scared of him and knew that if he was still angry he would turn on me.

He stopped in his tracks and stared at me. For a long moment I thought that this was it and I was going to get a beating and steeled myself for the pain that was to come. I've never had much courage and don't you think it's harder coming from someone you know? But I was lucky that afternoon. Father and Mr Pugh were within earshot and even our Billy had enough sense not show Father up in public.

'I'll get you later,' he hissed, and left it at that. I

silently breathed a sigh of relief because I knew he wouldn't. He would have forgotten about it by the evening, so it was with a light heart that I trailed along beside him back to where Father and Mr Pugh were standing by the bull's pen. We arrived just in time to witness the spit and slapping hand-shake that settled the deal. Father had bought the bull.

The rest of the afternoon passed quietly. Mrs Pugh made a high tea of boiled ham and pickled onions followed by Welsh cakes and gallons of tea. Kate Ann said nothing but I noticed that she had a dark bruise on her chin and scratches on her neck. Her teeth had gone through the skin on our Billy's arm and raised livid weals. I saw Father look at it while we ate our tea but he didn't mention it. I wonder if Mother had found an opportunity to tell him about the fight. Maybe not, because our journey home passed quietly with little conver-sation through the warm evening light, Peter trotting smartly through the hazy lanes until we arrived home and went straight to bed.

The bull came by train the following week and Father and Billy went to the station in the village to walk it home. It was a handsome animal but fiery and probably the most dangerous bull we ever had. Albert Baker found that out one Satur-day afternoon when he and Marian came for their tea.

'That bloody Welsh bull's got out and is run-ning in the home field,' yelled Herbert Lowe, running into the parlour in his stockinged feet, all excited and nervous. 'I need the boss because I'm not tackling that bugger on my own.'

'Oh, dear,' said Mother, putting down the silver teapot, 'Mr Wilde is in town at the public meeting. Only the boys are here.' Father had gone to listen to Mr Lloyd George who was speaking that afternoon at the town hall. Mother had said she would like to go – she was interested in politics – but Marian persuaded her against him. She said there'd been rumours about Lloyd George and women and she for one would never take notice of him again. 'That's silly,' said Mother, but it gave her pause for thought and she stayed at home and had a little tea party instead.

'Our Dick and I will come,' said Billy to Herbert, eager as anything, and jumped up to go into the scullery to get his boots. I got up too, but reluctantly. I was terrified of that bull. Mother looked concerned. 'I don't know,' she said. 'He's far too boisterous for the boys.' Boisterous wasn't a word I'd have used. Wickedly lethal was more like it. But someone would have to go otherwise that bull would run riot through the field and find his way into the cow pasture.

Mother stood up. 'Albert can go with you,' she said. 'I'll feel happier with that.' That was a facer for Albert. He'd been sitting quietly, his teacup on the little wine table and a plate of seed cake on his knee. He was a right townie and despite having been married to Marian now for five years he had no interest in farming. He was interested in the money it brought in, though, and when Father died and there was some talk that Mother might sell up, he made sure that he and Marian were in on every discussion. He was quite disappointed when she decided to carry on. But this

Saturday he was keeping quiet. Even Marian was hesitant. 'Albert doesn't know about bulls,' she said, trying to get him off. 'He'd be no help.'

'He could hold the gate open,' said Mother firmly. 'But if he won't, I'll do it.'

Well, after her saying that, Albert had to go, shod in a pair of Father's gumboots, which squeaked and rattled as he walked along, for he had quite dainty feet, much smaller than Father's.

The Welsh bull was at the top of the home field sniffing the air and deciding the best way to get among the cows on the other side of the fence. He had broken out of the side of his pen and straight into the field beside it. I suppose we were lucky that he hadn't been able to get into the yard and then out into the road. Then we would have been in trouble. Herbert had already put a piece of corrugated iron over the break so that if we could get him back in, he would be secure. The plan was that Billy and Herbert would approach with sticks and drive him down to the gate. Albert and I would stand ready to get him into the yard and then the four of us would drive him into the bull pen.

'Bloody Nora!' said Albert in alarm, looking across the field, and the bull cocked his head back at him and fixed his little red eyes on Albert's boater. My brother-in-law never went anywhere without a hat. Winter it was a bowler, summer a boater.

'Come on,' shouted Billy to Herbert and they walked cautiously along the hedge until they were at the top of the field behind the bull. Billy had armed himself with a piece of iron and

Herbert had a pitchfork.

'Now!' said Billy and they converged on the bull and fetched it great blows on its back so that first it started to trot and then began to gallop down the field. Fair play, he was a good-looking animal in full flight, a heavy red-and-white body on small feet and private parts that swung like great pendulums as he ran. Albert and I pulled the gate back and waited for him to get into the yard. I was scared, but I knew what I had to do and hung on to the gate, making sure that it was between me and the bastard bull. It was Albert's own fault what happened next. He let go of the gate and backed into the yard, going for the big hay barn, I think, but the bull was quicker and tore into the yard like an express train, head down and bellowing for all he was worth.

Albert was lucky. The Welsh bull missed his body altogether but caught the back of his Sunday best jacket in his horns and, lifting his head, tossed Albert high into the air where he performed a perfect somersault. Father's boots stayed behind in the yard. 'Aagh!' cried Albert as he flew across the yard and landed head first in the muck heap beside the trough. His boater spun away in the opposite direction, but the wind caught it and would you believe, it landed at a crazy angle on one of the bull's horns and the straw was pierced right through. Even though the bull was snorting and pawing at the ground, ready for round two, we were all, except Albert, doubled up with laughter and Mother and Marian, watching from the kitchen door, were clutching each other and screaming in mirth too.

Billy got to his senses first and bravely approached the fiery beast. 'Give over, you bugger,' he shouted, bringing the iron bar down on the bull's nose, and Herbert, taking his lead from Billy, used the back end of the pitchfork to push the beast towards the pen. The laughter seemed to have dissipated my fear, and still chuckling I grabbed a big stick and joined in with the prodding and pushing until we had the bull back in his pen.

'Well done, boys,' said Mother when we had the iron gate shut and the animal made safe, 'and thank you, Herbert. I'll make sure Mr Wilde knows how brave you've all been.' Marian had gone over to Albert and was helping him out of the muck heap... I could see that she was still dying to laugh but didn't like to hurt his feelings. That didn't stop Billy, though. He chortled and giggled, pinching his nose between his fingers.

'You'd have been all right if you'd stayed behind the gate, like our Dick,' he said scornfully when Albert trailed back towards the house, dripping with cowshit and smelling like a midden. 'I'd have thought you'd have more sense.'

'That's enough, William,' said Mother, and folded her lips severely so as not to laugh out loud. 'Come into the scullery, Albert dear, and we'll get you cleaned up.'

Oh, what memories. Those days are so clear in my mind.

'Why are you smiling, Mr Richard?' Thomas has taken to calling me that and I don't mind. I think he heard the rector call me by my first name when he came to call last week.

'I was thinking of something,' I said. 'Something funny.' We left it at that and stopped to look at the waterfall. It was still wonderful.

Chapter Seven

It is four o'clock in the morning and I am sitting at my desk. I can't sleep. Too many thoughts, too many memories, which I must get down before ... well, before it is too late.

I have no pain, not really, merely a constant sickness that prevents me from eating much, despite the tempting little snacks that Sharon prepares for me. She gets cross when I don't finish my dinner, but I have persuaded her to put less on my plate and she has now got the hang of it and only gives me titbits. I like those.

Elizabeth has been in my mind a lot. She would be an old, old lady now, if she was still alive, and perhaps I wouldn't find her as beautiful as I once did. I like young people these days. I like their fresh skin and clear eyes and hopefulness. The few middle-aged and elderly I meet, like those busybodies who come from the church, with heavy cakes and dried flowers in little baskets, are unbearable. Fortunately, now, I don't even need to answer the door to them. Sharon tells them I'm asleep and not to bother me and then I see from my window that she puts the dried flowers into the dustbin and picks me a few narcissus or primroses. She knows how much I love fresh living flowers. I think Thomas eats the cakes, though. A little gannet, that boy.

I remember the day Elizabeth first came to the house. I can see her now, walking up the drive, striding along with that floppy blue hat constraining her flying curls and swinging the little cardboard suitcase which contained all her possessions. A striking girl, confident and cheerful, which was strange, considering her background and upbringing. We watched her, Mother and I, from the front bedroom, where we were putting Father's clothes into a big box.

'They must go,' Mother had said, dry-eyed and determined. 'He has no use for them now and there's plenty in the village who might be glad of a warm jacket to see them through the rest of the winter.' She meant the likes of the Kirbys and the Raffertys who lived in the slum cottages by the abattoir. They were helplessly poor, especially the Raffertys since their father was killed in the war. Jimmy Rafferty had been in school with me. I liked him; he was clever but had to give up his lessons early to look for work, which was unfair because he could have easily got into the grammar school like I did. But you had to pay in those days, and then there was the uniform as well. That cost.

The Kirbys weren't such a deserving cause. They were what Mother called feckless. Him in the Golden Lion every night and her not much better with her little mugs of gin. 'Medicinal,' she used to say, if you met her outside the pub where she would sit, rocking the latest baby in a cast-off pram. She had loads of children, but I don't remember any of them at school. I think now that some of them might have been taken away from her by the authorities. I do know that I once saw her, later on, wearing one of Father's working coats, begging for handouts by the station. So the clothes did come to some use, but I hope the Raffertys had their share.

Father died in the January of 1917. He'd been ill for months, bedridden since the November previous and quite unable to speak, or even know who we were, after Christmas week. I'd had my eleventh birthday just before the holiday and he'd been able to whisper a greeting to me, although he got my name wrong and called me Philip. Mother said not to mind, it was good that he had given me his best wishes, but after that he never said anything sensible again.

Dr Guthrie was hopeless. He had no real idea of what ailed Father so Mother paid for a specialist to come down from Rodney Street in Liverpool. They arrived together one afternoon in a smart black car, driven by a chauffeur. We'd seen cars, of course, many times in the town and Father had been planning to buy one with the extra money he was making out of the vegetables, but he'd been taken ill before having the chance. Still, this car, a Wolseley, if I remember rightly, was impressive and Billy and I stood by it for half an hour, admiring every nut and bolt and asking the chauffeur about the buttons and dials on the dashboard. He was a nice bloke and let us sit in the front and touch everything until Marian came out and asked him to come into the kitchen for a cup of tea and a bite of lunch.

I kept my eye on the front bedroom windows, watching the shadows of people passing back and forth as the doctors examined Father. After a while, all movement stopped and I knew that the examination was over. I went inside then and sat on the bottom step of the staircase waiting for them to come down. It seemed to me that this was an important day in my life and so it turned out. The muttered conversation on the landing was hushed and when Mother led the doctors down the stairs I got up and went to sit quietly on the old settle which stood against the wall between the dining room and the parlour. Billy had gone into the yard and Marian was still in the kitchen, but I knew that someone other than Mother should be there to hear the verdict. She didn't say anything, but I recognised the strained look in her eyes as she beckoned me over to stand by her side while she waited for the specialist to speak.

'You must prepare yourself for the worst, my dear,' he said, not dressing up the bad news. 'Farmer Wilde has a growth in the brain. There is no cure. He will not recover. The medicine I have prescribed will only make his passing more comfortable.' He paused and reached out a kindly hand to touch hers. 'I wish I could tell you otherwise.'

Mother had reserves of strength which never failed to impress anyone who ever knew her and they didn't let her down now. No weeping and wailing for her or even a wobble in her voice when she spoke. She merely took a deep breath and said, 'Thank you, doctor, thank you for your honesty. If you'll excuse my being so forward,' she looked into his eyes in the way that she had,

90

that look that impelled truth and straight-forwardness, 'now I need to know how long he has left. How long will he live?'

'A few days, a week or so, maybe.' He shrugged and nervously twisted his silk hat round and round in his hands. I was impressed with his hands; they were the cleanest I'd ever seen. 'I doubt he'll see the month out. I am very sorry.'

Mother remained upright and brave, merely nodding her head at the dreadful news. 'Thank you, doctor. Will you take a cup of tea before you leave?'

He shook his head. It was plain to see that he wanted to be out of the house as quickly as possible and he folded her hand into a warm handshake. 'No, thank you, Mrs Wilde. I have other patients to see.'

He walked towards his car and I trailed after him. The chauffer held the door open for him, giving the smallest bow. That courtesy wasn't offered to Dr Guthrie, who had to get his own self in on the other side. The specialist bestowed a friendly smile on Billy, who had wandered back from the yard, and patted me on the head. Mother watched him from the front door.

'Chin up, little lady,' he called before getting into the back seat of his car, 'you have two fine boys here to carry on.'

I ask you. As though having children made up for the loss of a beloved husband. Mother said nothing, but I knew she took that very badly.

Anyway, after that Father went downhill fast. The medicine prescribed must have been strong stuff,

91

for it kept him asleep most of the time and it took all of Sammy and Mother's strength to get him on to the commode and to roll him from side to side while they changed the bed. Billy and I would go in and wish him goodnight, as we had always done, but it made no difference; he didn't know us and after the first couple of days of Father lying vacantly in the bed Billy refused to go near him again. 'He's finished,' he said hotly to me when we had gone to our bedroom after seeing him. 'There's no point in bothering with him any more.'

I was sorry about that, for they had been very close and always the best of pals, no matter what trouble Billy got himself into. Perhaps my brother was simply upset and that's why he stayed away. He did say that too much work had to be done around the farm, and that was true. Even though it was winter, with short days and some fields lying fallow, the beasts had to be seen to, and the milking. I helped as much as I could when I came home from school, but I still found time to go up to Father. He never knew me, though, and died one stormy night with only Mother sitting beside him. When we got up in the morning, she had laid him out and sent Herbert Lowe for the doctor and the undertaker.

A good crowd turned out for the funeral, not only people from the village but farmers and dealers whom Father had known at the markets and fairs. Amongst them I was surprised to see Mr Pugh from Rhaeadr, who had made quite a journey in the cold winter weather. 'My best respects to you, Mrs Wilde,' he said when Mother greeted him outside the church, 'and I bring the kind thoughts of Mrs Pugh.'

Mother shook his hand warmly. 'Thank you so much for coming,' she said quietly. 'Please come back to the house for a warm drink and a few sandwiches. This weather is not fit for journeying, really.'

Other people greeted her and she repeated the same offer of food and warmth. She had gone straight to St Winifred's from the house, not walking behind Father's coffin as Billy and I had done. In those days, women didn't walk or ride in the funeral procession. Some didn't go to the service at all, clinging to the old belief that funerals were entirely men's business and that women's grief was so private that it must not be shown outside the home. I wonder if they weren't right. Public show of emotion is now commonplace. And the world is none the better for it.

Granny was one of those old believers. She stayed at the house and attended to the meal, grumbling to the other women who had remained with her that Mother was making a show of herself. I didn't think so. She was, as ever, perfectly composed, and greeted the mourners with such respectability and control that none who saw her could doubt that she was behaving correctly.

I remember that I was not composed and cried bitterly at the graveside when the coffin was lowered into the frozen earth. It was a misty afternoon with an early red sunset and a small icy wind that stiffened against my damp cheeks. Spiderwebs had frozen in lacy strings across the yew trees that surrounded the silent churchyard and even the robins and starlings, which normally chattered noisily in the dense green branches, had gone early to roost. My crying seemed to be the only sound. I wanted to stop, fearing that I was spoiling the solemnity, but I couldn't and sobbed and snivelled like a stupid infant. Mother put her arm round my shoulders to comfort me but Billy and Marian stood dry-eyed and imperceptibly moved away. I think they were embarrassed.

Father's death was a terrible blow to me, because although Billy was his favourite he had never been other than kind and fair to me. He was the strength of our family, the best one of us, probably, for although I loved Mother with an almost pathetic childishness, I later found out that she had faults. But that was much later and for all my young years I strived to be more like her, more a Trevellyn and less a Wilde.

Elizabeth came to live with us in that early spring after Father died. We were keeping the farm going, Billy having given up school and Mother taking on more work in the yard. She was a good farmer with a broad knowledge of animal husbandry and never afraid of getting her hands dirty. It was her idea to get a servant. 'It would be cheaper to get a girl to do the cooking and housework,' she said, 'than to hire another farm hand.'

Even Billy, who was tight with money, couldn't fault her logic, so that's what they did. Mother asked Mr Kendrick if he knew of a suitable girl and he found Elizabeth. Elizabeth Nugent, who was the loveliest girl I ever met in all my life.

'Can you cook?' asked Mother after she had brought Elizabeth into the kitchen that first day and given her a cup of tea.

'I can.' The girl smiled and took off her hat so that the wild hair sprang to life and flowed around her head in dark curls. 'I can bake bread and make soup and scouse and fry eggs. They taught me that.'

'They' were the nuns at the orphanage in Liverpool where she had lived for the previous two years. It seemed that her mother had died and her father for some reason was not able to look after her. She was about thirteen then, older than me by nearly two years in time, but twenty in experience. I grinned at her and pushed forward the fruit cake that Mother had put on the table. 'Have some cake,' I said.

'Mm, lovely!' She took a big bite and sighed with pleasure. Her wrists were thin beneath the frayed cuffs of her cotton dress and I guessed she wasn't used to treats like cake. I thought she looked like fun.

Mother wasn't as smitten as I. 'What about cleaning and washing? We'd need all that done, and,' she looked sternly at Elizabeth, 'I'd want it done my way and properly. This is a busy household,' she warned her. 'We haven't time for idlers.'

Elizabeth put down her cake and looked calmly at Mother. 'I'm used to working hard, and I'm prepared to learn. Just tell me what you want me to do.'

As it turned out, Mother came to love Elizabeth almost as much, I think, as I did. Indeed, as she grew older, Elizabeth was the one person that Mother wanted to be with and I knew that she bitterly regretted that her actions caused them to

95

be estranged. Before Elizabeth came to live with us Mother and Marian had been very close, and Mother's new affection for Elizabeth led to some ill-feeling. But it wasn't really surprising because our Marian had become a bitter woman by then. Albert had turned into a disappointment for her, despite his wealth, and then they had no children for her to care for. The church became too important and coloured her thinking to a ridiculous degree.

Our Billy was quite uncomfortable with Elizabeth to begin with. He hated having her in the house and was always worried that he might find her in the bathroom, or, worse, that she might find him. She had taken the middle bedroom, the one that Eddie had vacated, and over the years made it her own. Granny was disgusted. 'She's a servant,' she said. 'Put her in one of the attic rooms. Carpet's too good for her.'

Granny was such a snobbish old woman and with no cause. She'd never had a servant in her life nor even the money to hire one but she always knew better than everybody else and was jealous of the relative comfort in which we lived. At one time, she suggested that she should move in with us, but Mother soon scotched that idea. 'I do think you'd be happier in your own cottage, Mother Wilde, with your daughters next door. After all, since Thomas passed on I'm in the yard a lot of the day and you would have no one to talk to. I'm sure May and Fanny would be heartbroken if you left the village.'

They wouldn't have been. May and Fanny, Granny's youngest daughters, who'd never mar-

96

ried nor barely had the chance with Granny disparaging every man who even looked their way, would have cheerfully given up their virginity to get rid of the old lady. I bet they'd have given up their virginity anyway, if someone had offered. Simply for the experience.

Granny knew Mother was right and didn't bring up the subject again, but she still interfered with our lives almost on a daily basis. Poor Aunty May and Aunty Fanny were made old before their time and when Granny died they were left in a sad condition. Aunty May only lived a few weeks after but her sister lingered on miserably until she was in her nineties, fifty more wasted years of a lonely out-of-step life, with no friends of her own age or anyone else's, for that matter.

Elizabeth fell in to work straight away. Without asking, she washed up those first cups of tea and went round lighting the lamps as it got dark. Mother showed her the pantry and the meat safe and said that a bit of bacon and potatoes and cabbage would make a supper, if Elizabeth could manage. It was a Saturday and we always had scraps on that day. Mother had a nice piece of our own pork for Sunday dinner.

'Sure I can, Mrs Wilde. Leave it to me.'

So, reluctantly at first, because she was a proud housewife, Mother did indeed leave it to Elizabeth and was rarely let down. The house was clean and warm, food was ready on time, clothes were washed and ironed and even our boots were polished in time for Sunday worship. Needless to say, Granny wasn't satisfied.

'I don't take to that girl,' she'd say, watching out

of the kitchen window as Elizabeth hung baskets of washing on the line. 'She thinks too much of herself.' Exactly how Elizabeth's 'thinking too much of herself' manifested itself Granny never divulged, but I suppose it could have been the fact that she cheerfully ignored Granny's remarks and refused to take offence. Following Granny's lead, Aunty May and Aunty Fanny started to be quite spiteful to Elizabeth but Mother soon stopped that. 'Elizabeth works for me, May,' she said sharply one afternoon when Aunty May criticised the way the washing was being folded, 'and I'll thank you to remember that.'

'Hoity toity!' said Granny, who had encouraged the criticism, bobbing her head up and down like one of our old chickens. 'There's no need for nastiness, Mary.'

'Every need,' said Mother. 'I won't have interference, Mother Wilde. I run this house and farm, as well you know.' Granny gave in then. She couldn't best Mother and seemingly never had been able to, even when Mother was a young bride first come to Manor Farm.

'Now then,' said Mother, her flurry of temper subsiding, 'What about a nice cup of tea?'

The only trouble was that having been cut off from having a go at Elizabeth, Granny turned on me. 'Why isn't this lad working yet?' she demanded.

I was at home that morning, the last day of my Easter holiday. This was my first year in the grammar. I loved school and was doing well. Amazingly, for a farm boy, I turned out to be good at classics, a useless skill in our village, but one which

98

fascinated me. A page of Latin translation held almost as much interest for me as a page from a favourite novel. I was good at French and German too. Science subjects were my downfall, and for all the excellent teaching I wasn't half as good at arithmetic as our Billy. Mother said she was proud of me and even Billy, although he teased me about using long words, never said a word against my staying on at school when he'd been working since he was barely thirteen. It was Granny and the aunties who scorned my education.

'Anyone would think he was the son of a gentleman,' said Granny, getting up from her chair and picking out my school shirt from the wash basket.

'He is,' said Mother fiercely, snatching the shirt and giving Granny such a look that the old lady turned away and picked up her stick ready for her walk back to the village. She paused at the door and straightened her hat while she waited until the aunties went through into the yard.

'All I can say, Mary Constance, is that you would know better than anyone else about that.'

When she'd gone I said, 'You know, Mother, she was right. Father was a farmer, not a gentleman.'

'He was both,' she said quietly. 'I only wish I'd realised it sooner.'

I didn't understand what she meant and even now I wonder about it. There must have been a part of her mind that I didn't know and she was the person I thought I knew better than any other. Even than my adored Elizabeth.

Well, Elizabeth stayed on despite Granny, or maybe even to actually spite her, and soon she

99

was as much a part of the family as any of us children. Mother taught her farm work as well as housework and within a year she was indispensable in the milking parlour and dairy. She made friends with Sammy Philips and he showed her how to deliver a calf and the quickest way to dispatch a cockerel.

'I can't,' she wailed, the first time, when she had the poor unwanted bird between her knees and her hands round its neck. 'Sure and it's too cruel.'

'Get on with it,' yelled Billy. We were sitting on the gate watching. Sammy had taught us how to do it years before when we were nippers and my brother cheerfully killed a few birds every week, ready for market. I, on the other hand, would never kill an animal if someone else was around to do it for me.

Sammy gave our Billy a hard look. 'Leave her alone, Billy Wilde,' he said.

'Well, she's being a babby.' Being a babby was Billy's most damning comment. It had been directed at me on many an occasion, usually called for, but not always.

'I'm not!' Elizabeth shouted, stung into action, and with a grunt she pulled and twisted the bird's neck until it snapped cleanly and it was dead. 'There,' she cried, 'I've done it.'

'Well done,' I said. I thought she was brave, but Billy only laughed.

'Babby!' he repeated.

'Oh, am I?' Elizabeth looked up from the quivering corpse now dangling from her hands and with a sudden movement sprang up and dashed

100

across to the gate. Before we had a chance to move she had lifted up the white cockerel by its twitching yellow feet and fetched Billy a wallop across the head with it.

'Bloody hell!' he yelled as he fell off the gate into the yard and rolled helplessly in the mud. Feathers flew everywhere and Elizabeth climbed into the place Billy had so precipitately left and gave a triumphant 'cock a doodle do'. Sammy Philips snorted with laughter and I laughed too but my laughter was tempered with nervousness. I recalled the little Pugh girl, Kate Ann, and how Billy had attacked her. He had been out of control on that occasion and this was exactly the sort of humiliation that he couldn't abide.

I watched as Billy got to his feet and wiped a dollop of mud away from his cheek. For the briefest moment I saw that look, that still, sickening look that I hated and others had learned to fear. But I needn't have worried. His face suddenly creased into a grin and he joined in the laughter.

'I'll give you "cock a doodle do",' he pretended to growl, and gave Elizabeth a gentle punch on the arm.

'Aah, away with you,' she said, still laughing, her eyes friendly and unafraid, and she slid over on the gate so that he could climb up again to join us. We were three healthy youngsters then with nothing coming between us and life was carefree. I don't think Elizabeth realised how close she'd been to a belting at that time, but I knew, and she came to know it too in later years.

Chapter Eight

It is the last day of April today and the weather is warm like July. I sat in the garden this morning, under the laburnum tree. Sharon put out the old Lloyd Loom chair from the back bedroom and padded it with cushions, so I spent a pleasant hour watching the sky and listening to the birds in the fruit trees. The laburnum isn't in flower yet, but the leaves are bursting through; pale green, finger-shaped leaves that carry happy memories for me. Thomas's dog, Phoebe, a silly half Labrador and half I don't know what, but black and placid, came to sit beside me. She puts her nose into my hand all the time, snuffling and grunting for affection, and I, foolishly, give her what she wants. I like the smell of her and the feel of her smooth coat on my skin.

Andrew Jones, the solicitor, came round. I had made the appointment last week, but to be honest I'd forgotten about it until Sharon showed him into the garden and offered to get him a chair.

'Don't bother, Sharon,' he said, casual about using first names like these young people are. 'I'll sit on the lawn. I'd like that.' Phoebe gave him a sniff and wagged her tail but came back to sit by me.

We talked and watched the sky together. These days, constant streaks of white criss-cross the blue heavens because of the planes flying over us.

Andrew said that we are on at least three flight paths but not near enough to the airports for us to see the jets properly. They are flying at many thousands of feet above us here. I haven't been on an aeroplane for years but I wouldn't mind a trip somewhere. I've always loved travelling.

The plane that brought me out of Burma was a Lancaster bomber and I lay on a stretcher, being shaken about even though it had been fastened with webbing straps to the fuselage. It had no stewardesses bringing me meals and champagne, like those passengers flying so high above me this morning. Only young army nurses, who, although looking almost as exhausted as me and my fellow stretcher cases, cared for us with dedicated compassion on that terrifyingly bumpy flight across the Hump.

The Scottish sister in charge of them was supposed to be a dragon, but I didn't find her so. 'Welcome to Chittagong, sergeant,' she said as I was loaded off the plane into the blinding sunshine and sweltering heat of the military airport. 'You'll be well looked after now,' and it wasn't only me who breathed a sigh of relief. I could hear a similar sigh coming from the nurse who had stood by me for most of the flight. She had a sweet babyish face and her dark hair reminded me a bit of Elizabeth's. She couldn't have been more than twenty years old.

That pleasant moment ended abruptly when Ted Potter, a private from my squad who was in the stretcher beneath me on the ambulance taking us from the airport to the hospital, grabbed her arm. 'I need a piss, nurse,' he said crudely. I saw

103

no need for that sort of talk, no matter that he'd lost a hand to gangrene and had malaria and dengue fever like the rest of us. I was embarrassed for her. She seemed too young and fresh to have to listen to that. But she took it in good heart and gave no indication that she found it distasteful but reached for and took away the bottle discreetly under a green towel.

'Take no notice of him, miss,' I said when she bent over me to see if I wanted a drink. 'He's not a bad chap. We couldn't have done without him in the jungle. It's just his hand that's bothering him.'

'I know,' she said with a kind smile. 'Don't worry.'

Later, I found out that she was terrified of flying, but had bravely pretended to me and the other wounded that she had enjoyed the experience. It was like that during the war, everyone trying to be devil-may-care, no matter what happened. Not many obvious cowards were about, at least not that I met. Men and women hid their feelings from each other, specially their fears. I often think that if one of us in the Naga Hills had given way we all might have done and, God knows what would have happened then. The Japs would have had a field day with us.

I got to know Lucy well in the following weeks and at one time I almost thought I might be in love with her. I think she was with me and was miserable when I was shipped home. Poor girl, she might have made me happy but she knew that my heart was elsewhere. She knew that from the start. I think I'd been mumbling things when I was feverish with the malaria.

I thought of Lucy again this morning while I was watching the vapour trails and wondered if she ever flew again after we parted. Probably not.

'I want to change something in my will,' I said to young Jones.

'Thought you might,' he said, a bit cheekily. 'That's what these calls out usually are.'

I looked down at him. He was lying on his back with his arms folded under his head. How wonderful to be that young and relaxed. Most of his life in front of him and an attitude that would allow him to enjoy it. 'Get your pen out,' I growled, 'and write this down.'

After he'd gone, I came inside and had a sleep. I feel better today than I have for a week or so. It's the warm weather, I know it. My old bones don't ache so much and I can rest easier in my bed. Life is still sweet on days like today.

Sharon has asked me if I mind if Thomas has a few friends in at the weekend for his birthday party.

'I don't mind,' I said, 'but I didn't know you knew anyone round here.'

'Well,' she said, 'it's just a few kids from his school; he goes to their parties, so I have to ask them back. Don't worry, I'll keep them out of your way, in the kitchen or in the garden, but if it would be a nuisance I can take them out to a burger bar.' She thought for a moment, chewing on the earpiece of the spectacles that she always carries with her. Every spare moment she has her head in a book. 'Yes, perhaps that's for the best.'

'No.' I wasn't going to let her disappoint the child. 'Don't do that. Ask them here. After all, it's

105

the only home the little lad's got. He has to have somewhere to feel he belongs.'

Sharon screwed her face up at that and for a moment I thought she was going to cry. She didn't, but she did lean over my desk where I'd come to sit after my sleep and dropped a little kiss on my forehead. 'You really are an old sweetie,' she said and left the room quickly. I have become stupidly fond of this girl and am tempted to believe that she is indeed a descendant of the Major. She has the same charm and nobility that he had. I do hope the rest of her behaviour is better than his was, though.

Birthday parties weren't celebrated much when we were children. Mother would make a cake and decorate it with a candle to make it different from the cakes she made every day and we would get a small present. Mine was always a book and that was fine because I have loved books from the day I learned to read. Our Billy used to get football boots and once a cricket bat, which was a big present because cricket bats weren't cheap. Maybe it was second hand, I don't remember, but he loved it and we played for hours in the field, although it was late in the year and well past the cricket season.

Elizabeth's birthday was in July and in later years we used to have parties for her. I remember one in particular when we had a swimming party. It was the last summer before I left the farm and the end of my childhood. I was seventeen then, tall and gawky with arms and legs that always seemed too long for my body. 'Don't worry,' Mother used to say, 'you'll grow into yourself.'

At the time, that old adage, which was what people always said in our village, was no comfort, but later, when I was in my twenties and had put on some weight to balance out my height, I understood. At twenty-five, I stood six foot three in my stockinged feet and weighed fourteen stone. Mind you, when I came out of Burma I was barely nine stone and must have looked like a skeleton.

Father and our Billy were heavy too, but they hadn't the height. I don't think Billy made five foot eight, but he was stronger than I was and a much better sportsman. If he'd been in the army, he would have been the boxing champion or some-thing like that and maybe even won more combat medals than me. He was never frightened of anything was our Billy and would have joined up, but being a farmer was in a reserved occupation so stayed at home for the duration. Fair play, though, he didn't complain. Simply got on with the job.

Anyway, that was later and I'm thinking now about that swimming party for Elizabeth. She was nineteen that July and the most beautiful girl in the area. I can't properly describe how lovely she was: you would have to see her. To watch her walk into a room with her easy grace, her soft curls bouncing down her back and those dark blue eyes so merry and cheerful, you would be dumbstruck with her loveliness. And yet she seemed not to care about her looks or her figure. I can't remember her spending hours looking in the mirror the way our Marian had done when she was a girl. Of course Marian wasn't as pretty, so perhaps her long stares into the looking-glass were more searching.

She wasn't plain, our Marian. In fact plenty of people thought her quite a catch and I remember being told that she was one of the most eligible girls in the village. I can tell you that Albert Baker wasn't the only young man who courted her; he was simply the one she decided on. The most suitable, I suppose. And they made a handsome couple coming down the aisle at St Winifred's, he in his best grey suit and stiff collar and she with a wreath of orange blossom circling her short brown hair. She wore Mother's lace wedding dress with a long veil flowing out behind her and that veil caused an incident that was talked about in the village for years afterwards. It had been an unseasonably cold March that year and the wind blew in cruelly from the open church door, making the delicate lace fly about and wrap itself closely about her narrow body and face. Albert struggled clumsily to free her and when she emerged from the winding sheet she was as pale as the dress. Even her lips, which parted in a controlled little smile as she bowed from side to side to our friends gathered in the pews, were pale. Some of the older people drew in their breaths and shook their heads.

'Oh my good gracious,' Granny whispered loudly to Aunt May, 'if that isn't an unlucky sign I don't know what is.'

'Hush, Mother Wilde,' said Mother, and gave Granny such a look that she was quiet and sulky for the rest of the day.

I didn't think that it was unlucky for the wind to tangle our Marian up in the veil, nor did I think she looked upset. She was always pale. It was as though she had never been out of doors in her life; you'd never have taken our Marian for a country girl. Father always called her his 'fine lady'.

But Elizabeth was cut from a different cloth. Where Marian's skin was papery white, Elizabeth's was thick and creamy like the milk that came from Mother's little Jersey house cow. I always thought she looked at her best in the summer when she had been out in the fields and her skin had taken on a warmer colour. Then her eyes seemed a deeper blue and her lips full and pink and I found it an endless pleasure to watch her and smell the fresh scent of meadow grass and lavender that wafted around her. I recall the corn-flower blue dress with what she and Mother called a 'sweetheart' neckline which she wore all one summer. Many's the teatime I sat opposite her at the kitchen table, staring at the creamy skin that rose and fell so carelessly above the fabric. Our Billy would be going on about the latest success he'd had with the cattle or one of the shires and Mother would be sitting behind the teapot listening and watching.

'Go and refill the pot,' she said crossly to me one afternoon when I'd been staring at Elizabeth, and I remember now the hot sting of embarrassment as the blood rushed into my face. Billy didn't notice. He always missed any by-play; it didn't interest him. I think Elizabeth guessed though, for as I came back with the pot a little smile played about her lips and she lowered her eyelashes when she turned to me with the plate of ginger cake. Was that flirting? It must have been. Unconscious on my part but probably not on hers. The beginnings, I suppose, of what was to be the driving force of my life for the next forty years. I would never experience happiness more exquisite than that which I shared with her nor yet such heartbreaking despair.

I went to buy a horse once at the Dublin horse show and saw women who looked a lot like Elizabeth. They were from the west of Ireland, strong confident girls who could judge horseflesh as well as any man and were never at a loss for words to answer you back. I suppose Elizabeth was from the same roots; a lot of Liverpudlians are Irish or Welsh, or a mixture of the two. What is it about the Celts? They are so different from us ordinary English. Their ability to achieve extreme joy and extreme sadness is unparalleled, as is their ability to pass it on. It would seem that you can't have one without the other and, what is so much worse, you are willing to bear the pain to get the ecstasy.

She had callers coming to the house, lots of them fine lads, friends of ours from the village, but she wouldn't look at them as anything other than pals. Groups of us would go on picnics and always a couple or two would be having a cuddle up in the heather, but not Elizabeth. She said she was saving herself for Mr Right. I never knew who she meant and I don't think she did either, but it was something Mother had taught her. She and Mother were very close.

'Will you come to the church social with me?' asked Johnny Lowe, Herbert's grandson, who had come home from the Great War with only one eye. He was a few years older than us, but lots of his friends had been killed at the front and in

110

those days he still lived at home. Never short of money was Johnny Lowe and the lads in the village whispered that he'd taken it from dead soldiers and not only the Hun, but I didn't think so. He was a straight sort of person with a good head on his shoulders. He had got into the buying and selling of supplies, blankets and biscuits and even wine, quite legally, I believe, even before his discharge and was now in business in the town. By the time he was thirty he was a millionaire living in London, and Elizabeth couldn't have done better than to have married him. She would have been a real lady, but she didn't want him.

'I'm going with Billy and Richard,' she answered, but added, letting him down lightly, 'I'll see you there.'

He'd nodded, grinning in his lopsided way, for the bullet that had taken out his eye had also cut a furrow through the nerves in his cheek and left a scar not only on the outside. 'All right,' he said. 'You can promise me the last waltz.'

Elizabeth smiled at that. The last waltz meant something in those days. It was nearly as important as an engagement ring. As it happened, she danced the last waltz with me at that social, but only because she was holding me up. I'd been drinking and she didn't want Mother to see.

Johnny was one of the group who came to her birthday picnic. He and my pal Fred Darlington, and some of the other boys. Our girl cousins from the village had been invited too although we weren't that close to them. They were dull but necessary as chaperons, if nothing else. Elizabeth was quite pally with Mary Phoenix, who was a sort

111

of cousin. Her granny was Granny's sister and a much nicer person, as I remember. She drank a bit, though, and Granny never had a good word for her. Mary was a nice girl, in service at a big house where she was learning to be a cook. She was jolly and giggled a lot over silly things. You'd always be sure of a good audience if you told Mary a joke. She'd scream with laughter even if she didn't get it. Some of the lads used to tell her dirty jokes which I'm sure, being quite an innocent, she didn't understand, but she would go into gales of laughter and the lads seemed to get more wicked pleasure out of that than from the pathetic joke itself. I must confess that I once sat in on one of those joke-telling sessions with Mary Phoenix and found it most amusing, but our Billy walked in on us in the back of the church hall and was really angry.

'Come away, Dick,' he said, furious and dragging me by the arm. 'Those are mucky stories, not fit to listen to.' He never liked anything even in the slightest bit salacious. For a farmer, he was prudish, and in that way quite like our Marian. As we left, the boys were still sniggering and Mary looking round all confused and pink-faced but laughing.

'You're a common slut, Mary Phoenix!' shouted Billy over his shoulder as we reached the door, 'listening to all that dirty talk.' I felt bad for her then and even the other lads looked embarrassed, but Mary seemed to think it was all part of the joke and carried on laughing. For a moment, I thought Billy would run back and hit her. He was shaking with rage, but I walked on towards the door and he followed me.

Elizabeth had also asked Jane Parry to come. She was the daughter of poor Mabel who had got pregnant at our house after I was born. Mother didn't like her, but I think Elizabeth was curious. She asked me a couple of times about the story and then said, 'Poor thing' in an indignant tone. She asked me who I thought the father could be but I had no idea and was no help.

The day of the party was glorious. A hot July day with cloudless skies and an eighty-degree temperature at midday. The swimming was to take place late in the afternoon when all the guests had finished work and school. Mother and Elizabeth spent most of the day making the picnic which we would take up to the river. Billy had harnessed up Peter, a grey and whiskery old horse now, but still willing and able and the easiest animal in the world to manage. They had put the food in grease-proof paper parcels into wicker baskets and loaded them on to a little cart which Peter would pull. Mother added towels and extra cardigans and shawls in case the girls felt cold, though it was baking hot and wasn't cooling off as the afternoon wore on. A crate of pop had been delivered from the Golden Lion, cherryade and Vimto and Billy's favourite, dandelion and burdock. Fred Darlington sneaked in some bottles of beer and Johnny Lowe brought a bottle of spirits. Our Billy didn't know about these; he wouldn't have approved, but I did and had a good few swigs. I've always liked a drink.

All of us youngsters gathered in the yard at about five o'clock and sang 'Happy Birthday' to

113

Elizabeth before trailing away in groups of two or three across the fields towards the river. Billy led the horse by its neck halter and I walked along beside him. I remember being excited, loving the occasion and burning with desire to give Elizabeth the present I had saved so hard to buy.

'What are you getting for her birthday?' I had asked Billy a few days earlier.

He looked at me quite astonished. 'I don't know,' he said. 'Never even thought about it.'

'Well, you should. She's like a sister to us. You always get Marian something.'

Billy nodded thoughtfully as he heaved bales of sweet-smelling meadow hay into the barn. At almost twenty he was in his prime. Rippling muscles moved strongly beneath the brown skin of his arms and his fresh face gleamed with good health. His brown hair curled at the nape of his neck and as I stood there watching him, I was envious. I wanted desperately to be that handsome. The only thing was that he didn't have a girlfriend and my pals used to discuss that for hours. They made all sorts of suggestions, most of them pretty coarse, and I had a regular job defending him.

'The farm takes up all his time,' I said, and that was true. We had a lot of land, more than most of the other farmers in the area, and in order to turn a profit you needed to be at it every hour of the day. Billy was making a good profit, so good in fact that he was talking of sending me to university. Mother was all for it and encouraged both of us to consider the proposal as a normal extension of my schooling. I was keen too, anxious to show off my academic prowess in front of the family and the village. I see now what foolish pride I had, and no shame. God knows, it has always been true that pride goes before a fall, but I don't think I deserved such a steep descent.

But back to Billy. Lots of girls lowered their eyes before him and giggled to each other when we walked into church or into the village hall, but he wasn't interested. He liked Elizabeth though, admiring the way she had with the beasts and her no-nonsense approach to life. We had a happy life at home, Mother, Elizabeth, Billy and me, all friends and close as any family could be. So when I mentioned her birthday gift, it gave Billy something to think about.

I had my present for her safely wrapped in tissue paper in my trouser pocket, and as I walked beside him towards the river I kept putting my hand into the pocket and touching the paper. I had bought her a necklace of blue and silver beads, which I had found in the market some weeks before.

'It's real silver, mister,' the gypsy woman said, 'and gemstones between.' She was often at the beast market, sitting behind a little table where oddments of jewellery and tarnished cutlery were on display. Our Billy would have it that everything she sold had been pinched, but I know Mother bought one or two things from the woman, so it seemed all right for me to do likewise.

I picked up the necklace. The links between the stones did look like silver, but the beads were probably glass. None the less they were the colour of Elizabeth's eyes and I knew that they were meant for her. 'How much?'

'Five shillings.'

This was a facer. Five shillings was all I'd saved since Easter when I'd spent my previous savings on a school trip to London. That had cost quite a bit, but I didn't regret a penny of it. I was the first person in the family to ever go to London. But I'd hoped to have some of that five shillings left to go to Patsy Collin's circus when it came to our town in September.

'I've got half a crown,' I fibbed, knowing as I said it that my face was flushing. My hair always prickled when I lied.

The gypsy woman laughed. 'You silly young bugger,' she said coarsely, 'you think I was born yesterday?'

I looked again at the necklace. It was meant for Elizabeth and I had to have it. 'All right,' I sighed, and taking the coins out of my pocket I dropped them on her table where they spun for a moment amongst the dirty spoons and brooches.

The gypsy gave a knowing little smile as she picked up the necklace and gave it a quick polish on the coloured fabric that covered her thin breast. A piece of tissue paper was produced from her pocket and the necklace wrapped securely. She looked at me again and then said, 'Go on then, son, you can have it for four,' but as I reached down to retrieve the extra shilling she suddenly grabbed hold of my hand and turned it over to look at the palm. When she looked up at me again her face had lost its sly grin.

'It won't do you any good, mister,' she said. 'She's meant for another.'

'The necklace is for my mother,' I said quickly, lying again, acting like the foolish young man I

116

was. But she had turned away to serve another customer and had, for all I knew, already forgotten what she'd said to me. Looking back now, I can't really remember if I took that warning to heart, or even if I took it seriously. But then, I suppose her prediction did find a pocket in my mind or else why would I have remembered it all these years on?

Chapter Nine

Dr Clewes came to see me yesterday and after his examination stayed for a bit of a chat. We sat in the kitchen, for the weather has turned dull and rainy this week.

'How am I doing?' I asked. I wasn't really interested in his reply because I know that I haven't long to go, but, perversely, I've felt better these last few weeks than I have for a long time. Maybe he would revise his previous diagnosis.

Dr Clewes pursed his lips and gave me a calculating stare before replying. 'Your illness is progressing,' he said, and added, in his no-nonsense way, 'as I told you at the outset, untreated cancer can only get worse.'

I shrugged. Treatment at my age is a pointless exercise. 'I feel not too bad,' I said. 'Some pain now and then but I'm still enjoying my food, and' – I tapped my head – 'I've still got my marbles.'

He smiled at that. 'So I gathered.'

A sudden squall of rain rattled on the window

and we both looked round. I like my kitchen, but then I always have done. In Mother's time it smelled of baking bread or maybe clean washing, for the wooden pulley was hoisted to the ceiling above the range and our clothes hung there on washdays to air. Now as I look up I can see a pair of Thomas's shorts and other bits and pieces of clothing hanging there. Very homely this room is, clean and fresh and a pleasure to be in once more. The old horse brasses around the range are polished and a vase of deep red tulips brightens up the back windowsill. Thomas's artwork decorates the door of the refrigerator.

Sharon was listening to our conversation while she made us a drink. 'I think Mr Wilde could do with some stronger painkillers,' she said, clearing her throat as though nervous about butting in and her face going slightly pink. I think she felt as though she were intruding on a private conversation, but I don't hide my medical condition from her. It would be impossible. I did at first. Not wanting her to know that I suffered, preferring to keep that to myself. But I was in a lot of pain one night and knocked over my carafe and glass in my efforts to get at the aspirin. Sharon came downstairs then and knocked gently at my door.

'It's all right,' I said, when she came in, 'I just barged into the table. Go back to bed.'

She said nothing for a moment, and then leant over and picked up the glass and carafe. 'Get into bed. I'll clear this up.'

She went for a cloth to mop the carpet and then vanished back into the hall. I thought she'd gone upstairs but after a little while she reappeared

118

with a cup of tea and a hot water bottle. 'Here,' she said, tucking the bottle against my back where it imparted a wonderfully comforting glow and settled some of my aches and pains. She opened the aspirin bottle and offered two on the palm of her slim hand. 'Better take these, if you've nothing stronger. They should help a bit.'

I grumbled that it didn't matter and she mustn't fuss, but I was glad that she had come in. After all these years of living on my own, I'd forgotten how cheering a bit of company is. Especially in those cold and lonely early morning hours.

Now she was speaking up for me, making sure that I don't pretend I can cope. I am a silly old man, vain as ever, trying to be braver than I am.

Dr Clewes nodded his head. 'I was going to suggest that,' he said, and got out his prescription pad to scribble out a new medicine. 'I think this will keep the pain at bay for a while. We might have to go on to something stronger in a month or so...' He left the rest of the sentence unsaid. It wasn't necessary. All three of us knew what he was talking about.

Sharon put a pot of coffee on the table with a plate of iced ginger cake, which she knows I love, before disappearing back to the dining room where she has set up her computer. That computer is a marvellous machine and I am amazed at the things it can do.

'Here,' she said the other day, after sitting me down in front of it, 'press that button and see what happens.' To my surprise a picture of the farm appeared, and then when I pressed again another replaced the first and then more, including one of me sitting under the laburnum tree with my old panama hat on. I remember Andrew Jones taking that photograph the day he came to change my will. He had just bought a fancy new camera and wanted to try it out. These lovely spring pictures are the result. Somehow, and although she tried to explain it to me I couldn't grasp the technical details, they have been able to transfer them on to the computer. Andrew and Sharon are good friends now.

'I suppose that's very clever,' I said grudgingly, for I like to tease her a bit, 'but I've got a photograph album up there in the bookshelf that I can look in any time I like. That's good enough for me.'

'Go on with you,' she laughed, 'you old Luddite!'

Now, I know what a Luddite is, but I have to say I was surprised that she did. I've been underestimating that girl. That college course she's taking must be having an effect. Anyway, we both laughed and she knows I'm only having a bit of fun with her. I pulled out the photograph album later that day and had a happy hour looking at the pictures. It was on the kitchen table when Dr Clewes came, for I had been showing snaps of the old shire horses to Thomas.

The doctor opened the album as he sipped his coffee. 'May I?' he asked.

I nodded and watched as he turned the stiff blue paper pages and peered closely at the faded pictures.

'Is this you?' he said, pointing at that old picture of me standing by the lychgate of St Winifred's in my school uniform. Mother was so proud when I went to the grammar school that she asked Mr Kendrick, who had a camera, to take a photograph.

I nodded. 'I was eleven then. First week at big school.'

He turned over a few more pages. 'Here you are again, I think. Older now.' He looked more closely. 'And these two people? Your brother and sister perhaps?'

I pulled the album over towards me and put on my glasses so that I could examine the photograph properly. It brought back such strong memories that sitting in the kitchen eighty years later I could almost smell the scent of wild flowers and hear the relentless buzz of honey bees. It was a scene taken on a summer's day and despite the sepia tones, to me it was all colour. Three young people leant over a wooden farm gate and looked into my eyes. One boy sturdy and solemn, one lanky and grinning like a fool with his head half turned towards the girl who gazed at the camera as though it were a lover returning from a voyage to faraway lands.

'No,' I said, my breath suddenly catching in my throat, 'not exactly. That boy was my brother, but the girl wasn't my sister.' The next words I said were cowardly and stupid. A denial of everything that came later. I took off my glasses and looked up at his plump earnest face. 'No, not my sister,' I repeated slowly. 'She was a girl who lived with us. A farm servant.'

After Dr Clewes had gone, I brought the album with me into my parlour and propped it open at that page on my desk, so that I could keep looking at it. It is staring at me now as I continue with my story. Oh, I so well remember that picture being taken. It was the day of the swimming picnic, which I was writing about a week ago. We had a camera of our own by then. We had lots of things, even a car. The farm was successful and Billy, for all his narrow-mindedness, was not mean.

Mother took that picture. 'My three children,' she said, looking from one to the other of us in turn and then quickly adding, thinking of Marian, I suppose, 'well, those that are at home, anyway.'

Then later on when we were walking Peter towards the river, Mother came running after us. 'Here,' she said, putting the box Brownie into my hands. 'Make sure you take some snaps.'

'His hands always wobble,' snorted our Billy. 'I'm better with the camera.'

'No they don't!'

'They do.'

Mother clucked her tongue and shook her head in mock anger. 'Boys! Boys! How old are you? Behave yourselves.'

I put the camera in the wagon with the picnic baskets and truth to tell I forgot about taking any photos. Too much happened that evening and I'm glad in a way. The one taken earlier couldn't be bettered.

Elizabeth and the others had reached the river by the time we arrived. We had to open and close gates for Peter and the wagon, so when we got to the place where the weeping willows dipped into the water beside a little dusty beach, the boys and girls had separated into two parties behind bushes so that they could change their clothes. Some of the girls didn't want to swim and emerged from

122

cover still in their summer frocks, but those who did had put on black one-piece suits and giggled shyly as they stepped carefully towards the sparkling river.

'Here I come, ready or not,' yelled Fred Darlington, leaping out from behind the boys' cover and running with huge steps straight into the water.

'Oh!' the girls screamed as they were splashed and then 'Oh' again as the other boys followed him and larked about tossing handfuls of water at each other and diving under the rippling surface to catch at unaware legs.

Mary Phoenix was the first of the girls to get in. 'It's lovely,' she said, stepping in and sinking down so that first her broad hips and then those generous breasts, which bulged out of the armholes of her costume, were submerged. She didn't seem to mind the heart-stopping cold of the water the way the rest of the girls did. They squeaked and cried as they hopped gingerly into the river making a dreadful fuss before settling into gentle swimming and paddling. Elizabeth herself squealed a bit but then sank into the slow-moving river and set out with broad strokes for the opposite shore.

Billy had taught her to swim a few summers before and she was as competent at that as she was at all practical things. When I had changed I ran into the water too and struck out after her, but the opposite bank was nearly two hundred yards away and she was already sitting under a stand of grey alders with Johnny Lowe when I reached her. We lay there, the three of us, in the evening sun, watching the antics of the others, our Billy leading the pack of dunkers and leg holders and Mary Phoenix happily letting the boys grab hold of her wherever they would. Elizabeth shook her head. 'Poor Mary,' she said with a sigh that made her sound older than her years. 'If she doesn't find a husband soon, who knows what might happen.'

I knew what she meant, but even though I regularly joined in the smutty talk with the other lads at the back of the Golden Lion, I couldn't really credit that sort of 'all the way' behaviour for Mary or any of our pals. As far as I was concerned, nobody ever really did it; it was all talk.

'I've got a present for you, Elizabeth,' Johnny said after we had turned away from contemplating Mary, 'but we'll have to go back to the other side to get it.'

She smiled at him, parting those pink lips and showing her even teeth. I felt a sudden burn in my stomach, a churning which travelled outwards so that my fists curled and the beginnings of hot tears pricked in my eyes. At the time I barely recognised it, thinking for a moment that perhaps I was ill or had swallowed too much river water, but of course it was jealousy. I couldn't bear the thought that anyone outside the family could be close to our girl.

Johnny jumped off the bank and held out his hand to her. 'Come on,' he said, and as I sat up, getting myself together, she slid off the edge and joined him in the water. For a moment they held hands before setting off back to the little beach. My swim across the river was hectic and rough, splashing more than swimming and getting nowhere fast, in my hurry to keep up with them.

They were drying themselves off when I scrambled out of the water, laughing and joining with all the others and behaving as though nothing had happened. Indeed, Elizabeth threw me a towel so nonchalantly that I was immediately ashamed of my previous feelings. The fact was, I realized, that nothing had happened and I was imagining everything.

We ate the picnic in the blue and pink glow of a summer evening, boys and girls lolling on the grass and talking on the cool river bank. Of the dozen of us, Elizabeth was the queen of the party.

'Present time!' cried Mary Phoenix, and leant over to get her Dorothy bag. The other girls did likewise and soon a small pile of parcels lay in front of Elizabeth's knees. The boys hung back, waiting and watching as Elizabeth opened the wrapped gifts. She had combs, ribbons and little bottles of scent, all pretty things that she exclaimed over with genuine pleasure. Even poor Jane Parry had managed to afford a dainty embroidered handkerchief and received a special kiss and a 'thank you'.

When it came to the boys' turn we looked at each other as gifts were shyly produced from jacket pockets: a photo album from Fred Darlington, a china lady from Harold Hyde and other things that I can't remember now.

'Close your eyes,' said Johnny Lowe as he placed a small box in Elizabeth's hands.

'What is it?' she said, laughing. 'Don't tease.'

We all leant over to see as she opened the blue velvet box and many sharp breaths were drawn, particularly from the girls, as we saw what lay within. It was a wristwatch, a rectangle of glittering stones, diamonds I think, on a moiré ribbon.

'Oh, Johnny,' whispered Elizabeth, 'this is too much. I can't possibly accept it.'

'Of course you can,' he laughed. 'Try it on.'

My heart was again in turmoil as she slipped the black silk band around her wrist and fastened the gold clasp. The watch face winked brightly in the dying light as the sun started to sink down below the mountain.

'I bet that cost a bit,' said Mary Phoenix. 'You'd better give him a thank you kiss too.'

'Yes,' said Elizabeth, 'I suppose I had,' and in the silence of us watching youngsters she leant over and kissed Johnny on the lips. 'Thank you,' she said. 'I'll treasure this.'

That kiss seemed to be a signal for everyone to pair up and soon couples slipped away for privacy. Even our Billy had gone off, with Mary Phoenix, of all people, considering that he had been so angry with her the week before. I was glad for him, in a way. It was time he had a girlfriend and I was pleased that he had made up his fight with her. It only left me because Jane Parry had said she didn't feel well and gone home straight after Elizabeth had given her a kiss. I sat alone on the river bank with my elbows on my knees, aching with jealousy and hating the blue and silver necklace that burned a hole in my pocket. How could I give it to her now? It would look like nothing after that diamond watch.

I sat on in the gathering dark, simmering with resentment and thinking of clever things I could have said if they'd only occurred to me at the time. I hated Johnny Lowe for being older and richer. He didn't even have to try to make amusing conversation to impress Elizabeth. A diamond watch was enough.

'Hello, our Dick,' said Billy, standing in front of me. He was on his own.

I nodded to him, too miserable to speak.

Billy started to pack up the picnic baskets. 'I'm going to lead Peter back home now,' he said. 'It's late and I've got to be up for the milking.'

'I thought you were with Mary,' I said as I stacked the plates inside one of the big wicker baskets.

Billy shook his head. 'She's gone home. Her mother was expecting her.'

'She's got the whole weekend off,' I said, trying to be kind and encouraging to him. 'You can see her tomorrow.'

He unhitched the rein from the alder tree and pulled Peter round so that he was facing home. 'Maybe,' was all he said.

Mother was still up when we got home and had a late supper laid out. I was surprised to see Elizabeth sitting at the table, her various presents displayed in front of her and no sign of Johnny Lowe.

'What a lucky girl you are,' said Mother, fingering a few of the items to examine them. I watched as she picked up the blue velvet box and, with a quick look for permission from Elizabeth, opened it.

'Goodness me,' she breathed as she held the watch up to the light, and then with a small frown creasing her forehead, 'Johnny Lowe, I suppose.'

'Yes,' said Elizabeth. 'Wasn't he generous?'

'Mm, very.'

Our Billy came in then from putting the horse and wagon away and stacked the picnic baskets by the door.

'We'll do those tomorrow,' Mother said. 'Let's have a nice cup of tea now.'

This would have been the time to give Elizabeth my present, but I felt perverse and angry. I sat brooding in my chair.

'I've got you something too,' said our Billy, kicking off his shoes and throwing himself in a chair beside her. 'But it isn't ready yet. You'll have to wait until next week.'

Fibber, I thought, I bet you forgot and plan to go to the town on Monday and buy something. I gave him a sneer to let him know that I'd seen through his lying words. He gave me a sneer back and lifted up the folded newspaper Mother had been reading, ready to hit me about the head. Our Billy never missed an opportunity for bullying. But I felt reckless that night, upset over what had happened and anxious to pass that upset around. 'Don't believe him,' I muttered. 'He hasn't got anything.'

Billy opened his mouth to answer me but I continued with a stupid grin on my face, 'He's been too busy thinking about lasses. You should have seen him at the picnic with...'

My sentence was cut off abruptly as Billy growled, 'Shut up, you,' his little brown eyes darkening, 'and mind your business.' He gave me a scowl and his fingers tightened on the paper. 'Anyway, where's your present? We haven't seen that yet.'

128

I could feel Mother and Elizabeth staring at me. 'Richard?' said Mother. 'You didn't forget, did you?'

'I might have.'

Elizabeth smiled gently. 'It doesn't matter. I've got plenty of lovely gifts.'

'Don't let him off that easy.' Billy laughed, but the laugh was mirthless. 'He's a mean young bugger. He wants to save his money for going out with his fancy friends from the grammar. He needs a telling off.' And putting words into deeds with cruel suddenness, he leant over the table and smacked the newspaper across my ear. It was only a sting, which normally I'd have ignored, but maddened by all that had happened that evening I threw back my chair and ran round the table to grab him.

'Bastard!' I shouted, pulling him off his chair and on to the floor. We often had these little scraps, it meant nothing, simply the sort of thing that lads did, but this night I was out of control. I curled my thin hands into sharp bony fists and pummelled him. He grunted with pain as one hit got him on the point of his nose and a spurt of blood shot out and sprayed into my face.

'What's the matter, you stupid bugger,' he yelled, surprised, I think, by the unexpected retaliation, and he struggled to gain his usual upper hand. We wrestled and punched, rolling over and over until eventually he fastened one fiercely strong hand round my neck and started to choke me. How I thrashed and flailed about, kicking my legs until they crashed into the kitchen table. Above my cries and Billy's grunts I could hear the cups and saucers rattling and out of the corner of my eye I saw the milk jug roll off and shatter on the floor beside us. My struggle was all in vain. Try as I might, I couldn't release Billy's hands from their deadly grip.

'Stop it!' yelled Mother, quite terrified, trying desperately to pull us apart. I was beginning to lose consciousness when suddenly I was blinded by a great shower of water and our Billy's hand loosed its hold. As I blinked the water away I saw Elizabeth standing over us with the mop-bucket that she had filled from the trough in the yard. 'You're mad, both of you,' she yelled, 'and I hate you. You've spoilt my birthday.'

Even now, after all these years, I feel ashamed. It was an awful thing to do and my old cheeks burn with the memory. I can see my seventeen-year-old self, gawky, snuffling and scrambling up from the floor, tears in my eyes and blood splattered over my best white shirt. 'Sorry,' I muttered, my voice hoarse, for the effort of speaking was painful. I think our Billy would have killed me, if we'd struggled further. 'Sorry,' I whispered again, and pushing through the debris of chair legs and water I ran out of the room.

'He'll be all right,' I heard Billy grunt carelessly as I went out of the door. ''Twas only a bit of fun. Our Dick and me are the best of pals. You know that, Mother. And you too, Elizabeth.'

Outside, the night was dark and cool and a light rain had begun to fall, plastering my hair to my throbbing head and mingling with the hot tears that now ran, uncontrolled, down my cheeks. What a fool I'd made of myself. Fighting Billy was always a mistake, I'd had cause to regret that on more than one occasion, but this business with Elizabeth and Johnny Lowe had really floored me. I'd had no idea before that I felt like that about her. She was part of the family, a cousin, a sister, as close as that. But of course she wasn't really. Nothing of the sort. I suppose that was the moment when I knew for certain that I loved her. Even the callow and inexperienced youth that I was, barely understanding what I was experiencing, I recognised the most important emotion that I would ever feel.

I was right. Through all the years and disappointments that followed, the times when I was angry and despaired of the things she did, I never stopped being totally and utterly in love with my Elizabeth.

But then, stupid boy that I was, this emotion was new and confusing and I didn't know how to handle it. All I knew was that I had wanted to please her more than anyone else in the world and that I had let the opportunity go.

'Richard?' She was walking across the yard towards me, the light from the open kitchen door behind her and her hair, released from the blue band with which she'd tied it back for the party, flowing like a cloud around her head. 'Richard?' she repeated, a puzzled note in her voice. 'That wasn't like you.'

'No,' I muttered, turning my back on her and clumsily wiping the tears from my face. 'Sorry.'

She stood so close beside me that I could smell the faint perfume of the lavender water in which she'd rinsed her hair. 'You know,' she said, 'there's nothing between me and Johnny Lowe. We're just pals, the way we all are.'

How did she know that I was upset about that? Had I shown myself to be jealous? Oh, God, what a fool I must have seemed at the party. I couldn't look at her and couldn't speak.

She put a hand on my arm. 'Come in now and make friends. Billy has got over it and your mother doesn't want you to go to bed upset.'

Did she know about it too? Mother? I was ready to run into the village and get on the first train that stopped. The embarrassment was too hard to bear.

'Your mother says it doesn't matter if you haven't bought me a present and you know I don't mind. Having the lovely swimming party was enough.'

I let out a breath of relief. If Mother thought I was only upset about the gift, then at least I could show my face again in the kitchen.

'Come on.' Elizabeth pulled at my sleeve. 'Let's go inside and you can give me your shirt to put into some salt water. That blood will stain if you leave it much longer.'

There was nothing else to do. I couldn't stay in the yard all night, I would look like a bigger fool, so I allowed myself to be turned and walked beside her back to the house. Just before we got to the door, I stopped. 'I did get you a present,' I said, still not looking at her but gazing at the damp patches on the cobbles beneath my shoes. 'I just didn't find the right time to give it to you.'

'Did you, Richard? That's really kind of you.'

Her voice in the still night was innocently happy and I loved her more for not making fun of me. I turned to face her and taking the little tissue paper parcel out of my trouser pocket put it into her hand. 'Here. Happy birthday, Elizabeth.'

The rain had stopped and the clouds that had covered the nearly full moon drifted away, so that we could see each other in light that was almost as bright as day. I watched nervously as she undid the tissue paper and revealed the necklace.

'Oh! It's lovely!' she breathed, and held it up to the moonlight. The silver links gleamed a pale cold colour and the blue beads seemed as dark as midnight. 'I love it!' she said, true excitement in her voice, and then, 'Thank you, Richard, for choosing this. Nobody in the whole world, except you, could have found something that would please me so well.'

The relief, the happiness I felt then is indescribable. I was so glad that I hadn't given it to her before. It was better this way, just between ourselves. It made the gift seem all the more precious. I grinned. 'I thought you might like it,' I said, the words tumbling from my mouth in relief, and I was going on to tell her about the gypsy but she stopped me with a finger over my lips...

'Put your face down,' she ordered, and as I lowered my head to hers she reached up and put her mouth on mine. Our kiss was long and heartfelt. It was my first, as I remember, but I had enough sense to savour every moment, putting my arms around her soft body and drawing her close to me. Owls hooted, and a fox barked somewhere in the copse beyond the nine-acre field, but otherwise the earth stopped spinning and time stood still.

How long we might have stood there, I don't know. Elizabeth gave no sign of pulling away and I could have stayed with my arms wrapped around her for ever.

She put her lips to my ear. 'You mustn't be jealous, Richard,' she breathed. 'You know I love you better than anyone else.'

I was dizzy with happiness. Elizabeth loved me and was to be mine. All her other followers were of no account. She had chosen me.

'What are you two doing out there?' It was Mother at the kitchen door and I sprang away from Elizabeth as though I'd been stung. She moved more slowly and looked round gently towards the yellow light that outlined Mother's thickening figure.

'We're just coming,' she said lightly. 'Our Dick has got over his bit of temper now and wants his supper. Don't you?' She looked back up at me and smiled.

If this was a ploy to fool Mother, it didn't work, for when I stumbled uneasily through the door she gave me a look that left me in no doubt that she wasn't pleased with my behaviour. She had seen the kiss, had probably been standing at the door for a while before she spoke, and had not liked what she saw.

Oh, Mother, you were so wrong in what you did. Why couldn't you have left well alone?

Chapter Ten

Sharon has gone out tonight to a summer ball and I'm left with the babysitter. The pretence is that the girl, Linda Parry, is looking after Thomas, but I know that I am also part of her remit. She has already been into my room twice offering cups of tea and sandwiches. I've refused, but nicely, because it has been kindly done and I wouldn't want Sharon to be upset. Young Linda is as nervous of me as I am of her so we have decided on a sort of armed truce. I won't bother her and I hope she won't bother me.

Sharon looked a picture going out. Her red hair was pinned up and she wore a long pale green dress with a skirt that floated as she walked and a tight bodice, which showed off her tanned shoulders. I liked to see her dressed up. Normally she wears jeans and T-shirts and marches around the house and yard in built-up training shoes. I hadn't realised that she had such dainty feet until I saw them tonight encased in gold high-heeled sandals.

'You look nice, Mummy,' said Thomas as she gave us a twirl in the kitchen to show off her outfit. 'Doesn't she, Mr Richard?'

I nodded. 'Yes. Charming. Quite lovely.' Oh, but she does have a look of the Major. I can see him now with those fine drawn cheekbones and intelligent blue eyes. I know Mother thought him a handsome man and I suppose he was. Sharon is a pretty woman and I'm not the only one who thinks so. She has followers.

'You know where I am, if you want me,' she said, picking up her little beaded handbag, 'and I've given Linda all the phone numbers.' She looked at me and Thomas as though we were the same age and frowned. 'Are you sure you'll be all right?'

'For goodness' sake go,' I growled. 'We'll manage perfectly, won't we, son?'

Thomas was leaning against my shoulder, eating a lolly ice that dripped unnoticed by him on to my shoes. I didn't mind. That child is such a joy to have about this old and dreary house. 'We're going to watch the telly, Mr Richard and me,' he said. 'There's a programme about cars. We'll like that.'

Sharon looked anxious. 'Make sure that you don't tire Mr Richard out, and I've told Linda what time you go to bed. You'll be a good boy for me? Promise?'

Jason Hyde knocked on the back door then and she went. They looked wonderful, young and full of life. I was almost envious.

Now Thomas is in bed and fast asleep and I'm looking over what I wrote the other day, feeling happy and sad at the same time. Those words I've written are strange. True memory I think, but then could I have really remembered owls hooting and foxes barking when I was so wrapped up with Elizabeth? Maybe I'm only adding impressions of what might have been, but I don't think so. That night stands out in my mind as clear as a picture.

I went to bed in a daze after the late supper that Mother had put on the table and watched us eat.

She'd seen the kiss and I could tell, from the way that her shoulders twitched and how she set her mouth, that she hadn't approved. I glanced at her nervously from the side of my eye as I picked at the plate of cold beef and bread she had set before me. Normally, my appetite knew no bounds; I was a growing boy and would eat everything on offer. But this night I could barely swallow a mouthful. My heart seemed so full that I had no room in my body for food. Mother clucked her tongue as she took the plate away and poured a cup of tea for me.

'Drink this and then go straight to bed, Richard,' she said, her, voice uncharacteristically cold. 'I don't want you coming down with something.'

The only thing I was in danger of coming down with was love and I knew that that was what she meant. 'Yes, Mother,' I said, gulping at the hot tea, ignoring the pain as it burnt my gullet, so anxious was I to get away from her disapproving eyes.

Elizabeth behaved as though nothing had happened. She chattered away about the picnic and what the other girls wore and how generous everyone had been with their gifts. She brought out the blue and silver necklace from her pocket and held it up. 'Dick gave me this.' Her voice was sweet and breathy. 'Isn't he kind?'

The silver gleamed in the smoky light of the kitchen oil lamps. We hadn't had the electricity put in then; that came later that year, after I'd gone. I loved those lamps. No doubt the electricity was more efficient and time saving but never as beautiful. Our lamps with their milky glass domes threw a light across a room that was so calm and comforting that I always see my childhood illuminated in that way. So when Elizabeth held up the necklace, it was shown off to its best advantage.

'Very nice,' said Mother. 'Cost him a pretty penny, I dare say.' She didn't ask to handle it as she had done Johnny Lowe's watch, but I didn't mind. Somehow, her hands on it would have detracted from its importance.

'That's champion,' said Billy generously. He had no malice in him now after our spat. He'd already forgotten it. He jerked his fork in the direction of the necklace. 'I knew he was getting you something. He told me. Good choice, I think. Those blue stones match your eyes.'

They did. As I looked from the necklace to Elizabeth's face, I knew I'd chosen well.

'And don't forget,' Billy added, wiping bread and butter round his plate and shovelling the last crumbs into his mouth, 'your present from me is on its way. Next week.' He pushed back his chair and went over to the door by the scullery where his working boots stood ready. 'There's a cow ready to calf, Mother. I'm just going out to look at her. Leave the back door for me.'

Alone in the bedroom I'd always shared with my brother, I went over the events of the evening. My thoughts were all of the necklace and the result it had produced. How clever I had been and how lucky I now was to have a girlfriend. Seventeen and a half years old and I knew everything. Did I picture the future? I'm sure not. Young men think only of the present day. So, as far as I was concerned, my life would continue along its set lines, school over and now university and then a job of

138

some sort. The only difference was that Elizabeth was mine and we had a relationship to explore. Even Mother's obvious misgivings could be set aside. She'd simply have to get used to the idea that I was grown up.

I slept deeply and with a contentment I hadn't experienced before. So much so that I didn't hear our Billy coming in, although he must have. His bedding was wrinkled and tossed aside when I woke up. He was already in the milking parlour.

Fred Darlington knocked at the kitchen door while we were eating breakfast.

'I fancy a couple of days in Snowdonia,' he said. Mother poured him a cup of tea and put another piece of bacon into the frying pan. 'Why don't you come with me? We can stay at my uncle David's and have some good climbing.'

Normally I'd have jumped at the offer. We'd had several weekends at his uncle David's in Llanberis and had climbed most of the prominent peaks in the area. I loved mountaineering, although I was an amateur and that term should not rightly have been applied to me. The struggle to get to a summit and the exultant feeling that surged through me when I stood on the top was something never bettered. Until now.

I was still thinking about how to let him down when Mother put her oar in. 'I think a couple of days in the mountains will do you good, Richard. You've been looking a bit out of sorts lately.'

If she thought I was ailing, then this was the first I'd heard of it. In fact, I don't think I'd ever felt better. 'I'm all right,' I said, giving Mother a frown, 'but I'm needed on the farm. There's a lot to do.'

Billy came in then for his breakfast. If anyone looked low that day it was him. His usual high colour was absent and he had dark circles under his eyes. I wasn't surprised really; he must have been up most of the night with the calving and our Billy did love his sleep. He slid into his place at the head of the table and poured himself a mug of tea.

'Morning, Fred,' he muttered, and nodded to Mother to show that he was ready for his breakfast.

'Richard's been kindly invited for a few days in the mountains. I think he should go.' Mother spoke with her back to me as she was dishing bacon and eggs on to Billy's plate. 'You don't need him about the yard this weekend, do you?'

'No. Nothing much doing.'

'But...' I searched for excuses. How could I go away now, when something so wonderful had just been added to my life? I wanted to take Elizabeth up on to the hillside and have another go at kissing her. I wanted her to tell me how much she loved me and how I had always been the one for her but she had been too shy to tell me before. I looked round the room and craned my neck to peer through the window. I hadn't seen her yet this morning. Trying to sound casual, I turned to Billy.

'Has Elizabeth been helping you with the milking?'

He shook his head. 'No. Old Lowe turned out, but he was no use. His arthritis is worse than ever.' He looked up at Mother who was bustling about with the teapot, keeping an ear on the conversation. 'That bugger will have to go, Mother.

140

He's worse than useless.'

'Careful, William. Make sure he's got enough to live on before you turn him out. We wouldn't like to be talked about in the village.'

Billy snorted. 'Don't worry about him, Mother. He's been putting money away for years. Anyway, George and Ivy will take care of him.' Herbert's son, George, hadn't gone into farming and now had a steady income from the pit. And it wasn't as if Herbert lived in one of our farm cottages. He'd moved into his own rented place years ago. His army pension paid for that.

But all this didn't solve my problem of Elizabeth's whereabouts. I was thinking about going upstairs and waking her up when Mother said, with maybe a note of triumph in her voice, 'Elizabeth has gone to see her father in Liverpool today. She went on the first train.' As I looked up in surprise, she added, 'Were you looking for her?'

'No. Not particularly,' I said, and returning to my breakfast carefully spread bramble jelly on a piece of bread.

Fred had made a sandwich with his rasher and bread and was folding it into his mouth. 'Well, are you coming?'

Perhaps I'd made too much of that kiss. Maybe it meant nothing to her and that she'd kiss anyone and probably had. My mind whirled in a froth of angry speculation and I could feel my give-away cheeks beginning to burn. 'Right,' I said making my mind up and nodding to Fred. 'I'm for going.'

Did I imagine Mother's little sigh of relief? Probably. I was becoming fanciful in my eagerness to have Elizabeth as my girl in the face of

Mother's obvious dismay. Our Billy showed no relief or any other sort of emotion. He was quiet today, seeming subdued and exhausted, but he did ask if I needed money. Even when I shook my head, he put a hand in his back pocket and peeled off a couple of notes from the roll he habitually kept there. 'You can't be a scrounger,' he said. 'Make sure you buy Fred's uncle a drink and take one of our cheeses for the auntie.' There was no bravado about this gesture; it was his way. He had been head of the family since Father had died, and though only two years older than me had made sure that I was never short.

When I came downstairs ten minutes later with my corduroy breeches, plimsolls and wash things in a bag, he had wandered back into the yard. Fred had run home to tell his parents that we were going and to get his things. We were meeting at the railway station, so I had a few minutes to spare.

'Have a good time,' called Mother from the pantry.

'I will,' I called back but I didn't go in to kiss her goodbye. I was angry for reasons I wasn't entirely sure about and, spoilt boy that I was, hated the feeling that I was no longer her special pet.

Billy was leaning against the door of the byre. Inside, one of the cows was bellowing and he was standing ready to assist the calving.

'Another one?' I asked.

'No. Same beast. I thought she'd be ready sooner.'

So he'd been up all night on a fruitless exercise. No wonder he looked badly. Mind you, night calving was always happening, so he should have been used to it.

'I'm off, then,' I said.

'Yes,' he said absently. The lowing was getting more urgent so he lifted the latch and went into the byre, concentrating entirely now on the cow. She was one of our best big milkers, a bony black-and-white Friesian, and would have cost a packet to replace if anything went wrong. As it happened, she delivered a fine heifer just after I'd gone, and Billy was well pleased.

The mountains worked their usual magic on me and I'm ashamed to say that I was such a shallow young man that I almost forgot about Elizabeth. Fred and I climbed Tryfan, struggling at one or two places with overhanging rock and unsure footholds, but youth and determination were on our side. I wonder now at how daring we were. Nobody had taught us how to climb, and as for safety equipment, well, we had none. I suppose it wouldn't be allowed today but those were less regulated times and if we had fallen no one would have been surprised or looked for blame. Life wasn't cheap but sudden death seemed less of a stranger. Could that have been the result of the Great War when so many young men died and nearly every family had an empty place at table? Perhaps. I don't know. All I know is that on that fine summer day we didn't concern ourselves with mortality.

'I could spend my entire life up here,' said Fred happily. He had grown into a hefty young man. Not as tall as me, but over six foot and strong with it. We had been friends all our lives and I felt as close to him as I felt to our Billy.

'Oh yes? And how would you eat?'

He laughed and stretched out on the rocky ground beneath us. 'I know,' he said, 'but I'm going to make sure that I come up here as often as possible. I never want to spend too many months away from these hills.'

I felt the same. Even though I was planning university, I couldn't see further than three years of study and then back to the village. The idea of travel, or even living elsewhere, had never occurred to me. I thought I was going to be a teacher, or perhaps a solicitor at the very most. But my life would be lived in the environs of the village or the town.

Fred wasn't planning university. We'd left school together, on the same day, and while I was hanging about waiting for the college term to begin, he was apprenticed to the auctioneer, Watson, and had already started work. He would do well, I knew that.

'I'm leaving Watson's,' he said suddenly as we sat looking at the panorama of mountain peaks around us.

'What?' I was astonished.

'I'm leaving,' he repeated. 'I've joined the police.' He sat up and got out a packet of cigarettes. He offered me one and I took it eagerly, sharing his match. Smoking had become one of my worst habits over the past year. That is, if you didn't count drinking.

'Watson's is boring. I want a bit of excitement.'

I couldn't understand him. What excitement did old Fairbrother, our local bobby, encounter? The odd drunk making a nuisance of himself at

144

closing time, arguments over ready cash at the market and the occasional lost cat or dog. Nothing more than that.

I looked at Fred with amazement. Surely he wouldn't want a life like that, traipsing about country villages and being separate, not one of the gang. I was positive that I had to put him off, show him that this was no life for him, but before I could say anything he spoke again. 'I'm going to London. I've joined the Metropolitan Police.' He laughed. 'That should be pretty exciting.'

Well, I couldn't doubt that, and I began to feel a new respect for my pal. Here I'd been thinking that I was the only one in the village with aspirations for advancement and Fred was beating me to it. I even felt a bit jealous. My enrolment at the university in Liverpool was certainly not so groundbreaking, now that Fred was off to London.

'We'll keep in touch; holidays, you know. And I'm coming home for as many weekends as I can.' He ground out his cigarette on a rock before tossing it away. 'My parents are all for it, now that I've explained the pay and all. It's secure, you know. Job for life.'

That was the thing, in those days. A job for life was important when so many people were on the dole.

We didn't talk much on the way down, but that evening, over pint jars in the smoky pub, he asked me about my plans.

'Well, the university first. Our Billy's going to pay. He said he would. I'm going to do English. That'll get me a job anywhere.' Of course, it would

145

have done then, but now, when I think back, I had such low expectations. I couldn't see further than the village school. What a duffer I was.

'And then you'll get married and stay on at the farm, or close to?'

'Yes,' I said, and a picture came into my head of Elizabeth and me sitting beside a fire, reading together, and Mother and our Billy close by.

'Elizabeth and I have kissed,' I said tentatively. 'She's going to be my girl.' Maybe Fred wasn't surprised or maybe I didn't notice a look or a gesture that would have told me different. All he did was nod slowly and stare into his pint of beer.

'That's good,' he said.

We went home on the train on the Monday afternoon and parted at the station, Fred striding off to his parents' house in the village to continue getting ready for the great move to London, and me hurrying home the quick way across the fields, eager to pick up on my burgeoning romance.

I was stopped on the route by old Fairbrother of all people who was standing mournfully under the big ash tree staring at the fields ahead.

'Hello, lad,' he said. 'What are you up to?'

'I'm going home, across the fields,' I said, and added rudely, 'What d'you think?'

'Watch your lip,' he growled, but as ever his bark was worse than his bite and he pulled out a cigarette and lit it with difficulty whilst trying to juggle with his helmet, which he had tucked under his arm. I was surprised to see him out here; this wasn't his usual beat.

'What's up?' I said.

He gave me long look. 'You haven't heard then,'

146

he said, and sighed when I shook my head.

'I've been away. In Snowdonia.'

'Ah. Well you won't have heard then.'

'No,' I repeated wearily. This was typical of Constable Fairbrother. Couldn't bring himself to the point.

'It's Mary Phoenix. She's run off.'

I was surprised. 'Where?' I asked foolishly, and the constable wasn't slow to give me a shake of the head and a deep draw at his Woodbine.

'Who knows,' he said, 'but she was last seen on your land. I've asked your brother and Mrs Wilde, but they don't know nothing.'

'Well, neither do I,' I said, and continued on my way.

By the time I reached the farm, the weather had broken. Rain poured relentlessly from a leaden sky and a cool east wind had set in, whistling under the rugs in the hall and threatening to blow out the pilot light on the new boiler. The kitchen was dark and gloomy and being only four o'clock in the afternoon the lamps hadn't been lit. Mother was feeding bits of stick and kindling into the range when I came in and looked up at me with an exasperated expression.

'Hello, Richard, love,' she said before turning back to her task. 'Did you have a nice time?'

'Yes,' I said. 'Where is everybody?'

'Oh, they'll be in for their tea in a minute.'

I threw myself anxiously into my seat at the table and then a voice from the rocker in the corner caused me to look round. 'You look remarkably well, Dick. The fresh air's done you good.'

It was Marian, sitting forward in the chair with

her small neat feet side by side beneath her. Not one for lolling, our Marian. She didn't get up and give me a kiss, she wasn't affectionate in that way, but she did smile at me. I was glad she was there: she would take Mother's mind off me and the chatter between her and Mother would allow me to talk to and look at Elizabeth in peace.

'I met Constable Fairbrother on my way home,' I said. 'He says Mary Phoenix has run away.'

'What a surprise!' said Marian, with a sniff. 'That girl is nothing but a slut. She's gone off with some man, mark my words.'

'Oh, don't say that, Marian,' said Mother. 'She is family, after all.'

Marian and Mother were somewhat estranged these days, not such good pals as they had once been. I didn't know why. Maybe it was because Marian was unhappy in her marriage, although I didn't know that then, or maybe it was because she was jealous of Elizabeth.

Marian lived a few miles away, with Albert Baker in their place in the town. They had moved on from the flat above the shop and now had a house in the best area, a large Edwardian villa with too many empty rooms and an enormous garden. We had gone there on Boxing Day for our dinner and Mother had sat on an upright chair, refusing to relax. I watched as she discreetly turned over the plates to examine the maker's name and looked for the silver mark on the cutlery, and I was surprised. This was not like her; she had never cared much for material wealth, preferring people's goodness to their possessions. But somehow she seemed to resent Marian's doing so well for herself

148

and becoming a 'lady' when Billy and I and Elizabeth were still farming folk.

Albert was doing well, had just bought another shop and had joined the Chamber of Commerce. The only thing that was unsettling was a rumour that Fred had told me in strictest confidence. Albert had a fancy woman. It was well known in the town, apparently. I didn't know whether to believe him. Albert was such a jolly fellow, polite and seemingly most affectionate with Marian, and she was still not thirty and not bad looking. Our Marian was worth ten of most women in the town. It was a secret I didn't tell. If it had been true, Billy would have killed him. He might have killed him only for the rumour.

I went upstairs to my room and quickly dropped my overnight bag. I didn't want to talk to Mother or particularly to Marian for that matter, but I couldn't wait to see Elizabeth and ran back into the kitchen after giving my hands the briefest wash in the bathroom. Would she give me a special look that would confirm our new relationship or would she pretend that nothing was different and wait until we were on our own to show me how she felt? I fancied the latter; she was always discreet. I paced restlessly about the kitchen as Mother got the tea ready, keeping an eye on the yard through the window, waiting for her to come in. When at last I saw her, hurrying across the cobbles, head down against the driving rain, my heart gave a huge lurch. I rapped on the window with a shaking fist to grab her attention and it seemed that she'd heard it for she stopped her running. But then as I started to wave, I saw that she wasn't looking at me. She had turned her head and was talking over her shoulder to Billy who was coming along behind her.

The window was all steaming up and I had to scrub my hand against it to get a clear view, but I could see that she was laughing at something he'd said and looking as full of life and happiness as I'd ever seen her.

'What d'you think of the news?' said Marian. She had got up from the rocking chair and was laying the table, quite roughly I realised, as each cup was rattled into its saucer and a teaspoon plonked noisily beside it. I turned round to look at her, puzzled. What news?

'Never mind that now,' said Mother, and brought a tray of scones straight from the oven and put them on a trivet beside the teapot. I can smell the hot buttery aroma of Mother's sultana scones now and my mouth waters. I could never resist them and darted from my place by the window to snatch one from the tray. Marian and Mother both said, 'Don't, Richard,' at the same time, but it was too late. The hot scone had gone in a twinkling and I was reaching for another. Mother swiped at my hand with the tea towel, but it was a half-hearted business. She seemed to have her mind on something else and when I glanced guiltily at Marian, expecting her to grumble at me too, she turned her face away.

The door burst open and Elizabeth and Billy came into the kitchen, panting from running through the rain and filling the kitchen with a sharp waft of wet air and wet animals. They were still laughing from whatever the joke had been in the yard and I was suddenly sick with nerves. How would she greet me? Would she say or do anything that would show the others how we felt about each other? At that moment I prayed that she wouldn't. The embarrassment would have been too much because, after all, I was a very callow youth. So in a way I was glad that when she saw me the laugh faded from her face and was replaced by a look of caution and concern. She gave me a brief 'hello' and went over to the sink to wash her hands.

No such shyness from my brother, though. 'Hello, Dick,' said Billy, giving me a punch on the arm. 'Have a good time?'

I nodded. 'Yes. Splendid.'

'Well,' he said, 'I'm glad of that, because you missed the excitement here.' He was bubbling over with something, I didn't know what, or why his mood had improved from Saturday morning. I looked from face to face wondering what on earth he was talking about. His was pleased and open, happy that he had some good news to impart. Mother had turned back to the stove and was busy with the kettle. Did I fancy that her back was resolutely stiff or have I imagined it?

Marian had come to sit at her old seat at the table where she gazed at her hands as she smoothed them against the skirt of her Macclesfield silk dress. When she looked up, I was suddenly struck by how like Father she'd grown. Her hair had been shingled and was brown and stiff as his had been and her face was similarly square and firm. She didn't seem to share Billy's excitement. Indeed, she looked as though she was in a temper.

'Well, what?' I wanted all this, whatever it was,

151

over, so that I could have a chance to talk to Elizabeth and find out what she really felt about us. 'Did one of the shires win a prize?'

'No, duffer,' Billy crowed, coming to sit in his place at the head of the table and holding up his cup for Mother to fill. 'Can't you guess? It's me. Me and Elizabeth. We're engaged!' and he pointed with his cup towards Elizabeth and called, 'Show him. Show him the ring!'

I wonder how I must have looked. Did I blush? Or did the colour drain from my face? My memory concentrates on how I felt and even now my stomach churns as I write about that afternoon. You see, I was only a boy, a boy in love and stupid in the ways of the world. I could only gape at him, trying to take in his words and to understand their meaning. Had I misheard? Could it be that he was engaged to someone else, some other girl from the village? Mary Phoenix, perhaps? But even as those doubts circled in my head I knew that I'd heard right and when finally I turned my head to gaze at Elizabeth and saw her flick her eyes down and a slight flush come into her cheek, I experienced the worst feeling of all. Betrayal.

I had to get out. Another moment and I don't know what might have happened. Acid bile had come into my mouth and I felt suddenly and violently sick. 'Excuse me,' I said, keeping my voice as steady as I could, and stood up. My chair fell over as I pushed it back but I didn't stop to pick it up. All I could do was choke out the words 'I'll be back in a minute' before running from the room.

'He'll be all right,' I heard Billy say, in an uncanny echo of the other night when I had walked out of a similar scene. 'He probably had too much ale over the weekend.'

Chapter Eleven

Betrayal. It is a terrible word. I think it sounds worse than murder. I felt that I could never forgive her, for I knew that she didn't love our Billy, not in that way. He was a brother, a friend, family even, but never a lover, not to her. And I knew too that he didn't feel for her the way I did. I don't think Billy ever felt like that for anyone.

It all happened a long time ago and I should have forgotten about that one day, for my life has held many other occasions that were sad and frightening. During my service years I saw and did some dreadful things, but I can't say I am ashamed of them; they were things we had to do. Now, though, it's as though that brutality happened to another person, not me. No, that is nothing like the feeling of betrayal, which remains sharp and fresh many years later.

A reporter from the local paper visited me yesterday and wanted me to give her an interview. She was doing a piece on the Burma railway and had been told by the vicar, of all people, that I'd been on it.

'I wasn't there, my dear,' I said. 'I can't help you.'

'I'm sorry, Mr Wilde,' she said, all polite, 'I'm only going by what the vicar told me. I'm a trainee, you see, and need a good story for my editor.' She flipped shut her notebook and put the tape recorder away in her shoulder bag.

I felt sorry for her; she was only a youngster and wanted to get on in her profession. 'I was in Burma during the war,' I said, 'but not on the railway. The men who built that were prisoners of war, you know. I was with the Chindits.'

You could see that she hadn't a clue what I was talking about, but then that war has been over for more than fifty years now so why should she. 'The Chindits fought behind the lines,' I explained. 'We were guerrillas; we blew up bridges and outposts. And any Jap soldier we could find.' I added that despite the look of distaste that had spread over her face.

'But you weren't a prisoner? Never captured?'

'No.'

She considered what I'd said for a moment and then shook her head. 'I don't think I can use that story. I was going for prisoner-of-war stuff. To tie in with the payments they're getting.'

Thomas had been sitting with me in the kitchen when the reporter came. He's on summer holiday now and because the weather is bad he's been hanging about the house. He's shot up a lot since coming to live here. His legs look all spindly and bumpy at the knees like the young colts when we first put them out into the big field. He'll be tall and thin like his mother. I wonder if there's anything of his father about him. I wouldn't know, of course, because I've never seen the man, but to me the lad looks all Cleeton.

'Tell me about the guerrillas, Mr Richard,' he

said after the young reporter had gone. 'Tell me about blowing things up.'

Where to start? And a harder question was where to finish. I didn't know what to tell him, for at nine he is too young to hear about what men do to each other during war, and how could I explain about blowing up an outpost without first saying how we bayoneted the Japs who had been manning it?

I stared at his eager face, quite perplexed, and wondered what to say, but fortunately I was saved, because Sharon came in from the yard then with her hands full of shopping bags. She'd been to the supermarket and one of Thomas's chores was always to help put the groceries away.

'I'll make you a cup of tea, in a minute,' she said while I sat and watched the proceedings. Thomas had been rewarded with a bag of sweeties for his efforts and had run off with his daft dog to eat them. He always shares his goodies. with that dog.

'No hurry.' I was thinking about that tape recorder the reporter had. If I had one, I could speak my memoirs into it and that would save me the trouble of writing. To tell the truth, writing is becoming difficult. My hands seem to be getting weaker and my pen goes all over the place so that half the time I can't read what I've written. Even sitting for any length of time in my chair is becoming more painful.

When we were having our tea, I mentioned the tape recorder to Sharon and asked her to buy me one when she went to the shops. 'Get a good one, mind,' I said. 'I don't mind paying for the best. And lots of tapes.'

155

She smiled. 'You and your old writing,' she said. 'You've been at it all year. What is it? Your life story?'

'Yes,' I said. 'It is.'

This is the first time we've talked about it although she has seen me scribbling for months now. She isn't an inquisitive girl and as far as possible doesn't interfere with what I'm doing. I like that. Privacy is a precious thing and after so many years of living on my own I have become used to not explaining my actions to anyone. It's none of their business. But Sharon is different. I think I could almost let her read what I've written. Not yet, perhaps, but sometime.

'I'll get it,' she said, 'don't worry.' She looked at me in the motherly way she does when Thomas has a cut knee and put her hand on my arm. 'Are you taking your medicines, Richard? They're important.'

I laughed. 'They won't cure me, you know that. I'm an old man and everything inside me is just about ready for the knacker's yard. But I am taking the painkillers. They just don't work as well as they did before.'

'I'll get Dr Clewes to give you the stronger ones. He's coming to see you tomorrow.'

I didn't argue. To be truthful, the pain is getting worse and sometimes I feel as though I'm burning up from the inside. I suppose I should have expected this; it isn't as though they didn't warn me, but I've still got so much of the story to write that I must be strong enough to carry on.

Sharon bought the tape recorder and showed me how it worked. It's really simple. I've got it on

156

the table in my room beside the window and I'm in my padded chair with the microphone lying beside me. I couldn't be more comfortable.

Yet even with the assistance of this machine I find it difficult to talk, or even think, of what happened between Elizabeth and me. Few things cut like the wounded vanity of a young man. Even now as I speak about it, that fool of a boy raises his head and his hurt and feeling of betrayal are still there, seeded in this old, old man.

It was truly that. They all betrayed me. Elizabeth, Billy and Mother. Our Billy I could forgive because he didn't know that his getting engaged to Elizabeth would mean heartache to me... But Elizabeth was guilty. After the way she had kissed me and told me that she loved me better than anyone else, how could she turn round and get herself engaged to Billy?

My flight from the kitchen ended behind the hay barn where I threw myself over an old barrel and sicked my guts up. I'd had more than my share of beer in that Welsh pub the night before, but not enough to make me like this. Tears mingled with the vomit and when I'd finished I crawled into the barn, lay on the sweet-smelling stack and cried my heart out.

It couldn't have been long before a shadow fell across the barn door. 'You silly young bugger!' Billy was there, his chunky body blocking out the sparse light that pierced the gloom of that rainy afternoon. I raised my head, too miserable to try to hide my tears, and saw that he was regarding me with a mixture of scorn and brotherly affection. 'You've spent the whole weekend drinking,'

157

he said. 'Don't try to tell me any different.'

I didn't. It was easier to let them all think that than to give away that my heart was broken. 'I had a bit,' I mumbled and he nodded and came over and hauled me to my feet.

'Come on, you silly fool. Come and have your tea. We'll tell Mother that you've eaten something that disagreed with you. You wouldn't want them upset.'

No, I thought, they mustn't be upset. It doesn't matter that I am. I don't matter. These selfish thoughts nearly set me off in childish tears again but Billy pulled me out of the barn and set me towards the water butt.

'Wash the sick off your face,' he commanded, and when I hesitated he grabbed the back of my neck and plunged my head into the water. Saving myself from drowning then became an imperative as I struggled to pull away from his steel-like grip and to stand up. 'There,' he said, cheerfully, 'that's better, isn't it?'

'You never guessed, did you,' he said as we walked back towards the house.

'No,' I said. I was using my hands to push water out of my hair and smooth back the cowlick that always flopped over my brow. Hopefully, I would look like someone who'd been ill, rather than someone who'd been crying.

Billy laughed. He was animated and excited, quite unlike his normal steady self. I didn't like him this way, it made me uncomfortable. Our Billy was not a person who found life amusing. 'Mother had the ring,' he said, 'it was just the business of taking it to the jeweller to have a different stone. She thought the pearl should come out because of the old saying.' I must have looked puzzled for he added with a shrug, 'Pearls for tears. She kept saying that. We had an opal put in instead.' Years later, Elizabeth told me that opals were unlucky, but I didn't know that then any more than our Billy did.

He stopped for a moment to look in the calf pen. I stood watching as he reached over to open the mouth of one of the little beasts and put an exploratory hand along its flank. My mind was full of rings and stones and wondering if she had worn the blue and silver necklace over the weekend. He re-joined me and we continued across the yard.

'That's why I hadn't got the present in time,' he said. 'Bloody jeweller took too long.'

'Was it Mother's idea?' I asked. I was positive I knew the answer.

He had the grace to flush so I didn't believe him when he protested, 'No, of course not. I thought of it. It was obvious. I need a wife to run the farm and Elizabeth is as good as anyone could possibly be. Besides, I'm right fond of her.'

What could I say? He'd only done what any young farmer would do. A knowledgeable wife was a necessity on a properly run dairy farm. Elizabeth had become as good as Mother in the dairy and as well as that, she was strong. In many ways she was better than the new herdsman we'd taken on. Certainly, she made two of old Herbert Lowe.

Mother was now sitting at her place in the kitchen and was serving a second cup of tea to Marian and Elizabeth. They looked at me searchingly as we came in, but Billy saved me the necessity of explanation. 'He's been sick,' he said casually. 'Eaten a bad crab sandwich over the weekend.'

That set off a discussion of the merits and otherwise of seafood in strange places and I was able to slide into my place without having to talk to anyone. I looked up once and caught Elizabeth's eye. If she was trying to send me a message, I wasn't inclined to be receptive. As far as I was concerned, anything between us was over, but I felt a squirming starting again in my stomach. I was grateful when Mother said, kindly, 'Are you feeling better now, son? Could you manage some bread and butter?'

It was when Marian was ready to go home that Billy brought up the subject of the engagement again. 'You haven't seen the ring,' he said, 'and neither has our Dick.' He turned to Elizabeth. 'Go and get it.'

Was it with some reluctance that she pushed back her chair and stood up? I don't know. She still hadn't said anything and, as far as my boyish mind could tell, hadn't shown any great excitement over this event. 'She keeps it in its box,' continued Billy as Elizabeth walked over to the dresser. 'In case it gets damaged when she's with the beasts.'

Marian looked at it closely when Elizabeth slipped the ring on her finger. 'I recognise that setting,' she said and looked at Mother with an almost accusatory glare. 'Wasn't that a pearl ring? You used to wear it sometimes.'

'Yes it was. It came to me from my mother and from hers before.' She had the grace to look

160

slightly flustered. 'These things must be kept in the family.'

'It's nice, isn't it, Marian?' said Billy, as ever unaware of any awkwardness.

My sister stood up and brushed a few crumbs from her dress. 'Very pretty,' she said and pulled on her hat, ready to go home. Her car must have been in the front drive for I hadn't noticed it when I came in from the yard. She had learned to drive in the past year and was now proficient.

'Goodbye, Richard, dear,' she said. 'I hope you feel better soon.' She gave me a searching look that I didn't like. I turned my head away to pick up another piece of cake. I was now suddenly ravenous again.

'Mother, Billy.' She nodded to them and walked through into the hall. The fact that she hadn't spoken to Elizabeth hung heavy on the air and Mother sighed. I saw her close her hand over Elizabeth's and the look that passed between them was one of relief, I think, that the difficulty of imparting the news was over.

The evening passed quietly at our house. I sat with one of my favourite books on my lap, a comforter of old, but tonight none of the words went in. My mind was dull, exhausted with my own real emotions and not ready to accept those foolish fictions of Thomas Hardy's. I knew that Squire Boldwood's heartache couldn't possibly be as bad as mine.

Billy and Elizabeth had gone out, I didn't know where, probably on to the hill, now that the rain had stopped and their work for the day was over. I wasn't invited and I wouldn't have gone with them anyway. I wondered if they were holding hands or even kissing. A picture of them lying close on the scrubby grass, arms clasped around each other, groaning in an agony of passion, came into my mind and I fought to swallow the huge lump in my throat. But even then in my despair, I couldn't quite believe in what I was imagining. Hugging and kissing weren't our Billy's way.

Mother came in from the dairy, having wrapped the cheeses in muslin, ready for market. She took off her apron and picked up her darning basket. It was habit that made me move the lamp closer to her, something I did most nights, but now I stole a look at her, wondering if she would say anything to me about today's happenings. She looked tired, older than I remembered, and for the first time I noticed that she had more grey than gold in her hair. Mother was a handsome woman and I had always been proud of her. She and I had a strong rapport, sharing a love of books and learning. Indeed it was she who had insisted on taking the Major's entire bequest, his library of books, even though Billy had said we hadn't room for them. 'I will have them,' she'd said. 'They can go in the parlour. I'll get the joiner in to make good shelves, nothing cheap, mind. Some of those books are very old and valuable.'

Billy had been silent for a moment before saying, 'You must do what you want, Mother, though I doubt whether having anything of Cleeton's in this house would have been to Father's liking.'

She had coloured at that. 'Leave me to decide what your father would or wouldn't have liked, William Wilde. Who knew him better than me?'

That was an end of it. The bookcases were built, with dark mahogany shelves smoothed like silk so that none of the pages or the carefully worked bindings could be damaged when the volumes were pulled out. The joiner had warmed to his task and added carved lintels and decorative scalloped edges to the upper shelves. It was a work of art really. A craftsman's job and it is here now in front of me nearly eighty years later. I remember that it was Mother and I who put the books away when they arrived in packing cases one day after the Gate House was emptied.

'When I die, Richard,' she said, 'these are yours. Remember. Don't let your brother try to tell you any different.'

I didn't want to listen to that. What young boy whose father had died only a couple of years previously wanted to hear about the death of his mother? I pretended to read one of the books and didn't answer. As it happened, when Mother did die, she had left me the books in her will, so there was never any doubt, but I often wondered what might have happened to them all those years when I was away if Billy had realised how valuable some of them were. If he had known that selling two or three of the best ones would have bought him a champion horse or a tractor, then I know they would have been down to the sale room in a trice.

And I was sitting with one of the Major's books on my knee that evening in the kitchen when Mother told me why Elizabeth couldn't be mine.

She plunged right into it, taking advantage of the fact that we were on our own. 'I know you're upset, Richard,' she said, 'but there's nothing to be done about it. This farm has to be kept going and it needs both William and Elizabeth.'

I was going to interrupt. I was going to say that they didn't love each other and it was wrong, but she held up her hand. 'You'll be going away to university in a few weeks. It'll be a new life for you. And this place could never be yours; you know that. There's room for only one family here and it has to be William's. It's his right. He is his father's heir.'

'Aren't I his heir too?' I said, my voice breaking. 'It can't all be Billy's.'

She shook her head. 'The farm mustn't be split up. It would lose its value, and,' here she faltered, 'there's something else you should know...'

I was a boy and had no patience to listen. 'But why Elizabeth?' I broke in, refusing to let her give another reason. 'Why must he marry her?'

Mother folded her lips in that determined way I recognised. 'Because she must stay here too. I want it. I want to have her near me.'

The tears that had been so near the surface all evening came rushing back into my eyes then. 'It's not fair,' I cried, like the silly fool that I was. 'You don't care about me. All that matters to you is Billy and Elizabeth. You've pushed Marian out and now you're pushing me.' I sobbed it out carelessly, in anger and frustration, without thinking of the meaning of my words, but once it was said and in the open I realised that I had spoken the truth. The old relationship I had enjoyed with Mother was finished for ever. My nearly eighteen years of childhood was over and things could never be the same. This brought me up sharp and the tears were over almost as quickly as they had started.

'You don't understand,' Mother said quietly.

'Yes I do.'

'No,' she said, and looked at me in a strange way. 'Elizabeth must stay here. She's William's best chance. She'll keep him safe.'

She was right, I didn't understand. Our Billy was the strongest, bravest man in the district and didn't need anyone to keep him safe. This was only a silly excuse that Mother had thought up, so she could have her own way. I knew she had made up her mind and then worked on Billy so that he believed it was all his idea. And she'd done the same to Elizabeth. I bet she'd told her that Billy would be wealthy. He was already the richest farmer in the district despite his youth and Elizabeth would never have to worry about the next meal. That would have played well. She had come to us gaunt and in rags. I doubt that she would want to go back to that.

These thoughts drove a spike of iron into my heart, and I gazed across at the mother I had once loved and admired so uncritically as one properly seeing her for the first time. I didn't know what to do. The spoilt boy I was only minutes before would have flung himself out of the kitchen in tears, hurt to destruction by the cruel actions of his beloved family. But suddenly I'd changed. Once I'd seen through Mother's tricks, then I didn't need to be her child any more. I had grown up.

Her chair creaked and her hand came out towards me. I could hear her breath shuddering

165

as though she was fighting to hold back tears, but I remained unmoved. 'I'm sorry, Mother,' I said coldly, lowering my eyes back on to my book, 'I don't want to talk about it any more.'

'But, Richard,' she started, pleading now, 'you must...' Her voice faded away as I put a finger in my place in the book and raised my face to look at her.

'Yes?' I said and I can remember now the dangerous edge my voice had taken. 'What must I do?'

For the first time in my life, I was in charge and she knew it. No further words came from her and after a while she got up and made some supper. Billy and Elizabeth came in, their behaviour entirely normal, chatting about the stock and the fields as though nothing exceptional had occurred. We sat around the table in the yellow pool of lamplight in the same way as we had for years, eating bread and cheese and home-made pickle, and of the four of us, only Billy didn't realise that our lives had changed for ever.

Did I sleep that night? Not much, as I remember. I went to my room well after everyone else, having stayed up late with my book. When I crept up the stairs, the house was quiet and Billy, who always slept soundly, didn't stir as I came into our room. The clouds of early evening had cleared and the bright moonlight, shining though the open curtains, fell upon my bed and the chest that I used as a table. It was on this chest that I kept all my treasures. The coin I'd found on the hillside, some of my favourite books, and the carved dagger that my uncle had given me all those Christmases ago. A ritual I'd started years before made me touch all these precious things before getting into bed. It was a comfort route to sleep and even tonight, in my newly found adulthood, I was compelled to perform it, but this time the moonlight worked some sort of magic. I knew, when I stroked my hand along the sharp raised pattern of the dagger, what I was going to do. The answer was obvious and welcome and I couldn't wait.

The next morning I was up early, but still not before our Billy. He had already gone down to the beasts and I had a good half-hour to sort out all my things. My new-found determination suffered a momentary lapse when Elizabeth came down to put the kettle on and we found ourselves together, alone in the kitchen. She looked as lovely as ever, fresh and smelling of soap and talcum with her curls held back in a blue ribbon and her fine body warm and glowing in the cornflower dress.

'Hello, Dick,' she said quietly and for the first time since yesterday teatime looked me straight in the face. Her eyes were large, sick with worry, I thought, and I could have taken her in my arms even then, despite all that had happened.

'Oh, Elizabeth,' I said, still eager to forgive her, 'what have you done?'

She stared at me for a long moment and then turned her head to see to the boiling kettle. 'What I had to do,' she replied with a finality that begged me not to argue.

That was an end to it as far as I was concerned. Later that morning I went into the yard to find Billy.

'I'm not going to university,' I said.

'Oh, aye?' He was feeding the weaners and they ran about his feet in the pig pen, squealing and creating as though they'd never seen a meal before. 'Why's that then?'

'I've got other plans.'

'And what would they be?'

'I'm going in the army.'

Before speaking again, he emptied the last scraps out of the bucket and came back into the yard, closing the gate of the pig pen behind him. 'Why?'

'Because I want to travel. I need to see other places than here.' I waved my arm around indicating the farm, the house and all the area around. Everywhere in fact under this marcher sky that Elizabeth had walked in. 'Anyway,' I added, 'I'll be earning my own living. You won't have to pay for me.'

'I never said I minded that,' he said gruffly, and when I looked at him closely I could see that his eyes were swimming. He didn't want me to go.

Why did I have to make it better for him? He was the older one; he had always looked after me, the weakling, the silly little brother, but now I felt that I had to comfort him, promise to come home regularly and persuade him that what I was proposing to do was the best thing for us all.

'I shall miss you,' he said, clumsily wiping his face with his mud-spattered sleeve.

'You'll have Elizabeth.' And that was the truth of it. He would have it all. The farm, the home, Mother and my Elizabeth.

I left later that afternoon, walking across the fields to the station. I had packed a small suitcase with a change of clothes and a couple of books, leaving everything else that represented my lifetime in the care of those who had rejected me.

My farewells were brief. Marian had been telephoned and rushed over to admonish me and try to change my mind, but Mother and Elizabeth seemed dumbstruck. We parted by the field gate on a lovely summer afternoon. Swallows dived for insects in the clear sky above us and the cattle watched us curiously from the long grass in the meadow. I was dry-eyed, that iron now well lodged in my heart, but Billy held me so long in a warm clasp that I thought we would have to be torn apart. Eventually Mother and Elizabeth took hold of him and with a brief kiss from Marian I walked away. It was eight years before I saw them all again.

Chapter Twelve

September has come in cold this year and my pleasant mornings of sitting in the Lloyd Loom chair under the laburnum tree have finished. Anyway, that damn nurse that Sharon has arranged to look after me won't let me go out. She prefers me to stay in my room, in case I fall, I suppose, and become even more of a nuisance. In a way, I can't blame her. As far as she is concerned I'm an old, very sick man and I play along, letting her fuss and fiddle because it allows me a vestige of privacy. The bits of me that still do work, my brain and my willpower, I've kept

169

hidden from her. It stops her from interfering with what I'm doing.

I laughed to myself when I realised from the first day of her being in charge that she thinks I'm listening to a story on this tape and not telling one. I suppose she thinks I'm just mumbling along with an invisible narrator.

Sharon and Thomas have gone on holiday and I hate them being away. They have become so precious to me that it took all of that willpower not to show my despair when they were leaving.

'Ten days will go in a flash, Richard,' said Sharon as she put their suitcases into the back of the taxi.

'I know, and I'm glad you're going. God knows, you need a break from me and this house.'

'I can call it off right now,' she said, coming back to the front door and giving me one of her searching looks. 'You only have to say the word.'

I would have loved to say the word. I would have loved to be able to tell her that she is as dear to me as my mother when I was a little boy and that I am frightened when she is out of my sight for any length of time. Why shouldn't I break down and say that she mustn't go? Tell her that I am scared of dying when she isn't here to hold my hand?

What an old fool I've become, and cowardly too. I've lived well past my allotted threescore and ten and should be ready to give up. A few months ago it wouldn't have mattered. I'd nothing left to live for; I hadn't met Sharon or Thomas and found the comfort and friendship that has been so lacking in my life for these many years. And now there is this account. It must be finished. My story deserves to be told.

So there it is. I can't voice my fears; nor would I. The girl needs time away and this offer of a holiday was so generously given that she would have been a fool to refuse it. She has gone with Andrew Jones and his mother to their house in Spain where Thomas will have a jolly time splashing in the swimming pool and I dare say Andrew will give the girl a few dinners out in a restaurant.

We've seen quite a lot of him lately and his visits haven't always been on my account. I know that I've been tinkering with my will and that requires him to act for me, but that bit of business was over weeks ago, so his continuous presence must have another cause. What with him and young Hyde and the interest shown by Dr Clewes, Sharon has her hands full. It beats me why she wasn't able to find a decent man earlier. She's a good-looking girl and well lettered. It's my opinion that previously she was fishing in the wrong waters.

This holiday house is in southern Spain, near Gibraltar. Thomas and I looked at the atlas and found the name of the town and the airport. He was so excited about it all, especially when I traced my finger across the countries to show him the way that the plane will go.

'Have you been there, Mr Richard?' he asked, jabbing his index finger on the flimsy paper of the old map book.

'No, lad,' I said, carefully pulling his grubby little hand away. The atlas belonged to the Major and it is old and fragile. 'Not to that town, but I went to Gibraltar many years ago and lots of other places.'

'Was it a holiday like we're going on?'

171

I shook my head and leant back in my chair remembering the excitement I had felt when our ship put into port and we were allowed to disembark and go into the town. Me and my pals, young men in rough army uniform and ready for every new experience that was going to come our way.

I loved the army. From the very first day when I joined up at the headquarters camp and surrendered my civilian clothes in exchange for badly fitting khakis, I felt at home. That was strange really, for I'd come from a good place and was used to much better than the bare barracks room where we slept and the terrible food that was slopped on to our tin plates three times a day. I was an exception. Most of my companions were simply grateful for the warmth and regular rations, such had been the scarcity of comfort they'd previously experienced.

'Bloody hell, Wilde,' my pal Lewis Wilton said, when I spoke about our farmhouse and the butter and cheeses Mother used to make, 'you must be mad to be here.'

I only laughed. Within two days of joining up, I was an army man and my civilian life something that I'd pushed into the back of my mind. Only at night, when the lights were out and the last few shouted remarks between the bunks had died away, did I think about home. I counted the passing days and weeks in what might be happening on the farm, thinking that now they would be ploughing and now the stock cattle would be going to market. As for the family, well, I preferred not to think of them. The bitterness still overwhelmed me.

But slowly, I began to forget. Well, not forget, exactly, but not to dwell on it and not to have my previous life to the front of my brain. So much was new every day; my companions became my interest and I started friendships that were to last for many years.

We were a proud bunch of a fine company. I had deliberately joined the same regiment as my uncle and hoped that I would be sent to join the main body of its force in India.

'Steady on, private,' said the colonel, when I put in my request, after taking the King's shilling, 'you're jumping the gun a bit. There's basic training to be done and I understand that you've had some education. We might find that you are more use to us in the offices.'

This was a setback, because being as yet ignorant in the ways of army life I had imagined that my request to be in India would be accommodated as soon as I made it. I wanted action, travel and what youngsters desire above all else, adventure. I must have shown my disappointment, for the colonel grinned and looked at his adjutant who was standing beside his desk. 'These lads are so eager, aren't they, Parker? Can't wait to get abroad, to the cushy life.'

The adjutant turned up his mouth in a semblance of a smile. I already didn't like him. The colonel was gentleman, but you couldn't say that of Parker.

'They're a man short in the admin block,' he said. 'I expect Wilde could make himself useful there, once he's completed basic training.'

He was a bastard, and later on, when we did get

173

some action, he was shown to be a coward too.

I completed my training and did right fine. Growing up on a farm fitted me well for an active life. The early risings were no bother and as for learning to handle a rifle, well, that was easy. I'd been using a shotgun on the farm since I was a lad. I came out top in my section on the rifle range and later on, when I went in to competitions, I won a few cups. It was these sorts of things, I think, that made me popular, for I never experienced any bullying although I knew that it did go on in some other barracks. The corporal in charge of ours was a tough old Irishman and wouldn't stand any nonsense. He wasn't above belting a squaddy who transgressed his given rules, and that included bullying.

My friend Lewis had been made a steward in the Officers' Mess after training and he would bring us titbits from their kitchen. By God, they ate better than us and no mistake. Many's the night when the old corporal was snoring that we picnicked in the dark on roast beef scraps and shank ends of lamb. In return, I taught him to read and write. I taught quite a few of the fellows to read, starting first with their letters from home and then getting on to some of the picture papers that were quite popular then.

Lewis came from near Durham where he'd been brought up in an orphanage and had no family. He always said that the army was his family but that he was the black sheep. He was, too; always in scrapes but never mean. Simply wild. If there was trouble to be got into, you could bet your last pound that once all the dust had cleared, there

174

would be Lewis's black curly head and humorous black eyes surveying the mayhem he'd wrought. I can't tell you how many times I had to drag him home from drunken brawls in pubs or away from angry prostitutes he'd propositioned without the money to pay for them. Later on he married and settled down. It was just before the war and I was the best man.

I went to see Sarah, his wife, after I'd been invalided out, to tell her what had happened. She was living back with her parents then, her and the little girl that Lewis had only seen once.

I lied. 'It was quick,' I said. 'He never even saw the bullet that hit him.'

'Thank you, Richard,' she said. Then, after she'd dabbed at her eyes, she said something that surprised me. 'I'm glad that you were with him at the end. Lewis always said that the men felt safe when you were around.'

I was thankful then that I hadn't told her how I'd had to leave him in the jungle, with his guts hanging out of a terrible wound and only a rifle between him and the approaching Japs.

'Go,' he'd said, fixing his terrified eyes on mine. 'Take the others and get out. I'm finished anyway.' He was, we all knew that and we couldn't have carried him, but I nearly broke down as I shook his hand. I told my platoon to go on while I stayed for a last farewell. I dare say it wasn't very manly, but I kissed him on the cheek before I left. We heard the shot a few minutes later. It wasn't a Jap gun.

We had been good friends, growing into manhood together, egging each other on as regards entertainment in the town. I was a virgin and I

175

suspect that he was too, but he always swore he'd had all the girls in that Durham orphanage. So when we made our first visit to the brothel, I relied on him to tell me what was expected. Hah! He disappeared when we went in and left me to pay the madam and get seen to by a scraggy old thing nearly as old as Mother. I nearly couldn't perform but she was kind enough to help me along and that hurdle was over.

There were other girls during the two years we spent in that garrison town, and not all of them had to be paid for. They were a common lot, though. Hanging around in the pubs and ready to do anything for a drink and a Woodbine. After the first few months of wenching, even Lewis got bored with it and we and some of our pals found that gambling and drinking held almost as much attraction.

I was a great drinker. I had been before I left home, much to Mother's chagrin, and I tell you now, I could drink anyone else in my company under the table. It must have been something to do with my size. Lewis was hopeless. He got drunk on four pints and would go looking for a fight. Civilians were his favourite meat and a wrong look or an accidental push at the bar would set him in a fighting mood. He could only have been about five foot five but I've seen him take on three big meat packers from the abattoir. Many's the time I had to carry him back to the barracks. Sober, though, he was the nicest lad you'd want to meet.

We got our orders to sail for India after two years. I'd almost lost hope and thought that my entire army career would be spent in the administration office of our regiment.

The colonel came in one morning after his usual ride and stopped by my desk. I'd been made a lance corporal by then, which was somewhat quick, but I'd proved useful and I think that was it.

'Morning, Wilde,' he said. The colonel was a good man. He knew us all by name and remembered incidents in which we'd been involved, even when some of us had long forgotten them.

I stood up smartly. 'Good morning, sir,' I said.

'Now, lad, you should be happy today.'

'Why's that, sir?'

'Don't you know?' He gazed around the room, surprised, and the other clerks standing beside their desks looked as mystified as I did. He frowned. 'I thought Parker would have told you by now. Oh, well.' He slapped his riding crop against his boots and grinned. 'Orders have come. We're transferring to Meerut.'

I must have looked puzzled for he added with a great laugh, 'India, Wilde. India. That's what you wanted, wasn't it, when you joined? You'll love it.'

Oh, and I did. I was truly excited about seeing the country that my uncle had described so lovingly and when we embarked on the troop ship at Liverpool I couldn't stop myself from grinning.

'Good God, Wilde,' said Lewis, 'you look like the fucking cat that's got the cream.' He had a rough tongue and taught me a few choice words, I'm ashamed to say, but I couldn't help but laugh.

'I have,' I said, stowing my gear and testing the wafer-thin bunk that was to be my bed for the next few weeks. My feet hung over the end if I stretched out and I couldn't do that for another bunk met

177

mine and another soldier wanted to lie down.

We were billeted in cabins that were probably below the water line; certainly we didn't have a porthole and for that I was quite glad. My pals were high spirited and no end of belongings might have gone missing through that window, if it had been there. Our equipment was stored in cabins on another deck, so those men who hadn't taken out their hot-weather gear in time had to go begging to the officer for permission to wade through the duffel bags.

The journey took a month, stopping in Gibraltar for a few days where some men disembarked and others came on board and then on through the Mediterranean towards the Suez Canal. Luckily we were on deck for most of the day and everyone's mood lightened as we sailed further south. It seemed that as the grey winter skies of Great Britain gave way to a brilliant blue, the spats of bad temper that affected confined men gave way to cheerful banter and good humour.

The sights I saw amazed me. A cheer went up when we saw our first camel. The animal was led by a man dressed in a long striped robe, who walked as casually as our Billy did when leading one of the horses across a field. The Arab gave us a wave as our ship slowly passed by. We saw another man and another camel, then more, and soon the sight became commonplace so the lads didn't bother to cheer and settled back to the card game that had been going on non-stop since we'd left Liverpool. I was fascinated, though. Did these people think like us, I wondered. Did they laugh and cry and do the things that we did? It didn't seem possible. I could only see them as figures who had dressed up in foreign outfits to entertain us.

I'd bought a book about India before we left and read it avidly, picking little sections with romantic or dramatic stories to read out to my mates. They listened amenably enough, but not many of them were as enchanted with it as I was. So I read my book and leant over the ship's rail watching Arab dhows sail by and sniffing the changing smell in the air. You see, it's true, you can smell a country before coming to it and I could smell India, spicy and enticing, for days before we reached port and our huge boat docked amid the cranes and busy wharves of Bombay.

Right from the moment we marched down the gangplank loaded down with equipment and still unsteady from four weeks at sea, I loved India. It was all that I had hoped for, exotic and different. Strange in so many ways, yet just as my uncle had described it to me. And where was I based? In the very same garrison as he was and within the first week I had found his grave in the military cemetery and established that most important link.

I wrote once to Mother, to tell her where I was – it seemed a right thing to do – and mentioned that I had seen the grave. We had corresponded since I'd left home but not much. A line to tell her when I joined up and where I was and a couple of Christmas greetings. She had written back several letters but I was disinclined to reply. I, who spent hours writing letters for my pals, telling their families fantastic stories of their abstinence and success, barely bothered to contact my own family.

Mother had written of Billy and Elizabeth's nuptials, which took place only months after I had left. 'They were married on Christmas Eve,' she wrote. 'It was a raw day, but Elizabeth looked very well in ivory silk and they went that afternoon for a few days to Ludlow. The hotel is open all year.' I closed my eyes, imagining Elizabeth in the ivory silk gown and wondering if she had worn my necklace. I doubted she had.

In the other letters I learned that Granny had died, the farm was doing well and the shire horse colt had won a prize. 'He's the spit of old Diamond,' wrote Mother. 'It's a grand line.'

So when I wrote to tell them that I was in India, it was with some triumph. I might have been rejected and thought of as only the second best at home, but I had achieved something that I knew none of them would ever do. I'd travelled, seen sights that would amaze them and lived amongst people who were not of my colour or religion.

Meerut was not far from Delhi and it had been a garrison town for nearly two hundred years. It teemed with life and was noisy and dirty with people vying for space on the dusty roads with bullock carts and bicycles. Open-air shops lined the main street and I was amused to see not only shopping being done but dentistry and medical procedures performed in full view of the passing crowds.

We lived in barracks again, but airy, open-ended buildings, with great bladed fans that drove in welcome draughts of air. Now even we, the lowest of the low in the army, had servants. Someone to do our washing and cleaning, and for a few rupees you could get almost any service you wanted. Even girls.

I was not surprised that my uncle had found himself a foreign wife; many of those Indian ladies were pretty. Sometimes I would find myself, when off duty and walking through the market place, watching them as they went about their business. They were like dainty birds in their multicoloured saris and gold jewellery, chattering, bargaining and flashing their kohl-lined eyes. I was as fascinated by them as I was by everything in India.

To my huge relief, when we joined the company I found that I was no longer required in the offices. They were over-staffed with old timers who had been given an easy billet due to illness. Malaria was a problem, but we had our quinine tablets, which if you remembered to take them kept you in good health. There were other things too. Cholera and dengue fever, but on the whole they weren't as much of a problem as the malaria. I was lucky. For most of my time in India, I suffered nothing more serious than sunburn. Later on, though, during the war, I did get ill, but that was because of the diet and the conditions. I had an ulcer on my leg that took an age to heal and I bear the scar of that today. I've other scars, but they were the result of battle.

No, once in India, I was back on the front line of my platoon and kept ready for action. The trouble was that none occurred. A few minor wars had cropped up in the past years, on the Afghan border and in a place I'd never heard of: Waziristan. Only three years before I went to India some small battles had taken place in this

181

little princedom, but now all was quiet. But we were expected to be ready for action at any time and kept busy, with exercises and trials of weaponry. We had some policing to do now and then, but I found it unpleasant work. It always seemed wrong to me, although I hadn't yet understood the politics of what we were doing. I loved this country almost as much as I loved my own and I hated to see the locals put down. My pals laughed at me, saying I was soft on the wogs, and they might have been right, but I didn't think so then and am proud of my feelings now.

But having no fighting to do we had to find some other occupations and that took the form of various entertainments. The boxing matches were popular, but although I was big the thought of fighting never appealed to me. Oh, I watched the bouts with pleasure, that's true, but no matter how much the lads tried to persuade me, I would never put myself forward. I used to think about our Billy when I saw the team from our regiment sparring. He could have made two of any of them and won a few cups as well.

And then there were the dances. We had lots of them and no shortage of young ladies to dance with, for plenty of Europeans were in and about the area and they had their families with them. These dances were held in the Recreation Hall, a vast bleak room that echoed when empty and needed at least a hundred people inside to instil a party atmosphere. Like most of the buildings in the camp, the Rec was built up on pillars and you had to climb steps to the entrance door. I suppose that was the best method of building out there, but two hundred feet doing the Charleston or a Highland reel made a tremendous racket. It had a wooden floor which was continuously being eaten by termites so always in danger of giving way.

On one occasion we went to Agra and I saw the Taj Mahal. I cannot express how exquisitely beautiful it was, especially as we saw it first thing in the morning in the cool part of the day. The early yellow light perfectly outlined the marble and showed up the intricate carvings to their best. We were told by an old European who was wandering around that the raja had built it as a memorial for his dead wife, to show how much he loved and missed her. To me this was a noble gesture and it played on my mind as we drove away.

'Would you do something like that?' I asked Lewis.

'Bloody hell, no,' he said. 'There isn't a woman alive worth that sort of thing.'

I said nothing, but thought about Elizabeth and how much I'd loved her. I was in my twenties now and hadn't seen her for five or six years, for the time had passed by almost without my realising it. She probably had a child or even two by now, taking up all her spare time. She would have become settled and matronly. Whatever else, I knew that she would have long forgotten about me. That brought a new thought. Was my name ever mentioned on the farm? Did they get out the old photos and point me out to the children and say, 'That's your uncle Richard,' or something like that? And did the people in the village ask how I was getting on; the vicar, perhaps, or Johnny Lowe and the lads I'd grown up with? I wondered about the family, all those silly girl cousins and the outrageous Mary Phoenix. Had she turned up from her disappearance and settled into a respectable marriage or run away to live in sin? I hadn't thought about the village for years and now it was nagging at my brain like an unresolved toothache. I wanted to go home.

'You're quiet,' said Lewis. He sat beside me in the cab, chain-smoking and drumming his hand against the open window frame.

'Mm,' I muttered, but didn't say more. Even after all these years of friendship I still hadn't spoken about Elizabeth to him. I think he knew that I'd been disappointed in love, but it was never mentioned. In the army, we respected privacy. It was the only way to live for men who were in each other's pockets most of the time.

'D'you think we'll get leave soon?' I said.

'Maybe. We've been out here a while.' He turned his head to look at me. 'You keen for home, now? I thought you finished with them years ago.'

I shrugged. 'I have. I was just thinking, that's all.'

As it turned out, we were recalled to England the following year, but I didn't go. I was made up to sergeant and offered a transfer into one of the companies who patrolled the North West Frontier. This was exciting work and I would have been a fool to turn it down. It was to be my first experience of real soldiering and however much I longed to see the family at Manor Farm, they had to take second place to my career.

Chapter Thirteen

They're home! Silly old fool that I am, I cried when I saw the taxi coming up the drive and watched Thomas jump out of the front passenger seat and wrap his small arms around Phoebe, that daft dog who has been looking for him each day. And I'm no better. Every morning, I've looked at the calendar and mentally counted off the dates.

She knew I would be watching and as she stepped out of the vehicle she looked over to the window and inclined her head to me in that strangely formal manner that has forced its way through her abysmal upbringing. Andrew Jones said something to her then and she looked away to point out their cases, but I didn't mind. I was already feeling better than I had for days.

'Mr Richard!' It was Thomas's high-pitched yell echoing through the house and a wonderful sound it was after days of quiet footsteps and carefully closed doors. 'I've got you a present.' He burst into my room, followed by the dog, and threw himself against my knees. I was winded for a moment, but didn't let him see it. I wouldn't put that child off, not for all the world.

'Look!' he said and pushed a hastily wrapped parcel into my hands.

'What is it?'

'Open it, open it,' he said, wriggling with excitement.

185

The sticky tape was difficult to undo and with an old-fashioned 'tut, tut' he snatched it away from my shaking hands and tore at the paper until the gift was exposed in all its glory. It was a bull and bullfighter, made of straw and garishly painted in bright reds and black. The bull had a silly grin on its face and the toreador a torn place on his trousers to show that he had already been thrown.

'Why, Thomas,' I said with a laugh, 'this is a wonderful gift. It will look well on my desk.'

'I knew you'd like it,' he said, and leant his head against my arm in that familiar pose that I have grown to love. I bent and kissed the mop of red hair and the tears came to my eyes again. The memories of another are so strong.

Sharon came in then and gave me a kiss. 'How are you?' Her eyes searched mine and she touched my shoulder in a most affectionate way. 'I've missed you,' she said. 'There was so much to see and I wished you could have seen it too.'

'Well, you must tell me about it all,' I said, hiding my watery eyes by looking down at the straw bullfighter. 'I shall enjoy hearing about everything you did and what you saw.'

Later that evening, when Thomas had gone up to bed, Sharon came to sit with me in my room. I have not been sleeping well and am tired and restless. These days I can only manage catnaps and then I'm suddenly wide awake and frightened. Dr Clewes is reluctant to give me sleeping pills because, he said, they don't mix well with the heavy painkillers. 'We might kill more than the pain,' he said in his sardonic voice, and put his prescription pad away.

I must accept his opinion, I suppose, because he is an educated man, but it is hard to bear. 'People don't sleep as much when they get older,' he added, staring through the window at the garden, which is dull and sodden from the early autumn rain. 'After all, you get no exercise.'

I was suddenly annoyed with him. Why was he treating me like an idiot? Did he disregard my intelligence? Or was it that he was bored with my living so long and forcing him to drive out here every week?

'I know that,' I said, drumming my hand angrily on my table, 'but that doesn't explain the feeling of fright.'

He still wouldn't take me seriously. 'No, I don't suppose it does,' he shrugged, 'and I don't know what to suggest. I'm just a humble GP.'

I couldn't conceal a snort. He has nothing humble about him. I thought he was vexed because Sharon wasn't there. She was the first person he asked for when he came in and showed surprise when the nurse explained that she was away on holiday. It was cruel, but I enjoyed telling him that she had gone with Andrew Jones. Perhaps I shouldn't have, because he got back at me when he was leaving.

'Guilty conscience,' he said, picking up his bag and covering his nastiness with a laugh, 'perhaps that's what it is. Why you wake up in a fright.'

I sat for some time after he left, outwardly composed, but quite unable to swallow my elevenses despite the nurse's pleading. Internally, my heart was jumping and my stomach lurched like a drunken sailor. Guilty conscience, he'd said, and

187

those words swirled worryingly in my brain. How could he have known? And worse, did everyone know? Was my secret, so carefully kept for so many years, common currency?

It took a couple of hours before I calmed down and realised that I'd been taking him too seriously. He'd made a joke, that's all. It was me, reading too much into his flippant words. But it didn't help my sleeplessness.

'You look tired,' said Sharon as we had a drink together on the night of her return.

'I'm not sleeping well,' I grunted, 'but it doesn't matter. Old men don't sleep much.'

'Well, I'm home now. You'll be better.'

I knew I would be and smiled gratefully at her. 'Tell me about you and Andrew Jones,' I said, my smile turning into a grin. 'Is it serious?'

She held up her glass to the light so that the crystal winked and the red wine glowed. This was one of the old glasses that Mother had brought from her father's vicarage and I had recently suggested that we must use. Too many things in the house had stayed in their boxes, cold and unappreciated.

'He is,' she said.

'And you?'

'I'm not sure. I'm inclined to be wary.'

Funny words, but correct, I thought. Andrew Jones knows too much to be entirely detached. But he would be a catch for her.

'Thomas likes him,' she said after a while. 'But then he likes most people.'

Thomas has a sweet nature and sees the best in everyone. I was like him when I was a boy. Later on I became cynical and careful in my dealings,

188

particularly with people I didn't know. It paid off, for on many occasions my lack of trust saved not only my life but those of my companions, officers as well as men. I remember some chieftains in the Afghan mountains who swore that they were on our side, but would happily sell out to a Russian with a bigger purse. I've seen a collection of heads in a sack, some poor souls who had most likely been promised safe conduct. Is it a wonder that I never trusted them?

That was when I was on the North West Frontier and dealing with the tribesmen who were engaged in a series of blood feuds while we were in the middle, trying to protect our British interests. What our interests were I didn't really know. I simply obeyed orders even though sometimes those orders were difficult to understand. But the work was exciting and what I'd joined up for.

Those tribesmen were a queer lot and could be frightening because they didn't think like us. They included some fanatics whose only desire was to kill Christians and they'd go about it with such serious intent that nothing would satisfy them until the deed was done. One day, a rebel jumped off the wall surrounding our camp and stabbed one of our sentries. The soldier was alerted by his colleague so that he managed to duck aside and the dagger only fetched him a glancing blow on the shoulder. I'm happy to report that the sentry survived, having nothing more than a scratch, and we managed to capture the rebel. Truth was, he didn't put up much of a fight and was quite peaceable once we had him in chains, but he was sentenced to death immediately.

But what I'm saying is this. When we captured him, his eyes were like those of an animal, wild, terrifying and so full of hatred that you could barely look him in the face without shivering. But on the scaffold, before the rope was looped round his neck, he was as docile as a baby and accepted his fate with something akin to joy. It was his religion. He thought he was going to his heaven and had no fear.

I thought about that, after I'd cut him down and laid his still quivering body in the dust, and mentioned it to the camp doctor who had come to formally pronounce him dead.

'Fanaticism, laddie,' said the doctor, 'it's like an illness. A mental illness. The blood lust turns on and off like a tap. It happens in Christians too.'

I wanted to know more, but our conversation was halted by the colonel, who had walked round to where we were kneeling beneath the scaffold. 'Wilde,' he said, 'you're new here, so you might not have heard. We bury a dead dog with the corpse. They think it will stop their soul going to heaven. Might put some of the other buggers off.'

The doctor raised his eyebrows and shook his head. 'They've been trying that for years,' he said when the colonel had gone. 'Doesn't seem to make any difference.'

I carried out my orders, though, getting a sepoy to shoot one of the diseased dogs that scavenged in packs around the camp and throwing it in the grave on top of the hanged rebel. Several locals watched as we did it and it caused much muttering and obvious dismay. They didn't like it.

It was in those days that I began to earn a new

190

respect from my colleagues. It was 'sarge, this' and 'sarge that' from the men as we trekked cautiously through the high passes in pursuit of the rebels. I was in my element out there in the mountains, confident and as surefooted as a goat on the craggy rocks, and my spirits soared in the thin air. It was easy for me, I think, because I'd done so much climbing in my youth, but it wasn't only that. I loved having the rank and the chance to think for myself. The men took their lead from me, generally without dispute, and we were a cheerful bunch who looked after each other. I didn't lose one of them in that first engagement with the Mahmoods, although one young private was badly injured and had to be invalided out. He was shot in his belly and suffered greatly. That was the first time I'd seen anyone shot and it was a facer, I can tell you.

The officers were less formal out there. We were led by a Colonel Barnes, an old India hand whose family had been soldiering in the sub-continent for two hundred years. I say old, but that was purely in experience. He can't have been more than fifty at the time, a strong, dark-haired man with a thick moustache and whip-tight muscles. We soon found out that he had no taste for shirkers.

'Keep them to it, sergeant,' he would say when I led the men on training exercises through the hills. 'It'll save their lives, one day.' I wonder if it did. Most of those men fought on through the Second World War, not in the high mountains of northern India but in the jungle thousands of miles further east where the problem of disease was almost as difficult to overcome as the Japs. I got to know the jungle too and suffered with malaria and other infections that could bring you so low that death seemed like a blessing. But I think the training did stand us in good stead: we learned to be more self-sufficient and we were all extremely fit.

Barnes could speak some of the languages of the hill tribes. We all picked up a word or two, but not like Barnes. He had long conversations with some of them and was very respectful of their elders, touching his head and heart in the way that they did and eating with his hands from the dishes of food he was offered. Once, when we were trying to stop a particular scrap that had been going on for years, I was chosen to go with him to negotiate with the elders of a warlike tribe.

We were to meet the men in a small high village, which entailed our riding through the mountains for a day and a half. A couple of bearers rode with us but no other soldiers and I thought it extremely risky, but not so the colonel. 'They won't hurt a guest,' he promised as we rode up the crumbling soil of the hillside, and I had no choice but to take him at his word. He seemed to feel no concern.

'Listen to what they say, Wilde,' he instructed me.

'But I can't understand their language,' I protested.

He sighed. 'That's not what I mean. Listen. Give them respect as you would any stranger, particularly when you are a visitor in their home. I'll interpret, but you make as though you know what's going on. It will be more impressive.'

The village was a poor place, a group of square

192

baked-mud houses with flat roofs built higgledy-piggledy on low rocky slopes, each abode surrounded by nothing but a bare patch of dusty ground. But beyond those simple dwellings, the river bottom opened into a lush and fertile valley. I could see fields of maize and barley waving in the cool breeze, and when I looked further I noticed sheep and goats roaming on the hillsides. Whatever else, these people weren't short of food.

That opinion was borne out when we rode into the village. The place was noisy with people and animals who watched us closely as we passed by towards the warlord's house. We had to duck under banners, some black and some striped in colours, which flew from improvised flagpoles while at the same time avoiding the brightly coloured clothes that lay drying in the sun on the ground. Thin dogs barked at us and fat babies sitting in the dust gazed on nonchalantly, sucking at their fists. The children and the few women we saw had fairish skin and round cheeks that were rough and red from the wind, although the women would hold their veils modestly over their faces if we glanced in their direction. But the men were tall, taller than the Indians who lived in the country around Meerut, and under their turbans their faces were lean and fierce-looking. Each man carried a rifle and had a variety of weapons, daggers and handguns and such, stuffed into the bandannas they wore round their waists. I thought of my single rifle and the colonel's pistol being our only defence and could feel my stomach curdling, but the colonel rode forward not a whit afraid.

As it turned out, my fears were groundless.

These people could be horribly cruel, but they had decided that we were the best bet in their fight with their neighbours, so for the time being we were safe. The colonel spoke to the elders for a long time and much laughter was exchanged, which I joined in when I deemed it right. I was keeping to the colonel's instruction and trying to listen. It wasn't so hard really. You could tell from how they gestured, towards the mountains and then over their shoulders towards the valley, what their fears were about. The opposing tribesmen were stealing their stock and wrecking the crops. They wanted protection and it seemed that in return for their staying faithful to the British and not the Russians, the colonel was prepared to give it to them.

'Go and look at the crops,' the colonel said to me at one point. 'They'll appreciate our showing some interest.' So, bowing to the warlord, I left the room and went back into the dusty street.

I was accompanied on my ride down the valley by a group of young men, and thank God I'd been brought up on a farm. I knew how to strip down the leaves of maize and examine the ears and how to rub the barley between my fingers to judge its readiness for harvest. I made a great hit by catching a sheep and looking at its feet. I guessed at that, for we had barely any sheep at home. The young men waved their rifles in the air on the ride back and chattered animatedly to the others we passed.

'Well done, sergeant,' said the colonel, when I returned. The news of my prowess as a farmer had preceded me back to the village. A feast was

194

prepared and we sat on the floor to eat sheep's head and rice, and very nice it was too. I was never squeamish about what was put in front of me.

A funny thing happened as we ate our meal. A very old man spoke to the colonel and nodded towards me. He had obviously been someone of importance, and as he wore a British army medal in his turban I could tell that he'd seen some service. The younger men fell silent when his wavering hand pointed at me and a few gravelly words were grunted out. To my astonishment, I thought I caught the word 'Cleeton' and I looked up quickly to the colonel for an explanation.

'Are you related to an officer called Cleeton?' he asked quietly, and just as I was about to shake my head he added, 'Might be a good idea if you agree. They would like that.' So I nodded vigorously and the old man opened his mouth and cackled a toothless laugh.

'He says that a Major Cleeton was up here at the turn of the century. A brave officer, apparently.' The colonel listened some more and then joined in the general laughter. 'It seems that your hair is the same colour his was and he was tall too.'

I thought back to the days when I had met the Major in the lanes as a child. He had looked big, but then to a child all adults are big, and I couldn't remember the colour of his hair. The last time I saw him was that day just before he died when Mother went to care for him, and then he had appeared sadly shrunken and pathetic.

On our ride back to the base at Peshawar, the colonel and I chatted in a friendly way. He spoke of his wife. 'She's an old India hand too,' he said, with a fond smile. 'Her family have been out here nearly as long as mine. Of course we were both educated back home and Caroline stayed on for a few years, but apart from that ... well, I don't know what we'd do if we had to leave.'

'Do you have children, sir?' I asked.

'We do. Three boys, all at school in England.' He gripped his reins tightly as we negotiated the stony track that was our way through the mountains. 'Caroline longs to see them, but we aren't due for home leave for another year.' He turned round in his saddle. 'What about you, Wilde? Family man, are you?'

I shook my head. 'No, sir. No wife. No children.' I paused to grin and dared another comment, for we were both men of the world and had no ladies present. 'That is, none that I know of.'

He laughed and we rode on in relaxed companionship. It was later that day, when we had made camp and were drinking tea after our meal, that he brought up the subject of Major Cleeton again. In truth, it had been on my mind during the ride and I was pleased to be able to talk about it.

'The name Cleeton is not entirely unknown to me,' he said, cradling his tin cup between his palms. It was cold in the mountains now that the sun had disappeared behind the peaks and I was glad of the sheepskin over-jacket that I'd bought in the market at Peshawar. The bearers had made us a fire out of the wood and kindling that we had brought with us, which made us more comfortable.

'Nor to me, sir,' I said. 'We had a Major Cleeton in our village. He was in the same regiment as you,

196

sir, but I know nothing about his service record. My brother bought his land and cottage when he died.'

The colonel was interested. 'Your brother is a landowner, then?' he asked.

Landowner. That sounded too important for what we were, but I suppose it was true. Our Billy did own more than four hundred acres of land, and with the house and the cottages he must be worth a bit. 'We have a farm,' I said.

'I gathered that, Wilde. It sounded as if you knew what you were doing back there.'

I tried to be dismissive. 'My brother's the farmer, not I. I left home before my eighteenth birthday.'

He answered nothing to that, recognising, I think, my difficulty with the subject, but he brought the conversation back to the Major. 'Cleeton had some adventures in these hills,' he said. 'I remember my father telling me about him. Fought bravely and cleverly. He cut quite a dashing figure, too, so I believe.'

I laughed. 'I wouldn't know about that, sir. The Major Cleeton I knew was something of a drunkard and his antics became a scandal in the village. My father and brother had little time for him.'

'And you?'

I was quiet for a moment, considering my answer. 'He left my mother his library of books,' I said, thinking about the legacy. 'He knew she and I were keen readers.' I leant back against my saddle and remembered the day he had taken me into his parlour and given me his own copy of *David Copperfield*. Then I thought about that winter day when he was dying. 'Mother cared for him on the day he died,' I continued. 'She made me run into the village for the doctor and bring him back to the Major's cottage. He was very poorly. She stayed with him until he died.'

'No wife?'

I shook my head.

We fell to talking about other things then, the village, the tribesmen and the recent fighting, and the subject of the Major wasn't mentioned between us again. But when I thought about it later, it struck me that neither of us had found the coincidence strange and the whole episode became something that I couldn't forget.

Back at camp, I went straight to the washrooms and looked at my face in the glass. I tried to picture the Major and looked closely for any recognisable similarities, but I could see none. I was glad. If the unspoken implication were true, it would make my mother something that I didn't want to think about. The only trouble was I could picture my father and our Billy quite clearly and I was nothing like them. They were dark stocky men with bull-like shoulders and square faces whereas I, now grown into adulthood, was tall and thin with a straight nose and that blasted red hair.

I went back to my quarters and took out my writing case. I felt that I must write some words to Mother and get this thing sorted out; the doubting was becoming too much to bear. But even before my pen had touched the paper I knew that it would be a senseless thing to do. What could I write? What could I say? How could I accuse her of infidelity? Of sleeping with another man? I baulked at the prospect. It was plain I couldn't and

I put my pen and paper away in their leather case.

Later that evening I went to the canteen and drank rum until the distasteful thoughts dissolved, and when I lay on my bunk that night I didn't think of Mother and Major Cleeton but of the tribesmen and the fat babies sitting in the dust.

After that incident, I threw myself into my work again. It had grown quieter though and very few skirmishes with the rebels occurred, so I didn't have much to take my mind off my thoughts of home. A new intake of men came out from England in the spring of the following year, a rough lot who had joined up because unemployment was high and had no real desire for soldiering but were prepared to do anything for three square meals a day. One man turned out to have been born in our town and we knew many of the same people. I asked for news of home. He had none of my immediate family, as he knew them only by name, but did tell me about Albert Baker, Marian's husband. He'd been made mayor and was now an important person.

I wondered if Marian was enjoying her new position as lady mayoress and all the socialising that went with it. On the whole, I thought that she probably wouldn't be; our Marian didn't suffer fools gladly and I imagined there would be plenty of fools in and about the council. Mother would be proud of her, though.

It was after hearing about Albert Baker that I decided to take my home leave. I had been out in India for six years now and was entitled to several months back home. The colonel was keen that I should take it when I put in my request. 'You have to get away at regular intervals, Wilde,' he said, 'otherwise you go a bit mad.'

Had I gone a bit mad? I didn't know. The years away from home had certainly changed me, but I would have changed anyway, by growing up. But a bit mad? Well, I would have to find out.

'My wife and I are going home too,' he said. 'She is yearning for our boys and for a few months in our house in Ireland.'

I had guessed that they might have a home in Ireland, for I had met Mrs Barnes at an evening of theatricals which both officers and men attended. The colonel had introduced me to her as 'the young sergeant who handled the Waziris so well the other month', and I couldn't help but blush.

'Ah, don't you be so modest, sergeant,' she said, and the lilt of the accent and the toss of her black curls put me so much in mind of Elizabeth that my breath caught in my throat and I took a moment to speak.

'I did nothing, ma'am,' I stuttered, 'just looked at a few ears of corn.'

She wagged her finger at me in a humorous gesture. 'But it's the way you looked at them that mattered, Mr Wilde. That's what told the story.'

I might have grown up, but my social graces were still poorly honed and I could do nothing but shuffle my feet and mutter, 'Yes, ma'am.'

'Stop teasing, Caroline,' the colonel laughed, and nodded pleasantly to me before they moved on to the next group.

'She was a real beauty when she was young and first came out here,' said an old sergeant who was standing beside me. 'I remember her well.'

I was sure that she had been, for she was still handsome and had a cheerful and gracious nature. Would Elizabeth grow older like that, I wondered, and for the first time in many years the old longing for her came rushing back.

So with that feeling, and the recent business of Major Cleeton, my need to be home was becoming overpowering.

'I'll sign the chitty now, Wilde,' the colonel said. 'You can entrain in a couple of days and be in Bombay by next week. There's a P&O ship going out. Mrs Barnes and I will be on it too.'

Needless to say, I saw little of them on the journey, for we were separated by rank, but the day before we docked at Southampton I was on deck watching the coastline loom out of the mist, a solitary figure in a heavy downpour, when a gloved hand gently touched my arm.

'Will there be someone to meet you, sergeant?' Mrs Barnes asked. She was holding an umbrella over her grey cloche hat, from which wisps of hair had escaped and curled into tiny damp ringlets. It was a sight I recognised and it added to my longing.

I shook my head. 'They don't know I'm arriving. Anyway, home's a long way away and they'll be busy on the farm.'

'Ah, sure,' she said, and leant over the rail to look at a single gull bobbing on the tossing waves.

'And you, ma'am?'

'My boys.' She looked up with a sweet smile. 'The boys will be there to meet us. All so grown up now.'

We were quiet for a moment, thinking, I suppose, of those we loved, and then she said, 'Do you have a sweetheart at home?'

I shook my head. 'Not now. I did once.'

'You will again.' She smiled and nodded good-bye as she strolled on.

It was afternoon when the train pulled into the local station and I stepped down on to the familiar platform. 'You can get a taxi over there, mate,' a porter said, indicating the one old cab that I remembered from eight years ago.

'I'll walk,' I replied, hoisting my kit bag on to my shoulder and climbing over the wooden fence behind the waiting room. I looked back once and he was still standing on the platform, watching me. It wouldn't take long before the news of a stranger, a soldier, had percolated through the village. How many would guess who it was?

The fields, green with spring growth, were squelchy beneath my boots. Must have had a bit of rain, I thought, but it'll make good grazing later on. I grinned. How strange that I should have dropped back so quickly into farming thoughts after years away. When soldiering, the state of the terrain was only of interest for getting safely across.

I paused at the gate where I'd said goodbye, suddenly scared and ready to turn round and head back to the station. What sort of reception I would get, I couldn't imagine. Would they want to know me after all these years? Perhaps not. Perhaps they'd forgotten I existed except for the odd occasion when someone mentioned my name. The confusion and fear grew and I stood holding the rough wood of the fence, unable to make the final step over.

'Hello!' a voice called from across the yard. 'Hello! Can I help you?'

I looked towards the sound and there she was, climbing over the far gate and walking towards me, an old jacket over her dress and a wool hat holding her hair away from her face. A dog trotted beside her and then, at her swift order, dashed forward until it was standing in front of me. It was a big dog, a wolfhound, not the sort we usually kept on the farm, but it was well trained and didn't touch me, merely waited for her.

She reached me. 'Can I help you?' she started again and then, suddenly, her hand went to her mouth and her eyes widened. For a moment the colour drained from her face, but it rushed back as she lifted her arms towards me. 'Richard?' she gasped. 'Richard, is it really you?'

'Hello, Elizabeth,' I said.

Chapter Fourteen

It was a moment I had alternately hoped for and feared during the past eight years. Sometimes I had seen myself walking up to the house, the door being flung open and the family standing in a group, welcoming me in as a prodigal son. On other and more frequent occasions my imaginings had taken a darker scenario where my return was greeted with disdain, if not downright anger. I couldn't blame them because I had, after all, left home in a childish rage and barely contacted them since. So this smiling welcome was better than I could have wished, even in my dreams.

'Oh, Richard, my dear,' Elizabeth crooned, and leaning over the fence she took me in her arms in an embrace that was both motherly and sisterly, but to my mind perhaps more. I chose to think that, right from the beginning.

I held her close, revelling in the softness of her body beneath that old jacket and breathing in the faint smell of spring flowers that I remembered so well. Her hat fell off and I moved one of my hands up to her hair and stroked it. It was shorter than before, cut to the nape of her neck, but still springy with life and energy.

It was she who broke off the embrace, leaning back from me but grasping my arms with both her hands and gazing into my face. 'You look so ... so grown up,' she said. 'So manly, but still our Dick.'

I stared back, smiling, and loving her as much as ever. She had changed. The girlishness had gone and with it the innocence and aura of fun that had helped to make her so attractive. Her face was angular and that perfect skin, still peaches and cream, was now finely drawn over her jawline so that the youthful softness that I remembered was gone. Now she was a woman; a beautiful woman, but quite different from the girl I'd left behind.

'Have I changed?' she said, frowning suddenly under my unwavering gaze.

'No. Not at all, really. Just as beautiful as I remember.' That last was true: she was as lovely as ever, but I lied when I said she hadn't changed. The person who stood before me wasn't my

Elizabeth. It wasn't the girl who had carelessly raced across the hillside and flirted with the boys at the local hop, and certainly not the one who had smacked our Billy in the face with a dead cockerel. But I smiled and gave her another hug. The old Elizabeth was in there, somewhere.

'Come on,' she said, turning towards the house. 'They'll be so excited to see you.'

Now I was nervous again, doubting my welcome. 'Are you sure?' I said. 'My leaving was so sudden. Maybe Mother and Billy would rather I'd stayed away.'

'What?' She stopped and looked up at me. 'Preferred that you stayed away? What can you be thinking of?' She grabbed hold of my arm again and gave it an irritated little shake. 'Listen to me, Richard. Your mother has missed you every day, and Billy ... well, he talks about you constantly. Don't be so soft.'

Reproved, I hoisted my kit bag and climbed over the fence. We walked, arm in arm, like brother and sister, towards the yard and the dog trotted obediently beside her. I was going to ask her about it but then I saw a heavyset figure, carrying a bucket, coming out of the shippon and walking into the yard. It could have been my father and a little gasp of shock escaped my lips. But Elizabeth gave my hand an encouraging squeeze and I came to my senses. I knew who it was.

He looked towards us and paused, putting his hand up to shield his eyes from the sun, which was now low in the sky. I couldn't wait any longer.

'Billy!' I called. 'Billy!' and running to the yard gate I vaulted over it in one easy leap, raced up to my brother and wrapped him in my arms.

'Oh, Dick,' he said, dropping the pail of feed, 'you've come home,' and his face worked agonisingly into a grin and then a frown before he burst into sudden and noisy tears. I held him for what seemed an age, smelling the muck from the cows on his jacket and the straw from the barn in his hair. All the years of our childhood, when we had shared our life and growing up, were encompassed in that long fraternal hug.

'You stayed away so long,' he sobbed.

'I'm back now.'

'Yes.' He stepped back and took a long shuddering breath while pulling out a large blue handkerchief to wipe his eyes. 'You silly bugger. You should have told us you were coming. We would have laid on a bit of a party,' he said, now resentful as he sniffed and blew his nose.

'I don't want a damn party,' I said, grinning. 'A cup of tea would go down a treat, though.'

He laughed too then, and grabbing hold of my shoulder dragged me across the yard towards the kitchen door. Elizabeth and her dog followed behind.

Mother was at the sink. She had her back to us and didn't turn round as we came in but carried on draining the pan of potatoes that she was getting ready for the evening meal.

'We've company for supper, Mother,' called Billy, the excitement bubbling out of his voice. 'I hope you've made enough.'

I think she knew. I think she'd guessed. Because when she turned round and looked at me, a smile was already spreading across her face and that smile was the one she had always reserved for me. No words were spoken. I walked across the room until I was standing before her.

'Hello, Mother,' I said, and now the tears began to gather in my eyes. All that resentment and the feelings of umbrage that I had nurtured for years faded away, not lost for ever, as it turned out, but pushed aside by the overwhelming realisation of how much I had missed her.

Slowly, she put down the saucepan and took up a cloth to wipe her hands. 'Oh, my son,' she said, 'my Richard.' She put her hand up to my face to stroke my cheek just as she'd done when I was a boy. Our embrace drove away all the reservations that I might have imagined about my right to return. I was home.

Supper was a jolly affair with much laughter and conversation. Thinking about it later, I realised that to begin with it was Billy and I who did most of the talking. Mother tut-tutted at my stories about the tribesmen and held her hand to her mouth in horror when I spoke about the heads in the sack. She compared my tales to those of Rudyard Kipling and I could tell, being a reader like her, that she would be going to the book-shelves later on to pull out a volume to re-read.

Elizabeth was almost silent. She served and cleared away, dishes of meat and potatoes followed by a treacle tart and the farm's own cream. Later she poured tea for us all, putting the requisite amount of sugar and milk in each person's cup without enquiry. She listened to my stories, I know, for I saw her eyes widen sometimes and a smile come to her lips when I recounted amusing tales of my fellow soldiers. But she seemed a shadow of the soft, funny girl that I remembered.

Before we'd finished pudding, Marian and Albert arrived, alerted by a telephone call from Mother. They had grown sleek with wealth and position and Albert, particularly, was almost unrecognisable. He was portly, if that word could be used to describe a man who had only just reached his fortieth birthday. His fair wavy hair had all but gone, except for a greying half-moon around the back of his head, leaving a bald pate which grew damper and shinier as the evening progressed. I'd always liked him and he was still as cheerful and friendly as ever.

Marian, on the other hand, had become sterner and older than her years. 'Praise be to God,' she said, giving me a dry kiss on the cheek, 'you've returned safely from a heathen land.'

I thought she was joking, and grinned, looking round the table for a supporting laugh, but Elizabeth gave a slight shake of her head and I realised that Marian was in deadly earnest.

'I've prayed for you,' she said, 'prayed to the Lord to watch over you.'

'Well, it seems that He was listening,' said Albert jovially, 'because Richard looks fit and has apparently had an exciting life.'

Marian pursed her lips at that. Her relationship with the Lord was not to be taken lightly. Mother poured her another cup of tea and brought out a fruit cake.

As the conversation ebbed and flowed between them, I settled back in my chair to watch and listen. It was almost like the old days. The family

208

together after supper, arguing and laughing under the soft light of the big oil lamp. Oh yes, that oil lamp was still there despite the fact that electricity had been put in when I was away.

'Best thing I ever did,' said Billy. 'Makes a hell of a difference in the milking parlour.'

I grinned, raising my eyebrows in Elizabeth's direction, commenting silently on Billy's remark, but apart from a brief smile back she made no response.

I turned to Mother instead. 'I expect you like it, Mother. Much easier than filling up the oil lamps.'

She nodded. 'It is easier, Richard, and cleaner. And look over there.' She pointed to the corner where a small blue-mottled electric stove stood between the dresser and her marble-topped baking slab. 'It makes lovely cakes.'

'But this?' I pointed to the big overhead oil lamp. 'You've kept it.'

'It's a kinder light,' she said, and everyone nodded in agreement. Change had to come in small steps towards my family.

So nothing had really changed. All was as ever, and I relaxed in the comfort that feeling brought me. I sighed deeply and looked lazily around the big kitchen, noting the light gleaming off the copper pans and the shirts and underwear hanging on the pulley. Billy's shirts, Mother or Elizabeth's underslips and blouses, just like the old days. Then I drew in a breath as it suddenly struck me. All those clothes belonged to adults. No children were in this house.

I turned back to the family, formulating a stupid question, and found Elizabeth's eyes fixed on me with a look so despairing that the enquiry died in my mouth. I glanced up again at the washing then back at her and received a little shake of the head in reply. How was it that she knew what I was thinking? I never knew, but she always had that ability. Fortunately, this by-play was unseen by the rest of the family who chattered on, discussing my adventures, so recently relayed to them. As I turned back to them and joined in the conversation, I thought about her quietness, her still girlish figure. All her affection seemed to be bestowed on the pet dog who was even now at her feet. Poor Elizabeth. Eight years married and as childless as Marian. No wonder she looked so sad.

It was late when Marian and Albert left and Mother had cleared away the last of the supper things. Billy had already gone, yawning, up to bed, promising to have a 'good old talk in the morning' and to take me on a tour of the farm to see the new additions and renovations. Elizabeth had said goodnight shortly after that and had gone up too, accompanied by her dog, whose name, I had now learned, was Tess.

'Where shall I sleep, Mother?' I asked, lifting my kit bag and taking my uniform jacket from the back of my chair.

'Why, in your old room, of course. I made up the bed while Elizabeth was washing up and I've put a bottle in, to air it.' She smiled at me. 'You should be comfortable in there.'

'I know I will,' I said, 'although I'm that tired, I could sleep on the washing line.'

'Go on with you.' She laughed and gave me a goodnight kiss before I made my way into the hall and up the familiar staircase to find again the bedroom where I'd slept for nearly eighteen years.

In the big room at the front which had been Mother and Father's I could hear a rumbling snore. Billy, who always slept the moment his head hit the pillow, must be in there. This was something I hadn't thought about, but of course it was obvious. The married couple should have the double bed.

Walking carefully now, so as not to wake them, I made my way across the landing to our old room but was stopped for a moment by a low growl that came from the little bedroom above the front door. Elizabeth's dog was in there.

My room looked as though I had left it only the night before. The two beds were made up and all my treasures there on my table, placed as I had left them and dusted clean. The curtains were drawn back and pale moonlight lay in a strip across my bed. I smiled. Mother had remembered how I liked to see the night and I stood for a while looking out on to the yard and the dark fields beyond. A breeze blew in through the slightly opened sash, bringing with it a fresh sweet smell of the hillside. How different from the cold, sterile wind that howled out of the Hindu Kush or the heavy spice-laden air that used to blanket my cot in Meerut.

When I slipped into bed, I was immediately back in childhood. I exulted in the feel of the heavy Irish linen sheets and my feet rubbed familiarly against the little slubs of cotton woven into the fabric. It was a pleasant change from the army where we slept under blankets, although in Meerut it was so hot that a pair of shorts was all that was necessary. But now I stretched out in pleasure as I closed my tired eyes and slept. Once in the middle of the night I woke, hearing the owl hooting in the oak tree, and readied myself for action. My arm reached out to lift up the mosquito netting before I realised where I was and, comforted, settled back into sleep.

I've been talking into this machine for hours and I must remember to ask Sharon to get new batteries in the morning. It is early morning now, still dark, and the birds haven't moved from their nests and neither have I. My bed is most comfortable now the special mattress has been delivered and set up. It works on an electric button and I can press it to sit me up or lie me down. Cost a few bob, but what of it? The money's there and should be spent. I've bought a new car for Sharon too. She played hell with me, saying that she didn't need it, but that old thing she's been driving is a death trap and I'm concerned for Thomas. Anyway, he loves the new one.

I've only slept for an hour or so, even though Sharon is home and I take comfort from the knowledge of her presence. She has been busy since her return from Spain, but hasn't neglected me. It was she who organised this bed, and after discussing it with me and Dr Clewes arranged for the nurse to come in every day to help me bathe. And she's started new studies.

'I'm going to the college in town to do a degree,' she told me a few days after she came home from her holiday. 'Do you think I'm mad?'

'No.'

'It's English and history,' she explained. 'Then I could do a teaching course. It would make me secure, money-wise, when...' she paused and swallowed before continuing, 'and I could give Thomas all the things that I never had.'

'What things?' I ignored the 'when' and wondered what it was that her parents had denied her. She rarely mentioned them and certainly never visited her mother, who I knew was still living on the big estate in town. Her father had disappeared years ago. Maybe even dead, by now.

'Books, trips to other places, holidays even. Better friends.' She looked at me, taking off her spectacles to polish the lenses on a corner of her T-shirt. 'Do you think I'm being stuck up?'

I shook my head. What could possibly be wrong with trying to better yourself? That's what most of us in the village had tried to do, years ago. I was going to be the first one in the family to go to university and Mother and Billy had been proud of me. Of course, I threw all that over when I joined up and I did regret it, later.

'I think you'll find it most satisfying, my dear,' I told her.

She grinned and stood up. 'Andrew thinks it will be a waste of time. He can't understand why I want to do it.'

Exactly, I thought. That man is no good for her.

And even as I thought it, she added, 'He doesn't understand me at all, really. Not like Jason.'

So it was Jason Hyde whom she preferred. I felt satisfaction at that and was about to tell her so, but then scolded myself. God knows, I should be the last one to offer advice. I got it wrong throughout my life. I loved one woman so much that it all but destroyed any other relationship that I embarked upon.

I thought of something else to take my mind off love. 'What will your mother think about it?' I asked. 'You going to college?'

She shrugged. 'I might not tell her. It's none of her business.'

It was stupid of me to bring it up. I knew she hated talking about her old life, and now she was picking up our teacups and taking them out to the kitchen. I watched her as she went through the door and thought again how recognisable that tall thin figure was and how evocative that cap of hair, which bobbed animatedly as she left.

Was it her mother or her father who was supposed to be related to the Major? I'd never found that out, but truly it didn't matter. The more I looked at her, the more I knew that she was indeed a great-granddaughter. She is so like him, and Thomas has that same red hair he had, and I did, once.

'Your hair has darkened,' said Mother the next morning when I came down to breakfast.

'Has it?' I mumbled, my mouth full of delicious bacon and softly fried eggs. 'I wouldn't know.'

I had slept deeply and come down when the day was well on. Outside, the weather was fine, still coolish, for it was only early April, but bright and sunny, and I could see Mother's little garden through the window, alive with bobbing tulips and the last of the daffodils. I stole a look at her in the harsh daylight and confirmed what I had suspected the night before. She had grown old, and yet was still only in her early sixties. All the gold had gone from her hair and her face was lined and tired. Or perhaps the expression couldn't be described as tired, but something else that I couldn't exactly put my finger on.

'Billy and Elizabeth have no children,' I said. 'I'm surprised.'

The expression on her face deepened and I now saw what it was. Disappointment. 'No,' she said, shortly. 'They haven't been blessed.'

I left it at that; it was obviously a sore subject. If she had hoped for grandchildren then she was unlucky. No chance from Marian, Billy and Elizabeth childless – and me? Well, I wasn't married and had no plans to be so.

I strolled out into the yard after breakfast and went to join Billy in the milking parlour. The last of the cattle had just been milked and he was whistling cheerfully as he slapped the bony haunches of the black-and-white cow to send her on her way. Changes had been made in the years I'd been away. The milking parlour had been extended and the walls replastered and distempered. Even the floor had been improved. I could see that the flagstones had been lifted and repositioned so that they were flat and properly cemented in. Much easier to keep clean.

I'd noticed other changes too. A new Dutch barn and an implement shed where a tractor held pride of place. I wondered if the heavy horses still pulled the plough or if they were now only kept as a hobby. If they were, then Billy had gone completely soft. He'd never been one for pets.

Somehow I fell into the old tasks without even realising it and found myself opening the gate into the field and urging the cows into the pasture. It felt good and I opened up my lungs and took a great gulp of air, so much indeed that my head swam for a moment and I wobbled on my feet.

Billy came out then and put an arm on my shoulder. He was quiet today, brooding, I think, over my return and the implications that it might have. He had become older, and his face was our father's face, as I recalled it from my earliest memories. He was heavier, too, with no sign left of the athletic boy he'd once been. He had an air of great strength about him, and rock-like immovability. But, oddly, his eyes seemed to have shrunk and were now like two chips of coal in his square, weather-beaten face.

'It's right good to see you,' he said, and I knew his words were sincere. 'I dread you going away again.'

'It won't be for a few months.' My reassurance seemed to help for he laughed when I added, 'And you'll be that bloody sick of me by then, you'll be setting the dogs on me.'

'Never,' he said.

We walked the farm that day and every day after that, as I became unpaid labour once more and glad of it. I learned all I knew about farming from our Billy. He had a knack of making money without stinting on the feed or on the welfare of the stock, although he hated waste and was still careful with every penny. When I went with him to market, the following Monday, I was almost embarrassed at the firmness of his dealings with

216

the other farmers and the way he browbeat them into giving him the best deals. The cattle at our farm were the finest in the district and any one of our heifers was guaranteed a good price. Our Billy made sure he got it.

The only trouble was that it made him unpopular and I could see that he had no friends in or out of the sale ring. I, on the other hand, was greeted most kindly by men I'd known as boys, and many offers of hospitality came my way. I promised to meet some of them in the Golden Lion that evening and even though I assured Billy that he would be welcome too, he declined the offer. I think he knew that I was wrong in my assurances.

'I've better things to do than sup pints,' he said, 'but you go along. You can catch up with all your old pals.'

I had a great surprise when I went into the pub. The first person to stand up and greet me was my old friend Fred Darlington. Oh, God, I was always glad to see Fred; he was a true friend to me. That night we talked and talked and after the others drifted away home to wives and children we stayed and caught up on the years we'd lost.

He was still in the police but had transferred up to our town a couple of years ago. 'I was sick of London,' he said, 'and after my dad died it was difficult for my mother. Now we all live together.'

He had married a girl he'd met in London, who was originally from Cornwall. A country girl at heart who had settled back happily into village life.

'She never liked London either,' he said. 'But her people are poor and she needed to make a living. Her father was a tin miner. He was killed a few years ago and Miranda had to go into service. Just round the corner from where I was stationed.'

I listened with interest, thinking what an exotic name Fred's wife had. Was she as fascinating as her name implied? I met her soon afterwards and a pretty lass she was, with curly black hair like a gypsy, but very housewifely and sensible and not a bit exotic in character. She was kind to me in later years, when I particularly needed it.

'What about you?' he asked. 'Got a wife somewhere?'

I shook my head. 'Too busy soldiering, and where I've been, well, not many English girls would like to go.'

'Besides which,' he said in a lowered voice and giving me a knowing smile, 'none of them is Elizabeth Nugent.'

I must have looked at him with amazement, because he laughed and got up to get us more drinks. When he came back I said, urgently, 'What d'you mean? There's nothing between me and Elizabeth.'

'I know that. But you did want her, didn't you?'

What could I say? He remembered my telling him about her on that weekend in Snowdonia. I nodded. 'I did once, but she's married to my brother now.'

'More's the pity.' Fred's normally pleasant face darkened. 'There's a marriage made in hell if ever there was one.'

Those words cut through the warm cheery atmosphere as though they had been chipped out of ice. I stared at him, scarcely believing what I was hearing. My best friend describing my brother's marriage as 'made in hell'. It was shocking.

'What?' I said, nearly choking on the last of my beer. I could feel my face getting hot and my fists clenching, but I was still not sure that I'd heard him right. 'What did you say about Billy and Elizabeth?'

We were almost the last people in the pub and I could see that the landlord was hanging the bar cloth across the taps, getting ready to ring the bell, but I had to know what Fred meant. I reached over and, not too gently, grabbed his coat lapel. 'What are you bloody talking about?'

He made an effort to shake me off. He'd grown stronger after his years in the police and was used to handling rowdies, but he still couldn't match me in strength. He had to put his hands down.

'Oh, look, Dick,' he sighed, 'I have to tell you something. There's been a lot of talk in the village about them. She's not happy, you must have noticed that, and early on everyone said that he was knocking her about. God! I saw her once with awful bruises on her neck.'

My jaw dropped in horrified amazement. This was something I'd never imagined and I could hardly believe it. My brother hitting his wife? Our Billy smacking my Elizabeth? It was impossible. Anyone would be mad to believe it.

But even as I was about to spring to my brother's defence, something stopped me. I thought about the quiet sad atmosphere at home and the almost forced jollity. I knew that something was wrong. Mother was strangely anxious and Billy seemed detached and vague. Then there was the business of the separate bedrooms. And the dog. Did

219

Elizabeth keep it by her for protection?

I kept my face down and stared into my empty glass. 'I know that Elizabeth is unhappy,' I muttered, 'but I can't believe that Billy hits her. He wouldn't.'

The landlord called time so we got up and made our way out into the damp night. The village was quiet; it was late and raining and most people had gone to bed. We should have parted company and each hurried home but now a genie's bottle had been opened and too much had burst out for me to let the discussion end.

Fred lived in the police house next to the school and it was on my way home anyway, so I walked along beside him, mulling over what I'd just learned.

'You must have got it wrong,' I said finally, breaking the silence. 'Neither Mother nor Elizabeth has said a word to me.'

He stopped at his gate. 'You need to keep your eyes open a bit more. I don't think I'm wrong, Dick, and I think you should see what you can do.'

That wasn't fair. What the hell could I do about something I didn't really believe? I muttered a 'goodnight' and walked on my way with a heavy heart.

Chapter Fifteen

I still think about that first time I was told my brother was a wife beater and my feelings of disgust and dismay. As far as I knew, people like us didn't take out our frustrations on those who were weaker.

Of course, I'd known about men in the village who knocked about their wives and children and, although we had regarded them with a certain contempt, it was accepted. These were the poor people who lived in the houses by the abattoir and, according to popular opinion, could do nothing right. The men were brutes, the women sluts, and the children, whom I knew at school, had nitty heads and scabs of impetigo.

I wonder if Sharon suffered in that way. Perhaps her father had been a beater and that is why she is so wary about Thomas's having anything to do with his own father. I tried to question her again, the other day, but she didn't say much. Only that Thomas's father was a student she'd met at a bar in the town.

'I went out with him for a few months,' she said. 'He met someone else and left. It was good riddance as far as I was concerned.'

I was taken aback by the casual cruelty of it all, but then who am I to be shocked by indifference? I've practised it for a lot of my life.

I've taken to sitting in the kitchen every morning now after breakfast. The dog and I hog the Aga and let the nurse and the new cleaner work around us. Sharon is at the college most mornings and Thomas is at school so I like to take my place as the one in charge. I've been feeling quite well lately: only another remission, I suppose, but welcome nevertheless.

The cleaner is a woman from the village, who comes in three days a week and scours the house with great energy.

'These books could do with a wipe,' she said one day, coming into my parlour and looking at my library.

'Not with water and bleach,' I said sternly. 'A soft cloth only!'

All she did was laugh. These young women have little respect for their elders, but she did use a cloth and spent a whole morning pulling out the books and piling them on the carpet. I sat and watched her polish the shelves and then made sure they all went back in the right places.

'Pass me that one, please,' I asked as she applied her cloth to the worn cover of a book I knew well.

This was a favourite, bought at an open-air stall in Meerut where I used to go regularly to buy second-hand books. *Plain Tales from the Hills* by Kiplin', fine stories of India that I'd carried with me in my saddle bags when I was on patrol on the Frontier. I was holding it on my knee when Sharon came home at lunchtime.

She came into my room carrying a tray with sandwiches and coffee for both of us, and glasses of sherry as a treat.

'What's that you're reading?' She picked up the

book I'd put aside while I sipped at my drink.

'Kipling,' I said. 'A book of short stories. It's a wonderful read.'

I thought back to that sultry day and the dusty market stall where I bought it. I could hear the noise of people and animals, smell the spice and dung in the air, and for a moment felt a longing for India. I was young there, strong and capable and unafraid. Everything that I'm not now.

'That book travelled all over India with me,' I said, 'and came home when I did. It was one of my favourites.'

She flicked through the pages, stopping now and then to examine the line drawings. 'I knew you were in India,' she said, reaching for a sandwich. 'Did you like it?'

Like it? Like is such a pathetic word to describe my feeling for that glorious place.

I sighed and looked through the window. It has been a raw day, sunny and clear, but the wind is blowing hard off the hill and bringing the last of the autumn leaves off the fruit trees.

'Did you, Richard?'

'Yes,' I muttered, 'I loved it. Apart from this farm, there is nowhere else on earth I would want to be.'

'But you came home.'

'I came and went a few times,' I said. 'I was a regular soldier and stationed out there. But I came home on leave. To see Mother, Billy and Elizabeth.'

Sharon was quiet, listening. That is the wonderful thing about her: she doesn't hurry my memories and I can get them in order in my mind.

223

'The first time I came home, I had been away for eight years and things had changed. The farm was bigger and more efficient and Billy was doing well. There shouldn't have been a thing to worry about. But there was. They weren't happy.'

I think I might have gone on to tell her more, but the phone rang then and she made a gesture of apology to me and left the room. When she came back, we ate our lunch and spoke about Thomas and the moment was lost. But that time of my return has been much on my mind and I must speak about it. Talking into this machine is easier, anyway, because I can speak the truth. I might have lied to Sharon. I don't want her to judge me. Not yet.

That next morning, after Fred told me about Billy and Elizabeth, I came down to the kitchen with a renewed awkwardness. I'd been home for four days and had just got back into the way of being part of a family when this bombshell had exploded. Fred had intimated that I had to sort the problem, but what could I do?

So I walked through the hall and into the kitchen passage quite downcast. All the bloom of my homecoming had been thoroughly wiped away. It was with relief that I saw Marian sitting at the table, drinking a cup of tea. She had a small diary in her hands and was pointing to a date.

'I want to take Mother on a little holiday,' she said after I'd given her a nod and kissed Mother's cheek. 'I thought Torquay would be nice.'

Mother put a plate of sausage and eggs in front of me. 'I can't go away,' she said. 'There's far too much to do.'

'Nonsense!' Marian straightened her hat, a severe brown cloche decorated with a black cock's feather. 'Richard is home for a few months and Elizabeth can easily do your tasks. I'm sure she can do more in the dairy and it wouldn't kill her to cook a few meals for her husband and brother-in-law. After all,' she added, her voice weighed down with import, 'she has plenty of time to take that dog for long walks.'

Mother said nothing, but sat down in front of the pot and poured me a cup of tea. Her face was tight, drawn about the lips, and she kept her eyes firmly on the cups and saucers in front of her.

'What d'you think, Richard?' Marian said, giving me one of her meaningful looks to make sure that I agreed with her.

As ever, I took the easy way out. 'Good idea,' I muttered through a mouthful of food. 'You've always enjoyed the seaside, Mother.'

She looked up, shaking her head slowly. 'But you've only just come home.'

I drank my tea. 'I'll be here for a good while yet. A week,' I stopped and looked at Marian for confirmation, and she nodded, 'a week away won't make a difference.'

'I'll think about it.'

'I need a decision now,' said Marian. 'I've got a full diary.'

'But it's the week after next,' Mother complained. 'I'd have to get everything ready; there'd be washing, and I'll need a dress for going down to dinner if we're staying in a nice hotel.' Her voice trailed away and I knew that Marian had won. A lot of the spark had gone out of my mother.

Marian made a note in her diary and put it back in her handbag. 'Good,' she said, 'it's decided. I'll pick you up on Thursday afternoon and we'll go into town to buy you a dress.'

Mother shrugged and that was an end to discussion. She had given in.

I accompanied Marian to her car.

'You look better today,' she said, surprising me, for everyone else had thought my tan quite winning and said how well I looked. 'Not so yellow,' she added.

I ignored that but took the opportunity of our being alone to raise the question. 'Have you noticed anything odd between Billy and Elizabeth?' I said tentatively.

Her face clouded. 'I was never in favour of that match,' she said.

'But I've heard,' I started anxiously, 'I've heard that he's...'

She put a finger to my mouth so that I couldn't finish what I was saying. 'Take no notice of gossips,' she warned. 'You'll never hear anything good.'

'It isn't gossip,' I said, angry that she was dismissing it so casually. 'Fred Darlington told me that there has been violence.'

My sister flinched as though someone had struck her and her mouth pursed even smaller. 'Whatever has happened,' she said in an unnecessarily lowered voice, 'isn't to be talked about. Mind me, Richard. It's family business and no one else's. Besides,' she got into her car and waited impatiently while I cranked the starting handle, 'besides, Elizabeth hasn't complained, so there's probably nothing to it.'

When I got back into the kitchen, Elizabeth was sitting in the chair Marian had vacated, pasting butter and marmalade on a piece of toast. She looked almost like her old self this morning, the wind having added some colour to her cheeks and pulled her hair about. She wore a grey skirt and a pale blue jumper, and when she lifted her head to smile at me I saw a flash of silver and blue, just showing over her collar.

'Oh,' I said, 'you've still got that old necklace. I thought you might have got rid of it by now.'

'Of course I wouldn't.' She bridled and put up her hand to touch the silver links.

'She wears it all the time,' said Mother. 'It was a nice present.'

I kept what I thought of that remark to myself. Mother hadn't been so keen at the time; indeed, she hadn't been keen on anything that might make Elizabeth and me closer. I gazed at her, wondering what she thought of the rumours of trouble and if she knew that they were true. I doubted that she would say anything, even if she had the facts laid out before her. In that respect she was as closed off as our Marian. Family matters had never been spoken abroad, but now it seemed that they could not be spoken here either. I changed the subject.

'Mother's going with Marian to Torquay. The week after next.'

Elizabeth put down her knife and looked up, genuinely pleased. 'Well, I'm very glad to hear that, Mother. It'll do you good, a few days away, and I've heard that Devon is mild at this time of the year. They've got palm trees on the prom-enade.'

Mother laughed. 'I don't know about palm trees. I expect they'll be nice, but our Marian is planning to take us to a grand hotel and I'm not sure I have the clothes.'

Elizabeth shook her head, still smiling. 'You can easily buy some new things if you feel like it. Go to Clays.'

I listened to them chattering, the two women I'd loved best in the world, but now somehow removed from me. Only Billy had taken me back into the family as though nothing had happened. With Mother and Elizabeth I sensed a distance.

I got up then, bored with women's talk about clothes and trips, and wandered out into the yard where I was immediately grabbed by my brother who put me to work shifting hay. He was revving up the tractor ready to go into the fields.

'I'm going down the Major's land,' he said. 'There's peas to plant. Come and join me when you've finished here.'

Billy had three farm hands working with him now and all were kept busy. One was a lad; about fourteen, I suppose, and a bit mental. The men were kind to him and helped him with his jobs, but Billy gave him hell day and night. I didn't like to hear him shout and swear at the boy and said so on the third day I was home. Billy ignored my protests.

'He's got to learn,' he said, 'and he's so thick that I have to tell him the same things over and over again. I wouldn't have taken him on if Mother and the vicar hadn't begged me. I can't abide him.'

I remembered Billy's contempt for the disabled and disfigured, which had bordered on the downright cruel. He had teased Herbert Lowe unmercifully as a lad, and once our father had belted him for poking a stick at Herbert's bad leg. And he hadn't been much better about Johnny Lowe. 'That empty eye socket is horrible,' he'd told Elizabeth the day before her party. 'I don't know why you want him at your do.'

She had tossed her head in her usual way. 'I like him,' she said. 'What difference does an eye make? He's still handsome.'

I had been jealous when I heard her say that, but Billy had snorted angrily and yelled that she was going out with an 'ugly bugger' as he ran into the field followed by the turnip that Elizabeth threw at him.

But I think my complaint about Billy's treatment of the boy had some effect because he stopped shouting at him and left him in the charge of the other farm hands.

I wondered about Johnny Lowe, and that was when I found out about how rich he had become. Billy still despised him but Mother said he had done well for himself and had looked after his family like a gentleman.

I was thinking about that as I forked the hay into the stalls, so after finishing I changed my mind about helping Billy with the peas and decided to walk into the village to see Herbert Lowe. He was long retired now and living in some comfort, thanks to Johnny's regular contributions. To my great pleasure I was greeted like a long lost son by the old man. He had changed greatly and looked aged and in poor health, but was still able to carry on a conversation.

'You're a grown man,' he said in a breathless wavering voice, and then gave a dry little chuckle. 'The image of your father, I'd say.'

My heart sank. I'd put all that business behind me, deciding once I'd got home that those fancies which I'd dwelt on so miserably were simply those. Fancies. No matter what an ignorant old tribesman had suggested. But here was someone who'd known me from birth, speaking about it as if it were quite accepted.

'How have you been keeping?' I asked, hoping to divert him.

'I'll do,' he said.

'The farm's doing well,' I ventured again.

'Maybe.' He stared into the fire for so long that I thought he must've fallen asleep. I was just about to get up and quietly leave when he said, 'I haven't seen Miss Elizabeth for some time. How is she?'

'Well,' I said. 'She seems very well.'

'Taking care of herself at last, is she? I told her that. Don't provoke him, and keep a damn big dog with you at all times. That way you'll be safe. That's what I told her, poor lass.' He cleared his throat and spat a glob of phlegm into the fireplace where it sizzled noisily on the hot grate. I stared at it as he weakly raised his arm and wiped his mouth on the sleeve of his cardigan.

I wanted to go now, I'd heard enough. But he started speaking again.

'Your mother was downright wicked allowing that match. I told her so myself. And you were no use. Clearing off like you did.'

I felt helpless. Here was the suggestion again, out loud and from a source that I had to believe. I stood up. 'I have to go now, Herbert, but I'm glad to have found you in good health.'

He grunted and gave a little chuckle. 'I reckon you came just in time, son. I'm not far off from meeting my Maker.'

I bent over and shook his hand before leaving, but he fastened his fingers around mine and looked up into my face. 'By God, lad,' he repeated, cranking out a breathless laugh. 'You are the very image of him. Don't worry, I always respected him, really, no matter what I pretended to Mr Wilde.'

As I walked through the village, accepting the greetings and good wishes of several old acquaintances, I was troubled. So many problems in front of me and none of my making. Not only the question of my parentage, which, if I was honest, was the reason I had come home, but now this monstrous accusation against Billy. I had no doubt that I was expected to do or say something about it, but it was so unfair.

And I couldn't let it go, particularly when I made myself think of what Billy might have done to Elizabeth to cause so much gossip. The evidence of his brutality must have been horribly obvious, because I knew my girl. She would never have complained to outsiders. If Fred had seen bruises when he lived down the road in the village, what had Herbert seen when he was about the farm daily? He might have been retired, but I knew that he would have remained a fixture at the kitchen table at midday dinnertimes for as long as he was able to get out.

The road out of the village led past the Gate House, now an abandoned place with the downstairs windows boarded up and the little garden in front overgrown and full of weeds. Billy had bought it along with the land and I wondered that he hadn't put a tenant in there. It would have brought in a few bob and he wasn't one to let that sort of money go. I stopped for a moment at the spot where I had stumbled over the Major's book and that whole episode came flooding back.

I saw the inside of the house clearly, the polished tables and colourful rugs. Those rugs I'd seen more recently in the bazaars in Peshawar, similar colours and patterns, timeless and exquisite. The idea that the Major had bought them in that same market made me smile. How strange that we should have been in the same place and doing the same thing. I wondered what he would have thought of that small boy if he had known what was coming to him. Did he know who the boy really was? Possibly. Mother could tell me, perhaps, but could I bring myself to ask her?

I tried to picture the Major's face. Tried to see through the gloom of that dim room to the thin stooping figure who had pointed me towards the leather stool before almost falling into his chair. Was his hair red; did he have a sharp bridge to his nose, and blue eyes? It was no good: my memory was blank. All I could remember were the smooth pale hands, so unlike Father's, presenting me with the book. I looked down at my own hands and my stomach turned.

It had clouded over and a few drops of fine rain were coming in on the wind. I shivered as I hurried on along the lane towards the farm. I wasn't going to help Billy with the peas. I could hardly bear to look him in the face, not before I'd spoken to Mother. But once I was home, my determination filtered away as I tried desperately to think of questions to pose or accusations to make that wouldn't sound foolish.

Marian telephoned after supper to tell Mother that she had booked the hotel, so there could be no backing out.

'I wasn't going to,' said Mother, but the indignant tone in her voice gave the lie to her assertion. She had been nervous about telling Billy at supper, but with no reason, as it turned out. He was all for it, telling her that he also was going away for a few days to take Diamond to the Three Counties Show.

'Our Dick can be in charge,' he said, and gave me a slap on the back. 'After all, he's been an important man in the army, in charge of more than a couple of farm workers.'

I was less confident, but Billy had no doubts.

'Get out the vet if you need to, but you'll be all right. The men are used to dealing with animals.'

Only Elizabeth was silent. She hadn't been invited on either trip and seemingly there was no thought that she should have been. I stole a look at her and was astonished to see the secret look of joy which bathed her face. The look disappeared almost immediately but I'd seen it.

The night before Mother's trip, I ventured a question about Billy and Elizabeth. They had both gone up and Mother was just finishing off her ironing, ready for her holiday. She looked tired and dispirited and not at all ready for a jaunt. I tried to jolly her along.

'You'll love it,' I said. To tell the truth, I was becoming bored with her uncertainty. The Mother I remembered never dithered like this. 'It'll be somewhere different to see, and Marian will make it all comfortable.'

'I know you're right, Richard, love. But I do think I'm needed here.'

This was my opportunity and I grabbed it with both hands. 'Is it because of the trouble between Billy and Elizabeth?' I asked.

She gasped and her hands froze on the iron. 'What have you heard?' she said.

'Quite a lot.'

The colour drained from her face as she stared at me in dismay. I didn't like to see her upset, but once I'd started I couldn't stop. 'For God's sake, Mother,' I said, 'tell me.'

I thought that there would be another rebuttal, for she shook her head and said nothing for a couple of minutes but hung up the blouse she had been ironing and unplugged the iron. That was a new addition since I'd been away. The old flat irons that Mother used to heat up on the range had been put away, no longer of any use. And now she took her time, winding the brown cloth-covered flex into a figure of eight and folding up the white blanket she used as an ironing cloth.

'Mother,' I said, getting angry now. I suddenly couldn't wait any longer, now that I had braved the citadel of silence. 'Come and sit down.'

She sat in her chair, opposite mine in front of the range, and took a deep breath. 'I think it started on their honeymoon,' she said, her voice quiet and reluctant. 'Elizabeth said nothing, but she seemed so low when they came back, even though they'd only been away for a couple of days, that I knew something had gone wrong.' She shifted, uncomfortable about talking of such intimate things, but finally ready to break a long silence. 'I thought at first that it was just maidenly embarrassment and that after a while all would be well. But then, one night, I heard her crying. It woke me up and I came downstairs. I thought a cup of hot milk would settle me, but I found her here, in the kitchen, shaking with fright. "He tried to kill me," she said. "Your son tried to kill me."'

I felt sick. I knew how violent my brother could be when he was in a temper and my next words were foolish. 'What had she done to anger him?' I said.

'Nothing!' Mother almost shouted the word at me. 'She'd done nothing. Your brother can't control himself.'

'But you knew he had a bad temper,' I said, not letting her off, 'and you wanted the marriage.'

'Yes, I did,' she replied, sitting forward in her chair. 'I told you at the time, I thought it would keep him safe. I thought it would stop him from...'

'From what?' I was so confused, so childish in my ignorance. 'What did he need saving from?'

This is where she stopped for thought. 'I don't think that William is quite normal,' she said eventually. 'Before, I imagined that he needed a wife to keep him steady. The way the stallion

235

needs frequent coupling.'

She stopped then, looking up at my face, which I'm sure registered my utter disgust. Did she realise what she had just said? And if she did, when had she changed? This wasn't the Mother of my childhood, the woman who had oft times flouted convention and had a brain and a will of her own. I found it hard to believe that she placed her son and his wife on the same plane as the beasts they looked after and I couldn't imagine that she had been so uncaring of Elizabeth that she had urged her into that sort of arrangement. Worse than that, almost, was the fact that she had preferred the possibility of the girl's being in danger to my timorously offered suit.

'You knew I loved her,' I said bitterly.

She sighed, almost annoyed that I had brought it up. 'Of course I did, but what would have been the use? You had nothing here and would have had to take her away. I couldn't let that happen.'

'I could have stayed,' I cried. 'Come back after university and lived in the village. What would have been so wrong about that?'

If I thought that she would admit her foolish behaviour, I was wrong. Admitting that she had been stupid was impossible for her. 'It wouldn't have worked,' she said, astonished that I was questioning it now. 'You wouldn't have earned enough. Besides...'

'Besides what?' Was this the time? Was she going to tell me about my father? For the briefest moment, I think she nearly did. Indeed, her mouth opened and her hands spread out in a sort of entreaty for understanding and I waited, heart

236

beating, for the truth.

It never came. Instead, she closed her mouth and, folding her hands on her lap, let the moment pass. Too many years of silence and denial couldn't be overcome. I knew then that she would never tell me.

'What's to do, then?' I had to get on to practical things now. 'How do we stop him beating her?'

'Oh, he's stopped.' Mother was quite sure. 'He stopped all that years ago,' she said as though it were a problem solved. 'He never touches her now. Not in any way.'

That last remark meant exactly what I thought it did and I knew that it was the real and possibly only cause of her sadness. Ours was a truly unhappy household which continued, unchanging, from day to day. There would be no children, no one to carry on the farm, and she would die knowing that she had allowed it to happen.

'Should I say something to Billy?'

For the first time a little smile came to her lips. 'I don't think so, Richard, love. He wouldn't know what you were talking about. He forgets his little tempers almost as soon as they are over. They never last for long.' She got up and moved the kettle on to the hot plate. 'He bears Elizabeth no grudge, you know,' she murmured as an afterthought, 'for being how she is.'

I think my mouth dropped open at that remark. I realised then that whatever happened she wouldn't change. No matter how much she loved Elizabeth, the farm – and that meant Billy – mattered more. But I couldn't let it go. How could she dare to transfer the responsibility?

237

'And what's that then?' I asked, my anger only just beneath the surface and ready to explode at any minute. 'How is she?'

'Why, Richard, love,' she said, pouring boiling water into the teapot, 'our Elizabeth is barren. Surely you realised that?'

Chapter Sixteen

We went out today, Sharon, Thomas and me. It was her idea, this little expedition, and I confess that at first I was very reluctant. It's been weeks since I left the house, and to be honest I had resigned myself to the fact that my days of going out were gone for ever. It's no fun being old and sick and trapped within four walls, specially when you have been active like me. Up until a couple of years ago I was still driving my car; not far, mind, towards the end, just into town and to see friends locally. But since my illness I've stayed pretty much around the house and garden. And now my legs are gone. They're like rubber and barely keep me upright. Even walking the short distance from my room to the bathroom or the kitchen I need help. It's shaming.

But Sharon has organised a wheelchair. She brought it into my room the other afternoon after the nurse had left. I hated to look at it and made a bit of a fool of myself, railing against it, being the stupid old bugger that I am.

'I'm not going in that,' I said to her. 'I do have

some pride left.'

She shook her head, exasperated. 'What the hell is wrong with you?' she grumbled. 'I was trying to do something nice for you.'

I ignored her anger and blustered back, 'Nice? What's nice about a wheelchair? For God's sake, woman, you can't imagine that I would be seen dead in that.'

'No,' she said evenly, 'you'll be seen dead in your coffin and good riddance when you're in a mood like this. But until then, give me a break and allow me to take you out.' She turned the chair round and marched out of the room. Her rare displays of temper are most unsettling and I don't like it. Despite that red hair, she's generally calm and not at all quick to take offence.

I realised how ridiculous I was being. What does it matter if I have to sit in a wheelchair? Have I become such a vain and silly old man that my precious dignity can be so easily offended? I called her back and apologised.

'I'm sorry,' I said, 'that was wrong of me. I find it hard to think of myself as, well, as old, I suppose.'

She was still simmering, I think, but accepted my apology nicely. These last few days she seems to be quieter than usual. It's as though she has something on her mind that needs sorting out and keeps popping up, unbidden, to confront her. I heard her snapping at Thomas yesterday, when he came in from the field, covered in mud, and ran through into the hall without taking off his boots. 'For goodness' sake,' she yelled at him, yanking off his boots and throwing them into the scullery, 'how many times do you have to be told the same thing?'

So I was somewhat concerned about her and recognised that I should have been more conciliatory when she suggested a day out. Perhaps she needed time away from the house to get things into perspective.

We decided to go to the coast. The weather is clear at the moment, quite cold, but not raining, and we thought that the views'd be wonderful.

'Don't bother with a picnic,' I said when I saw Sharon, at breakfast time, looking under the sink for the flask. 'I'm going to buy us lunch out at a hotel.'

'Lovely!' She smiled. 'But I haven't told you yet, I've invited Jason to come with us. Do you mind? I'll pay for his lunch.'

'You'll do no such thing,' I said firmly. 'It's my treat.'

So we set out, not in Sharon's car but in Jason's big four-wheel drive and very comfortable it is too. Thomas and I sat in the back with the blessed wheelchair folded up behind us, while Sharon sat beside young Hyde in the front. I looked at the back of his head and chuckled. He is like his grandfather, the same thick fair hair and broad shoulders. Eddie hated farming, although he worked well for us, upward of ten years. After the war the pit paid better, but that's not the only reason he didn't come back. He didn't get on with my brother and I remember several occasions of bitter arguments and clenched fists.

He was much happier down the mine where he loved the camaraderie of the other colliers. It did him little good though in the end because he died of the chest disease that many of them suffered. I didn't know his son well, only to nod to, but this young man is at our house almost daily. I detect more than a spark between him and Sharon.

We were right about the views. Even from the big windows of the hotel dining room where we ate our lunch, we could see far out on to Cardigan Bay. It was calm and blue and the headlands to the north and south were clear and sharp against a cloudless sky. I remembered bringing Elizabeth here once when we were a lot older. She liked this hotel enormously, and sitting today with the young people I had to smile at the memory of Elizabeth and me drinking whisky, sunk deep into chintz armchairs and looking out on to this very same view. I loved that memory and wanted to keep it in my head, so I bought another bottle of wine and Sharon and I helped ourselves. I gave a sip of mine to Thomas but he wasn't keen, preferring his cola, and Jason refused, because of driving.

After lunch, we walked along the promenade, me in the wheelchair, well wrapped up against the keen wind, breathing in the fresh cold air. I took so many gulps that I found myself getting quite giddy and was glad when Sharon spotted a sheltered bench.

'I'm going to sit for a bit,' she said. 'Jason will wheel you for a while.'

'I'd rather stay here,' I said, 'and look at the view.' She nodded, and pulled my chair close to where she had settled.

'I'll take Thomas on the beach,' said Jason. He is

241

a generous man and I think he could see that Sharon wanted a moment or two away from him. He put a hand on Thomas's shoulder. 'Come on, lad,' he said, 'let's see what we can find down there.'

The boy needed no urging and ran down the steps to the sand with a squawk of delight, followed no less eagerly by young Jason, who leapt athletically over the barrier and ran laughing towards the sea.

'He's nothing but a big kid himself,' said Sharon, smiling indulgently.

I reached for her hand and squeezed it. 'You like him, I think,' I said.

She nodded and then turned to look at me with a troubled look on her face. 'He's asked me to marry him,' she said. 'I don't know what to say.'

This was a facer, but in a way I should have been expecting it. My Sharon has a coterie of followers and is bound to get tied up with one of them sooner or later. But selfishly, at that moment, I felt nothing but the old familiar dismay. Wasn't it ever thus? The girl I loved had to belong to someone else.

She waited for me to say something, but I was quiet. Myriad thoughts raced through my mind and foremost among them was the one which frightened me most. If she married Jason, she would have to leave me.

'What d'you think?' she asked. 'Tell me, please.'

I sank in my chair, feeling cold and miserable. 'I don't know,' I said. 'Do you love him?'

'I think so.'

'But what about your other suitors? Andrew

Jones seems very keen and the doctor only comes to see me in the hope of catching a glimpse of you.'

She laughed at that and moved further towards me so that our shoulders were touching and her long hair fell over the front of my coat. 'I'm not really interested in them,' she said. 'At least, I don't think so.'

I swallowed. 'I'll miss you and Thomas, if you do marry Jason. I'm used to you about the house, and the boy...' Here I had to stop because the tears with which I have always had trouble threatened to overwhelm me. But I pulled myself together and finished my sentence. 'The boy is very close to my heart,' I said, and didn't care that my voice wobbled. It was cowardly of me to speak of my fears, but I couldn't stop myself. This girl and her son have become very dear to me.

She sat up abruptly and when she spoke her voice was fierce. 'Listen to me, Richard. We won't leave you. Nothing will change, and you must know that you are equally dear to us.' She stopped and gazed out to sea where the tide was coming in and the late autumn light beginning to fade. 'We shall be heartbroken when you leave us,' she added in a small voice.

It was kind of her to say that and, comforted, I was able to enjoy the rest of the day. When the boys came back, happy and smelling sharply of brine and seaweed, we walked back to the hotel and sat beside a big log fire to have our tea.

I dozed on the drive home but woke up close to the village, confused and disorientated, looking at the back view of Jason in his tweed jacket. I thought of our Billy in his tweeds, worn smartly to the horse show with a soft brown hat pulled low on his head and Father's watch and chain hanging across a mustard yellow waistcoat.

That's how he looked on that May day when he set off to the Three Counties with Diamond. I had helped him load the big horse into the box and listened patiently while he had run through the latest list of instructions. They were no different really from the ones he'd given me the night before, and he'd been in the milking parlour telling the men since before seven. But he was most keen to go and wouldn't let the fact that I'd been away for nearly eight years and was no farmer anyway put him off.

Mother had left on the Monday with Marian, still pretending reluctance, but patently excited.

Elizabeth had said, 'Off you do go,' when Mother had tried yet again to find reasons for delaying the departure. She would brook no further nonsense. 'I can manage, and you know it.'

So Mother and Marian had driven away and Billy, after giving them a brief wave, had returned to the stable where he was gathering all the implements necessary for showing Diamond to his best advantage. My brother had become an important man at the horse shows and according to Mother really loved the attention. This year he had been appointed to judge the colt class and been bursting with pride ever since the invitation had arrived.

'My God,' he'd said when I'd asked him about the standard of entries, 'I'll make sure I sort out the quality and conformation. The whole breeding will go downhill, else.'

Elizabeth had gone about her usual duties in the

dairy and the chicken houses. The cheeses she produced equalled Mother's and she had a fine reputation at the market. When I went with them I was proud of my name, so many people came to ask for Manor Farm cheeses and butter. 'I'll only take Wilde's cheese,' said one of the shoppers. 'Are you sure it's straight from the farm?'

'Of course.' Elizabeth smiled. 'I made it myself.'

I watched her dealing with the customers at our stall. She was charming and friendly and I'm sure everyone who met her came away with a good impression. She looked so attractive, standing behind the trestle table in her blue striped apron with a white band holding her hair away from her face. I saw people shake their heads in admiration at the way she wrapped the wedges of cheese into greaseproof paper parcels and cleverly cut slabs of butter into accurate pounds. There was no doubt, she was the star of the beast market.

But that was her away from home. Within the four walls of our house she was a different creature, quiet, distant and keeping herself to herself. We had barely talked alone in all the three weeks that I'd been home. To tell the truth, I was a bit frightened of her. Of all the family, she was the one who had changed the most and was almost a stranger. Oh, I would've known her anywhere, her face was painted on to my memory and will never leave me, but her personality had disappeared.

So when Billy drove out of the yard with the big box rattling behind him, I felt nervous. All those hopes and dreams I'd harboured on many lonely nights, of being alone with Elizabeth, had come to pass and I was petrified.

We had a chicken pie the first night, one that Mother had made and put in the pantry ready. It was delicious and we sat at the table, only the two of us, and ate in virtual silence.

'Very nice,' I said finally, wiping round my plate with a chunk of home-made bread.

'Mother made it,' Elizabeth said, gathering the plates. 'You'll have to put up with my cooking tomorrow.'

'That should be all right. I seem to remember that you could cook just as well as her.'

She nodded, but didn't enter into the spirit of the conversation, and even later, when the chores were done and we sat together with a cup of tea and a round of toast, she barely spoke. It was almost as if she had forgotten how normal chatter was done. I went to bed, still confused and sad for her, that she had become a shadow of herself.

It was late on the next afternoon when we finally got round to talking. She was taking her dog for a walk and I asked if I could go with her.

'If you like,' she said, and set off along the edge of the top field, mindful that Billy had planted barley crop in there. I followed, Indian fashion, for the space left between the hedge and the growing crop was small. Our Billy didn't believe in waste.

'Where are we going?' I asked as she turned away from the hill where we used to play and headed for the lower slopes where the rowan and gorse grew.

'I prefer to take her here,' she said, indicating the dog, who had run on ahead and was sniffing eagerly at the warren of rabbit holes in the next field. 'She tries to go in the caves on the hillside.'

Her face clouded. 'I don't like her doing that.'

I said nothing. It was a reasonable answer, I supposed, although the dog seemed pretty amenable and I didn't think she would wander far. She was no terrier, and presumably Elizabeth hadn't brought her up to go rabbiting; she was only a big soppy hound who adored her mistress.

We walked together across the damp grass towards the trees, ducking now and then beneath the low branches of the rowans and stepping carefully through the bramble traps that had infiltrated the little wood. We weren't on our land here, but it didn't matter. No one would object. These few acres were part of a parcel Father had sold to the mining company when there was talk of putting a railway line through here to take the coal directly from the pit head to the station. They'd never gone ahead with the plan and the land had been left to go wild. Even in the days since I'd been home on leave, Billy had grumbled about it.

'Criminal waste of useful land,' he'd said, his voice withering in its contempt. 'But what else would you expect from townies?'

'I like it wild,' Elizabeth had said, unexpectedly, surprising me with her offered opinion. It was so strange to hear her speak at the table. I looked nervously towards Billy to see how he would respond to her arguing against him. Please don't let there be a row, I silently prayed. I needn't have worried. My brother merely shook his head and carried on eating. He couldn't bring himself to debate with her.

Now, as we walked amongst the brushwood and small trees, coming across patches of wild pansies

247

and lady's slipper, I could see what she meant. Sometimes wild areas are better than cultivated fields. I had loved my time in the stark mountains of the Frontier, even though when walking or riding through them I had been anxious that the bare rocks would be good hiding places for rebels. It was a grandeur made by an almighty and better than man could do.

The dog, who had been springing happily ahead of us, startled a nesting bird, so that it flew suddenly out of a young tree straight towards us.

'Oh!' gasped Elizabeth. She stepped aside, bumping into me so that in order to keep my feet I had to grab hold of her. This was the first time I had touched her since the hug on my arrival and I should have seized the opportunity that I had so longed for. But I couldn't. Even as my arms folded round her thin shoulders and her head sought the shelter of my neck, my shyness and ever present cowardice took over. I dropped my arms and stepped away. My hands felt almost burnt from the contact with her body.

We carried on walking, me singing a stupid little ditty about 'the birdies in the sycamore tree', quite idiotic, but I was nervous and would have been grateful if she had joined in, but she was quiet. It occurred to me then that she may not be listening to me, but away in her own thoughts as she so often seemed to be around the house and farm. But when I snatched a quick look at her, I was startled by the hurt expression that had spread across her face. Had she wanted me to hold her?

We had reached the end of the little wood where the path opened out and the roofs of the village houses could be seen in the distance. 'Where now?' I asked.

'I usually walk into the village and back home along the lane,' Elizabeth said in a low voice. 'But you can go back the same way, if you want.'

'No.' I suddenly felt angry. I'd done nothing wrong and she was sulking in a way that was ridiculously childish. Indeed, her behaviour was constantly awkward and could be described as spoilt. Maybe she was entirely the cause of her own misery, no matter what Mother said. 'No,' I repeated, determined not to be fobbed off. 'I'll come with you.'

The village was quiet. Most of the men were at work, either on farms or down the pit, and the women had done their shopping and were in their houses, getting the evening meal ready. A few people were about and greeted us politely. Fred waved from the garden of the police house where he was watering a bed of flowers and holding his small daughter by the hand. He had two children then, both girls.

It was nearly five o'clock when we walked past the Gate House and, as ever, memories drew me to the place, so that I paused in our walk and looked carefully at the door and windows.

'It looks as if someone has been trying to get in,' I said. One of the boards Billy had put across the small drawing-room window had been prised away and was hanging loosely on the one remaining nail. 'I'm just going to have a recce.'

I didn't know if she understood the military language but it didn't matter. She waited with the dog while I walked into the overgrown garden and peered through the exposed window. The glass was intact, but because of the gathering gloom and the dirt on the window I couldn't see through the diamond panes. I struggled through the weeds to the front door and tried the handle. To my dismay, it turned easily and the door swung open as it had all those years ago.

For a moment I paused, unwilling to confront the ghosts that always assailed me when I passed this house, but squaring my shoulders I pushed the door wider and stepped inside.

I can't tell you how strange I felt inside that house. First I was a child again, sitting in front of a man who wanted to give me a glass of whisky, and then a lad trying to stop his mother climbing the narrow stairs to tend a man she so obviously cared for. But all that had to be put aside. Now I was a man. An empty house should hold no fears, but you don't choose your fears: they come upon you and you deal with them as best you can. When I stepped further into that hall I was able to put aside what I'd previously felt. After all, it was only a house.

'Has anyone been in?'

Elizabeth was in the doorway behind me, holding the dog on a lead now and sounding quite concerned.

'I'm not sure,' I said, and walked into the drawing room, where the furniture was still in place and apart from the absence of books from the huge bookshelves nothing had changed. There were the rugs which I'd thought about when I was in Peshawar, their bright colours dull under a thick coating of dust, as were the ornate sideboard and the ironwork flower stand. The Major's arm-chair stood next to a cold and dirty fireplace and I smiled when I noticed that the little table beside it still held a tray with a decanter and a glass. The decanter was empty, and when I looked closer I saw a little pool of liquid spilt on to the table and down one of the legs. That must have happened recently because the rest of the room was crackling with dust and cobwebs and any old liquid would have dried up years ago.

'Someone's been in here,' I said, pointing to the table. 'Had a bit of a drink.'

'That window board was in place yesterday,' said Elizabeth. 'I came along the lane. I would have noticed if it had been hanging down like that.'

I nodded. 'Lads from the village is my bet,' I said. 'Probably broke in for a lark and drank what was left of the Major's brandy.' I looked round. 'Nothing else seems to be disturbed.'

Elizabeth walked into the hall and gazed up the narrow staircase. 'What about up there?'

Our shoulders touched as I brushed past her to climb up the creaking stairs. A waft of her soap, or talcum or whatever it was that she used to give her that sweet rose and lavender scent, came to my nose and I breathed it in. It was still in my head as I looked round the door of the gloomy bedroom.

The room was as bleak as I remembered it. The bare floor and the little cot bed, now with its mattress rolled up, and the few pieces of furniture. Nobody had been in here for years, I could see that. When I turned round, I could see my own footprints in the dust.

'It's fine,' I called. 'Nothing here,' and I turned

251

to go out of the room. To my surprise, Elizabeth was on the tiny landing, having come up without my hearing. She had left Tess by the front door and was standing at the top of the narrow stairs.

'What's in there?' she asked.

'The bedroom.'

She moved forward and looked over my shoulder into the little room where I had watched my mother cradle the Major in her arms.

'It's very spartan,' she said after a moment, 'compared to the room downstairs.'

I nodded. 'He was on his own; no wife to make it comfortable.' I looked again at the narrow cot. Was this where I was conceived? Did Mother come up here with that mad old man and allow him to have his way with her? I shuddered, suddenly hating the thought that she had joined in willingly, wanted to be made love to by the Major. How could she possibly have preferred him to Father?

'Let's get out of here,' I said, and turned swiftly, brushing clumsily against Elizabeth again so that she put up her hands to my chest to stop herself being knocked over. Her face was close to mine, eyes wide in sudden surprise and that lovely mouth open in a silent O. Before I realised what I was doing, I had bent my head and closed my own mouth over hers.

She made no resistance, only a gasping sigh as she slowly put her arms round my back and pushed her thin body into mine. I held her closer and closer, wrapping my arms about her so that it seemed that she became almost a part of me. Once she groaned, but I couldn't tell if it was in pleasure or regret. I didn't care; all I knew was that I felt as though I was sucking in renewed life and it was wonderful.

I think we broke away at the same time and the realisation of what I'd done broke through the ecstatic feeling that had washed over me.

'I'm sorry,' I muttered. 'So sorry. I don't know what came over me.'

'It came over both of us,' she said quietly, and lifted up her hand to brush away a strand of hair that had fallen over her face. A pink flush suffused her cheeks and when she looked directly into my eyes I could see that hers had softened and become a more intense blue. She looked almost as young as the girl I had left eight years before.

The desire to take her in my arms again was overwhelming and it took all my poor reserve of moral correctness to stop myself.

'We'd better go,' I grunted, not looking at her but forcing myself to slide past her and go down the stairs. 'I'll come back later and nail up that board again.'

'Yes,' she said, and followed me down and out of the cottage.

Chapter Seventeen

We ate our supper in virtual silence that evening. My mind was full of what had happened and I knew that Elizabeth was thinking of it too. She had made a casserole of lamb and leeks and left it stewing in the range while we went for our walk. I'm sure it was delicious but I ate it automatically, one forkful after another, barely tasting a morsel. After a while I pushed my plate aside and got up. I couldn't sit opposite her in that silent kitchen any longer.

'I'll go and fix the window,' I said, 'before it gets too dark.'

She nodded but said nothing. She had pushed her plate aside too and I could see that she had eaten less than me.

All the way along the lane, I thought about that kiss and was overcome with shame. What had I done to her? She was a person who, according to all reports, was repelled by physical contact and I, in my jealousy and stupid longing, had violated her just as cruelly as my brother had. I hated to imagine what she must be thinking about me.

'Hello, Dick!' A voice broke through my thoughts and I looked up to see Fred Darlington, attired in his police sergeant's uniform, walking along towards me. 'I was just coming round to your house,' he said. 'The Gate House has been broken into.'

I held up the hammer and the jar of nails I'd taken from Billy's workshop. 'I know,' I said. 'I was just going to fix the board.'

'I'll come with you, then.'

Elizabeth had found the front door key to the Gate House in a kitchen drawer and I had it in my pocket. In those days we never locked our doors, but I thought that perhaps now it might be a good idea. Something of a deterrent to the village louts if they tried to break in again.

254

I was glad Fred was with me once we got to the cottage and started on the repair, for the board was heavy and I'd have struggled to hold it up on my own and to hammer in the nails at the same time. 'Damned youngsters,' Fred growled as he held the heavy piece of wood in place for me. 'It was probably the Kirby boys and some of their pals. Right tearaways. Jeff Kirby will end up inside sooner or later.'

I thought about the children Mrs Kirby used to leave in the pram outside the Golden Lion and remembered how Mother had condemned her. Jeff must have been one of them, poor lad. Dragged up, fostered out, sent to children's homes, always in trouble, and his brothers and sisters the same. As it happened, he did go prison later on. He got a couple of years for breaking into the mine office and stealing the wages, but after that he came home and behaved himself until he joined up. He was killed at Tobruk, leaving a nice wife and a school-age boy. Young Mrs Kirby used to do a bit of housework for me, until she married again.

But that evening, repairing the board in a sharp rainfall that had set in for the night, I had nothing but anger for the whole Kirby family.

'Thanks, Fred,' I said when we'd finished and I'd locked the door securely. 'Our Billy's away, you know. I'm in charge and don't want to let anyone down.'

Fred pursed his lips and shook his head. 'Wouldn't do to upset him,' he said, and grinned to let me know that it was a joke. I think he felt embarrassed about what he'd told me before.

I laughed too. 'You're right there.'

Still grinning, he picked up his helmet and brushed down his jacket. I thought he looked smart in his navy blue uniform. Authoritative. But then I supposed I did too in mine, although the material that our khakis were made from was very rough and you had to work hard to get the creases into the trousers. Our tropical clothes were better, but of course out East we had dhobi wallahs to do the washing and ironing. I hadn't worn my uniform since I came home, managing for the first week on my one civilian suit and a couple of shirts, but our Billy was having none of that.

'Come into town with me,' he'd said on the Friday and we'd gone to the men's outfitters in town where he bought me a Harris tweed jacket and two pairs of slacks. He even paid for new underwear and a good pair of shoes.

'I can't accept all this,' I'd hissed when the sales assistant had moved away. I was ashamed of having to be supplied with clothes as though I wasn't able to pay for my own.

'You can and you will,' said Billy. He wouldn't brook that sort of nonsense. 'You can work off your debt,' he added, 'if it makes you feel better. And there are spare overalls and boots in the scullery so you can keep this lot clean.'

Mother had kept some of my old clothes in the press in my bedroom, but they no longer fitted me. I had grown a lot both in height and breadth in the eight years away and these schoolboy's clothes were good for nothing except a jumble sale. I had a good look at myself in the glass too while I was searching for socks in my old dressing table. The face that looked back at me was almost that of a stranger, although, uncomfortably, another face flickered through from the depths of my memory. It wasn't as if this was the first time I'd seen myself in all the years I'd been away, but here, in this old familiar setting, who I was and who I had been seemed desperately distant from each other. Now it was a man who stared back. A man with dark red hair and tanned skin with lines around his eyes even though he wasn't yet thirty, a man of some experience and a man who could hold his own in a company of rough soldiery. I thought of the pale carroty youth I'd been and alone in my bedroom I laughed. How could I have possibly imagined that Elizabeth could have loved me then? I'd been nothing more than a child.

Fred broke through my thoughts again. 'Come and have a bite of supper with Miranda and me,' he said. 'She'd love to meet you and I want to introduce her to my best friend.'

I was touched. He still regarded me as his best friend and I was glad of that, but I knew that I mustn't go this night. Things had to be said between Elizabeth and me. I wasn't going to allow what had happened earlier to become another subject in the Wilde household that wasn't talked about.

'Thanks, Fred,' I said, 'but can we make it another night? Perhaps tomorrow? I've got things to sort out at home.'

'Tomorrow night, yes,' he said, 'even better. I'm off duty and it will give Miranda time to prepare something.'

We parted at the gate, him turning towards the village and me back to the farm. 'Dick,' he called, as I walked away, 'bring Elizabeth with you.'

The light was on in the kitchen when I got home but the room was empty. The supper things had been cleared away and a fresh pile of ironed clothes lay on the table, smelling sweetly of washing soap and the outdoors where they had blown about on the washing line in the morning air. I wondered if Elizabeth had gone to bed but as I stood, frustrated that she had escaped further discussion, I heard a noise at the scullery door. The dog, Tess, trotted into the kitchen, wagging her tail and shaking her coat. It was damp and redolent of the fields.

Elizabeth walked in after the dog and once again I could feel my heart melting. In the soft light she looked younger, her hair curling after the rain and her cheeks pink from the recent exercise. I could no longer wait.

'We have to talk,' I said.

'What about?'

I groaned. 'You know what about.' She was so frustrating. How could I make her sit down and talk to me?

She took off her mackintosh and went into the scullery to hang it on the row of hooks. When she came back in she still wouldn't look at me but went to the range to move the kettle on to the hot plate. I waited anxiously for her to speak and watched her face. But when she did open her mouth, I was further frustrated.

'Do you want tea?' was all she muttered. I could feel the blood rushing to my head and knew that my fists were curling.

'No!' I shouted. 'I don't want fucking tea!'

258

The shouting and the expletive shocked her and when she turned round to stare at me I could see fright in her eyes. I was immediately ashamed.

'I'm sorry,' I apologised. 'I didn't mean to swear. Forgive me.'

Her nodded agreement was slow and wary and I was sick with myself for upsetting her so. I knew what she was thinking. That I was the same as my brother and maybe the next thing I would do was hit her. I swallowed and forced myself to calm down. This was the last thing I'd intended.

Cautiously, I walked across the room to her side and took her hand in mine. She flinched and tried to draw away but I gently held on.

'Look, Elizabeth,' I said softly. 'I am truly sorry about what happened in the Major's cottage. It was wrong of me, but...' and here I faltered, uncertain about saying what I was really thinking. So many feelings in this house were hidden, so much was never said, that the occupants lived in it flat and unreal, like two-dimensional figures. In our home, all was on the surface. Nothing beneath could be explored, and if I didn't speak now it wouldn't matter. Billy would be home in three days, Mother at the end of the week, and in a month I would be gone. Everything would stay the same and life would carry on as usual. Perhaps that was indeed the best way.

But as I looked up at her, preparing to apologise again and leave it at that, I saw the glint of the necklace showing through the open neck of her blouse and knew that she had once felt something for me. I had to speak.

259

'I have loved you since I was twelve years old,' I said, now not daring to look at her but addressing my words to the shadows in the corner of the room. 'Before I went away, I had planned to tell you, but I was too young, stupid and cowardly to speak up. And then you chose to marry Billy and I lost my chance. But I have never stopped loving you, not once. I don't think I ever will.'

I took a deep breath; it was out. The secret I'd kept from her all these years I'd finally managed to admit, and in a way I did feel better. Maybe, I thought foolishly, she might laugh about my childishness and tease me out of my solemnity and then we could get on with our lives as before. My passion would somehow magically transform itself into simple filial affection.

But first I would have to make sure that she realised that this afternoon had been a mistake. 'I don't know what came over me in the cottage,' I said again, and gave a short laugh. 'I think that place holds too many memories for me. Unsettles me. You know.'

I dropped her hand and plunged mine into my pockets, waiting for her to say something, but she was silent, her face turned down towards the kettle. My heart was bumping. We weren't a family who expressed emotions; that's how we'd been brought up and I'd broken a lifelong habit. I was scared and desperately wanted her to respond. But I knew that she wouldn't. She had lived with our family for far too long.

But there, as ever, I was mistaken. Elizabeth slowly reached out her hand to move the kettle off the hot plate and turned round. When she looked up at me her eyes were glittering with unshed tears and before I could speak again she put her face to mine and gently kissed my cheek.

'Don't say you're sorry, Dick,' she said, 'for I'm not. What we did this afternoon was the best thing that has happened to me in eight years. I'm glad you held me. I'm glad you kissed me. I wanted you to.'

It's hard for me to say how exultant I felt then. Elizabeth had wanted me to kiss her. She had wanted to be held and loved. Loved. That was what it was. She loved me, as I loved her; now I knew it and it was bliss. Any thoughts of Billy and Mother flew from my mind and I bent over her again and took her in my arms.

All these years on I can still remember that rapturous feeling. It was glorious, so exciting and breathtaking. Our embrace now had a sense of urgency, quite different from how it had been in the cottage. There, it was a sudden snapping of the moral sense of two people who had been taken by surprise. Now it was passion. We tore at each other, mouths and hands exploring and intimate, and I knew that we couldn't stop. No words were needed as we walked hand in hand out of the kitchen and up to the little bedroom above the front door.

These things are difficult to talk about, but still so alive in my memory. The smell of my sweat mingled with her fresh scent, the feel of her delicate hands on my bare skin and the softness of her body as I crushed it beneath mine. I have only to close my eyes to see and feel that surging emotion, and even all these years afterwards the breath catches in my throat as I remember that first time I made love to Elizabeth.

She cried afterwards but I knew that they weren't tears of fright or shame. It was as if a great dam had burst and all that she had been holding in and hiding from the world had exploded into the light.

'Don't cry, my darling,' I crooned, holding her closely in my arms, 'Don't cry.'

But she sobbed as if she could never stop and all I could do was lie there in the narrow bed, rocking her and kissing the soft skin of her neck until eventually the shuddering breaths subsided and she became more peaceful.

'Don't worry,' she whispered after a while and, managing a small laugh, 'I'm all right now.'

'You're better than all right,' I growled. 'You're wonderful. I love you.'

She laughed out loud then and when we made love again it was glorious and joyous. We were two young people enjoying the most natural act in the world and, for the moment, not caring about the consequences. When we'd finished, the bed groaned in relief as we collapsed back against the pillows.

'I am so...' Elizabeth sighed, giggling gently.

'So what?'

'So relaxed. I can't believe anyone could feel like this.'

'Mm.' For once I couldn't speak. My heart was so full that I felt in danger of those stupid tears that I had been so prone to as a lad. Nobody could have been as happy as I was, that night. So happy that I refused to think about Billy or the inevitable consequence of what had just happened. I would leave that until tomorrow. Now all I wanted was to drop off to sleep with Elizabeth in my arms and wake up to the first morning of my new life.

I turned my head to look at her. Her eyes were closed and she was beginning to breathe deeply. I couldn't resist tracing my finger across her smooth jawline and kissing those dark lashes that rested so tenderly on her flushed cheek. She gave a little wriggle and tucked her body more closely next to mine so that we were like two spoons in a velvet-lined box. We slept.

I woke next morning, at first confused about the strangeness of my surroundings and then as I remembered, happy. It was light and I was alone in the bed. I rolled over to look at my wristwatch, which I'd left on the floor with my hastily thrown clothes.

'God!' I said. It was already eight o'clock and the men would have been at work in the milking parlour and the barns for two hours. Elizabeth must have got up and brought the cows in from the field, a job that I'd been doing since I came home, so that they would be ready for milking when the men came. She had let me sleep on.

When I rushed into the kitchen, barely washed and still buttoning my shirt, Elizabeth was dishing up breakfast to the farm hands. She paused, holding the big black frying pan, which held half a dozen fried eggs, poised above the table. The three men turned round to look at me. I was surprised to see that they uniformly had expressions of sympathy on their faces.

'You feeling better, Mr Richard?' said the oldest of the men. He was facing a plate piled high with eggs and bacon and reaching for a piece of home-made bread. The mere sight of it made my stomach growl, and nodding a good morning to them all I went to sit at my usual place.

'Miss Elizabeth said you'd been taken with a bit of a fever.' This from the younger man. 'Having a lie-in.'

Ernie, the lad, said nothing but just gazed bovinely at me while he chewed on a piece of bacon. His life had improved with Billy's absence and that's all he cared about; he couldn't have guessed that I had spent the night with the master's wife. The others might, though, if I wasn't careful. I looked up to Elizabeth and saw the grin hovering at the corner of her mouth. She'd covered for me.

'Yes,' I said seriously, 'a touch of malaria. You get it out East.'

'Aah!' They nodded sagely as though they knew all about tropical diseases and were absolutely prepared to believe that I was ill. That was all very well, but I was famished and wanted to join in on the breakfast.

'I'd go back to me bed if I were you,' said the first man. 'You'll do no use about the yard.'

I shook my head. 'Oh, I'll be all right. When you've been soldiering, you get used to worse than this. A bite of food will set me up.' And I nodded to Elizabeth, who kept her eyes away from mine. I could tell she was working hard not to burst out laughing while she set a plate in front of me and poured me a big cup of tea.

I was kept busy for the rest of the morning in

264

and about the farm, trying hard to give the impression of a person bravely carrying on in spite of illness. Elizabeth spent her time in the dairy, preparing cheeses and butter for market and the gallon of cream for the weekly delivery to the best hotel in town. I managed once to pop my head round the door and ask how she was this morning.

'I'm wonderful,' she said, not bothering to lower her voice, and indeed she looked it. She had a lightness about her, a grace of step that hadn't been there before, and her face? Well, her face was lovelier than I could ever have imagined. The flush that had followed our lovemaking remained and she seemed to be glowing with health and happiness.

I wondered if the men had noticed and remarked on it to each other as they worked in the big field. How would they put it, I mused, after I'd left her and gone back to my tasks in the stables? 'Miss Elizabeth looks right bonny today, mind,' one of them might say.

'Aye,' the other would answer. 'Must be because the master's away and Mr Richard is seeing to her.'

My own cheeks flushed at this imaginary conversation and the coarse laughter that could ensue. In no time the gossip'd be all over the village, and in two days' time, when Billy returned, the scenes that might follow didn't bear thinking about.

The men left at five o'clock and we were finally on our own again. I stood aimlessly in the kitchen and watched her as she packed the baskets ready for the market and took them to the pantry.

'Fred Darlington wants me to go for supper at his house,' I said, following her into the long narrow room. I had forgotten about his invitation until now. 'He invited you too.' She said nothing but I could see her back stiffening. Elizabeth had become something of a recluse and now didn't socialise about the village. In all the years since she and Billy had been married I doubted that they had had more than a couple of meals away from our own kitchen.

'I don't know,' she said.

'Oh, come on,' I said. 'We'll have a bit of fun.' In truth, I would have preferred to stay in the house with her. We hadn't touched since last night and I think we both felt shy but I knew we were going to. I put my hand on her shoulder and immediately a frisson of excitement ran through my stomach and into my loins. I bent her back against the cold slate slab and nearly devoured her with fervent kisses. This time there was no coy walking upstairs hand in hand. I took her on the quarry tiles as bold as one of the farm animals and she put up no resistance. She was equally keen, crying and panting out her enjoyment. Then we laughed like two naughty children and struggled to our feet.

'Oh, Elizabeth,' I said, holding her to me. 'I do love you. You must be mine for ever.'

That wiped the smile from her face. She pulled away from me and walked back into the kitchen and sat heavily in the chair at the head of the table.

'I can't, Dick,' she said with that old sad look. 'You must know that. I'm a married woman.'

'Married!' I exploded. 'What sort of a marriage is it when you don't sleep with your husband for fear he'll hurt you?'

She looked away and her head drooped on to

266

her chest.

I pulled one of the other chairs close and sat in front of her, taking her hands in mine. 'It's true, isn't it? He beats you. Everyone in the village knows it and even Mother told me that you were frightened of him. You just won't admit it.'

For a moment I thought she was going to cry again but when she looked up her eyes were dry and cold. All the happiness and passion we'd just experienced had disappeared and been replaced by such melancholy that I could have bitten out my tongue for having spoken. Like the impulsive boy I'd once been, I'd gone too fast with her and spoilt her happiness.

'I'm sorry,' I muttered, 'I shouldn't have said that. I wouldn't hurt you for the world.' And I got to my knees on the stone flags to put my arms round her waist so that she was, once again, close to me.

When she spoke, her voice was clear but seemed to come from a long way off, as though she was reciting something she'd thought long and hard about for years. 'He can't really help it, you know,' she said slowly, putting her hands round my shoulders and resting her head on mine. 'It's as though he confuses passion with violence and once he loses control he can't stop himself. William thinks lovemaking is something dirty, and he's that sickened by it that when he's done he has to take his revenge. He thinks I'm a slut, you know. He told me on that first night of our honeymoon when I got into bed. "How can you lie there, barely dressed," he shouted, so that I thought that all the people in the hotel'd hear him. "But, Billy, love," I said, "it's our honeymoon. This is what happens."'

She shuddered at the memory. '"I know that," he said. "But I never thought you'd be that eager." And afterwards, he gave me a slap on the face as a warning. "Don't you be bold again."'

I groaned. Poor Elizabeth, what a terrible way to start a marriage. She'd only been a young girl and it should have been the happiest time of her life.

'I put up with it for a year,' she said. 'The slaps and punches and the cruel way he had with me. I was no better than one of the animals, in his mind. I was to be rutted with and then ignored, if I was lucky. If I wasn't, then I got what I deserved.'

I felt a teardrop splash down the side of my face. Was it mine or hers? It could have been either because now she was crying, her shoulders shaking in agony, and great drops had gathered at the corners of my eyes too. I wanted her to stop. It was an awful tale to tell and I couldn't bear her to be so broken-hearted. But she had kept it to herself for so long that now it all had to be said.

'One night he came in from the barn after he'd had to shoot one of the cows,' she continued. 'He was in such a temper that when he came to bed he nearly killed me. "Slut," he yelled, "common whore," and words far worse than that. I jumped out of bed and tried to get out of the room but he grabbed me round the throat and started squeezing and squeezing until the room was spinning and I couldn't see. I don't know where I found the strength to lift my knee, but I did, and caught him a right kick in his privates. He screamed and let me go and in that minute I managed to open the door and run downstairs.

That's where your mother found me.'

'Couldn't she do anything? Couldn't she have spoken to him?' I was shocked to think that Mother must have known that this was going on and done nothing.

Elizabeth gave a bitter laugh. 'Mother likes to pretend,' she said. 'Haven't you noticed? She's got so many secrets of her own that she is terrified of anything being brought into the open.'

That was it, of course. I could see it now. 'But you could have gone to the authorities.' My voice petered out even as I spoke. I knew that that would have been the last thing anyone in my family would have done.

'We're all right now.' Her tears had abated and her voice was stronger. 'We don't bother each other any more. Now that I'm in my own room and he's in his, he can pretend that I'm just a farm servant again and have nothing really to do with me. I do my work and he gives me wages every month. It works well. As far as anyone else is concerned we are a respectable couple.' She took a deep breath, and when she spoke again her voice was low and awfully sad. 'Although unfortunately not blessed with children.'

It was a dreadful story. I wanted to ask so many questions, but they would have to be for later, because she got up and smoothed her hand down my cheek.

'I love you too, Dick,' she said, 'but I can't leave here. I couldn't shame him. As I said, I don't think he can help how he is.' She walked towards the hall. 'I've changed my mind. I'd enjoy that supper with Fred. I'll go up and change.'

We could have been any young couple walking down the lane towards the police house. I held her hand when we were alone but respectability demanded that we moved further apart as we came into the village. Few people were about, but the ones who were greeted us normally, without any suspicion, although I was sure that I must have looked different. With the facility that lovers have, I had somehow managed to put aside Elizabeth's sad story and simply think about what had happened between us.

'You look like the cat that's got the cream,' said Fred while we were sitting at his table. Miranda had made a grand spread and was a cheerful girl with a nice nature and I liked her straight away. Once Elizabeth had got over her initial awkwardness the two women had talked comfortably and were even now chattering in the scullery as they washed the dishes.

'You give Richard another glass of beer,' Miranda had instructed her husband from round the scullery door. She had an uncommon accent and I had enjoyed listening to it. It made everything she said sound exciting and exotic and I could see why Fred had been entranced. 'Elizabeth and I have pickled walnuts to talk about.'

Fred raised his eyebrows at that and jerked his head towards the door. 'She tends towards bossiness. Perhaps you've noticed.'

I laughed. 'I think she's very nice. She suits you well. You couldn't have found better anywhere.'

'I know,' he said, and then, looking at the stupid grin that kept stretching my lips, he mentioned the cat and the cream.

'I'm just happy, that's all.'

He was quiet for a moment and then looked slyly towards the scullery. 'Elizabeth looks lovely tonight. Better than I've seen her for ages.'

She had dressed in a white lace blouse and a slim mauve skirt and she did look radiant. The temptation to tell him, to tell anyone, was almost overwhelming. A wonderful thing had happened to me in the last twenty-four hours, something that should be shouted about from the rooftops. But I knew it couldn't be. Like everything in the Wilde household, it would have to stay a secret. So I merely shrugged my shoulders. 'I don't know why you think that,' I said.

The smile faded suddenly from Fred's strong face. 'Be careful, Dick,' he said.

That night, when we got home, we were calmer and lay quietly in each other's arms, exhausted by powerful emotion. I don't know what Elizabeth was thinking, but my mind whirled with plans of how I was to get her away from there. Now that I had got her, I was never going to let her go no matter what might happen.

Chapter Eighteen

It has gone very cold these past two days and wet with it. Every morning I wake up hoping for some sunlight but the Lord presents me with another dank, raw day under a miserably grey

271

sky. I don't ever remember it raining so much, and even in the bad years the fields weren't as sodden as they are now. Jason Hyde tells me that the water meadows are flooded to a depth of several feet and it is dangerous to walk down there for fear of losing your footing and being swept away. What a shame that is.

I have always loved that place and I think that he and Sharon do too. They have walked out there on several occasions. Mother used to say that it was the most beautiful part of our land. In the summer Billy and I used to go there with our friends in the early evening for swimming, although then we didn't appreciate the scenery. We took our pleasure hiding amongst the willow trees whose branches hung over the river and jumping out on one another. Later, as shy young people, those same branches offered us shelter for changing purposes. Our Billy was private. He didn't even like me, his brother, looking at him nude.

In the winter it was a different place but I loved it then too. I think of the lonely days after the war, when Nell and I walked daily through those meadows down to the river, even when icicles hung from the bare branches and frost sparkled on the carpet of dead leaves beneath our feet. Old Nell chased happily around the tree trunks but there were no rabbits for her to raise. They were all below ground keeping out of the weather. Lucky them, I used to think, cosy at home with their families. I found it hard to stay in my house for long, in those days. My head was too full and my heart broken.

But now the land is unusable and the river

272

poisoned by an overflow from Jason's slurry lake. He is sick with it all and is threatening to get out of farming. I heard him tell Sharon that it was a mug's game. He'd be better off selling his acreage to the developers. 'I could retire to Spain,' he said. 'Play golf all day.'

Sharon laughed. 'You'd hate it,' she said and then added with a pretend sneer, 'and who would you get to play with you? From what I hear, you're not much cop.'

I waited for an explosion of temper, but he is a calm young man and doesn't seem to take offence easily. All he did was give her a teasing slap on the backside as she walked past.

'Stop it,' she giggled. 'I don't know what Richard will be thinking of us.'

I was in the kitchen with them. We'd just had a cup of coffee and Jason had come round to collect Thomas. It's Saturday and he has tickets to a football match.

My coffee tasted so awful I couldn't drink it and Sharon gave me a searching look when she picked up my cup to take it to the sink. Just lately I've been off my food and I'm bone tired, but what can I expect? Death is just round the corner. But here is the thing. My life has become interesting in these last months, more than it has been for forty years, and I don't want to leave it. It isn't fair.

A knock came at the door and who should come in but Andrew Jones. I haven't seen him for a few weeks since I gave him my latest instructions and I don't know whether he has seen Sharon either. He didn't look pleased to see Jason sitting at the table.

'Morning, Mr Wilde,' he said. 'How are things?'

'I'm still alive, if that's what you mean,' I growled, and Sharon left her computer for a moment and came to stand beside me, worried, I suppose, in case I was upset. She has a laptop computer now, given to her by Jason as a birthday present. An expensive present, and one that she was all for refusing even though it was exactly what she wanted for college. It was only when he asked her to keep track of his milk yield on it for him that she accepted.

'I don't have the time, and I can't afford to take on another man,' he said. 'It would help me no end if you could load my accounts and farm business on to it. When you have the time.' This last was added hastily, but Sharon was trapped. She wanted the computer, and agreeing to his request was her method of payment.

She and Thomas spend quite a bit of time at Jason's house and he is here by the minute. He is paying suit, as my mother would have put it, and Sharon is showing no signs of rejecting him.

But I can see that this affair doesn't please Andrew Jones at all. In the spring and summer he must have thought that he was the chosen suitor, taking her on holiday and all. I'm wary of him, though. He knows too much about my business. 'What d'you want?' I asked.

'Nothing in particular,' he said, pulling out a chair and sitting beside my wheelchair. 'Just a social call.'

'Well, you'd better stay to dinner.' Sharon was in one of her restless moods. 'Jason and Thomas are off to the football and they're leaving any minute.'

I saw Jason's face cloud over, but if she noticed she ignored it and went to the hall to call for Thomas. 'Hurry up, love,' she called. 'You'll be late getting to the ground.'

I could hear his footsteps coming down the stairs and into the hall and waited for him to burst into the kitchen. He looks so well and is growing apace. Every week he seems to need new shoes and I have been glad to help with the cost. Sharon argues, of course, insisting that she isn't a sponger, but I tell her not to be so silly. What's the price of a pair of children's shoes to me, when I've money in the bank just gathering interest? I'd rather spend it on Thomas than give it to the government.

I watched Jason and Thomas leave. Jason was reluctant and Thomas had to almost drag him out of the house. It's not that he didn't want to go to the match, but Andrew Jones was staying for lunch and that didn't go down well.

'Bye, Mummy, bye, Mr Richard,' the boy called as he took Jason's hand.

I shuffled a hand in my pocket. 'Wait a minute, son,' I said. 'Come here and open your hand.' I poured some pound coins into his palm and closed his fingers over them. 'Buy some sweeties.'

'Thank you,' he breathed, looking to his mother for permission to take the money. She nodded and he said 'thank you' again and put his wiry little arms round my neck and gave me a hug. I live for these moments.

Andrew Jones only stayed for his dinner and left soon after. I think he'd hoped for an afternoon alone with Sharon but she was having none of it.

'I've work to do,' she said after he'd finished the

fruit salad she'd made for pudding, 'so I'm going to throw you out.' She looked at me. 'That is, unless Richard needs to talk to you.'

I jerked my head over my shoulder towards my room. I was tired and needed my afternoon sleep, so that was that. He had to go.

When I woke up, Sharon was bringing in some tea and scones.

'Hello,' she said. 'Feeling better?'

'Yes,' I said. 'How did you know I was badly?'

She shrugged. 'I've known you long enough now to tell. Do you need the doctor?'

'I don't think so, not yet. The painkillers are keeping me pretty comfortable, but I am increasingly tired.'

'Gone off your food, too.'

I nodded. 'Nothing tastes good any more.'

Her face drooped and she gazed at me in a distracted way. 'I wish I could do something. Something to help. Make you something you could fancy.'

I laughed. 'Unless you can make up some special elixir of life, then I wouldn't bother. It's *anno domini*, my dear. It comes to all of us.'

For her sake I drank my tea and ate a scone and we sat happily for an hour while the sky darkened and the late autumn night closed in. On my instructions, she changed the tape in my recorder and put in a new battery.

'Still at it?' she asked.

'Yes,' I said, 'still telling my story.'

'Will I hear it sometime?'

I nodded. 'When it's finished and if I'm brave enough.'

I've never thought of myself as a brave person, despite that double row of medals lying in my desk drawer. I got those both before and during the war, but what I did to earn them was very much spur-of-the-moment stuff because I doubt I'd have had the necessary courage if I'd had time to think about it beforehand. I have been cowardly about lots of things, particularly when it comes to people. It was the way we were brought up, no doubt, keeping everything to yourself and not speaking up. My heart sinks even now when I remember how I lay awake beside Elizabeth on that second night and wondered how to get her away from the farm. I know that part of my concern was how to break the news to our Billy and face his wrath. Even after all those years of being away and growing up bigger than my brother, I was still scared of him.

Elizabeth was nervous too. When we lay together the next morning in the first light, we indulged in little conversation. Somehow, the first excitement had faded and now we were into something that was almost too big to cope with. We had one more day before Billy came home and then the day after that Mother would descend on us. There would be no keeping of secrets from her. Her instinct was far too acute.

'Elizabeth,' I started, 'I've been thinking.' I wanted to talk about what we should do, but she wasn't in the mood.

'Got to get up,' she said, rolling out of bed and pulling on her shift. She was lovely. Her body was smooth and perfectly straight. That's how she walked, too, upright, straight, like a lad, with

277

none of those mincing steps that some women make. She never bustled like Mother, or wobbled her hips like the women who hung around the barracks, she simply walked without fuss.

'We could go to Canada,' I said, getting up too and pulling on my work trousers. 'Or Australia. They want workers in those countries. We could make a new life.'

But she shook her head and left the room and all that day, at the market and then back at the farm, the subject wasn't mentioned again. I did try once, after supper when we were sitting in the kitchen having a cup of tea.

'Will you think about leaving?' I begged, but she wouldn't answer me. It was a lovely evening, still warm after a fine spring day, and the air was scented with the smell of flowers. The laburnum tree had just blossomed and I had cut a spray to bring into the house. It was there in a jug on the table.

'Let's go out,' she said suddenly. 'Let's go on the hill.'

'I thought you didn't like it up there now.'

'I'll like it with you.'

We were like youngsters again, running up the hillside with her dog galloping beside us while the birds swooped around the trees for a last supper before bedtime. We made love on a bare patch of scrubby land close to the top and our cries were as natural as those of the old fox who had started to bark and the owls who were just waking up.

'I love you so much,' I said, holding her close in my arms.

'I know, and I you.' Her voice was soft but sad

and I now realise that her mind wasn't running along the same lines as mine. I was all for going away, but she was for staying, and talking about it would spoil everything.

The next day we stood in the yard as Billy unloaded Diamond from the box and came over to join us.

'Everything all right?' he asked, scanning the barns and the home field.

I nodded. 'Gone like clockwork.'

'Good. Knew you'd be able to manage.'

'And you?' I hoped my voice sounded normal. 'How did you get on? Did the old horse win again?'

He frowned. 'No. Runner-up. Some bloke from the north brought down a fine pair of nags and one of them took the cup. It was fair enough, though. I would have judged it the same.'

He told us more at supper, extolling the youngsters coming up which he had judged. 'I might buy a young 'un. Diamond's had his day and it's time for new blood.'

The words were too close to home and I sneaked a look at Elizabeth to see if she had found them so, but she was looking down at her plate, not joining in the conversation.

Suddenly, Billy turned to her. 'You look very well, our Elizabeth. What you been doing to yourself?'

My breath caught in my throat and I thought my heart would jump out of my chest. Did he know? Had he somehow found out? I was almost shaking with fright as I gazed at her, awaiting her reply.

I shouldn't have worried; she was as calm as ever. 'My work as usual,' she said. 'Nothing different.'

Billy turned back to me. 'It's having you around, I expect.' He laughed. 'Reminds her of the old days when we were silly lads and lasses. Mind you, her face does look as if she's been rouging. I can't abide that. Paint and powder. It's common.'

Elizabeth got up then and cleared the dishes. 'You know I don't wear that sort of thing,' she said, over her shoulder. 'You must be mixing me up with someone else.'

He froze, his eyebrows lowering and his mouth going into a thin straight line. This was a bit of by-play I hadn't seen before. Was she suggesting that he had another woman? Our Billy?

No, I thought, not him. From what Elizabeth had said, I didn't think he even liked women much. But I didn't want a row so I changed the subject rapidly and we went back to talking about the horse show and the people he'd met there.

That night I slept alone in my old room. I longed to creep across the landing and join Elizabeth in her narrow bed in the room above the front door, but I was too scared. Suppose the dog barked or the floorboards creaked under my footsteps? What if we woke Billy with our cries of pleasure? It didn't bear thinking about and I lay sleepless and angry with myself in my empty room until long after the owl had gone to sleep and the moon was on the wane.

Mother came home on the Saturday and it was clear from the off that she had truly enjoyed herself. She was full of the delights of Devon, and when Marian carried in her suitcase Mother gave her a thank-you kiss and a pat on the hand. It was obvious that the week away together had rekindled their old closeness and I was glad of it. They had been great friends when Billy and I were children and, fair play, Marian did have a big part in bringing us up. The memories of us as two baby boys must still have been between them.

'I loved Torquay,' said Mother that evening after supper, 'and you would love it too, Elizabeth.' I think she was feeling guilty that Elizabeth had not been invited on the holiday. She had been especially attentive to her all through supper. 'You would think you were in a foreign country,' she added, 'with all those palm trees along the front. And the gardens, well, I have to say, they were the best I've ever seen.'

'What's the land like down there?' Billy asked.

'Oh, it's so red,' she said. 'You wouldn't believe it. The earth is rich and the pasture is deep and in such good heart. The cattle seemed most contented.'

Billy grunted. 'I don't suppose they get the rain we do, though. Our grass is the best in the country.'

Mother smiled and shook her head. She knew our Billy; he was never able to accept that anywhere could be better than our farm. 'And how have you been, Richard?' she said, turning to me. 'Almost back to your old self. I didn't like that colour you had when you first came home. Marian agreed with me. We thought you looked quite yellow.'

'Cold fresh air, that's what it is,' I muttered,

hoping that she couldn't see the new light in my eye, which I was sure must be obvious to all. I ached for Elizabeth, wanted her naked in my arms, needed to feel her cool lithe body under mine, and all my desire must have shone out of my face for when I turned to look at her, sitting quietly in her chair at the end of the table, the look she returned was one of both joy and caution. She gave a slight shake of her head and reluctantly I turned away, back to Mother.

And there I met another pair of eyes, full of alarm. In that moment of my recklessly letting Elizabeth see how much I loved her, I had given away our secret to the person who knew me best. I saw her snap her head round to Elizabeth and then back to me and then reluctantly over to Billy. I followed her eyes. If she had guessed, had Billy?

He hadn't. My brother could never pick up on a glance, never hear a nuance, and we were quite safe, for now. But Mother looked almost frightened and I had to break the atmosphere.

'The Gate House was broken into,' I said, 'three nights ago.'

That certainly changed the atmosphere in the room. 'Damn and blast it,' Billy exploded in one of his sudden tempers, banging his fist down on the table, his cheerful mood flying away. 'Hooligans from the village, I'll be bound. It'll be that young Kirby and his pals. By God, I'll give them what for.'

'Calm down,' I said. 'You don't know that.'

'I can guess,' he growled.

'Was there any damage done?' said Mother tentatively.

282

'No, not much. A board was torn off one of the windows and some bugger had drunk what was left of the Major's brandy.' I turned to my brother. 'Why don't you tidy the place up and let it? God knows, it would be safer with a tenant in place. Otherwise it'll just go to rack and ruin.'

He shrugged. 'I might sell it. Get it off my hands. I never could abide the place, anyway.'

Mother stood up and started to gather the dishes. 'You'll do no such thing, William,' she said, her face troubled. 'Your father always planned to add the Gate House and its land to our holding and I was glad when you managed to do it. I won't let you go against his wishes.'

The room simmered with anger and accusation and I was both glad and sorry I'd brought up the subject. Billy's tempers could be fearsome but at least it had stopped Mother thinking about me and Elizabeth. 'Well,' I said, 'you could just get the garden done up. It won't look so abandoned then.'

'I'll do that,' said Elizabeth suddenly. 'I'll get Ernie to help me.'

Billy wasn't pleased, I could see that, but he pushed his chair away from the table and got up. 'Do what you like,' he said, 'but I might still go ahead and sell it.'

He never did. That cottage is still part of the farm today and I do have tenants in it. They are a couple of retired schoolteachers who came up from London over twenty years ago. I put in heating and a new bathroom and they have kept the place very nicely. The garden is a picture.

It was the following day when I realised what Elizabeth was up to. 'Meet me at the Gate House after dinner,' she whispered when I put my head round the dairy door.

The lad was there as ordered, digging the garden, and he nodded to me in his vacant way. Elizabeth was nowhere in sight but the boy jerked his head towards the door. 'Miss Elizabeth's indoors,' he said, 'if you're looking for her.'

She was in the bedroom and I noticed straight away that she had unrolled the mattress and put an old quilt over it. 'I found this in the chest,' she giggled. 'I hope it doesn't give us our death of cold.'

And for the three weeks left of my leave, we met there every day. If the boy wondered why his mistress and her brother-in-law 'moved furniture' so often, he didn't say, and I'm positive he didn't think about it. His brain worked slowly, barely able to manage the job in hand and never ready to go on to the next. Of course, if anyone had come to the cottage and asked for us he would have told them that we were inside. But we were lucky; nobody came.

Towards the end, we became bold and careless, creeping out of the farmhouse after Mother and Billy had gone to bed and racing hand in hand down the lane to spend our nights together on that narrow army bed. I had sneaked a blanket out of my room and she had found a small candleholder and a supply of candles. It was there in the flickering yellow light of those few stolen nights that I experienced the most powerful emotions I would ever have. My passion for Elizabeth knew no bounds and hers seemed equally intense. Our lovemaking was fervent and at times so crudely animalistic that I was left exhausted by my ardour. But every day I came back eagerly for more and found my girl equally ready and joyous.

One early morning, when I had only two days left before I had to report back to headquarters, I asked her again to leave the farm and come with me. 'Please, please, my love,' I begged. 'I can't bear the thought of being parted from you again.'

She wouldn't. She talked about the shame of being found out and the hurt it would give to all our family, particularly Mother.

'But that wouldn't matter,' I said. 'We'd be in India, where no one would know. We could marry out there.'

She rolled over away from me and her next words were so quiet that I could barely hear them. 'But I'd be a bigamist,' she said, and her voice choked on a sob. 'I made vows, in church. I promised.'

'Billy made vows too,' I cried, desperate now to convince her. 'Hasn't he broken them? You owe him nothing.'

She turned back to me. 'That would make me as bad as him then, wouldn't it? I'm a better person than that.'

I was angry and spoke hastily. 'Sleeping with your brother-in-law doesn't make you a better person.'

As soon as the words were out of my mouth, I was sorry. She gasped and I saw her face cloud over and her mouth droop. When she raised her eyes, I was sick to see that old distant expression she normally reserved for Billy.

Quickly, I took her in my arms and held her

close. 'Oh, God, I'm sorry, so sorry,' I said, horrified at my cruel and clumsy remark. 'That was stupid of me and I didn't mean it. I'm desperate, can't you see? I don't think I can live without you.'

Her body softened then and she held me too. We lay back on the bed listening to the birds beginning to twitter in the oak trees at the back of the house and saw the first rays of light creep in through the small Gothic window. 'You will,' she said, dreamily, 'and so will I. In a way, we've been lucky, can you see that? Our love is so strong, so deep, that even when we are thousands of miles apart I'll just have to close my eyes and I'll be back here, in this little room, feeling your body next to mine. For the rest of my life, I'll know that someone loved me and I'll never let that go. I am yours and you are mine. We'll never be free.'

She was so right. I have never been free from her. Even now, when she has been dead for more than thirty years, I think about her every day. I can see her lying on that bed, her dark hair wild and tousled and her naked body relaxed and offered willingly to me. Elizabeth was both the best and worst thing that ever happened to me.

Mother knew. As I said, she guessed straight away, but she kept it to herself. I think she became more careful, and certainly her relationship with Elizabeth changed. It was if she felt that she had lost control and that from now on everything that happened was without her input or even her permission.

Outwardly, she was her old bustling, interfering self, but now she watched all the time. When Marian and Albert came round for Sunday

286

dinner, she kept up a constant chatter about inconsequential things, so that they were kept occupied in answering her and given no opportunity to consider the other people at the table.

'For heaven's sake, Mother,' said Billy as he attacked the huge joint of beef with the carving knife, 'give it a rest. I can't think what I'm doing.'

'Don't you be so cheeky, William Wilde,' she said, her face all red and her shoulders twitching like one of her bantam hens. 'You're not so big that I can't give you a clep.'

'What?' said Billy, the carving knife and fork held aloft as astonishment swept over his face. We all sat in silence, contemplating the scene of our little mother giving Billy a clep, and suddenly the dam of awkwardness burst and we all collapsed with laughter.

'By God, that would be a sight to see, Mother Wilde,' said Albert as he eagerly accepted a loaded plate of juicy rib meat from Billy. 'You could sell tickets for that. Five rounds in the beast market.'

'Well,' Mother grumbled, forced also into a smile, 'there was no call for that,' but she calmed down and we were able to enjoy a family get-together as in the old days.

Later, before the visitors left to get back to their smart house in town, Albert and I took a turn round the garden. He was getter fatter by the week and had that smooth, cared for look that the rich always seem to achieve. He hadn't changed in temperament, though; he was still jolly and kindly. I knew that he and Marian had their differences, but he remained friendly with us and didn't blame us really. It was only once, when he let drop that remark about Marian's being put off babies by being present at my birth, that he gave the game away about their married life. If it was true that he had other women, then who was I to blame him.

'Back to the barracks next week, then,' he said as we leant over the field gate.

I nodded. 'Got to report next Monday, eleven o'clock.'

'Then what? Back out East?'

'Maybe.' I shrugged. 'My regiment is still out there and I can't believe that they will let me stay back here. I've got special experience now.'

He lit up a cigarette and offered me one. 'If you like, I could have a word with one or two people. I'm not without influence, you know.'

I suppose I should have taken up his offer. If I'd remained at headquarters, visiting home every two weeks or so, in time I might have been able to persuade Elizabeth to leave. But somehow, I couldn't. Albert was a civilian and I was a soldier and eight years of indoctrination into loyalty and respect for doing things the army way stopped me. To tell the truth, apart from wanting to be with Elizabeth, I was sick of hanging around at home, being a general dogsbody. I missed the responsibility of my rank and the regimented lifestyle. It surprised me to realise this for I'd always considered myself something of an outsider, being teased for my book reading and wanting to look at the sights, but when I thought about it now I could see that the teasing was only good-natured banter. I missed my mates.

So I shook my head and rejected Albert's offer.

'I don't think so, thanks,' I said. 'I'm a twenty-year man, through and through.'

He took the brush-off well, and reached up a podgy hand to clap me about the shoulder. 'Ah well, Richard, remember, the offer is still open, if you change your mind.'

I left in the early hours of the following Monday morning, walking across the fields to catch the milk train. Mother and I had said goodbye the night before, but although she cried and pressed me to her, I think she was glad I was going. Maybe the atmosphere at home would go back to normal with my departure.

'It's time you found a nice wife,' she said, mopping her eyes. 'Someone to take care of you in that heathen land.'

'Right.' I laughed. 'Next time you see me, I'll be accompanied by a lovely Indian girl. Sari, bangles and nose ring. The lot. And you couldn't complain; I'd have just been following orders.'

She put her hand to her mouth and looked at me with genuine concern. 'You wouldn't do that, Richard, love, would you? You'd break my heart.'

I shook my head and gave her a kiss. 'No, Mother, don't worry. It's too cold here for Indian girls.'

Elizabeth met me at the Gate House later on. Billy had been up with a calving and she had stayed to make him tea and a sandwich. He was kinder with her than he had been when I'd first come home. Almost as they'd been when we were youngsters. I think she was more relaxed and it allowed him to be also. As long as there was no sexual contact, they could live in the same house almost happily.

She was quiet as we undressed and got into the bed and our joining was silent and desperate. I started to plead with her again but she put her hand gently over my mouth. 'Don't, Richard,' she begged, 'no more. I couldn't bear it.'

So I just held her and we lay sleepless until it was time for me to go.

'You know,' she said suddenly as we were getting up, 'my mother left my father. She ran away with a soldier who took her to South Africa.'

I was surprised. This was the first I'd heard of it and I paused with one shoe on and the other on the floor. 'I thought you said she was dead.'

'I did,' she said. 'I told everyone that. My father was too ashamed to let people know. That's why we had to leave home.' She thought for a moment and then added, 'Maybe she is dead now.'

It was a secret I had never even thought about. I remembered her arriving at our house in those first months after Father died. Elizabeth striding up our drive with that hat jammed over her long wild curls and the ragged cuffs of that pretty blue dress. I loved her then, too young to realise that her boldness was only a front. And now I loved and had loved her even more.

'Shall I write to you?' I asked. 'Will you write back?'

She shook her head. 'What would be the point? It's better to have a clean break, don't you think?'

No, my heart cried, I don't want a clean break. I want you to feel as bad as me. I want you to hurt and ache and long for me every day as I have for you. But I said nothing. And when we parted, all we did was hold each other for a moment before I walked back to the house down the lane and she hurried through the woods to slide quietly through the kitchen door before Mother rose.

I took my farewell of Billy in the milking parlour in full view of the men who were bringing the herd through. 'Goodbye, Billy,' I said, wrapping my arms round him in an embrace.

He looked miserable. 'Look after yourself, our Dick,' he mumbled. 'I shall miss you.' Tears gathered in his eyes and dropped unheeded on his cheeks.

'Come on, none of that,' I said. 'I'm going to keep in touch.'

He thrust a hand in his pocket and took out a roll of notes. 'Here,' he said, 'take this. I'll brook no refusal, mind. It'll get you started saving or something, ready for when you come out.'

When I examined the money later, sitting in the deserted compartment of my train, I saw that he had given me two hundred pounds, a very generous sum in those days. My stomach turned when I thought what I'd done to him. I'd made him a cuckold even though he didn't know it and here he was, kind-heartedly giving me money. I didn't spend that money for years. It went into the bank and lay there with bits and pieces I had spare over the years, gathering interest until years later, when I found a proper use for it.

So we hugged and shook hands and I left. I could hear him shouting at the lad as I walked away but I didn't look back for fear of seeing Elizabeth in the window or at the dairy door. I didn't have the guts for that.

My spell at headquarters lasted less than two weeks. Just long enough to get examined by the doctor and re-kitted with new hot-weather clothes. By the end of the month I was on the P&O, sailing east, back to India.

Chapter Nineteen

I got back to Meerut at the beginning of July when the monsoon season had just started. Warm rain beat down incessantly, soaking through our uniforms when we were on the parade ground and dripping through the holes in the roofs of our barracks. For some, it brought a welcome relief from the exhaustingly dry heat of the months leading up to it, but the humidity sapped the strength of those not used to it. I was one of those for the first few weeks and suffered quite a bit until I got back in the swing of things.

My mate Lewis Wilton welcomed me back. It had been nearly two years since we'd seen each other, because he'd stayed behind on the plains when I was seconded to the Frontier force. In my absence he too had been made up to sergeant and proudly showed off his stripes. How he'd achieved the rank I don't know, for he was as keen as ever on the drink and unless restrained by more cautious pals would look for a fight as enthusiastically as before.

I asked the colonel if I was to be sent back to the Frontier. I wanted that posting; the call of the mountains was very strong and I longed for the clean cold air. But I was to be disappointed.

'No, Wilde,' the colonel said, 'it's pretty quiet up there at the moment. It's here that we have trouble.'

I knew about the Freedom Movement, of course. We had been pretty ruthless, I think, in putting it down over the previous few years and it should have petered out by rights. But we had reckoned without Mr Gandhi, who had such determination and bravery. His non-cooperation movement kept us constantly on the hop. It didn't matter how many we imprisoned or even executed, there were always more to take up the banner of independence. I know now that we were fighting a losing battle and that it was one we deserved to lose, but attitudes were different then and we thought we were doing the right thing. After all, many Indians agreed with us, but they were the rich ones, the merchants and some of the Westernised rajas. Our leaders listened too much to them.

I hated this form of soldiering, pushing people around and escorting well-educated men to prison. Once, I had to take three men to the prison on the Andaman Islands. What a trip that was. There was me, three privates and our officer to accompany the prisoners. We went first by train to Calcutta and then boarded a ship for the three-day sail to the islands. I played chess with one of the prisoners, a doctor he was, on the train. He had the set in his suitcase along with a selection of books. I took to him immediately, partly because he seemed to be such a good and

293

gentle man. He had studied in England, and except for his looks you would have thought he was the same as one of us. We talked about books. He loved Dickens and Hardy too, and he introduced me to the works of E. M. Forster.

The officer, Captain Parker, didn't like this chat about books. He was always a bastard, poorly educated but moneyed and a show-off. I knew no one who respected him, certainly not the colonel, although he went to great lengths to hide his contempt and I think had sent him on this mission to get him away from the company for a few weeks.

'Wilde,' he said, 'haven't you got something better to do than hang around this prisoner?'

I dared to be obstructive. 'I don't think it does any harm, sir. We're just passing the time.'

No orders existed about how to treat these prisoners and I was within my rights. But he didn't like fraternisation and had to think up some excuse to get me away.

'Go and relieve the men so they can get their meal,' he said, and marched back to his compartment.

'It doesn't matter,' said the prisoner. 'We can talk later, if you like.'

On board ship we talked a lot. One day we stood by the rail watching the huge wash of scrambled water leaving a white trail in the flat blue sea. He asked me if I was married.

'No,' I said.

'Have you not found a suitable young lady yet?'

I thought of Elizabeth and sighed. 'I have, doctor,' I said, 'but she is already married.'

'Oh dear.' He shook his head and patted my

arm. 'There will be someone else, maybe.'

'I don't think so.'

He looked so sorry for me and quizzical at the same time that I found myself telling him about Elizabeth and my brother. Why I should have done so, when I never talked about my home circumstances to anybody, I don't know. Perhaps it was because I knew I would never see him again.

'So you see,' I said, when I had finished my tale of doomed love, 'she won't leave the farm, no matter how unhappy she is.'

For a while he said nothing, simply stared out to sea where flying fish had now appeared to accompany the boat. They leapt in and out of the waves, droplets from their jagged fins glistening like diamonds in the bright sunlight as they kept in line with the passage of the ship.

'I think you and she have done the honourable thing,' he said finally. 'Keeping the family from shame is more important than personal happiness.'

The fact was that I hadn't told him the whole story. In my version, Elizabeth and I loved each other from a distance; it sounded more romantic that way. And after that I didn't mention my home life again because I felt guilty pretending to be honourable.

When he and I weren't talking, he spent his time with the other two prisoners, both younger than he and one of them, a lad of about eighteen, frightened of what was in store. I watched one afternoon from a distance as the doctor spoke quietly and encouragingly to them, patting the youngest man on the arm and pointing towards me and smiling. Later I had an opportunity to ask what he had been saying.

'I was telling them not to be too alarmed. I said, "Look, there is an English soldier who is an educated man and not a bully. There will be others like him."'

I doubted that. From what I understood, the government generally chose the firmest sort of men to run the prisons. I couldn't imagine many literary discussions taking place between prisoners and guards in the Cellular Jail. But it would be an unkindness to tell him that so I merely nodded.

'I'm not an educated man, as such,' I said, 'just a farm boy who has read a lot. You have been to university and mixed with clever people. That is what I would call educated.'

Dr Rai considered this slowly, as he did nearly everything I said. I could imagine him with his patients. They would come into his surgery and tell him their problem and he would sit back in his chair and think for at least a minute. I wondered if their illnesses would make them impatient, anxious for an instant answer with relief of symptoms, or whether they knew what they must expect when they consulted this man. Probably the latter. What is a minute in a lifetime?

'The word education has many interpretations,' he said. 'Your interest in the world of literature allows me to think of you as an educated man. And following on from that, I am sure that many other facets of life pass through your mind and make you think.'

I looked quickly across the deck of the ship to where Captain Parker was sitting back on a chair with a glass of whisky in his hand. He had stopped trying to tell me not to fraternise, but I knew that he would put it in the report he would hand to the colonel on our return.

I lowered my voice. 'There is one thing I have been thinking about more and more.' I swallowed, wondering how to put it, not wanting to cause offence. 'I don't fully understand your struggle.' The words came out haltingly and I was nervous. Discussing what was tantamount to treason was probably treason of itself, and if the captain took it into his head he could have me slapped in irons.

Silence again as the doctor thought. He was a small man, with a round face and round spectacles, and even though we were both sitting cross-legged on the scrubbed sun-bleached deck, I towered over him. I watched a bird flying above us and realised that we must be nearing land. I could smell it, anyway. Not the heavy spice-laden air that I remembered from my approach to Bombay but a green smell, a sweaty dark odour of rotting vegetation. I could imagine lush jungle and I was right, because the islands just over the horizon were off the coast of Burma and I went there a few years later.

Dr Rai suddenly spoke and I tore my gaze away from the seabirds streaking across the hot blue sky.

'Imagine, Mr Wilde,' he said, 'that Britain had been conquered by France two hundred years ago. The French had brought their laws, their customs, their language even. You Britons had become a subject race, not allowed any more to do things in the old way. Now, the French could argue that you were not badly treated, that they had, indeed, civilised you. That their laws were more modern than yours and that their ways of conducting commerce, medicine, education and all aspects of life were better. What would you do?'

I laughed. The French could never conquer us. It was an impossible picture, but at the same time I could see what he meant and the laugh began to die. I suppose that is what we had done, and even if we had brought some good and made some sense of a hugely diverse continent, had it been ours to do?

'It isn't exactly like that,' I said, 'is it?'

He didn't reply, but sat still with his hands casually folded on his lap and let me work it out for myself.

'But you won't succeed,' I whispered, now conscious that Captain Parker had turned his head and was watching us. 'We have the army.'

Dr Rai permitted himself a small smile. 'So you have, Mr Wilde. But not only do we have right on our side, you must know that we have many millions of people.' He looked back to his two friends who were sitting a little way off. 'You are taking us three to jail, but twenty will take our place; one hundred more will take their place, and a thousand after that. In the long run, can you win?'

We didn't talk about the struggle again. He had done his job and sown a seed in my mind and I didn't need it reinforced. And as the islands grew larger on the horizon, he spent the remaining time with his companions. I was concerned for the lad, for he looked ill and I was pretty sure that he wouldn't get proper treatment in the prison. I wondered if Dr Rai would be given access to medicines and allowed to care for his fellow captives.

We disembarked at Port Blair and were taken by lorry to the prison. Despite the awful use it was put to, I was impressed by the building. It was built of red sandstone and its seven towers soared over the surrounding buildings, which were mostly poor housing and shops. Everything else that I saw of the island was primitive, as though the indigenous islanders had tried to carry on their own life of fishing and animal husbandry and ignored the fact that prisoners were being transported into their midst.

I learned, however, that despite its impressive exterior the inside of the jail was hellish, and some of the things that went on in there didn't bear thinking about. Saying farewell to our three men was made doubly difficult by this knowledge and it took an effort on my part to try to impart an encouraging word.

'Good luck, doctor,' I said to my friend as the prison guard marched forward to take command of our captives. The youngster was ghastly pale and I could see him trembling. The other man was holding him by the arm.

'Here,' I growled to the guard, who was a corporal and had to listen to me, 'take care with that man. Can't you see he's sick?'

The corporal sniggered and jerked his head back towards the prison gate. 'He'll be in good company then. All the bastards in there are sick. Or say they are.'

Dr Rai stepped forward and held out his hand. 'Goodbye, Mr Wilde,' he said. 'Thank you for your graciousness.'

I took his hand and lowering my voice said, 'Keep your chin up, sir. It won't be for ever,' and he smiled and turned towards the arched and studded door. Captain Parker bestowed a hard look on me, but I didn't care. I watched as the prisoners were marched away. I learned later that the doctor had died in jail.

When we got back to camp I had letters from home. Nothing from Elizabeth but two from Mother. The first was written a couple of weeks after I had left, saying that they had enjoyed my visit and that all was well. Billy had bought a new filly and called her Beauty. Elizabeth had been working at the Gate House and had cleaned it up lovely and improved the garden. Billy was coming round to the idea of having a tenant.

The second letter was considerably more worrying. I had been back in India now for eight months and this letter had been written six weeks previously. 'I must tell you,' wrote Mother, 'that we are to expect a happy event. Elizabeth is expecting a child and we are all very excited. It will be born in the early spring.' She went on then to talk about Marian and Albert's holiday in Biarritz and to tell me that old Aunty Fanny had been taken into hospital with pneumonia.

I could barely take any of that in. All that concerned me was the expected baby. I was frightened. What had I done? What further shame and peril had I heaped on Elizabeth? I wrung my hands in despair, crumpling the letter up into a tight little ball, so sick was I with how dangerously foolish I'd been. And then after a while another

300

thought struck me and I carefully uncrumpled the letter and smoothed it out. As I re-read the words that Mother had written, 'we are all very excited', it occurred to me that she'd not written of danger here, only happiness and anticipation.

Now I was in a quandary. Maybe the child wasn't mine. I had thought that Elizabeth and Billy seemed better friends in the couple of weeks before I left, so maybe they had resolved their differences and gone back to sleeping together.

I hated that thought. I couldn't bear to think of my brother's stubby, dirt-encrusted fingers on her smooth white body, and as for more than that, well, my heart and stomach lurched and I felt suddenly sick. It would have been she, I knew it, who would have made the first approach. She'd acquired a taste for it.

It was that night that I went out of the camp and down to the brothel by the market. I was angry, so angry that I wanted to wipe all thought of Elizabeth out of my head, and in a fever of confusion and rage I searched for my pal Lewis and dragged him out with me.

'This isn't like you, mate,' he said, but he was game for anything and happily joined in with the debauchery until we had used up all our rupees. The next day I was disgusted with myself, and in the days following even sorrier as I had to be treated for a dose of the pox. But it did take Elizabeth from the front of my mind and I was able to get on with my life in India without having one foot constantly back at the farm.

I heard some months later that Elizabeth had been delivered of a boy, John Edward, a fine strong child who was causing havoc in the previously quiet household. 'Elizabeth did suffer quite badly,' Mother wrote, 'and the doctor said that there must be no more children. So we must cherish this little boy. William is very proud of him, and has named you as godfather. We had the baptism last Sunday and Fred Darlington stood as proxy for you. I'm enclosing a photograph.'

The black-and-white snap showed Elizabeth holding a bundle wrapped in a white shawl. I could make out a baby's face but the features were indistinct and Mother hadn't said whom he favoured. Elizabeth looked solemn, her face hidden under a Sunday hat, but it was the only photograph I had of her so it went in my wallet and stayed there. I have it still.

The funny thing was that these people had become almost strangers to me after my great disappointment in what I perceived as Elizabeth's unfaithfulness. I read Mother's letters, which came every couple of months, with interest and noted the growth and progress of the child and the comings and goings of life on the farm. But my life was in India and my family seemed far away.

The years that followed were happy ones for me in many ways. I enjoyed military life and was given more and more responsibility. At one point I was offered the chance of a commission and I thought long and hard about it. I wasn't worried about my ability to mix comfortably with the other younger officers; I knew that if not as well bred as some of them I was certainly as well read, and after all these years I had plenty of experience. But I liked my life as a senior sergeant and felt satisfied with my lot, so I declined.

'I think you've done the right thing,' said the colonel when I went to him with my decision. 'It can be awkward.'

I smiled inwardly. He had been the one who had put me up for it, but I think that had been simply to keep me contented. The colonel was always conscious of the happiness of his men.

'Hang on a minute, sergeant,' he said, as I saluted and prepared to about-turn. He shuffled some papers on his desk. 'I've got an order here for you. Came up this morning. Now.' He put on his spectacles and scanned an army telegraphic message. 'Colonel Barnes has requested some men. He mentions you particularly. Are you up for another tour of duty on the Frontier?'

Was I? By God, I whooped with delight once I'd left his office and got back to my room in the barracks. This was what I'd been longing for.

I took twenty men with me to Peshawar, including Lewis Wilton, who wanted a change from the oppressive heat of Meerut. We had kitted ourselves out at the quartermaster's stores and I was able to let the men know what they would need for the entirely different conditions. As I had when I was first posted to the mountains, they found it hard to imagine that they would need thick jackets and padded sleeping bags.

'Bloody hell,' said Lewis, when he staggered from the stores with a great bundle of equipment, 'I'm beginning to be sorry I volunteered.'

I learned that more trouble had occurred on the Frontier. Not the tribesmen this time, but supporters of Mr Gandhi who had started a similar non-cooperation movement. They were led by a charismatic local man who had been called the Frontier Gandhi. What was really concerning was the attitude of our native regiments. They were not prepared to fire on their fellow countrymen.

Our trip north took nearly a week as the trains had to be guarded against insurgents and we missed a normally easy connection. But when we finally got into Peshawar and breathed the sharp cold air, all those difficulties were forgotten and I was happy.

'Bloody Nora,' Lewis grumbled, pulling his jacket closely round his chest and looking around him in amazement. 'Brass monkey weather here.'

I laughed. 'You've been too long in the same place,' I said. 'Time for a change.'

He looked up at the mountains rising abruptly from brief foothills. On this September morning they were clear against a brilliant blue sky and seemed close enough to touch.

'I hope you're not going to tell me that we patrol up them hills,' he said, and the other men who had volunteered looked at me with concern in their faces.

'You'll love it,' I said, and did a little show of callisthenics. 'Just as soon as you get fit.' I ignored their looks of dismay and hurried them into the lorry that was to take us to our camp. For me, it was like coming home, and as soon as I'd found my billet and brushed the dust of travelling off my uniform I went to report our arrival.

'Well,' said Colonel Barnes when I was shown into his office. 'Young Wilde, as I live and breathe.'

'Yes, sir,' I replied, saluting smartly. 'I'm very

pleased to back here and to see you, sir.'

'And I you,' he said kindly and shook my hand.

He looked older, tired and drawn as though he hadn't the enthusiasm for the struggle that he had before. As I searched for further conversation my eye lit upon the photograph of his wife on his desk.

'I trust that Mrs Barnes and the boys are well, sir.'

His face darkened and he turned away to look out of the window at the magnificent scene of snow-covered peaks. 'I'm afraid Mrs Barnes has passed away,' he said, his voice faltering.

I was shocked. I thought of the lovely woman who had reminded me so much of Elizabeth and had been kind to me on the journey home. No wonder the colonel looked so awful.

'I am greatly sorry to hear that, sir,' I said. 'Mrs Barnes was a very nice lady. I'm sure she's a sad loss to both you and the regiment.'

'Thank you, Wilde. Damned decent of you to say that.' He took out a handkerchief and blew his nose. 'I won't deny that it has been a dreadful blow to me. But you have to carry on, don't you? For the boys' sake.'

I found out that Mrs Barnes had been thrown from her horse while out hunting in Ireland, soon after they arrived home on leave. While I'd been experiencing the happiest time of my life, her family had been in mourning. What a tragedy.

Well, we did carry on. Friends, I dared to think, despite the difference in rank. I learned all the best things I knew of soldiering from him and when he went home for good, which he did a couple of years later, I was sorry.

I met a girl in Peshawar on that second tour of duty. Zahira, I think her name was, a pretty little thing whose father helped with the horses at the camp. He kept inviting me for a meal at their house in the town and one night I took him up on it. I took a bottle of whisky as a gift, but he was a Muslim and wouldn't drink it, but he thanked me anyway. He said he would trade it for something in the bazaar, if I didn't mind.

His wife and daughters didn't eat with us but I spotted Zahira almost immediately and smiled at her when she put the dishes of food on the table. We used to meet after that, sometimes, in the town and one day I was bold enough to speak to her. To my relief, she had some English and dared to use it but she was scared that our conversations would be reported back to her father. They were extremely strict, religiously. But one day she managed to escape her house and we rendezvoused away from the town, on the road out towards the border. I made love to her in the mountains, under a cold blue sky where buzzards squealed overhead and circled lazily on the thermals. I was guilty about it and careful, for in her faith the penalty for what she was doing was death by stoning. After that I didn't see her again, by my choice. It was too dangerous. I expect she is long dead by now. Those native women had difficult lives.

I stayed on the Frontier for four years, dealing with the petty squabbles of the tribesmen, which were only petty until one of our soldiers was wounded or even killed. The Freedom Movement was beginning to cause us far more trouble and was much more difficult to deal with than the tribal excursions of the Pathans. On the whole, these protesters were peaceable but that didn't make things easier. If we were rough moving them on we were considered cruel and despotic, which in a way I suppose we were. I didn't know how else to do it and neither did the officers. We were fighting a losing battle.

One day orders came to return to Meerut. Our regiment was being sent home. What a shock and a disappointment. I was an old India hand now and I had considered whether to buy myself out and transfer permanently to one of the Indian companies. The one I was seconded to would have been fine and I was sorely tempted. In the end, though, I stayed with my regiment and went back with them.

This time, my return to England was less exciting. Somehow I felt in no hurry to visit the family and put off my leave for several months. Our regimental headquarters, where I was stationed, was only about fifty miles away from home and I could easily have gone there and back in a day, but I never did. I suppose I was frightened, didn't want to see our Billy and Elizabeth being loving together and happily bringing up their little boy. Mother, I knew, would be triumphant that her plan had finally worked out and that the brief passion that had flared so hotly between me and Elizabeth had indeed only been that. Brief.

Instead of going home, I joined a climbing club and when I had days or weekends off I went with my new friends to the Lake District and Snowdonia and indulged in that passion for the mountains which has lived with me since childhood. Up in the clean air, all the murky complications of my life seemed to blow away and I could feel that I was truly happy. When I returned to the garrison after a couple of days' climbing, I could be contented for a while reliving every foothold and grip until thoughts of my Elizabeth and her child began to invade my peace of mind.

But I stayed on in the barracks, getting re-acclimatised to English life and more involved with my new duties as training sergeant. At thirty years of age, which does seem so young to me now, I was a hardened veteran of several campaigns and a figure of some importance within our regiment. The new recruits looked soft to me, mere shadows of the men they could have been. Things in the country weren't good: the terrible days of mass unemployment were only slowly disappearing and many young men were joining up for the sake of three square meals a day. They weren't dedicated to soldiering and it was my hard task to make something of them.

Our Billy would have been amazed if he could have seen me then, yelling and screaming at young fellows in an attempt to teach them the proper army way. 'He's a right bastard,' I heard one man say to his mate as I took them through the physical exercises that we had set up. And I suppose I was, but it was necessary. I think being able to run fast is just as worthwhile in a battle situation as is having the guts to stand and fight. I came to know that even more surely when I was fighting through Burma later on. By God, I made a good many hasty retreats.

One late autumn afternoon I was on the parade ground with my latest batch of recruits when a corporal came to tell me that I was wanted in the office. New orders from the War Office was my first thought. We were always getting conflicting instructions, because two points of view were abroad in the land. One lot said that war was imminent and that we should be ready for action at any minute. The other thought that peace would last for ever. Diplomacy was the key.

'Sir!' I said, arriving in the office and saluting to the young captain who was sitting at a desk reading a newspaper.

He put his head round the paper and I saw that a cigarette was hanging from the corner of his mouth. My God, if he'd been one of mine I'd have seen to it that he was less of a shambles. He wasn't a bad officer, later on when it mattered, but he was wounded in our first foray into enemy territory and invalided out. He was glad to go, but then we all were.

But now he couldn't be bothered to put his paper down. 'I believe there's a visitor for you, Mr Wilde. The corporal let them in when I was in the mess arranging the colonel's little dinner.' Our colonel was entertaining the city dignitaries that evening. Fortunately, I was off duty and wouldn't have to attend the welcome party in any capacity. He nodded towards the inner office. 'In there.'

I was perplexed. Who would come to see me? The family knew I was home; I'd written to Mother and promised to visit when duties allowed, but no one had ever come to headquarters before. My first thought was illness, or, God forbid, a death, in the family. My heart lurched. 'Please God,' I whispered to myself, 'not her.'

So it was a reluctant hand that turned the door handle and entered the room. This was the office that the colonel used when he was on the camp. But as I said, he was busy that day, getting ready for his party.

At first I couldn't see anyone. It was a large room with windows all along one wall and the afternoon sun was shining straight in, casting a brilliant glow that made objects difficult to make out. Then I noticed movement on the far wall beside the stack of filing cabinets and a figure that I knew almost better than my own swam into my view.

'Elizabeth?' I said, my breath short and difficult to produce from what felt like collapsing lungs.

'Hello, Richard.'

She was there, in the flesh and as lovely as ever. I should have run over to her and taken her in my arms but I couldn't. She wasn't mine now. All I did was walk to her side and drop a brotherly kiss on her cheek.

'This is a surprise,' I said coolly, regaining my composure and behaving as though I'd seen her only a few days ago and five years hadn't passed. 'There's nothing wrong at home, I hope?'

If she was disappointed by my lack of enthusiasm for seeing her, she didn't show it. She had changed again in the intervening years and now looked more mature, even matronly. Not that she had put on weight – Elizabeth was slim till the day she died – but she seemed less girlish. Her clothes were smart, a maroon coat with a fur collar and a fur hat that bore a gold brooch in the shape of a panther. And for the first time, I saw her in make-up. It suited her, for it was skilfully applied, but somehow it made her even more remote from the girl I had loved.

'No.' She smiled and the room became even more brilliant. My Elizabeth had grown into a beautiful woman. 'No, nothing like that.' She leant against the colonel's desk. 'It's just that you haven't been to see us since your return, and,' here for the first time her voice faltered slightly and a glimpse of the old Elizabeth peeped out from this newly sophisticated person, 'I couldn't wait any longer.'

Couldn't wait any longer? This was the woman I'd loved to distraction, who the moment my back was turned had gone back to her husband in the most intimate way possible. I swallowed, confused and wondering what to say. Surely she wasn't expecting us to rekindle the old relationship?

I struggled for the correct words and then settled on the obvious question. 'What couldn't you wait for?'

'Why, to introduce you to my son,' and she gave me a long steady look. I stood there gaping in that sunny uncomfortably furnished office as she turned her head and, putting out her hand, gently withdrew a small boy from where he had been hiding behind a wooden filing cabinet. 'Say hello to John.'

I looked down to see a bright little face topped with a thick tumble of carroty red hair grinning up at me. There could be no doubt. He was mine.

Chapter Twenty

Sharon has insisted that I stay in bed and I'm not sorry. These last days I've been feeling very rough, coughing a lot when I'm eating and breathless most of the time. It is a shame because it's my birthday tomorrow and should I live through the night I will have achieved the great age of ninety-five. What a thought. How long I've lived. Born right at the beginning of the century when it was a different world. And a kinder one, I've heard said? Well, maybe. People prefer to think that, but I'm not sure; being poor was cruel when I was a child. We had plenty of folk in our village who had to live worse than animals, if they weren't prepared to accept charity. The government did very little for them after the Great War. It was women like Mother and men like Mr Kendrick, the vicar, who kept some of our villagers from starvation.

But that was a long time ago and I'm meandering. That's what happens to you when you get old. Mind you, I'm not as old as the Queen Mother. She's made the hundred. A real lady, she is. I met her once and she kindly shook my hand. She and the King entertained some of our company after the war and seemed interested in what we had done in Burma. Of course, I didn't tell them much. You didn't speak of those things in front of royalty, and anyway, in those days, I couldn't speak of them to anyone. Man's inhumanity to man is not something that you want spread abroad.

It is cold today and dark with it. It's only about eleven o'clock in the morning, but the light is poor and through my window I can see low cloud over the hill and the beginnings of rain. What a year. Non-stop rain and flooded fields. Flooded towns too, judging by the pictures on the television. Thomas told me he has been having lessons at school about something called global warming and what did I think about it.

'Very little, son,' I replied, and maybe I was a little abrupt with him and I'm sorry for that. But the truth is that I'm not really sure what it's all about. It's too late for me to start learning new things but it still makes me angry not knowing. So, selfishly, I've chosen to ignore it.

Fancy teaching a ten-year-old about global warming. In my day, we had a nature studies lesson once a week, where we learned how to identify different trees and wild flowers. We brought in catkins and frogspawn in the spring and beech nuts and mushrooms in the autumn. Mr Cutts knew the names of everything and woe betide you if he told you and you forgot. By God it stuck in your head, if you knew what was good for you, and even today I bet I could tell you the names of every wild flower in a summer meadow.

I remember, once, Mr Cutts giving us a lesson about beetles and telling us to keep an eye out for the different ones that lived in our area. Well, when we got home, our Billy said we had to look for some and find as many as possible. I got loads, especially around the old tree stumps in the home field; all types, including those big ones with the crab claws at the front. Stag beetles.

'What d'you want them for?' I asked when I took my tin can full of crawlers into the machinery shed where Billy was waiting. He was busy punching holes into the lid of one of the big jars that Mother used for pickling onions.

'Just wait and see,' he said, and poured the beetles into the jar. The next day he put them in his satchel and took them to school.

I knew he was going to let them go but I didn't know when. Who would have guessed that it was to be in the middle of morning prayers? Right after 'Our Father' and before 'All Things Bright and Beautiful', he took the lid off the jar and shook the beetles out into the lap of the boy sitting next to him. It was Jackie Tyler, a fat little lad whose mother ran the village shop, being a widow after the first war.

'Bloody hell!' shouted Jackie as the freed stag beetles and their smaller mates ran over his bare knees and down his legs. All the children craned their necks to see what was happening, and when the girls on the other side of the aisle caught sight of about a hundred beetles crawling towards them, pandemonium broke loose.

'Silence! Silence!' howled Mr Cutts, but the girls were screaming and hopping from foot to foot and the boys all shrieking with laughter. I laughed fit to burst, and catching our Billy's eye saw him give a little grin of evil satisfaction. I think he was the only one in the school who remained in control. Of course he got a beating later on, when Mr Cutts had got to the bottom of it. I was going to get one too, but our Billy told

314

Cutts that it was nothing to do with me. I was grateful at the time, but afterwards in the school yard when Billy was being congratulated for the prank, and surrounded by admiring girls, I almost wished I'd had a beating too.

Oh, but it was funny and even now I can laugh about it, though it makes my chest ache and my head spin.

I've been ill for four days since I recorded that last piece. Sharon came in, saw me gasping for breath and had to sit me up to pat my back. She sent for Dr Clewes straight away. He was all for hospital, but I told him to go to hell, so I'm still here but with that damn nurse, back full time.

'You've got pneumonia,' said the doctor after listening to my chest and seeing what I was coughing up.

'The old man's friend,' I gasped, but I think he's too young to know about that. Anyway, I've been dosed with antibiotics and some other pills for my heart and I now have an oxygen bottle beside my bed for use in emergency. Thomas is fascinated with it, so I let him have a go with the mask. The nurse told us off.

Today I feel a lot better. Sad that I missed my birthday but Sharon has said that she will make an occasion of it on Sunday, which is Christmas Eve, with a cake and some alcohol. I told her not to bother, but she wants to and Thomas will enjoy it.

'You'll have to give up the recordings,' said Sharon last night when she came down to see how I was. The arrangement is that the nurse stays on duty until eight o'clock and then is free until half past eight in the morning. She has the use of the back bedroom where Mother used to sleep, but often she goes back to her modern house in town. I know she much prefers her place to this; once she said she couldn't imagine living permanently in such an ancient house.

'Old houses encourage ghosts,' she said, changing the bed while I sat in my chair beside the window.

That gave me pause for thought. Was she simply prattling, her usual aimless nonsense, or had she seen something? Was that why she didn't like sleeping here?

I didn't ask her. I don't want to know, because if the stories of troubled souls coming back to haunt the living are true, then this house would be crowded to overflowing. Generations of them, I bet, from long before I was born, but I've never seen or felt anything strange. I have wondered about it when I'm at my lowest and thought that a sight of Mother or Elizabeth could be a comfort. But then if I could see those two dear people I would have to see Father, who might be critical of me and even our Billy. Perhaps Nurse has come across Billy in one of his moods. Oh, dear, that would be a funny sight to see. I'm not sure who would come off best.

Sharon says she can manage me on her own at night, and although I don't care for her attending to me I have got over my embarrassment of the bottle. Those first two days I was reluctant about using it and handing it back to her all warm and dribbled over the edge.

'For God's sake stop making things so bloody

316

difficult,' she said when I tried to refuse the bottle, even though I was dying for a pee. 'Lie back and think of England. Women have to all the time,' she added, and that made me laugh, so I don't mind now.

But last night she was more serious after she came in when I was coughing again. 'You can't keep talking into the tape recorder,' she said. 'It makes you too breathless.'

I shook my head. 'I must,' I said. 'I haven't finished.'

She helped me with my cup of tea and wiped my mouth afterwards. Why don't I mind that? I've always been so independent and it is so unlike me not to rail against the loss. Perhaps I'm just too tired now.

'But is it so important?' she asked. 'There are plenty of people who knew you and you won't be forgotten.'

How strange. She thinks I'm writing this memoir in order to keep my name alive. As though I was someone of note whose life was one of heroic deeds and good works that deserved a written biography, and not what I really am: someone making a last confession.

'It's important to me,' I muttered. 'I have to tell what happened.'

She didn't understand, and why would she? She doesn't know more than anyone else. Only two people knew and they are both dead. But she is right about talking into the tape; it does make me breathless and I can no longer hold the microphone. Today I have it pinned to my pyjama jacket, but when I move my head I think the sound

317

is muffled, and added to that I can't lean over to look at the machine and I don't know when the tapes are running out. So I came to a decision.

'Sharon,' I said, after we'd sat in silence for a few minutes, 'will you do something for me? It's a lot to ask, and I know you are busy with Thomas and your course. But it would make me a lot easier.' Why did I feel as if I was blackmailing her? I knew she wouldn't refuse; she's too decent.

'You know I'll do whatever you want,' she said.

'I want you to read what I've written and listen to the tapes. And then type it all on to your computer so that I have a properly written record.'

'Yes,' she said, 'of course I will. But I thought you didn't want anyone to see it.'

'I didn't. Now I do. I haven't got much longer to live.'

She put her head down and looked miserably at the empty cup in her hands. I was suddenly exasperated. This girl and I have already come to an understanding about my demise. We both know it's imminent. I gave her a fierce look and was ready to shout at her with all the breath I could muster, but then I held back. She is too close to my heart.

'Oh, Sharon love, don't look like that,' was all I said. 'If I can lie back and think of England, so can you. We haven't time for stupid pretence.'

She nodded her head and gave me a small strained smile. 'Sorry, Richard.'

'Right. Well, read my story and I'll carry on as long as I can. I have to finish it some way.'

'You could speak it to me and I can type it straight on to the computer, if you like.' That was her idea and it's not a bad one. When I get too weak, that's what I'll do.

It was late, after midnight, when she left me and I could see that she was tired. She works hard, that girl, and I'm piling more and more on her shoulders. 'Sharon,' I said as she put her hand on the doorknob, 'you mustn't worry about how you'll manage after I'm gone. I've seen to it that you and Thomas will be all right.'

When she turned back to me, I was astonished by the anger in her face and the very sparks that seemed to fly off her bright hair.

'I don't want to hear that, Richard. I don't care about money and that isn't why I stay on here. Haven't you realised yet that Thomas and I love you?'

What a girl. I smiled to myself in the silent room after she had gone upstairs to the big bedroom. We are so alike. Same blood, you see, a family trait that we share, handed down from the Cleetons. It goes with the red hair. We start quiet and then begin to want our own way. I expect Thomas will be the same. I think John would have been too, if he'd been allowed to live. My son, John Edward Wilde, whom I only saw a few times in my life and could never acknowledge. To all the world, we were uncle and nephew, and for Elizabeth's sake I never wavered from that arrangement, but she and I knew and held that knowledge and love for him between us like a precious jewel. The boy felt it too, I think, for he treated me with the same trusting affection he gave to his mother. I loved him from the very first, on that autumn day in the colonel's office.

319

I can feel that swelling in my chest now as I did then, looking down at the child who had just been presented to me. Happiness it was, I suppose, and pride that I had been instrumental in giving life to this bright little spark. I dare say I was nervous too. I wanted him to like me.

'Hello, John,' I stammered, holding out my hand to the boy who stood beside his mother.

'You're my uncle Richard,' he said, and his face broke into a cheeky grin. 'Mummy said you'd get a surprise. That's why I hid behind the cupboard.'

I cleared my throat and swallowed the lump that had suddenly formed. The sun had made my eyes prickle and when I looked up at Elizabeth I could only see her through a mist. She smiled and looked down towards her son and then back up at me. Her deliberate nod was all I needed. She confirmed my belief.

'Everyone at home is dying to see you,' Elizabeth said, helping me out, for I was too emotional to speak and could only stand stupidly and gaze down at the little chap who was now looking out of the window at my recruits, who were being led through marching drill by two corporals.

'Look at the soldiers, Mummy,' John piped, and marched around the office trying to match the beat.

'Yes, love,' Elizabeth said. 'Aren't they smart?'

He nodded and then turned to me. 'Can you march like that, Uncle Richard?'

'Yes,' I said, and, turning to Elizabeth for permission, bent and picked him up. I then marched smartly with him on my shoulders, round the desk and backwards and forwards across the office until he squealed with laughter. His little body was alive and wiry and his legs in their small boots bashed in time against my chest. It was almost the best thing that had happened to me in all my life.

'He's wonderful,' I said to Elizabeth when I'd put him down. 'A grand boy.'

'I think so,' she said. 'Just like his father.'

I was nearly overcome again then, and had to take a deep breath before carrying on. 'Can you stay another hour?' I said. 'I'll be off duty then and we can go into the city and get a meal. We have a lot to talk about.'

It was only then that she put out her cool hand and gently touched my cheek. John was back at the window staring at the parade ground and didn't see the kiss that I placed tenderly and in gratitude upon her lips. Whatever had happened in the past five years, we were still the same. Our relationship had changed, but not for the worse. All that was different was that we had grown up.

Elizabeth pulled on her gloves and beckoned to her son to take her hand. 'We, that is John and I, are staying at the Northern Hotel. Why don't you come and join us there, when you get off duty? I've so much to tell you.'

The young captain had the good manners to get to his feet when I led Elizabeth and John from the colonel's office.

'Captain Bellis, may I introduce you to my sister-in-law, Mrs William Wilde, and my nephew, John Wilde?'

He held out his hand and Elizabeth took it graciously like the lady she instinctively was. 'How d'you do, Captain Bellis?' she said. 'I'm so

321

happy to meet you.'

'And you too, ma'am.' He was a decent sort, as I said. Just too casual for my liking. 'I don't know what we'd do without Sergeant Wilde,' he said, making conversation. 'This company would be lost without him.'

'I think we feel much the same at home,' said Elizabeth, and her face broke into a lovely smile which made Captain Bellis rock slightly on his feet. He was still gaping when she nodded her goodbye.

Outside, a well polished black Rover waited. I'd seen it on my way from the parade ground but never dreamed that it could belong to anyone from my family.

'Is this Billy's?' I whispered as I helped her into the driving seat and then took John round to the other side.

'This is my car,' she said with a grin of pure delight, which suddenly revealed my girl from our youth. 'Billy's got his own.'

That evening when I got to the hotel I was shown up to a suite of rooms on the first floor. Elizabeth was sitting by the window of the larger bedroom, reading a story to John, and the porter who let me in after Elizabeth's call of 'come in' looked at the scene with pleasure.

'A lucky young man, that, sir,' he said, and I agreed.

'Shall we get our supper first?' said Elizabeth after I'd said hello to them both. 'Then I can put John to bed and we can catch up on all the news.'

John had a good appetite and made short work of a small piece of steak and fried potatoes while

322

Elizabeth and I ate Dover sole. Neither of us wanted a pudding but John did. The waitress brought him a dish of jelly and blancmange and he wolfed that down too.

'That boy's got hollow legs,' I grinned.

'That's what we all say, don't we, John?'

He nodded, too busy licking the last of the pink blancmange off his spoon to answer. 'That was nice, Mummy,' he said. 'Just like Granny makes it.'

That reminded me of home again. 'How is Mother?' I asked.

'Very well indeed,' said Elizabeth. 'She dotes on this child. Spoils him to death.'

'And Billy?'

'He's fine. The farm is making money, particularly from the milk. Those Friesians that your father invested in have really paid off. We have the best milking herd in the county. And now we've put up some greenhouses. I read an article about fresh vegetables in the *Farming News* and we're giving it a go. It's our third season. We do lettuce and tomatoes and I'm bringing on early potatoes down on the Major's land. I'm enjoying it.'

When John had said goodnight, kissing me as well as his mother, and going to bed without demur, Elizabeth and I finally sat down to talk.

'I have to know,' I said urgently. 'Does Billy think...'

She didn't let me finish. 'Billy prefers to think that John is his. He has no reason to, and in his heart of hearts he knows it, but it makes no difference. As far as he's concerned, John is his son and he loves him.'

At first, I couldn't take it in. Our Billy knew the

323

facts of life; he'd been a stockman from childhood and witnessed every aspect of animal reproduction. He must have known that Elizabeth had been sleeping with someone else.

'Do you think he knows it was me?' I hoped my voice didn't sound as nervous as I felt. I was over thirty years of age and a six-foot-three hardened veteran of several violent skirmishes, but I still dreaded the prospect of fighting my brother. Mind you, I would have, if it had become necessary.

'I think he does, and in a way that makes it better. All in the family, you see.'

I didn't see. If things had been different, I couldn't have accepted the situation. Did that make me or Billy the odd one? It had to be Billy. Mother had almost hinted to me that something wasn't quite right about him. But I'd thought that it was his moods and violent behaviour she was referring to. That brought a new consideration.

'And Mother? I bet she hasn't got a clue.' I'd forgotten the look she'd given me the night she came home from her holiday with Marian.

Elizabeth shrugged. 'You're wrong. She knows, though she never says a word. But after John was born and the doctor went downstairs to tell Billy, she held him up and stared into his little face. Then she turned and smiled at me. "He's the image of Richard," she said. "He'll be a lovely child." I think that's why she loves him so. You were always her favourite.'

I could feel my face flushing and suddenly noticed how warm and stuffy the hotel room was. But my thoughts still dwelt on home. What must Mother have thought of me, and how could I face her again? I was glad then that I hadn't gone home to be shamed by her fierce condemnation. I'd let everyone down. But then, amidst these thoughts of embarrassment and remorse, I remembered that she'd probably fallen from grace also. If my suspicions were true, it meant that she'd slept with a man who wasn't her husband. Could it be that she was pleased that the Cleeton line had been continued?

'Who chose the lad's name?' I wondered.

'Oh, I did,' said Elizabeth. 'John was my grandfather's name and also your mother's brother. Billy liked it too. It's a manly name, he said.'

'But why Edward?'

She thought for a while and then grinned, 'Why, that was Mother, now I come to think of it. She said that she'd always liked the name Edward. There was something of history about it.'

Was there, I thought. My history, no doubt, and I sat back in the chair with myriad thoughts racing through my overworked brain. After a while I gave up thinking and went to sit beside Elizabeth on the settee. She was wearing a delphinium blue dress of the exact same colour as the one she used to wear all those years ago, and round her neck was the blue and silver necklace. I put my finger on one of the silver links. It was warm and smooth and I followed the chain round, allowing my fingers to trail on to her neck. She offered no resistance, merely a little sigh as I bent my head down to kiss the place where my fingers had been. Immediately I was drowning in the scent of lavender and wild flowers, and that evoked such memories that, closing my eyes, I felt almost as though we were

325

back in the Major's little bare bedroom.

'Oh, Richard,' she breathed and her mouth was on mine and we were lost again in such all-consuming passion that nothing else in the world mattered. Our union was as feverish as it had been the first night we made love. I tore at our clothes, groaning in pleasure as her slim fingers helped, pulling at my rough army trousers and raking my naked back. When I finally stretched across her slim body, I felt as though I was coming home.

We lay in each other's arms for many minutes afterwards. She was sobbing quietly and I felt dizzy with the release of pent-up emotion. 'I love you, Elizabeth,' I said. 'I always have.'

'I know.' Her voice was small, girlish and sad. 'And I love you.'

The truth was that what I felt for her was more than love. It came from a darker place where the sweet open affection of a man for a woman was unknown. I craved her, hungered for her body and mind as an addict yearns for opium. I knew I would never be free of her and that made me desperate and content at the same time.

Did she feel the same? I don't honestly know. She desired me, I'm sure of that much. Her physical passion matched mine so closely that our love-making soared to heights I never knew with other women. She could make me lose my mind with a touch of her hands or the feel of her lips on my flesh, and even the women I'd paid for in bazaars and markets across India couldn't bring me to such an explosion of fervour as she did. But she was prepared to leave me and eventually did, even when we could have been together. That showed that my love was stronger than hers. Didn't it?

I had no thoughts like that, then. In that stuffy hotel room, in the centre of a dirty industrial city, my mind was occupied only with what mattered at that time. Elizabeth lying in the curve of my arm and the child sleeping in the little room beyond. Even the complexities of our situation were forgotten for the while, pushed into the background while we gloried in passion rediscovered.

We slept for a while after, drained by elation and rapture, so that by the time I got out of the tumbled bed the sounds of traffic in the busy street outside had died away. Elizabeth lay with a smile of pure contentment on her face and a pink flush on her naked breasts.

'I have to go,' I said, bending down to kiss the soft flesh. 'I must get back to the barracks.'

Her face fell. 'Oh,' she said, 'I thought we'd have the whole night.'

I shook my head. 'I've only got a pass until midnight. But I can see you tomorrow evening.'

'I'm going home tomorrow. This is just a shopping trip. They don't know I was coming to see you.'

I groaned. Wasn't it always the way? As soon as I regained her, she was taken from me. 'I'll come home then, in a few weeks. I've got leave owing. I'll come home for Christmas.'

'Yes,' she said, her smile slightly less bright than before. 'We'd all like that.'

Oh, Elizabeth, you could turn the passion on and off like a tap. How did you do it? She was back in family mode now and worried that my presence might upset the careful pretence with

327

which they all lived.

'Don't worry,' I said as I pulled on my clothes and smoothed my hair. 'I won't give us away. I'll be just the brother coming home on leave.'

I looked into John's room before I left. He was asleep on his side with a white teddy bear tucked in beside him. I longed to creep over and kiss his hot little cheek, but I didn't. Perhaps I hadn't the right, not being able to acknowledge him, and besides, Elizabeth had got out of bed and put a warning hand on my arm. 'Don't wake him,' she said. 'He may get a fright.'

I raised my eyebrows.

'You know,' she said. 'Seeing a stranger.'

Well, it was a fact, wasn't it? I was a stranger, and as long as things stayed the same I would never be anything other than an uncle, and one who was rarely on the scene. How I envied our Billy. In the years to come, he would have this little chap at his elbow when he went to market or to church and would be able to introduce him as 'my son'. And later on, when John was grown up, he would be the master of Manor Hill Farm and tell everyone that his father had been the best farmer in the district. 'What about your uncle Richard?' they might say.

'Oh, he's just a soldier, you know. We don't see him often.'

My leave started the day before my birthday but I didn't go home straight away. I needed to go into the city to do some shopping. It had been a long time since I'd spent any money and my balance was healthy, so I took myself off to the best men's outfitters and collected the bespoke suit I'd been measured for the day after Elizabeth's visit and a new overcoat and shoes. I still had the clothes that Billy had bought me on my last leave, but I hated to think that the family would recognise them and see me as some sort of skinflint who was too mean to buy himself a decent suit.

After that I walked round the shops looking for Christmas presents for the family. I remembered my uncle John coming home from India and bringing us all Christmas gifts. I still had my dagger, and I wanted to get special presents that everyone would love. Especially John.

Billy met me at the station. I had telephoned the night before and told them my time of arrival and could hear the excited chatter at the other end of the line as the news was relayed from Billy, who had answered my call, to Mother and Elizabeth.

'This will be the best Christmas ever!' he had said, with such conviction and generosity that I forgot that I was both jealous and nervous of him.

I saw him waiting on the platform before I stepped from the train. His likeness to my father was uncanny and I felt like a little boy again when I walked up to him and put out my hand.

'Never mind your hand, our Dick,' he said excitedly, and wrapped his brawny arms around me in a great hug. There was no doubt that he didn't bear me a grudge and that our relationship was as before.

I relaxed a bit then. 'I'm looking forward to seeing the family,' I said.

'No more than they are you. And,' Billy started his car, a Morris, smaller than Elizabeth's smart motor, 'you have yet to meet our young John.'

The words were said with such pride that you would have been the hardest-hearted person in the world if you didn't feel some joy for his happiness.

'I can't wait!' I said, and I meant it.

It was a cold, wet day with a low blue mist made worse by the smoke from the forest of chimneys in the village. Since the pit had been sunk, cheap coal had come into the district. It was a perk that went with the job, and a welcome one. Nobody went cold at home in our village.

I saw that new houses were being built along the lane towards our farm, solid-looking semi-detached villas, some already occupied. As we drove past at Billy's regular snail's pace, I noticed a young man screwing a name plate to a gate at one of them. I could even read it. 'The Limes', it announced proudly, and not a lime tree in sight. I suppose he just liked the sound of it.

'We've made a few changes,' said Billy as he drove into the yard, and I could already see some of them. Where a tumbledown barn had been rotting away since Father's time, a smart brick garage now stood, and through the open door I could see Elizabeth's black car.

A fifty-yard run of greenhouses stood out bleakly in the home field, the glass misted from the installed heaters. 'My God.' I whistled. 'That must have cost a bob or two.'

'It did.' Billy grabbed my cases and swung them out of the car. 'But our Elizabeth is making it pay, so I won't grumble.'

Mother met me at the kitchen door. 'Well, Richard,' she said, raising her arms to give me a hug, 'home again, is it? So soon after your last visit.'

I laughed and so did she and I was relieved to find that the old easy relationship had returned. She wasn't going to make life difficult for me.

'I've got someone for you to meet.' Her giggle was almost girlish as she said that and Billy, coming in through the door behind me, gave me a huge slap on the back and chuckled too.

Elizabeth was waiting inside and John stood beside her with a great big grin on his face.

'Say hello to your uncle Richard,' Billy boomed from behind me.

For a moment the little boy didn't speak but looked from face to face, still grinning. I was nervous again now. Supposing he gave the game away by saying that he had already met me? That would make my homecoming a disaster. But I needn't have worried. The child had been well coached, and as we all stood waiting he suddenly broke into a run and dashed across the kitchen towards me. I was already swinging him into the air before he managed to shout out, 'Hello, Uncle Richard!'

'Hello, son,' I replied, and hugged him.

Chapter Twenty-One

Christmas has come and gone and it has been the best one for years. That and my birthday party which Sharon organised on Christmas Eve, have proved to me that there are still people around who care for me and make my life, such as it is, worth living.

For my birthday celebration, held a week late because of my sudden incapacity, she invited several old friends of mine, whom I hadn't seen for some time. We opened up the drawing room and lit a fire in the big stone grate. It's a pleasant room, still furnished with Mother's best sofa and matching chair. The old Welsh dresser and an oak corner cupboard which I brought from the Gate House, take their place nicely in that large room, particularly the dresser, which is loaded with Mother's Spode and Ironware china. The Major's leather armchair and stool are by the fire, and although not as comfortable as the one I have in the parlour, the chair is attractive to look at. I felt quite the grandee in that chair, with a tartan rug over my knees and my feet up on the stool. The same stool that I sat on as a boy when I went to see the Major.

The first to arrive was Jennifer Williams, Darlington as was, Fred's youngest daughter. I've known her nearly all her life and would have been her godfather if the war hadn't intervened. She is so like her mother, gypsy-like, but with a gentle heart. She still lives in the village with her husband, a retired vet. Fred's older girls moved away, but I had a card from each of them. That was kind.

Jennifer gave me a kiss on the cheek and her husband produced a bottle of whisky. 'We'll break that open before you go,' I promised, but I forgot. Still, we had plenty to drink. I saw Sharon coming in and out of the room at frequent intervals with trays of wine and orange juice.

Lots of people from the village came and I knew

332

all of them by sight. The names are beginning to escape me, but they gave me kindly greetings and wished me all the best. One or two even brought presents, stupid really at my time of life, but well meant, and it would have been churlish of me not to accept them graciously... I hope Thomas likes the sweeties and Sharon can save the sherry for a suitable occasion. Perhaps my funeral. That reminds me. Some silly bugger brought me a next year's diary!

Mary Phoenix's brother, Charlie, who must be nearly as old as I am, turned up, helped by his daughter. I don't like him, never have, and I am still wary of all the Phoenix family despite the fact that they are my cousins. I think they know, or suspect, that Mary didn't go south with that man friend as everyone in the village assumed, and never miss an opportunity to drop a hint. Charlie looks terrible, nearly bent double with arthritis, and I expect that doesn't help his temper, which is as disagreeable as ever. Even though it was my party and he had come to my house as an invited guest, he still couldn't greet me properly. 'How do, Wilde?' he said, but it wasn't asked nicely.

'Not bad,' I replied. 'Still alive.'

That seemed to upset him and he tightened his hand on the knob of his stick until his knuckles showed white through the liver-spotted skin. 'Aye,' he grunted, 'you are. Not like my sister.'

Will he never give up?

'Happy birthday!' I turned with some relief to see Andrew Jones standing beside me. I shook his hand.

'Thank you,' I said. 'I'm glad to see you.' He

didn't know how glad. His fresh clever face is infinitely better to look at than Charlie Phoenix's sour old mug. Charlie gripped his daughter's arm and struggled off to the table where Sharon had laid a decent spread of sandwiches and sausage rolls. My appetite has returned these past couple of days.

'How are you feeling?' said Andrew.

'I'm better,' I said, and I am. Last week I was ready to give up, but today I feel well. Dr Clewes has some magic pills in his bag. The nurse is still here, though, because my bloody legs have gone.

'Here.' Sharon came by with a glass of whisky and put it in my hand. 'You OK?' she asked, and looked into my face in that way she has, stripping away all the pretence that you put on, until you feel that absolutely nothing can be kept secret from her.

'I'm fine,' I said, and looked away towards young Jones. 'But here's a man who could do with a drink.'

'There's wine on the table,' she said. 'Help yourself.'

It was dismissive and I could see from his face that he was hurt. I wondered what he had done to upset her so, but at that moment Jason Hyde came over and gripped my hand.

'Well, Richard,' he said. 'Ninety-five years, not out.' A smile creased his big weather-beaten face. He seemed to dwarf the other guests, and as I slowly rubbed my squeezed hand I breathed in the smell that emanated from his sweater and trousers. It was a cold sharp odour, as though he had come directly from his hay barn and brought all the strong flavour of penned cattle with him. I saw Andrew wrinkle up his nose, trying not to show his distaste. This wasn't for him. He is a city boy through and through, and will never get used to it, but to me the smell was nectar. I could close my eyes and be back in the milking parlour in an instant, or mucking out the calf pen on a cold winter morning before school so that I could get my Saturday penny. Oh, I like Jason.

Sharon wasn't so friendly. 'There's wine on the table; help yourself,' she repeated, as dismissive of Jason as she had been of Andrew. I was bewildered, but then women have always had the ability to confuse me. All it needed now was for Dr Clewes to walk in and the prospective suitors would be all together. He did come, later, when we were attending to the cake. When she made it I have no idea, but it was a proper iced cake with lit candles, carried into the drawing room on one of the silver platters that I brought from the Gate House.

'You must blow out your candles,' said Jennifer Darlington as was. Silly girl. I have barely enough puff to speak.

I looked round the gathering until I saw the cheeky young face I'd been seeking. He was standing close to the table with a sausage roll in each hand and one in his mouth, judging by the bulge in his cheek. 'Come here, Thomas, lad,' I called. 'Come and be my breath.'

'Happy birthday to you,' they all sang as Thomas hurriedly swallowed his sausage roll and blew out the candles. Sharon put her hand over mine and together we cut the cake.

'Hurrah!' shouted Thomas, as the other children had at his party, and my older guests, stung into a reply, clapped discreetly and swigged at their drinks. I took a big gulp from my glass and was immediately overcome by a bout of coughing.

'Go easy, old chap,' said Dr Clewes, who had appeared at my side, and Sharon let go the cake knife and took the glass from my hand.

'I'm all right,' I gasped. 'Stop fussing.' But I wasn't and couldn't get my breath for ages. In the end, Dr Clewes went into the parlour and brought back my oxygen.

That brought the party to an abrupt end and people started drifting away. 'Goodbye, Mr Wilde,' they called. 'Best if we go now. Don't want to tire you.'

I stayed in the chair with the oxygen mask on, watching them downing last drinks and surreptiously grabbing a sandwich or two to eat on the way home. People are greedy, especially when it's a free meal.

'You should go to bed,' said Sharon, and looked at Clewes for his agreement. He nodded and she went off to get my wheelchair.

Later, when I was propped up in bed with Thomas sitting beside me, busily examining the contents of one of the boxes of sweets, I asked him if he'd enjoyed himself.

'Mm,' he said, mouth full of chocolate raisins. I watched as he dropped a handful on the floor for his daft dog. She cleaned them up in a trice. That dog is getting very fat; I must tell Thomas to take her for more walks and to stop feeding her titbits.

'Christmas Day tomorrow, young man. Are you

looking forward to it?'

This time he spoke properly. 'Oh, yes, Mr Richard. It'll be the best ever.' He climbed up on my bed and lay beside me with his head on my pillow. 'You are going to get up for the turkey, aren't you?'

I nodded. I would if it killed me. I wasn't going to spend what will certainly be my last Christmas on this earth in bed. 'I'll be there, lad, to pull a cracker with you.'

'Jason's coming,' he said.

'Good. I like him.'

'Mummy does too, better than that Mr Jones who took us to Spain. But yesterday she said that Jason takes things for granted. When I said what things, she wouldn't tell me.' He took another mouthful of sweets and lay looking at my ceiling.

'I wouldn't worry, son,' I said, patting his arm. 'Women are funny creatures.'

They are; everyone knows that. Even my Elizabeth was a funny creature, never the same two days running and always surprising. That Christmas when I went home, she was playing at being a respectable farmer's wife and I had been there for two days before she would even make an opportunity for us to be alone together. That was Christmas Eve and she suddenly decided that she didn't want to go to Midnight Mass. 'John's got a bit of a chill,' she said. 'I don't want him ill for tomorrow. There's no question of him going out so late at night.'

You could see that Billy was disappointed. He never lost any opportunity to be with his son, he was that proud of him. But he was as careful of the lad's health as was Elizabeth and he gave in

337

without a murmur.

It was before supper when Elizabeth said that and it was forgotten by the time we sat down. Mother had made her traditional giblet pie, which I hadn't had for years and was tucking into with gusto. The conversation turned to the subject of the King and Mrs Simpson. Well, he wasn't king by now for he had recently abdicated and we had King George to rule us. However, it took us a while to get used to calling him the Duke of Windsor.

'That woman is a witch,' said Billy. 'An evil temptress who has taken our king away.' His face had gone quite red, for in the spirit of Christmas he'd had a couple of glasses of whisky, something that I hadn't remembered him doing before. He was never a boozer, our Billy. Needless to say, I matched him drink for drink and more.

'He must have wanted to go,' I said, quite mildly. 'I doubt she could have forced him.'

That seemed to make him angry and his brown eyes glittered in a sudden rage. 'I repeat,' he said, and crashed his fist on the table with such force that his fork jumped off his plate and clattered on to the floor. Mother and I both bent at the same time to pick it up and when I met her eyes she gave me a warning look.

'I repeat,' he said again, 'that woman is an evil witch and deserves being taught a lesson. I know what I would do with her.'

It was an uncomfortable moment and I was glad that John had gone to bed early. Elizabeth said nothing, but that guarded look had come like a shadow over her face and in the hollow silence that ensued the only sound that echoed around the room was the heavy ticking of the grandfather clock in the front hall. I hoped that Billy had finished with Mrs Simpson and we could get on to another topic, but he hadn't.

'Yes,' he continued, his voice low and threatening as though Mrs Simpson were here in the room with us. 'Women like her should get what they deserve.'

I looked at him in astonishment. He was behaving as though poor Mrs Simpson had affected him personally and it was his task to reprove her. I searched my mind for something that would jolly him out of his sudden nasty mood, but I couldn't think of anything cheerful to say and stared down helplessly at the table. But after a moment I remembered a question I had wanted to ask earlier in the day and turned to Elizabeth.

'Where's that dog of yours? I haven't seen her about.'

If I'd thought that a simple remark about a dog would clear the atmosphere, I couldn't have been more wrong. The colour drained from Elizabeth's face and Mother bit her lips anxiously.

I looked from face to face waiting for an answer until Elizabeth cleared her throat and said, in a low voice, 'She died. A few years ago.'

'Shame,' I said. 'She can't have been that old. What happened?'

'She was shot.'

The words dropped like sharp stones into the listening silence that had consumed the kitchen and the pleasant mealtime mood disappeared.

Mother broke the silence by starting to clear

away the plates and Elizabeth got up to help her. It was a nasty moment and I looked anxiously at my brother from beneath lowered eyelids. He had changed quite a lot in the five years I'd been away. Apart from these occasional outbursts, he was much quieter and seemed lost in thought for much of the time. He would find himself jobs about the farm that he could do on his own.

His behaviour to the men hadn't improved either. I could excuse him by remembering that he'd had to take on a man's task at the age of thirteen and had been forced to grow hard, but as a younger man he had been ready for a laugh with his mates and enjoyed having people round to the house. Now, apart from his intense love for John, he seemed to prefer living in a world of his own: a world that only spoke when he spoke to it.

The previous morning I'd heard him tell off the men in the milking parlour for chatting. 'Get on with your work,' he'd growled, and as he walked off to inspect the sows I heard one of the men say, 'That bastard's heading for one of his moods again.'

The other one sniggered, not realising that I was on the other side of the door hoping to catch a glimpse of Elizabeth as she came out of the dairy. 'It's time he went into town,' he laughed, 'and got a bit of paid-for how's your father. That generally settles him down.'

'I heard that the girls in the flats are scared of him. Comes on rough like.'

'Oh yes? You been playing away from home, then? Knowing what those girls say? I think your missus should hear about this.'

A bit of a scuffle followed that remark, but soon they were back to work and as I left I could hear them both singing something they'd heard on the wireless.

When I went out with Billy later that day to help him do his Christmas shopping he was in a better temper and we enjoyed ourselves like two silly children at the toy shop while he chose a present for John. It was as though we were young again and he was able to relax in my company. The thing was that I never questioned him or any of his actions. You see, he'd looked after me all those years ago and I was grateful for that.

He bought Elizabeth a small amethyst brooch, which in the years to come I never saw her wear, and a string of jet beads for Mother, who wore those a lot.

But now, on Christmas Eve, his bad mood had returned and he was in danger of spoiling the whole evening. Mother put a lemon pudding on the table with a jug of cream.

'Here, William,' she said, and her voice was one of forced jollity, 'dish out this pudding while I put the kettle on.'

But he got up and pushed his chair back. 'Nothing for me, Mother.' His voice was shaking. 'I have to go out.'

'On Christmas Eve?' she cried, ready, I think, to argue with him, but Elizabeth put a hand on hers and turned her back to the range so that Billy could get out of the room without further harassment. In a moment, we heard his car roar into life and go trundling out down the drive.

That spoilt the whole dinner, and after we'd

cleared up Mother said that she didn't feel like church either and thought an early night would be a good idea. 'After all,' she said, giving me a goodnight kiss on the cheek, 'I'm sure you and Elizabeth have a lot of catching up to do.'

My cheeks were on fire when she said that. What could she possibly mean, I wondered. Surely she wasn't expecting us to leap into each other's arms like some sex-starved youngsters. Elizabeth a respectable married woman and her own daughter-in-law, and me ... well. I must have looked like an idiot, for when Mother left the kitchen and we could hear her going up the stairs, Elizabeth broke into muffled laughter.

'You should see your face,' she gasped, wiping her eyes on the corner of her apron.

'What the hell did she mean?' I asked, aghast.

'Exactly what you thought she did,' said Elizabeth, looking at me with a broad smile. 'She wants you to be happy. So do I.'

'Come here, you,' I said and grabbed her. Her generous mouth was still smiling when I lowered mine on to it and kissed the laughter away. We stood like that for many minutes, straining at each other's bodies, trying to get closer than was physically possible.

'I want you,' I said, and started to unbutton her silk blouse.

'No. Not here.' She broke away and put a hand on my mouth. Her breath was coming as fast as mine was and I knew that she wanted me too. 'Come to my room, in a minute. We'll be safe there.'

I barely gave her time to get up the stairs before

342

I put out the lights and followed her. There was a new double bed in her room above the front door, and in one of my rare lucid moments that night the thought flitted through my head that she had bought it especially for my visit. If she had, then it was a good choice, for we were as comfortable in our lovemaking as anyone could dare to hope for. I think I heard our Billy come in, much, much later, but he didn't disturb us and when I heard him again I knew he was getting up for early milking. For some reason, I wasn't a bit afraid of being caught. I turned over into Elizabeth's welcoming arms.

'Happy Christmas, my darling,' she whispered as I nuzzled my mouth into the warm hollow of her neck, and then she said, 'You'd better go. John will be up. He's that excited.'

'So am I,' I laughed, 'as you can see.' But she wouldn't let me have my way, too scared that John might come in, I think.

'I love you,' I said, rolling out of the bed with a stifled groan, 'and you've just given me the best Christmas present anyone could possibly have.'

She giggled at that and whispered, 'Go, go. Before the house is up.'

Billy's mood was much improved when he came in for breakfast. 'Happy Christmas!' he shouted, grinning broadly, and picking John up he swung him round. He smacked a big kiss on the boy's cheek. 'We'll open the presents after dinner,' he told him, 'but here's something to be going on with,' and he produced a small wooden car from his pocket.

'Oh!' cried John. 'Thank you, Father.' He

scrambled down and ran to show Elizabeth and Mother.

This morning, Elizabeth was wearing that delphinium blue dress with my necklace and I could have rushed over to her with the same enthusiasm. How I longed to pick her up and swing her round as our Billy had done with John. Her cheeks were pink because she had been bending down in front of the range to look at the couple of geese that Mother was roasting for our Christmas dinner. Marian and Albert were joining us, fresh back from their latest trip abroad. According to Mother, Albert had taken to foreign travel in the last few years, and despite Marian's lack of enthusiasm she always went with him.

'Well, well, well,' said Albert when we were all seated round the dining-room table, not eating in the kitchen because this was a special day. 'The traveller returns.'

'You too,' I said. 'Where was it this time?'

'America,' he said, beaming round at the assembled family. 'New York, and a wonderful town it is too. And the journey was as good as a holiday in itself. You'd go far to get service as good as we had on the *Queen Mary*.'

'You did go far,' said Elizabeth. Everyone stopped eating for a moment and looked at her. She rarely joined in general conversation and her making a little joke was most unusual.

Albert laughed and raised his glass to her. 'So we did, Elizabeth, my dear. So we did.'

Her cheeks became quite pink then and she looked quickly across at Billy to see what he thought, but he was busy helping John cut the

344

meat off his portion of goose and wasn't listening to the conversation at the other end of the table. Marian, who was sitting next to him, was though and she gazed at Elizabeth through the wire-rimmed spectacles she now wore.

'You're looking very well, Elizabeth,' she said, but the compliment sounded almost like a condemnation.

'Thank you.'

'And you,' she turned to me, 'not as yellow as last time. You've filled out.'

'Well, I've been home for a while,' I said. 'The tan has worn off.'

'We thought you'd get leave as soon as you returned. I'm surprised that you had to wait so long.'

Mother tutted. 'He's home now, Marian. That's all that matters.'

Albert turned the conversation to India and asked me what I thought of the 'rebels'.

'They're a peaceful lot, on the whole,' I said. 'I think they have a lot of right on their side.'

That surprised him and stayed his hand for a moment as he was helping himself to another pile of roast potatoes. 'You amaze me, Richard. I've been told on very good authority that those men are nothing but terrorists and communists ready to turn India into another Russia.'

I felt angry, thinking about Dr Rai, who had died in that dreadful jail in the Andamans. He would have made ten of Albert's so-called authorities. 'Their leaders are respectable, educated men,' I said. 'They deserve their freedom and will have it, one day. You'll see.'

Now it was me spoiling the jolly atmosphere and I was sorry when I saw Mother's face fall. But Albert was a better man than many. He resumed spooning potatoes on to his plate and gave me a smile. 'I'm sure you know better, Richard. I won't argue.' He turned towards the top of the table and winked at John. 'Now, I expect this young man wants his gifts. I'd better get a move on.'

We opened our presents by the Christmas tree in the drawing room. I was touched by the generosity I'd been shown by my family and was glad that I'd made the effort to get them decent gifts. Billy had given me Father's duelling pistols, which had come to him after Father's death. I had always admired them. And I had books from Mother and Elizabeth. Gold cuff links with my initials came from Albert and Marian.

'Thank you, thank you,' I said, and sat back to watch them open theirs. Elizabeth gave me a special smile when she opened the packet containing the blue cashmere cardigan. She liked it, I could see, and Mother liked her leather writing case and Billy the big book of horse breeding that I had found. I was glad that I had chosen well but all I was really interested in was whether John liked what I'd got for him, so when he tore excitedly at the paper covering the box I think I was biting my tongue.

'A train set,' said Elizabeth when he finally got it open. 'You lucky boy.'

'Thank you, Uncle Richard,' he said, his face red with excitement. 'Thank you.' He pulled the engine out and looked at it with solemn pleasure and then slowly and almost reverently touched all the other coaches and accoutrements that came in the set. He was almost squeaking with joy and everyone put down their own presents to watch him. Elizabeth bent down and whispered something in his ear and he gave a little nod. I nearly wept when he came over to me and wrapping his arms round my neck gave me a big kiss. It was a special moment.

'That was very generous, our Dick,' said Billy, his hanky at the ready as ever. These sorts of occasions always moved him. He had given the boy a beautifully carved rocking horse, with the name 'Diamond' painted on the rockers. He must have paid a fortune for it and it's still in the nursery rooms on the top floor. John sat on it often, rocking away and shouting that he was the winner in the race, but he always had one of the Hornby coaches in his hand.

The rest of Christmas passed quickly. I had another week of nights with Elizabeth but it went in a flash. This time I didn't beg her to leave. It would have been a hopeless task, for she wouldn't do anything that might make things difficult for John. She didn't love our Billy, but I don't think she was afraid of him any more. They had come to an arrangement.

'He goes to prostitutes,' she said one night when we lay together after a passionate session of love-making. 'Every now and then. It keeps him quiet.'

I said nothing. I didn't even ask how she knew. It seemed a strange way to behave, but I supposed that I was as much to blame as anyone. His wife was in love with someone else and wouldn't have anything to do with him. What else could he do?

I wanted to know about another thing too.

'What did happen to your dog?' I asked. 'Who shot her?'

'Who d'you think?' she replied sadly and I sat up on my elbow to look at her face. She sighed and moved closer to me. 'That was my punishment for getting pregnant. He wanted a child too much to damage me, but I had to be chastised.'

All I could do was hold her. I felt guilty. What distress we two brothers had visited upon her.

'Oh, God!' I said, smoothing my hand down the soft skin that covered her slim back. 'I hope I haven't left you pregnant again.'

'So do I,' she said quietly. I hadn't. She never had another child.

Fred Darlington came to see me one morning. He was looking older and more serious but greeted me as an old friend. 'When are you coming back home?' he said.

'I don't know,' I replied. 'I'm a twenty-year man. My life is in the army.'

He shrugged and looked away up to the hillside. 'Pity,' he said. 'It would be better if you were here.'

I was puzzled. 'Why?'

'You could keep an eye on Billy.'

'What?'

We were in the yard by the gate leading to the home field. I knew Billy was in the stables with the horses and Elizabeth was busy in the dairy, yet I felt I had to lower my voice.

'What are you talking about?' I whispered.

He stared, at me for a moment as though considering whether to carry on. 'He beat up a prossie on Christmas Eve. Nearly killed her. She's still

348

in hospital.'

I could barely believe what I was hearing, but the conversation that I'd heard between the farm hands trickled into my mind.

Still, he was my brother and I couldn't have people talking about him like that. 'Rubbish,' I protested. 'I don't believe you. If it was true you would have arrested him by now.'

Fred sighed. 'She won't bring charges, but I know it was him. It isn't the first time.'

This was dreadful news and I could barely take it in. I knew Billy had a violent temper, but I couldn't believe that he would get so out of control that he would beat up a young girl. Elizabeth had said that he went with prostitutes. I wondered if she knew about the beatings as well. Of course she did. He'd beaten her, hadn't he?

'Oh, God,' I groaned, 'this is terrible.'

Fred nodded 'Yes, it is. And you have to do something about it. You're the only one who can.'

It wasn't fair to put that responsibility on me. Billy was my brother, but he was older than me and all my life he had told me what to do. We didn't have a relationship that would have allowed me to reprove him. I shook my head. 'I can't,' I said. 'He wouldn't listen to me. And anyway, there isn't any proof.' It was cowardly of me, but then I was never a brave person, especially where the family was concerned.

'Well,' said Fred, 'then he'll just get worse until someone, somewhere, is brave enough to tackle him.'

We didn't talk about it again and when I called at his house the next day to say hello to Miranda

349

and the children, the subject wasn't mentioned. All the talk was about the possibility of war.

I didn't tell them that I was pretty sure it was on the cards. She was frightened for her children, and when I looked round their comfortable house and saw how happy they were I couldn't bring myself to spoil things for them. My own life was a mess, in some ways, but I had no need to make anyone else's as bad.

'Young John is a fine boy,' said Fred, seeing me to his gate when my visit was over.

I nodded. 'Yes, he is.'

We shook hands then and nothing more was said or needed to be. Fred knew whose child John was. I dare say all the village did too. The mark of the Cleetons is very strong.

Chapter Twenty-Two

I went back to my company in the first week of January. We had celebrated quietly at home, staying up to welcome in the New Year with glasses of whisky for Billy and me and port wine for Mother and Elizabeth. Billy went outside with a piece of coal and some bread and salt, so that in the first minute of the year he could come in with provisions. It was for luck, because Mother was always concerned with doing things 'for luck'. If salt was spilled she threw it over her left shoulder. She would bow to the new moon and turn her money over and sometimes, if she had accidentally caught sight of the moon through glass, the whole palaver of bowing and money and turning round three times had to be performed.

Other superstitions existed too, but as a child I never thought them odd. It was simply the way we lived, and to a certain extent I followed Mother's rules. Even now I can't put shoes on the table or allow lilac or ivy into the house, and I still look anxiously at the little jasper elephants on the mantelpiece in the kitchen to make sure that they're facing the door. Mother used to say that there would be ructions if they couldn't find their way out.

I thought about her superstitions on the day of her funeral. Someone had sent a wreath of white lilac, and when I came down the stairs after showing the undertaker where Mother's body lay, I saw the wreath propped up against a chair in our hall. I think the sight of those white flowers, actually in the house, was almost as upsetting as the fact of Mother's death. The driver of the hearse, who was sitting patiently behind the wheel, waiting for the coffin, must have thought me mad when he saw me throw open the front door and fling the wreath out of the house. We watched together as those flowers flew into the air, petals loosening and spinning away before the whole thing came down in a messy heap on the gravel.

I went and picked it up before Mother's coffin came down, carefully collecting all the broken flowers and bits of leaf. I was ashamed of my loss of control but I made sure that that horrible wreath didn't come to the churchyard. I had stuffed the card in my pocket and took it out and read it later that evening when I was putting my good suit away in the wardrobe. The wreath was from the Phoenix family. I might have known.

When I got back to barracks that early January, I wasn't as upset as I might have been. Elizabeth and I had come to some sort of arrangement, so that we could behave like any other married couple who had to be parted. I felt married to her, felt that we had a child together and the fact that we were merely brother and sister-in-law was an obstacle that we had to live with. It was simply that nobody else knew, or said it. So I returned to my soldiering life not as reluctantly as I might have and greeted my friends without wishing I was elsewhere.

Lewis Wilton had met a girl in the town over the Christmas holidays and this time, he said, it was serious.

'I'm going to get married,' he told me, when we met up in the Sergeants' Mess for our tea.

'You?' I said, shaking my head. 'That'll be the day.'

'No. I mean it. Sarah's the best thing that's ever happened to me.' He brought out a photograph of a fair, studious-looking girl. The picture had been taken outside a large building, and when I looked closely I recognised it as the central library.

'Where did you meet?' I was curious, because as far as I knew Lewis had never set foot in a library. Anyway, this girl didn't look like his usual type. He liked them noisy and up for anything.

'In the library.'

I must have looked amazed because he laughed

and punched me on the arm. 'I was outside the recruiting office in town, showing off the dress uniform, you know, and trying to drum up some new recruits, when it came on to rain. I sheltered in the doorway of the library and she came out with a cup of tea for me. She works there. After that we got talking and I went back the next day to see her. I borrowed a book.'

'Good God!' I laughed. 'What was it?'

'*A Passage to India.*'

'Have you read it?'

He shook his head. 'Not a word, it's so fucking boring, but she thought I would be interested, seeing as how I'd been there. She said she would love to travel.'

He chattered on, telling me how wonderful Sarah was and how in only two weeks she had changed his life. He'd even met her parents. 'I minded my p's and q's that day, I can tell you. Barely spoke a fucking word, too scared of swearing.'

'Have you asked for her?'

'Yes, and got permission. The wedding is set for Easter Saturday and we'll move into married quarters here on the base. Sarah will have to give up her job, but my sergeant's pay will give us enough to live on. And, by the way, I want you to be the best man.'

It was a quiet wedding, held in the Methodist chapel in town. The girl's parents were strict observers of their faith, so we had no alcohol to toast the happy couple, but they were nice people and had welcomed Lewis into their family as another son. I sat next to the fat bridesmaid at the small reception and later, after Lewis and his new wife had left for their honeymoon in London, I took her out to a pub in the town.

'I don't drink much,' she said, but she did and tried to get off with me. I wasn't having that and took her home as soon as I decently could.

Elizabeth came to see me sometimes and we would put up for the night at the Northern Hotel and enjoy each other's company in relative anonymity. These were her 'shopping trips' recognised as necessary outings by Mother and Billy because our local town was a poor place and the shops didn't carry anything smart. She played the game by taking home new clothes for herself and John and little gifts for Mother. She never bought anything for Billy. 'He gets clothes when he goes off to the shows,' she said. 'Always buying himself new jackets and overcoats. He likes to look smart when judging.'

It was true that he liked to look smart. I rarely saw my brother in anything worn or dirty, even when he was mucking about the yard. He wore brown overalls on the farm that Mother boiled up in the copper, so that every other day he had a clean pair to put on. Even his boots were hosed off each evening. He couldn't abide dirt.

'Did you hear about that girl on Christmas Eve?' I asked her. I'd been thinking about what Fred told me, on and off, in the months since I'd been back and it troubled me a lot. Half the time I didn't really believe it but then I remembered the rage that had left Billy shaking as he slammed out of the house.

'I heard,' she nodded. 'Miranda Darlington

354

told me at the church jumble sale. She said she thought I ought to know because all the village was talking about it.'

'Do you believe it?'

'Of course.' She propped herself up on one elbow and looked at me pityingly. 'Don't you?'

I said nothing and lay looking at the ceiling of the hotel bedroom. I did believe it, I suppose, but I didn't want to. It's hard to admit that a person whom you have known all your life, played with, grown up with and loved could do things as cruel as what he was being accused of.

As if reading my mind, Elizabeth said quietly, 'Think what he did to me, if you want proof.'

I turned to face her. 'I don't understand it. I don't know why he does it.'

She lay back down again and curled her body into mine. 'He's ill,' she sighed, 'in his head. Your mother knew it years ago; that's why she wanted us married. She thought it would calm him down. Didn't you realise?'

I held her close and thought of the conversation I'd had all those years ago with Mother. She'd tried to tell me, but I wouldn't listen. I'd been too wrapped up in my own callow jealousy. And later, I'd assumed that the organised marriage was to do with the circumstances of my birth. As ever, I'd only been concerned with myself.

That night in the warm hotel bed, lying next to the only girl I could ever love, I was stupid enough to feel sorry for Mother, having to bear all that knowledge alone. I didn't think then of the dreadful thing she'd done to Elizabeth. It was only when I heard a little choke and looked and saw that she was crying that I realised she was the person whose life had been most affected.

'Leave him,' I begged. 'Bring John to me and we'll start a new life here.'

She shook her head. 'He wouldn't let him go,' she sobbed. 'Besides, the shame of it all would kill your mother.'

I could say nothing that would persuade her and the only concession I was ever able to get out of her was a promise to leave, with John, if Billy ever got dangerous with her.

'I will,' she said, and added fiercely, 'And believe me, Richard, if he ever lays one finger on my son, I'll kill him.'

He was my son too, so why couldn't I have said that? I didn't. It was a circumstance that I simply couldn't imagine, and anyway, the fraternal bonds were so strong that even the thought of harming my brother was something beyond contemplation.

Rumours of war were rife all the time in those days and we were expecting orders for a general mobilisation at any time. When we did get them, at the beginning of 1939, I actually felt relief in a way because we'd been waiting for so long. We were being sent to Gibraltar to strengthen the garrison there, a good posting because it is a nice place, with good weather and plenty of bars.

Lewis didn't want to go. Sarah was expecting their first and, as it turned out, their only child any day and he tried all ways to get out of leaving England. In the end, the colonel allowed him a month's compassionate leave and he was able to be at home when his daughter was born. He re-joined the company later.

'Look,' he'd say excitedly to anyone he could grab when he had caught up with us, 'look at my daughter.' And he would produce a now dog-eared photograph of a baby girl, held proudly in her mother's arms. 'I'm going to bring them out here in a few months when the baby's able to travel.'

'She's a lovely child,' I said kindly when I'd admired the photograph for the tenth time. 'Now do you think you can move your arse and get the men on parade before the colonel comes back from headquarters.'

I liked Gibraltar. Everything seemed to be comfortable there. We had good quarters and plenty of free time to visit the town. I sent a box of oranges home and I had a note from Mother to say that they'd arrived and that John loved them. After that, I'd send the odd gift for him, clockwork toys when I could get them and once a little bull-fighter's uniform. Elizabeth wrote once, very affectionate and grateful for the toys. 'But he still loves the train set best,' she said. John had written 'love from John' in higgledy-piggledy pencil on the bottom of her letter. I kept that letter for ages, in my breast pocket, until it disintegrated in the blood that spread from my chest when I was wounded.

When war was declared in September, I thought we would be sent home to get ready to face the Germans, but to my surprise we had orders for India and were to enship within three weeks. Immediately there was a to-do with Lewis. He went berserk at the thought of being sent even further away from his Sarah and their baby.

'I can't go,' he said, white-faced, wild-eyed, pac-

357

ing around the Sergeants' Mess. 'I won't. I can't leave them at home if there's going to be a war.'

'Be reasonable,' I said, trying to calm him. 'You're a twenty-year man like me; you have to obey orders. Sarah will be fine. Her mother and father are only ten minutes away from her in the town. They'll look after her.'

But my words weren't enough. He went to the colonel and begged and pleaded, but to no avail, and in the end he ran out of the camp and into the town. It was a terrible shame, because even before he'd married Sarah he'd started to reform his ways, and since the wedding my pal had been a model of temperance and good sense. But that night he lost it all. By the time I'd found him, sent urgently by the colonel who knew of our friendship and wished to spare the regiment any embarrassment, it was too late. Lewis was fighting drunk and had already broken up one bar and was on to his next. It took me and two redcaps to get him back to camp, where he was immediately clapped into jail.

He lost his stripes and spent the entire voyage to India in the hot stinking cells on the lowest deck of the ship and I could do nothing to make his imprisonment easier. I did send an airmail letter to Sarah explaining the situation and asking her to write to him, saying she was all right. Fair play to her, she was a champion girl that and wrote a sensible letter that arrived in India only a week after we did. Lewis showed it to me when he was back in barracks, head shaved and very low. 'I'm proud of you,' she'd written, 'and glad I'm married to a soldier. I'm knitting socks for sailors and Mum and I go to first aid classes. I know we all have to do our bit. Baby Carol sends her best love to her darling Daddy and God willing we'll all be together soon.'

He was all right after that, but quiet and not the old Lewis we used to know. But anyway, we two had grown up by then and left the carousing to the youngsters who now made up the bulk of our company. These were my recruits on whom I'd been quite hard the past two or three years and I was glad to see that my training had paid off, for they were fit and well prepared for anything.

'Will there be snakes, sarge?' they had asked when we were on board the P&O liner on our way to India, 'Elephants? Tigers?'

I nodded yes to all these questions. 'There will, and a lot of hard work too, so don't think you're going on a holiday. Remember what I told you about taking your malaria tablets and don't drink mucky water. And if you want to go with the whores make sure you report to the MO the next day.'

They laughed at that. 'I'll be all right, sarge,' said one cocky young fellow. 'I've had everything those women can give me already.'

'Suit yourself,' I said, 'but don't come crying to me when your piss is burning a hole through your cock.'

We talked like that in the army, all men together. It meant nothing and I rarely heard even the worst blasphemer use such words in front of a respectable lady, but it was normal day-to-day language for us so they took no offence. I watched them gather together around the table in the centre of their narrow quarters, noisily debating what I'd said and boasting about the women they'd had or said they'd had.

For my part, I was as excited as they were, because I was returning to my beloved India, but I kept that a secret. It wouldn't have done to let them know. As we neared Bombay, though, I went on deck to look for the first sight of land and found myself in tears. It could have been the spice-laden air or maybe the sight of the cheerful semi-naked fishermen in their wooden dhows, weaving in and out of the path of our ship, that caused my emotion, but whatever it was I felt as though I was coming home. How strange, that I should have two equally important places in my heart.

We'd only been back at the Meerut camp for a couple of months when the colonel called me to his office.

'I've orders here, sergeant. You are to report to Major Derry in Rangoon. They want you to train for jungle warfare.'

Rangoon was across the border in Burma and a long trip from Meerut but I enjoyed the journey, looking out of the train window and holding my breath in excitement when we passed exquisite pagodas and Buddhist shrines. I was proud that I'd been chosen and keen for a new experience, but was aware of one fly in the ointment. That bastard Captain Parker was sent with me.

'This will be considerably different from your Frontier adventures,' he said with his usual sneer. 'You'll be very much the new boy here. No opportunity to show off, I'm afraid.'

I nodded, not bothering to reply, other than a courteous 'Sir'. I never knew why he had it in for me, although, in truth, he had it in for anyone who saw through the veneer of outward flash to the cowardly heart beneath. I turned back to the scenery, leaving him to read his newspaper for the umpteenth time. He had no interest in where we were going; only what he could get out of it.

He was lucky. The admin officer had gone down with a bad case of fever, and as soon as we reported for duty Parker was given a cushy office job. Consequently, he didn't do any training. But I did.

'I've heard impressive things about you, Wilde,' said Major Derry when I reported to his office, 'from my good friend Colonel Barnes. I sought you out particularly when I was assembling this team.'

'Thank you, sir. How is the colonel?'

'Retired. At home, and fretting for action. I've got his eldest son here, Lieutenant Jack Barnes. Nice lad. Eager to please.'

Jack Barnes and I got on famously, although we made sure that we were lieutenant and sergeant at all times and never let our friendship interfere with the chain of command. He was dark like his mother and had the same sweet personality. He never had any side to him and I used to think that he'd never be able to kill anyone, but he foiled me, being as brave and adventurous an officer as you could wish. Those public schools taught more than Latin and Greek, I realised later, when I saw him cut throats without blanching. That was two or three years later, when we got into real action.

'One yellow bastard less,' he would grunt, wiping blood off his bayonet, and God help any Jap who put his hands up to surrender. We didn't take prisoners. I know because I did my fair share in disposing of them. It was different then. They killed us, we killed them.

'I do hate this war,' Jack said one night, when we were resting up in a cave on our retreat. 'It's made me coarse when all I want to be is decent.' He sighed and looked out on to the thickly wooded hills beneath us. 'My mama would not have approved.'

I was glad that I got him out alive when we were retreating from the Japs. He lost a leg but I carried him through the jungle. I couldn't leave him. He had a chance, not like poor Lewis.

When I got home, after the war, I had a nice letter from Colonel Barnes inviting me to visit him and Jack at their home in Ireland. His middle son had emigrated to New Zealand having survived the war intact, but the youngest, a boy of only eighteen, had been killed in Normandy. I did see them once or twice, stopping off on my way to stay with Elizabeth, but I never stayed more than a couple of hours. It didn't seem fitting, somehow. Besides, on my trips to Ireland all I wanted to do was to be with her.

But back to the training. It was hard and I didn't like the jungle. The heat and humidity was overpowering and regulated everything we did. You would be wet with sweat after a few minutes on patrol and the humid air sapped the strength of even the fittest man.

'Keep your eyes open at all times,' warned Major

362

Derry as we went on patrol through the dripping green forest. 'Everything is your enemy.'

It was, too. The trees hid all manner of wildlife: snakes, spiders and leopards. I saw tigers a few times and bloody huge they were, but surprisingly shy, considering that they could be man-eaters. Above us, where the canopy thinned out, the trees were home to monkeys and bright-coloured birds who were always ready to give your position away. I learned to cope with it but I would have given anything to be back on the Frontier where the enemy might be just as deadly but at least you could breathe.

However, when we pushed further into the country, the landscape changed, becoming drier, with sparse vegetation and dusty open spaces. Here the sun blazed down and baked us. Even the protection of our wide-brimmed bush hats offered little relief. Then we were begging again for the shelter of the jungle.

Eventually, our training took us into the Naga hills where we climbed up through rocky escarpments and scrubby trees into country that I could understand.

It was up there that we came across tribesmen who were friendly and keen to take us to their villages. They were good people – simple, but nothing wrong with that – and the men were as good fighters, when it mattered, as any of us.

I've eaten monkey stew served by young women in ragged clothes and not even noticed how pretty some of them were, I was that hungry. It just shows you. When it matters, food and drink is what's important. They were kind, though. The cuts and bruises that I'd gathered almost un-noticed on my patrol through the hills were treated by them with unguents pasted on to strange leaves and wrapped over the affected part. The pus-filled cuts healed within days and I was grateful.

The training lasted for nearly six months and then we had a lull, back in barracks at Rangoon, where we sat about, ready for action which was not forthcoming. I went on a course to learn Japanese, but it was difficult. I only picked up a few words, commands and suchlike and the polite way to converse with a stranger. That seemed ridiculous. Any Japanese stranger we might meet out there would never have been greeted politely.

Rangoon is an exotic city, full of pagodas and strangely decorated temples. I wandered about, having bought myself a camera so that I could take photographs, and posted some of them home so that Elizabeth and Mother could see where I was. I lost the camera when we evacuated the camp later on. It was a funny business being in Asia, doing nothing much, when we knew that in Europe a terrible war was raging. I worried about my people at home, but not as much as some of the men whose families lived in cities. We heard of bombing and that was worrying. One of the lads came to tell me one day that he'd heard that his brother had been killed at Dunkirk. That was the first that I'd heard of the place.

I had news of home too. 'We are all right and have built an air-raid shelter in the garden,' Mother, wrote. 'Silly of me, I know, but I can't bear the thought of being stuck in the cellar with the house crashed down on top of me. We've been lucky, though, with very few raids.' Her letter went on in that vein, lucky to be in the country rather than the town, but nevertheless things were difficult. 'Jeff and Peter have joined up and Billy is managing with the lad and some casual labour from the village. He is very tired.'

It was the PS that worried me. 'I've taken over the dairy again with Miranda Darlington to help me. Elizabeth has taken John to see her father in Liverpool.'

Why would she need Miranda Darlington if Elizabeth had only gone on a visit? I pondered this letter for several days trying to guess what it was that Mother had left out. I didn't have to wonder for long. A letter from Elizabeth herself arrived, postmarked Liverpool and sent about six weeks previously.

'I've left home,' she wrote, 'and come to stay with my father. Billy is difficult again and although, so far, he has left me alone, I don't feel I can trust him any more. He is worked to death, you see, because of the war and no one to help with the beasts. I would help, if he would let me, but things have got bad again between us. Mother tells people that I've come to take care of my father, which in a way is true. He is homesick for Ireland and keeps saying that he'll die if he can't get back. John is well and growing out of his clothes rapidly. He loves his grandfather and that is a relief because I've joined up as a nursing auxiliary and Da takes care of him. I show John his uncle Richard's photograph all the time and we try to imagine where you are. Father has guessed about us but I don't mind. I love you.'

A photograph was enclosed of her, John and an older man who I presumed was her father. They were all smiling and standing in front of a small red-brick terraced house. Beyond them, I could see the street running downhill, houses on either side, until it met a T-junction. And there across that road was the unmistakable hull of a big ship. Elizabeth's father lived right by the docks.

I worried about this letter for a week, starting a reply which insisted that she go back home to be safe in the country and then tearing it up and starting another with completely different advice. I couldn't work out what she meant about Billy's being 'difficult'. Mother had said he was tired so perhaps he had only been a bit more bad-tempered than usual. And no one had said that he had been unkind to John. I wondered, not for the first time, if Elizabeth was exaggerating.

In the end, I didn't write to her at all. I put it off and waited to see if I would get another letter from Mother. It was typical of me, I suppose, but I've never been one for confronting that sort of problem. They'd sort it out themselves, I was sure of it. After all, they'd managed without my help for years. But, as I lay on my bunk, sweating and sleepless in the insect-laden night, I would think of Fred Darlington's warnings and my stomach would turn over. I was ready to believe the worst then.

My posting home came as a complete surprise. Jack Barnes and I were offered commando training and we both jumped at the chance. I never had any qualms about joining those sorts of units. I was a soldier through and through and always loved action. But it involved more training and that was to be done back home.

We flew out of Burma in the December, leaving behind sweltering heat, pagodas and the glorious yellow rhododendrons that lined most of the roads, and four days later, after a nerve-racking journey across war-torn countries, landed at a bleak and wintry Scottish airfield. What a change. I was permanently cold for the first couple of weeks until I became acclimatised and would spend my free time wrapped in one of my blankets. Some of the other men thought I was soft, I think, but I soon showed them.

We were barracked at a remote camp and many of my fellow recruits to this new force had already seen combat in Europe. At first, I felt very much the outsider, but I needn't have worried. My recent jungle training and my experience on the Frontier held me in good stead and I was well able to keep up with my fellow trainees. The only thing that caused me trouble was the terrible cold. It was a bad winter.

We went into Glasgow when we had a weekend pass and the city was a sad sight what with the blackout and the rubble everywhere. The people all looked exhausted, as though the war had taken a personal toll even on those who weren't actually fighting. But they displayed a deliberate cheerfulness, even though everyone looked as if their skin was stretched too tight over their bones. They had the same sense of purpose as we soldiers did.

Those people scurrying about the windy streets suffered like us but managed to live with it. Their sons and husbands were away, some killed, some taken prisoner and some, worst of all, posted missing. It was something I had to learn, being new to Britain in the war. And then there was the bombing. I was frightened when the air-raid warnings sounded, but after a few days I got used to it like everyone else.

I knew I was going back to Burma; my training couldn't be wasted, but I was envious of some of the others who were being sent on secret missions in Europe and would be properly in the war. I was being kept in waiting.

'Three weeks' leave, Wilde,' said the major who was in charge of our section. It was the beginning of May and the weather had warmed up. 'When you come back we'll work out how to send you back East. Go and pick up your travel warrant.'

Where to go? That was my immediate problem. I didn't know if Elizabeth had returned home or was still in Liverpool and she and John were the ones I wanted to see. So I took the train to Liverpool and with Elizabeth's last letter, with the dockside address on the top, in my hand found my way to the house.

'Uncle Richard!' crowed the red-headed youngster who answered my nervous knock on the front door. He must have been coming up ten years old then and was as awkward and leggy as a young horse. But he recognised me and threw himself into my arms.

'Mum!' he yelled, turning his head into the house. 'Mum! It's Uncle Richard.'

Oh, but she was thin. Dressed now in a grey nurse's uniform with all her lovely hair covered by a white triangle of cloth and her legs and feet in thick lisle stockings and heavy black shoes. I barely recognised her.

'Elizabeth?' I said, knowing that it was, but unsure at the same time.

She didn't answer but put up her arms so that I could put mine round her and hold her tight. We didn't kiss as lovers, not in front of the boy, but pressing her to me in that close embrace was almost as good.

'Thank God you've come home,' she whispered. 'I've prayed for your safety every night.' Tears had gathered on her lower lids and as we looked at each other, examining every new line on each other's face, they overflowed and fell unchecked down her cheeks.

'Mum?' said John after a moment. 'Mum? Are you all right?'

She pulled herself together then and laughed. 'Of course, silly. I'm just glad that Uncle Richard has come to see us.' And she put up her hand and quickly wiped at her cheek. 'Now, Richard. Come inside and let me get you a cup of tea and something to eat.'

John followed us into the small front room and then as we carried on to the room at the back he squeezed past me to stand beside his mother.

'Are you a commando?' he asked after he had examined the flashes on my battledress and taken notice of my new green beret. I nodded. I was surprised that he knew of this new force, but I shouldn't have been. The children during the war knew everything about the military.

'Golly!' he said, and gazed at me with renewed

respect. His eyes lit upon the bayonet that I kept in a canvas sheath on my belt. 'Can you use that,' he breathed, 'as well as your rifle?'

I nodded and he let out a little whistle. He turned towards the back door. 'Mum,' he said, 'can I go and tell Colin next door about Uncle Richard? Can he come and have a look?'

She nodded and he darted out of the door, leaving us together in that small dark kitchen. I dropped my kit bag on the floor and took her properly in my arms and kissed her until my lips felt bruised. 'Elizabeth,' I murmured, 'I've missed you so much.'

'Me too,' she said, and sought my mouth again.

'Now would this be Richard?' said a voice behind me and, alarmed, I dropped my arms and turned round. An old man stood there, leaning on a stick and grinning.

'Oh, Da,' said Elizabeth, and when I looked back at her I could see that she was blushing. 'We didn't hear you. Yes, this is Richard.'

'Well, I'm pleased to hear that. How d'you do, young feller?'

I shook his hand. 'I'm well, Mr Nugent, thank you.'

'Good,' he said. 'Give him some tea, Lizzie, and some for me, now. I'm parched from walking into town. Look in the bag and see what I've got you.'

I stood back and watched as Elizabeth took the canvas bag from him and delved inside it. 'Da!' she cried joyfully. 'Butter! Wherever did you get it?'

'Don't ask, darling, but would you ever put some on a slice of bread and give this man a decent tea.'

No fuss, no questions from old Mr Nugent. He knew that I was Elizabeth's man and that I made her and John happy. What else could matter?

Chapter Twenty-Three

I'm tired, so very tired. My breath keeps catching in my chest and sometimes I haven't enough to get to the end of a sentence. I don't think I can carry on with this story. What's the point anyway? Who wants to know about the pathetic comings and goings of a foolish man, most of which happened so long ago that the circumstances in which they occurred have been forgotten? It's not as if I am an important person. I've never done anything that mattered to the world, unless you count that one thing. So why on earth should I bother to struggle with this any more? Better to leave the story where it was. Those three happy days with Elizabeth and John, the last I ever had.

Sharon has been irritated with me. 'You're no worse than you were before Christmas,' she said, 'so why are you sitting in your chair and staring out of the window? It's a waste of time. You said you wanted to tell this story and I'm writing it up. What is the problem?'

Of course, she doesn't know. She can't possibly imagine that I can barely bring myself to recount what happened next. How my heart was broken and left in jagged pieces that have never properly healed.

371

'Tell me,' Sharon said, 'did John bring his friend to see you?'

'Yes.'

'And ... what did he say?'

Who cares? I don't even want to think about it. I'd rather look out of the window. And what a sickening sight that is. Bare trees and rain-sodden fields. The hillside is covered in cloud so that I can't even see halfway up. I hate January; it's longer and gloomier than any other month of the year.

When we were young, we used to walk to school in the dark in January and come home likewise and I was always glad when spring began to burst through. I can remember Father taking lamps with him to the byre when he milked the cows. I had the chore of attending to those lamp wicks. I didn't mind that so much. It was a job that was done indoors.

'Get up,' Mother used to shout in the early morning and we would roll out of bed reluctantly and trail across the landing to the new bathroom. When I was a baby, we had no lavatory inside and had to run out of the back door and across the garden to the privy. I don't remember it, but Billy did and would tell me about sitting on the wooden seat doing number twos with snow banked up against the door.

'How horrible,' I would shiver, glad that Father had installed a bathroom with a flushing lavatory, but Billy shrugged.

'I didn't mind it. That sort of thing never bothered me. You're just a sissy.'

Now this house has three bathrooms, two upstairs and one down. I converted the butler's pantry, off the back corridor, into a room exclusively for me. Even Thomas doesn't use it, although I would let him if he asked. I've seen him pee outside, against the laburnum tree, but that doesn't matter. Herbert Lowe always peed on the vegetable patch. He said it was good for the earth and he made a point of doing it on his own vegetable garden. It improved the growth, he said. I told Mother and Marian one day when they were shelling peas in the garden and eating some of them straight out of the pods.

'Little liar,' said Marian hotly, but nevertheless she shook the peas off her lap, where they'd been lying in the cradle of her apron, and stood up. She was heading into the kitchen to wash her hands and probably swill out her mouth.

'He does,' I insisted. 'I've seen him.'

'Oh!' wailed Marian as she flew out through the back door, and after that, whenever she had to pick vegetables, she made sure that her hands were thoroughly washed before she touched anything else. Mother didn't make a fuss; she only smiled. In those days, Mother smiled a lot; it was later, when we were grown up, that she forgot how to do it.

Before she died, the smile did come back. Her last few years were pleasant, I think. I certainly tried to make them so. It was only the two of us then at the farm and I made sure that Mother had two holidays every year. A summer week in Torquay, which is a place she loved, and then another, Easter holiday when I would take her to different places. She liked sightseeing and I would

373

drive to York or Stratford-upon-Avon, places like that, so that she could buy a guidebook and follow in the footsteps of people from history.

She died a few weeks after one of those Easter holidays. We'd been to Edinburgh, quite a long drive, but she was keen to go and had re-read Scott's Waverley novels all through the spring in preparation for a Scottish holiday. It was good weather while we were there, bright sunshine but cold, with a keen wind blowing off the firth.

Mother was in her early seventies and fit from a life of hard work, but that week she did look bad. Her chest hurt, she said, after we'd climbed up to Arthur's Seat to get a panoramic view of the city.

'But it's worth it,' she said, sinking on to a bench and gazing out. 'So beautiful.'

When I took her home, I insisted that she see Dr Trevor.

'He's just a youngster,' she said, getting into the car when I went to collect her. 'Makes too much fuss.' But she did take the pills he prescribed and took his advice to rest more.

She died in her sleep. Heart attack, they said, and a kind death. I was glad for her that she hadn't suffered, but I was lonely afterwards.

'Richard!' It's Sharon. I'd dropped off to sleep and here she is with my supper. Cheese on toast; one of my favourites.

'Are you feeling better?' she asks.

'Yes. I am.' I look at her out of the side of my eye. I feel guilty for being so bad tempered earlier and wonder if she's going to take offence. I needn't worry. Sharon is her usual loving self with me. I'm so blessed, having her. God was smiling on me the day that Sharon and Thomas came into my life.

'Do you feel up to continuing the story now?' she asks after supper is finished and I have a cup of tea on the table beside me. I'm nodding and she fastens the microphone to my jumper.

'Did you stay in Liverpool with Elizabeth and John for your whole leave?' she prompts, taking me back to that late April when I found them again.

'No. I went home for a few days to see Mother and Billy.'

I didn't want to go. In Liverpool, I could pretend that Elizabeth and I were man and wife, although John told all his friends that I was his uncle. Mr Nugent treated me most kindly, and the first night that I was there he took John with him to the Irish club so that Elizabeth and I could have some hours to ourselves.

She had been due to go on duty at the hospital, indeed she was just on her way into the city when I arrived, but she telephoned and got her hours changed.

Colin, John's friend, came round and gazed wide-eyed at the commando insignia on my battle-dress. 'Uncle Richard has been in fights with tribesmen who carry knives. He lives in India where there are tigers and elephants,' said John proudly, showing me off to his young pal.

'Have you really seen a tiger?' the lad asked.

I nodded. 'Several times. And leopards and monkeys. The snakes are as big as this.' I demonstrated the length by stretching out my arms as far as possible.

'Golly!' said the boys, laughing and punching each other the way our Billy and I did when we were excited.

'It's teatime now,' said Elizabeth. 'Off you go, Colin; I expect your mother will be looking for you.'

'She won't,' he said. 'She's taken on an extra shift at the munitions factory. But she's left me some Spam sandwiches.'

'Jesus!' groaned old Mr Nugent. 'For God's sake, feed the boy here, Lizzie darlin'. We've got enough.'

There was barely enough. Hardly any meat in the stew and mostly carrots and potatoes to thicken out the gravy, but it was tasty and we made up the shortfall with bread and butter. The two boys made short work of it.

After tea the children went out and Mr Nugent and I sat in front of the small fire in the front room while Elizabeth washed the dishes in the scullery.

'Are you going to see your brother?' the old man asked, tapping his thumb into the bowl of his pipe.

'Yes,' I said. 'I must visit Mother. Besides, I thought I'd see for myself just what's been going on.'

'Lizzie won't talk about him, you know. I don't understand it.'

'Neither do I,' I said with a sigh, and it was true.

Later, when he and John had gone to the Irish club, Elizabeth took me up to her bedroom. It was small and cold with brown lino on the floor and only room for the bed and the clothes cupboard. It seemed that John slept downstairs on the sofa but he didn't mind. I thought of the space and comfort of the farmhouse and realised that she hadn't made the decision to leave lightly. But all of that came later, after we had made love. It was quiet and gentle lovemaking performed by two people who were deeply in need of each other but exhausted by the circumstances that surrounded them. It didn't make it any less wonderful.

Afterwards, we got up and went downstairs. John and her father might be in at any minute. But we had time for talk.

'Tell me,' I said. 'What made you leave? Was it because of Billy?'

She nodded, pushing a hand through her hair. It had grown again and she wore it tied into a knot at the base of her neck. Our lovemaking had loosened it so that curling strands fell over her thin shoulders.

'It was the work,' she said. 'He couldn't do it all. We're milking too many cows and he's planted up thirty acres of vegetables. With only Ernie, Mother and me, we couldn't get round it all. It was all falling into a mess. We got a couple of men in from the village, but they were poor sorts, not keen to put their backs into anything, and Billy blew his top and told them to clear off.'

She took a deep breath, and when she continued her voice sounded as though it was coming from far away. 'He's started talking to himself, all the time. Sometimes shouting and yelling at the top of his voice, so that John was afraid to go near him.'

'And you?' I asked, sickened by this story of my brother's mental deterioration. 'Did he harm you?'

'He hit me. The day before I left. I heard a shot and went into the yard to see what had happened and he was coming out of the stable with the shotgun in his hand. He had this terrible look on his face, cruel and desperate at the same time. "What is it?" I asked. "What have you done?"

'"I've got rid of Diamond," he said, and then he laughed. "That bloody horse was eating too much and doing nothing for it."

'"You're mad," I shouted, and I tried to get past him to look in the stable to see if he was telling me the truth but he grabbed my arm to stop me going. "Stay out of the yard, you filthy slut," he snarled and fetched me a blow across my head that sent me spinning.

'I was seeing stars and wanted to get into the house, but he levelled the shotgun at me. "I'm not finished," he said as I scrambled to my feet. "I'm going to get rid of everything that doesn't earn its keep or I can't abide." His eyes were tiny and glittering and as he narrowed them to take aim, I believe I nearly died of fright. I knew then that he wanted to kill me. All those years of hating me had boiled up to this one minute and I really think he would have given me the other barrel if it wasn't for Mother coming out of the house.

'"William!" she shouted. "What on earth are you doing?"

'She's the only one who can control him. She saved my life. "Go inside, Elizabeth," she said, and as I hurried past her she whispered, "Phone for Dr Guthrie."

'He came straight away and gave Billy an injection, and he wrote a prescription for tranquillisers and pills that he must take every day. Mother says he's calmer now, but I wasn't going to take the chance. As soon as John came home from school, we left.'

It was a shocking story and I felt truly numb with despair. What a state of affairs – and what condition could the farm possibly be in? I knew I would have to go and see. There must be something I could do.

'Will you go home?' I asked, knowing the answer even before she replied.

She shook her head. 'I don't think so. Despite what Mother says, I think he will try to kill me, some day. He's been wanting to for years.'

'It's my fault,' I groaned. 'Getting you pregnant and you having John. You'd have been safe if it wasn't for me. I'm so, so sorry.'

'It's nothing to do with you,' she said. 'It's because I'm a woman who once showed him her naked body. He'll never get over that.'

I stayed in Liverpool for another couple of days and then took the train home. 'I'll come back before my leave is up,' I said when Elizabeth waved me off at the station. 'Then we can talk about our future.'

You see, we had a future then. She had left our Billy and there was nothing to stop her getting a divorce and marrying me. We would be a family. After the war, I would leave the army and get a job in Liverpool, or anywhere else that she fancied. Our lives would begin anew.

The farm was a mess. It was the hedges that I noticed first as I walked up the lane, all over-

379

grown and untidy. The yard was littered with bits of machinery and rubbish and even the cattle lowing restlessly by the gate looked muddy and unkempt. The smell from the barns and pigsties was overpowering and I had to put my hand to my nose to save myself from the stench of soured milk and the ammonia-laden air. It wasn't my brother's usual way of farming. He'd learned from Father and they were both tidy men.

I could see Elizabeth's car in the machine shed. The wheels had been removed and the car was up on bricks. I don't suppose they had the petrol for two vehicles, but Billy's car was there, parked askew beside the front of the house and filthy from mud and cowshit.

'Richard!' shouted Mother in a joyful voice when I walked into the kitchen. 'Thank God!' She got up from the table where she had been sitting with the farm account books spread out in front of her and reached up to kiss me. 'You're like a blessing from heaven.'

This last surprised me, for Mother wasn't a religious woman at all and never used expressions like that. I expect all the tribulations of the past few months had taken their toll on her normal good sense.

'I hear there's been trouble,' I said when we'd exchanged the usual greetings and I'd explained about my few days' leave. 'I've been to see Elizabeth in Liverpool and she told me.'

Mother nodded, not questioning that visit. She knew where my heart lay, so simply got on with telling me what was going on. The war changed us all. We were becoming more open and honest about things that didn't matter to anyone save the participants.

'William can't manage, you see. He expanded so much before the war, and now that there isn't any labour it's all going to ruin. He's not well, either.' She lowered her voice even though we were the only people in the room. 'He's had a bit of a breakdown.'

'Where is he?' I asked, looking round. The cattle were bellowing in the yard but I could hear no humans about. 'Gone into town?'

'No,' said Mother, 'he's upstairs, in bed. Having a sleep. He does that a lot these days. I think it's the pills that the doctor gives him.'

It was worse than I thought. If Billy wasn't running the farm, who was? Just the lad? And Mother?

'Have you got help?'

She shook her head and, to my great distress, began to cry. 'No one will come,' she sobbed, lifting the corner of her apron to her eyes. 'If I do find someone, he gets rid of them before they've been here a day. There's only Ernie and me. We do the milking, I feed the chickens and he sees to the pigs, I think. But we've had to leave the fields.'

'What about Marian?' I asked. 'And Albert? Can't they help?'

'Albert's useless, you know that, but Marian comes to help in the house and the dairy. Miranda has gone. Fred wouldn't let her stay any longer.'

I put my arms round her and comforted her as best I could. I didn't know what to do. I only had another ten days' leave and then I would have to go back to Scotland. And back East any time

381

after that.

'Right,' I said. 'You wipe your eyes, Mother, and put the kettle on, while I go up and find a change of clothes. I'll milk tonight and then tomorrow I'll go to the village and see if I can't rustle up some labour. There's bound to be someone who could do with an extra bob or two. I dare say some of them would work for a pound of butter or a few eggs. Don't you worry any more.'

I tried to sound confident, but truth to tell I doubted my own words. Our Billy had a bad reputation as a hard master, and if the word had got round that he was a bit barmy getting labour would be impossible.

The lad, Ernie, had crept into the yard from God knows where when I came down in my old clothes. I had heard Billy snoring in the big bedroom but I didn't bother disturbing him. I'd leave him for later.

'Hello, Mr Richard,' the lad said, his big brown animal eyes staring at me unquestioningly as though I'd only seen him the day before. 'Shall I bring the beasts in?'

We got through the milking slowly. I was rusty and he was stupid, but we did it and I hosed down the cattle for good measure and made him fork out the stinking hay and bring in fresh. After that, I went over to the pig pens and had a look round. It was worse in there. An old sow had overlain her litter and I saw decomposing corpses lying amongst the few healthy pigs. 'Jesus!' I said in trepidation, for I'd never liked pigs much, but I got into the pen and gathered up the dead piglets.

'Ernie!' I called, sounding for all the world like

my father. 'When you've finished in the barn, come and help me clean up the sties.'

Fair play, that boy was a good worker when he was given instruction, and even though it was getting dark we worked together to get those two areas of the farmyard decently clean.

'Right,' I said, and reaching in my pocket gave him two half-crowns. 'This is for doing extra work and I thank you very much. Make sure you're here bright and early in the morning.'

'Thank you, Mr Richard.' He opened his mouth in a sweet, gap-toothed smile and stared at the silver coins in his dirty hand. 'My mother will like this money.'

Billy was sitting in the kitchen when I went in. 'Hello, our Dick,' he said, getting up to give me a hug. 'Mother said you were home. I'm right glad to see you.' These words of welcome brought on a bout of tears and he sat down again and sobbed into his handkerchief.

'Never mind crying,' said Mother, practical as ever, 'come to the table now, for I'm sure Richard is starving after all that work.'

He nodded, noisily blowing his nose, and we sat in our old places at the table while Mother dished up a cheese pudding and a couple of sausages each. I looked at Billy out of the side of my eye as we ate. He seemed to have shrunk, somehow. His broad shoulders had lost much of their bulk and even his arms, normally bursting with muscle and power, looked strangely wasted.

'How have you been?' I said.

'Not very well. I've had a funny do.'

'I heard that was a while ago. You should have

got over it by now.'

Mother looked at me anxiously and shook her head, but I carried on. I couldn't help myself. 'The farm looks a bugger. You've let it go badly.'

Wasn't it odd? I was no longer scared of my brother. For the first time in my life I didn't feel inferior to him. I was his equal and, being such, could talk to him man to man.

He took it too, not curling his fists and letting his eyes bulge as they usually did when he was ready for a fight, but quite manfully in a way, accepting that he'd fallen by the wayside. Yet all the time I was talking he kept eating, taking the last scrapings of the pudding from the dish as was his wont. There was nothing wrong with his appetite.

'Father would have a fit if he could see how you've left things,' I continued. 'All his hard work, and your own, is going downhill fast.'

Mother cleared her throat. 'William has been quite poorly,' she said, hoping that I'd let up. 'It's been very difficult for him.'

'Well, he's better now, isn't he? He looks all right.' He didn't, but I chose to ignore that. As far as I could see, nothing was wrong with him that a few days of hard work wouldn't fix. I'd never seen such a pallor on a working man. You could tell that he had been spending too much time indoors. And he hadn't bothered to shave himself for days. That was slacking, something that I wouldn't have put up with in my men.

'Back to work tomorrow, our Billy. And leave off those pills; I reckon you've had enough. What d'you say?'

All this time he hadn't spoken, just sat in front

of his empty plate with his head down. I thought he might be crying again and indeed when he did lift his head I noticed a glimmer of tears in his eyes. But, to my relief, he managed a grin and nodded his head. 'Yes, sergeant,' he said, 'I promise,' and with his old short barked laugh he turned to Mother and added, 'This bugger's better than any of old Guthrie's tonic, eh?'

My last thought before I closed my eyes that night was whether he would do as he promised but, good as his word, he was in the yard before six the next morning and we milked the cows and turned them out on to fresh pasture. He then turned his attention to the bull pen, a place of which I was still terrified, but which my brother treated as though it were as unconcerning as a box full of kittens. I stayed to watch as he swiftly hooked the big bull through the nose and led him into the small enclosure, so that he could sort out the pen. The lad was set to cleaning up all the bits of machinery and feed sacks that were lying around, and later that day, when I drove back in from the town, he had hosed down the yard, so that the cobbles glistened in the bright spring sunlight. Already the place smelt better.

I went first to Fred Darlington, to get the truth of what had happened from him. I knew Elizabeth's version, but Mother had only said that Billy had been ill. She'd said nothing about the shotgun.

'Good to see you home, Dick,' said Fred, pumping my hand. He was in his uniform and was home for a mid-morning cuppa before going out again. 'You've just missed Miranda; she's gone shopping

385

in town.'

When I asked him about Billy he said, 'He's been terrible for a couple of years, ever since the war started. Worse than that damn bull he keeps. Everyone is scared to death of him.' He poured two cups of tea, and clearing a child's colouring book off the table put them down in front of us. 'I'm not surprised that Elizabeth went,' he continued. 'Miranda said she didn't mind going to help your mother for a while, but Billy got worse and I took her away. I got old Guthrie out to him again and he increased the dose of pills. Now I hear he stays in bed all day.'

'He did the milking this morning,' I said, a trifle smugly. 'Nice as pie.' Now I was worried that I'd told Billy to stop taking the pills. My thought had been that he was cured, but now I wondered whether his illness hadn't got a cure and the pills just kept him calm. I didn't know, but whatever our Billy needed it wasn't stuff that kept him in bed all day. I was certain of that.

Fred pursed his lips, wondering, I suppose, whether I was being over-confident. 'How long are you home for?' he asked. 'He needs keeping an eye on.'

'I'm going back to Liverpool next week for a couple of days and then I have to re-join my unit. I've come into the village to find some help. The farm is too big for just Billy and Ernie Fellows. Can you think of anyone?'

Fred shook his head. 'Your brother is a bastard to work for. Always looking for a fight and as tight as hell with money. Besides, most of the able-bodied men have joined up. There are Land

386

Girls on some of the farms but that wouldn't do for yours.'

'Why not?' I asked. I'd forgotten about the Land Army. A couple of healthy girls would work a treat on our farm and we had plenty of empty bedrooms to put them up. That brought another thought. Why hadn't we had any evacuees?

'For God's sake, Dick, surely I don't have to tell you.' Fred sounded exasperated. 'That damn brother of yours isn't safe with women.' I must have looked angry because he put up a hand. 'I know. There isn't any proof, but I for one don't need any. And the people who assign the Land Girls to places in the village know too. That's why none have been offered, nor evacuee children either, for that matter.'

I left his house in a state of turmoil. What on earth was I supposed to do now? Billy had a bad reputation, so our farm, which in normal times produced the best milk in the county and wonderful vegetables, was to be left in a state of disrepair. I couldn't let it happen. It was my home too and I felt I must do something. If the village couldn't help I had to go further afield, so I turned the car towards the main road and headed into town.

At supper that night, I told Mother and Billy what I'd arranged. 'Two young women from the Land Army are coming here tomorrow. They'll sleep upstairs and you, Mother, will be in charge of them.' She looked surprised. 'Like a chaperon,' I explained. 'They will work on the farm and be paid mostly by the government, so you won't be out of pocket. I've met and engaged two suitable girls.'

I'd picked them out specially when I went to the recruiting office where they had registered. One was an older girl, plain, with tortoiseshell glasses and of nun-like quietness. The other was a jolly, heavyset young woman who answered me back in such a way that I was sure she wouldn't take any nonsense from anyone.

Billy appeared to be concentrating on his food. He looked better tonight; the sunshine had added some colour to his skin and he moved more easily around the room. The sleepy lumbering gait of yesterday had all but disappeared. He had enjoyed his day, I could see that, and before I'd raised the subject of the Land Girls he had been speaking quite animatedly about planting up the greenhouses. Now he looked up again.

'I don't want young sluts about the place.' His voice was chilling and I was sickened to hear it. What had gone wrong in his head that made him think of women as sluts? If this was how he planned to behave, then my plan was turning to poison before my eyes. I couldn't allow it to happen.

'Mother,' I said, 'do you mind going upstairs and looking in my kit bag? There are photographs in there that I'd like you to see.' She understood me straight away and left the room with such alacrity that I knew she was glad to go. I stood up and walked round to my brother's chair. 'Listen to me,' I said, grabbing a chunk of his shirt front and pulling him upright. I was boiling with anger at his hateful stupidity. How dare he spoil all the arrangements I'd made on his behalf, just because of some half-cocked ideas he had about women. I wouldn't have it.

'These girls are not sluts,' I said, and I can remember now how nasty my voice sounded. 'They are ordinary, decent young women who are ready and willing to help us stop this farm from going to the dogs, which is what you are letting it do. No one in the village will work for you because you've become such a bastard, but I won't let you destroy all that Father worked for. These girls are coming to the farm and mark my words, our Billy, I've told Fred Darlington that if you so much as lay one finger on either of them, he is to arrest you straight away. Do you understand?'

For a moment I thought the old Billy would burst into life and take me on, for he had a dangerous glint in his eye and he was moving his lips as though in his head he was telling me exactly what he thought of my plan. I sized him up. He was still pretty strong but I reckoned I could best him now if it came to a fight, and when he shook off my hand and heaved himself upright I readied myself. But it proved unnecessary; he was already simmering down.

'All right,' he grunted, and went to the scullery to get his coat. 'I'll have them here. But they're to keep out of my way.'

'Where are you going?' I was worried again, because he was shaking slightly in that way he had once before.

'Nowhere. Just a walk round the stock before dark.' His mood suddenly lightened. He was like that. One moment in a towering rage and the next as calm as could be. 'Come with me,' he said, and gave me a boyish grin. 'I'd like a bit of company.'

Mother came back into the kitchen, just as we were going out. I gave her a little nod behind Billy's back and I could see her chest move as she took in a big breath of relief.

I picked up the girls the next afternoon. The one with the glasses was called Gloria. An incongruous name for such a plain quiet girl, but she didn't seem nervous or anything so I wasn't worried about taking her home. I was pretty sure now that Billy would behave himself. I'd done what Fred had told me to all those years ago and I'd been too scared to do at the time. Someone telling our Billy off, for once, was all that was needed.

The other girl, Ida, was completely different from her companion. She talked all the five miles home, expressing her opinion on how the war was going, what films she'd liked at the picture house and whether this car, Billy's, was worth the money. After a while I ceased listening and allowed her to gabble on unchecked and unanswered. I was thinking about Elizabeth and John. With these two extra people in the house and Billy given a firm warning, it would be safe for them to come home now. I had to get them out of Liverpool and away from the bombing. Surely Elizabeth would agree to that, if only for John's sake.

I stayed at home for another five days, and by the time I left the Land Girls had got into the swing of things and were already working hard. Ida was strong and could easily do the work of a man. She was a huge asset as long as you weren't in earshot, but to Mother's relief she was quiet in the evenings. Apparently she'd been brought up by her father not to talk during mealtimes. We silently thanked that father.

Gloria pulled her weight also. She knew nothing about farming and at first was frightened of the cows. I thought she was going to turn out to be useless, but she had a hidden bit of steel about her and buckled down to the work. As it turned out, she was the one to whom the cows grew attached and the milk yields steadied and then rose as she took over their management.

Billy ignored the girls most of the time, giving them instructions and showing them how to do things but otherwise leaving them alone. He was attending to the fields, which had been left unplanted this spring. It was late on, really, but he thought he could get something in and growing. He cleaned out the greenhouses too and sowed a crop of tomatoes and cucumbers.

It would take a few months, I reckoned, but our farm would get back to normal.

'You've worked a miracle, praise the Lord,' said Marian when she came round the day after the Land Girls came. She had changed the most of all our family. Her hair was grey like Mother's but she now wore it dragged back in a tight bun and she had given up wearing even the merest scrap of make-up. All those smart clothes that she'd worn as Lady Mayoress had disappeared and she now dressed in plain dark jumpers and skirts. Her religion had begun to take over her life.

'God is love,' she would say, apropos of nothing, when sitting in our kitchen having a cup of tea, and when she was in the dairy, separating the cream and putting up the cheeses, she would repeat whole passages of the New Testament.

391

Mother said nothing and would carry on as though this was all entirely normal, but one afternoon, after two hours of Marian's company, she stood with me by the field gate and breathed a great sigh.

'Sometimes, I think that you are the only normal one of the family,' she said to me, linking her arm in mine as we walked through the gate and along the edge of the field. 'Perhaps I was too hard on the other two when they were growing up.'

'You treated me just the same,' I laughed, but I knew she hadn't. I'd been her favourite and spoiled. Of course, it could have been that I had a different father. That fact was left, as ever, unsaid.

We sat on a fallen willow tree by the river. It was a lovely day, the first warm one of the year, and the water sparkled in the afternoon sun.

'Is Elizabeth well?' said Mother, looking away from me and up to the hillside. 'And John?'

I nodded. 'They're fine. John is growing so quickly. He's going to be tall.'

She said nothing for a few minutes and we sat listening to the birds twittering in the alders and the occasional plop of a fish leaping for an insect.

'I was so wrong.' The words came out painfully, and as if for comfort she reached out for my hand. 'Can you forgive me?'

'Yes. That was all over years ago.' It was a lie. I never forgave her, but I couldn't hurt her by saying so.

'Thank you, son.'

We sat a little longer and then got up to walk back to the house. She stopped by the gate where I'd waved her goodbye when I'd first left home.

'Give Elizabeth and John my best love, won't you?' she said. 'I miss them terribly.'

'Not for much longer. I'm going to bring them home,' I said. 'You'll see them in a few days.' The joy that came into her face then was nothing compared to the excitement and relief I felt. I was so proud of myself for what I'd achieved in the last few days. Everything would be all right now.

Chapter Twenty-Four

It was late afternoon when I got back to Liverpool. Elizabeth and John had been sitting having their tea in the little kitchen when I knocked at the door but John ran into the hall when Elizabeth let me in and threw himself into my arms.

'Oh, Uncle Richard,' he cried, 'I'm glad you've come back.'

'So am I, son,' I said and it was true. Much as I loved the farm, this was where I really wanted to be, with Elizabeth and John. If it weren't for the bombing, nothing on earth would make me persuade them to go back.

I could see myself settling in a little house like this, after the war, where everything was open and simple and spoken out loud. Me, Elizabeth and our son. So it was with a glad heart that I joined them at the small table squeezed in between the gas stove and the kitchen cupboard and tucked into jam sandwiches.

'How about going to the pictures tonight?' I said

to Elizabeth, when John had gone upstairs to find his homework books. It occurred to me that she and I had never been out together as a couple. Indeed, we'd never done any of the normal things that young couples in love did. We'd had sex, but in those days that wasn't as normal out of wedlock as it is now. The fear of pregnancy was far too great. But we hadn't been to parties or pictures, or even walked in a park, just holding hands.

She looked doubtful. 'What if there's bombing again?'

'I'm sure they won't come tonight,' I said confidently. 'They've been over three times lately. It's someone else's turn.' I took her in my arms and nuzzled my lips into her neck. 'What about it? There'll be something on in town,' I urged. 'Let's go.'

She grinned. The old Elizabeth was back, relaxed and happy. 'Yes,' she said. 'I'd really like that.'

John came into the kitchen. 'I've got arithmetic and geography tonight,' he groaned. 'It'll take me ages, and Grandfather said he would take me to the ceilidh at the Irish club. Colin and his mother are going too. You could come, Uncle Richard, you and Mummy.'

'Uncle Richard and I are going to the pictures tonight, love, but tomorrow I'm going to make a picnic and we're all going to the seaside for the day. You'll like that, won't you?'

'Yes!' he yelled and I joined him in his little war dance of joy, up and down the narrow hallway.

'Now,' I said, 'let's have a look at that homework. See if I can help you a bit.'

Mr Nugent came home half an hour later, with two oranges and half a pound of sugar in a blue paper bag. Nobody asked where these rations came from, but Elizabeth gave him a little kiss as she took them from his hands and put them safely away in the cupboard. I wondered about Mr Nugent. He seemed to be a gentle old man and was obviously a doting grandfather, but from the little I knew about Elizabeth's childhood, there had been a time when he had been a drunken and neglectful parent. Something had changed him.

'Come on, young feller me lad,' he said after John had put away his books, homework all neatly written out, 'go and get your coat. 'Tis time for the ceilidh.' He looked back at us as he went through the door. 'Don't you two be worrying now; I'll bring the boy home by ten o'clock and make sure he goes to bed. You have a nice night out.'

'Goodbye, Mummy,' called John, chasing after the old man who was striding out, with his slightly rolling gait, down the road towards the docks. 'Goodbye, Uncle Richard.'

It was a fine spring evening with the sun low in a pale sky as Elizabeth and I walked hand in hand through the damaged streets up into the centre of town. Liverpool had been bombed regularly in the past few months, the docks catching the bulk of it though a few stray bombs had done damage further into town. But if you didn't see the collapsed buildings or catch the whiff of acrid smoke which hung around the dockside, you would never guess that this was a city in fear of its life. The people were as cheerful and funny as ever, couples like us, arm in arm, racing up the streets so that they

395

could be in time for the start of the picture show.

Elizabeth was as girlish and relaxed as I'd ever seen her. She wore a dark green coat over a white blouse and a checked green-and-red skirt. Her hair was caught back in two combs and bounced freely on her shoulders, the way it used to in the old days. In later years, when I have seen things about the war on the telly, it always appears in black and white, and I think that is how most young people think of it. But it was brightly coloured, maybe more than the years just before. I felt proud and happy at the same time. Here I was, a strapping young sergeant with flashes on my uniform drawing respectful glances from other servicemen, and on my arm was the prettiest woman in town. I couldn't have been happier.

'Let's see this one,' said Elizabeth, looking at the poster outside the cinema. 'The girls at the hospital have seen it. They say it's wonderful.'

We went in and I can remember that film now. It was *The Philadelphia Story* with Katharine Hepburn and Cary Grant. It was on television only a few weeks ago and I started to watch it, but after ten minutes I turned the set off. It brought so much to the front of my mind. Things that I wasn't prepared to think about, and such overwhelming sadness and despair.

The cinema was full, and at the interval, after the news and cartoon, the lights came on. Elizabeth and I held hands like youngsters, foolish I suppose, but our love life up to now had been difficult and we had been constantly separated. Was it surprising that we couldn't behave like sensible thirty-year-olds? I longed to lean over and kiss her, but she would have been embarrassed in front of all these people. Instead, she talked about her child, our child, who was always to the forefront of her mind.

'I hope John enjoys the ceilidh.'

'Your father will make sure of that,' I replied absently, examining her fingers one by one, admiring the oval of her nails, and after a swift look round I drew her hand to my mouth for a kiss.

She giggled and snuggled up to me. 'Dada loves him. I think he feels that he didn't give my poor brother enough time and is making up for it. You knew I had a brother, didn't you?'

Did I? Maybe. I couldn't remember. Selfishly, at this moment, I didn't care.

'My little brother Ulick. I looked after him when Mammy left. He died of diphtheria,' she said. 'He was only six. I was ten and Dada was out drinking. There was nobody to help me, no neighbours that I knew. No doctor.' The fingers in mine squeezed tight. 'It was horrible watching him, Richard. He was clawing for breath and I couldn't help him because I didn't know what to do. He choked to death.'

I stopped kissing her fingers and looked at her face. It was troubled, but still lovely. My Elizabeth was always the loveliest woman in any room, and even when we were standing in the lobby of the cinema, waiting to buy our tickets, some men had turned to look at her. I don't think she'd noticed. That was the thing about her. She wasn't aware of anyone outside her immediate circle of interest. I was lucky; she loved me so my interests had become hers. Maybe this was the time for our chat about home, and I practised a few sentences in my head as I decided how to broach the subject. But it was no good; she was still thinking about her childhood.

'I vowed then that I would never allow myself to be poor like that again.' She gave a short laugh. 'And I haven't been poor, have I? Not in money. Just, well ... you know.'

I did know, but here I was planning to send her back to where she would be miserable. My words were pap, but the best I could do. 'You've got me, sweetheart,' I said, 'for the rest of our lives.'

We were quiet then, sitting together in that crowded theatre as the lights went down and the curtains swished open.

The funny thing was that I didn't really watch the film. My eyes were on the screen, but of course my mind was elsewhere, planning how to tell her that she must go back to the farm and take John with her. They must be safe at all costs. With the two Land Girls and Mother about the place all the time, our Billy wouldn't dare touch her. Perhaps her father would like to go with them. Then she wouldn't have to worry about him either. Yes, that was it. That was what I was going to suggest. After the film was over, we would go for a supper at the Kardomah café and I would explain what I had arranged at the farm and that she had to go. It was relief in a way to have thought it all out and I sat back then to try to catch up with the unfolding story in front of me.

But I was too late. Suddenly, a message was flashed across the screen and the lights went up. An air-raid warning was sounding outside and we were instructed to get up calmly and walk to the nearest shelter.

'Oh,' whispered Elizabeth, and when I looked down at her I saw that the colour had drained from her face and that her lips were beginning to wobble. 'John,' she murmured. 'I must get home.'

There wasn't time. The sirens were wailing as we left the cinema and the ARP wardens were insistent in their directing us to the shelters. We had no choice but to join the throng hurrying down into a damp and smelly underground place of safety. What a dreadful place it was too. For Elizabeth's sake, I kept my feelings of disgust to myself. This was my first experience of being in an air-raid shelter and I fervently hoped it would be my last, and hers too. We could hear the sickening crump of bombs falling so close by that plaster and brick dust was shaken loose from the ceiling and showered down on our heads.

I put my arm round Elizabeth's shoulder and muttered some words that I hoped would comfort her as we sat huddled together on the slatted bench. She was white with anxiety and flinched each time the distant thud of an explosion echoed through the cavern. 'Will they be all right, Richard?' she kept saying, and then, 'We should never have left them.'

'Don't worry,' I said, trying to keep my voice as light and cheerful as possible, 'your father will look after John. They'll be fine.'

She nodded, but I could see that my words had not reassured her.

It was nearly two hours later when we were able to leave the shelter and climb nervously up the steps and out into a dusty night. The city was a horrible sight, bleak and dark around us, with people scurrying away, shouting desperate good-byes to each other as they hurried home. To the south, down by the river, the sky was lit up by huge fires stretching like burning fingers into the sky and the air was full of acrid smoke.

'Quick!' said Elizabeth, tugging at my hand. Her eyes were wild as she looked towards the dock area.

The closer we got to the docks, the brighter the night became. A red glow suffused the sky, and it seemed that everything in front of us was part of a great inferno. The noise was tremendous, with further explosions and the sound of collapsing buildings, and above all the banging and crashing the incessant ringing of ambulance and fire-engine bells told a frightening story. These appliances kept passing us, backwards and forwards, swerving round corners in their terrible haste, and each time an ambulance screamed past Elizabeth would whimper in terror and increase her head-long dash to the little terraced house that had become her refuge.

'Get your breath,' I said, taking her arm in an attempt to halt her reckless flight, but she shook me off as though I were nothing but an un-necessary hindrance.

'I have to get to John,' she gasped. 'Don't try to stop me.'

I wasn't, but it would have been useless trying to point that out so I hurried along beside her, jost-ling now and then with other frightened people who were running in the same direction. I knew that they were the same people we had seen laughing and joking on their way into town only a few hours earlier. Then they had been enjoying the peace of a spring evening and now they were grim-faced and terrified. The fate of their families was all that concerned them.

We came to the top of the street where Elizabeth lived and to my relief I saw that the houses were standing. There was damage. Most of the windows were out and the road was littered with bricks and slates from the roofs, but you could see that none of these houses had taken a hit.

'It's all right,' I said. 'It hasn't been touched. You can stop worrying.'

'Thank God,' she whispered, and she took my hand again while we walked, slower now, towards the little red-brick terraced dwelling.

People were out in the street, standing back to look up at their houses, pointing out broken windows and chimneys to their neighbours. Relief was almost tangible and within minutes you could hear the shouted jokes and good humour returning to these brave men and women. But my heart sank when I looked towards the bottom of the street where a huge fire was burning. It would seem that a docked ship had taken a direct hit, and even as we reached Elizabeth's front door an ambulance, bell clanging dementedly, rattled past us up the hill.

'Poor souls, whoever they are,' said Elizabeth sympathetically, her eyes following the white vehicle as she opened her front door. She paused and turned back to me. 'I think I'd better go in to the hospital. I expect I'll be wanted.'

'Yes.' She was right, I suppose. In war we all had to do our bit, but I had hoped to spend the night in her arms and I was bitterly disappointed.

'John, Dada,' she called as we went into the hall. The house was dark. The electricity had gone from the whole street and a keen draught was coming in through the smashed front windowpanes.

'John, we're home. Where are you?'

I could hear the wind getting up and the crackling of wood in the distance. Flecks of soot danced in through the windows, bringing a sour hot smell of burning paint. I could imagine the mess down at the docks, see the mangled ironwork and smashed buildings. I could even picture grey paint curling and squirming into vapour as it burnt off the hulls of docked ships. But that was down there. Here, the house was not that badly damaged and could be repaired quickly. The only thing was that it was empty. We received no reply to Elizabeth's call and I think I knew then. The silent house presaged the silent years to come.

'John!' Elizabeth's voice was getting more hysterical and I could only stand back helplessly as she tore up the steep narrow staircase and then down again and into the little back kitchen.

'They're not here,' she wailed, and ran out of the house into the street.

'John,' she called again, looking up and down, searching the faces of the people who were standing around for the two she wanted to see. 'Dada,' she screamed, her voice growing more and more desperate.

I took her arm. 'Stop it,' I said. 'Pull yourself together.'

She had started to cry and I reached for her and took her into my arms, but it was no good. She didn't want me. She wanted her son.

'They'll be at the club,' I said. 'I expect they went into the shelter when the warning came and then continued the dance when the all-clear sounded. Look,' I pointed to my watch, 'it isn't even ten o'clock yet.'

'Oh, do you think so?' Her face relaxed and she clung to my hand. 'That'll be it, won't it?'

I nodded, but truth to tell even then I was doubtful. The docks had taken a fearful hammering and the Irish club was right there, beside the shipping offices.

'You stay here,' I said. 'I'll go down and find them and bring them home. I'll give your father what for for frightening you so.'

She wouldn't have it, of course, determined to accompany me down the street until we came to the T-junction and the broad road that bordered the dock. It was a dreadful sight down there. Burning ships and buildings crackling and splitting in the ferocious heat and people running about like demented animals. It's hard to be brave when your fellow man is suffering and you can't do anything about it.

We were stopped about a hundred yards along the road by an ARP warden and a policeman.

'You can't go any further, sergeant,' said the warden, putting up his hand to stop us. 'It's too dangerous.'

Elizabeth spread her arms in a pleading gesture. 'Please,' she said, 'please. My son and my father came down here tonight. To the Irish club. It's just

403

over there. I want to see if they're all right.'

I caught the look that passed between the two men and my heart turned to ice. The place she had indicated was a smouldering ruin of broken bricks and roof tiles.

'Best not,' said the policeman, looking meaningfully at me. 'I think you should take the lady into the church there.' He pointed towards a wretched little chapel that stood at right angles to the road and bore a large sign which read 'Accounting Station'. 'There'll be people in there who can help you.'

'Oh, God,' said Elizabeth brokenly and I took her arm and half carried her into the church.

Inside, it was very quiet. Two or three stunned-looking women sat on the pews and, towards the back, where the font should have been, a couple of men sat at a table and stared fixedly at a list of names. I sat Elizabeth in the nearest pew and went to the table.

'I'm looking for John Wilde, a young lad, and his grandfather, Ulick Nugent,' I said. 'They came down here this evening.'

'Were they in the Irish club?' said the older man. I noticed he wore a dog collar and that the cuffs of his jacket were worn and dirty. A smear of soot painted one eyelid and cheek and his white hair was full of dark specks.

'Yes.'

'I'm sorry.' He had an educated voice that sounded strange here, but it was full of compassion. 'It took a direct hit. No survivors.'

I wanted to vomit. My stomach lurched and heaved like the worst case of seasickness, and when I turned to look at Elizabeth it felt as though the world had suddenly turned to slow motion and that every sound was coming to me from a long way off.

'No!' she was shouting. 'No!' and she was getting up from the pew and racing towards the church door.

With legs like lead I followed her, my steps seemingly huge but somehow not covering the ground, and I feared I would never catch her. To my relief, the man sitting beside the minister jumped from his chair, took her in his arms and brought her to a halt.

'Steady, missus,' he breathed. 'There's nowt you can do out there.'

She started screaming then and, coming to my senses, I took over from the young man and held her in my arms, shushing her cries and stroking her hair until the screaming stopped and she was still.

After a minute she whispered with renewed confidence and determination, 'It isn't true, Richard. They must have already left and gone into town to find us.'

What could I say? Only that it was possible and that when we went back to the house we would find them there waiting. But I knew that it would be a lie, so I put my arms around her again and pressed my face into her hair.

The minister pushed back his chair. 'If I can have a word,' he said, touching my elbow and jerking his head towards the vestry.

I straightened up and whispered to Elizabeth, 'I won't be a moment,' and walked to where the old man was indicating.

'There are a few bodies in here,' he said, pointing towards the closed door. 'They need to be identified.'

I swallowed and could feel myself backing away. I couldn't do this. I couldn't look at smashed and broken corpses that only a few hours earlier had been alive and joyful. But I glanced back over my shoulder to where Elizabeth was sitting alone and desolate in the hard polished pew and took a deep breath. I had to do it. I couldn't let her look at her son and father in the state they were probably in. So I nodded and allowed the old minister to lead me into the little room behind the chapel.

It was lit by an oil lamp like the one we used to have in the kitchen, and as I sniffed the oily smoke comforting memories of home flashed into my head. These were soon dashed when I looked down. About ten bodies lay on the floor, covered in red ambulance blankets.

'Are these all of them?' My words were foolish but hope began to spring. There must have been more people than this at the ceilidh. Obviously, some had escaped

The minister cleared his throat. 'These are the only ones that could possibly be identified,' he said. 'The others were too,' he stopped and looked at me, hoping, I suppose, for some measure of understanding, 'badly damaged. Please look for your loved ones.'

I didn't find Mr Nugent but John's was the third body in the back row. The minister had gently lifted the blankets one by one until I stayed his arm when he came to our boy. He lay like a sleeping child, half on his side and barely marked, apart from a large gash stretching the length of his white forehead and trailing up into his dusty thatch of red hair.

'Oh, my God,' I groaned, as I knelt beside him and put a trembling hand on his cheek. He was already cold and getting stiff.

'Can you identify this child?' said the minister formally.

At first I couldn't speak. I had so desperately hoped that Elizabeth would be found to be right and that they had escaped. But here, lying before me, was the lie to that and I was obliged to answer. 'Yes,' I said, my voice hollow and weak. I suddenly felt unbearably tired. 'This is my son, John Edward Wilde.'

And do you see? With those words, I had been allowed to acknowledge my own child for the first time. It was almost a comfort.

The tears came then, not noisy or hysterical but deep and wrenching as though a part of me had been torn out and thrown into oblivion. I mourned him then and for ever after. He was a lovely boy and would have been a fine man, had he been allowed to live. He would be here now to see me through this last journey.

'I must tell his mother,' I said, wearily standing up and moving carefully away from the kind hand that the minister had laid on my shoulder. 'She might want to see him.'

When I went back into the church, she looked up at me and her eyes searched mine vainly for some inkling of hope. It was dreadful having to witness her distress and I think the hours that followed were the hardest I ever had in my life. There was nothing I could do but just sit beside her and put my arm round her thin shoulders.

'Have you found him?' she asked.

I nodded. 'You must go in. It would be better.'

'Is he...?'

'He looks all right,' I said. 'As though he's sleeping.' I pulled her to her feet. 'Come on, my love. Come and say goodbye to our little lad.'

I was proud of her. She didn't scream or fuss as I took her gently by the arm and led her into the vestry. The minister was there standing beside the still little body and at Elizabeth's approach he lifted the blanket away from John's face.

'Oh, my son,' she crooned, kneeling on the floor beside him, 'my baby boy.' And while I stood there, helplessly, beside her, she gathered his small stiff body into her arms and rocked him and stroked the hair from his darkening face.

After a while, it was more than I could bear and I knelt down beside her. 'Leave him, Elizabeth, and come home. You can't stay here any more.'

But she had changed again. Her face was terrifying when she looked up. 'Take your hands off me,' she snarled. 'This is my son and I'll stay here as long as I want.' And she went back to her rocking and crooning, for all the world like some wounded animal.

I looked up to the minister, hoping for some words from him that would persuade her, but he folded his lips and turned away. Another man had come into the vestry and was standing looking at the blanketed corpses with an expression of disbelief.

'Can I help you?' the minister was saying, but I lost the rest of the quiet conversation because Elizabeth had started to cry with great racking sobs and I had to comfort her.

'Oh, come now, sweetheart,' I said. 'Leave him, he's safe here,' and I gently pulled my son from her arms and laid him back on the scratched wooden floorboards. 'We'll take him home when I've found some decent transport. I'm not carrying him through the streets in front of all your neighbours. It's not dignified.' I led her away, out of the little chapel and up through the now deserted streets to the dark and empty house.

An ambulance brought him to the house a couple of hours later and I laid him on the bed that had belonged to his grandfather. My Elizabeth never spoke, but got a basin and cloth and washed him, kissing his face and hands all the while. Later she dressed him in clean clothes and bringing a chair from her bedroom sat beside him through the last few hours of the night.

We buried him two days later in the churchyard of the sailors' church not far from where he'd died. I'd managed to telephone home and tell them the sad news. I thought that Billy might come to the funeral, but he wouldn't.

'I can't,' he said brokenly. 'It would be too hard. You must be in charge.'

'Elizabeth won't bring him home,' I said. 'He's to be buried here.'

There was silence at the end of the line and then Billy cleared his throat. 'It doesn't matter.

I'll put a memorial for him in the churchyard. His name won't be forgot.'

Mother came on the phone then and cried so bitterly that we had very little conversation. 'She must bring him home,' she sobbed.

But I told her what had been decided. 'It's Elizabeth's choice,' I said. 'Her comfort is all that matters, now.'

I did try to persuade her otherwise. 'We must take him home,' I said, on the morning after his death. 'He must be buried in St Winifred's.'

'No!' Her voice was cold and strange. 'I don't want him alone with all those Wildes he never knew. He can rest here until I take him back to his people.'

'What people?' I said, confused.

She meant Ireland, and that is where he is now. With her and her grandparents and the little plaque added to the gravestone that remembers her father, whose body was never found. There's space there for me too and I have made all the arrangements. In eternity, Elizabeth and John and I will be together.

Mother came to the funeral, arriving by train. She was in the church before the hearse arrived and Elizabeth and I, walking side by side behind the coffin that contained our son, were surprised to see her.

'Thank you for coming, Mother,' said Elizabeth, placing her cold face against Mother's tear-stained one. 'It is a comfort.'

I don't think it was. Elizabeth had retreated into her own self and drawn up a barrier around her

410

that shut out everyone, including me. Our brief conversations in the two days following John's death had dealt with practical details. I had arranged the funeral, ordered the single wreath and asked the kind minister who had been present in the temporary mortuary to conduct a short service.

But all of this I did on my own. Elizabeth drifted around her little house like a ghost, never in the room that I was in but leaving an aura of her sadness that was almost tangible. She couldn't be comforted.

I thought about asking the minister to speak to her; maybe he would know the words that would give her some measure of peace.

Poor man, he did try. 'Maybe,' he said, kindly, 'the Lord in His goodness will bless you with another child. Not to make up for this sweet soul gone to glory but another child who will be loved for his own sake.'

Of course he didn't know the true circumstances, but Elizabeth turned away from him and me and went back up the stairs to sit beside her son.

He tried again at the funeral. 'You have had your son for ten years,' he said to us, as we sat numbly in the bare church staring at the small coffin. 'That is what you must carry in your heart. He has given you a love that will never die.'

I can't remember anything else, but I do know that he was as good at conducting a funeral as any other priest I've ever met. The words were kindly meant and if we couldn't appreciate them it wasn't his fault.

Elizabeth, Mother and I followed the little coffin to the cemetery where my son was temporarily laid to rest in a small grave close to others who had died on the same night. Several funerals were taking place that afternoon and our little procession was swamped by the grieving families of other victims. But it was all properly done and I think Elizabeth understood that the fortunes of war led to scenes like this.

'I have to go,' I said the day after. My leave was over and I had to go back to war. 'I don't want to leave you, but I have to return to my unit.'

'Yes,' she said. But I don't think she cared. Her mind was totally wrapped up in the deaths and nothing else mattered.

'Will you go back to the farm?' I asked. 'Mother needs you.'

'The hospital needs me.'

I shook my head. 'They've got volunteers. You must go home. It's not safe here.'

But she wouldn't listen, and when I hugged her and kissed her goodbye all that I got in return was a disinterested request to look after myself.

I went back to war confused and heavy of heart. I had lost my only son, and with him all my plans for our happy future had blown away like blossom on a cold northern wind. And there was no comfort for that.

Chapter Twenty-Five

This is no longer Richard, this is Sharon. I came into his room first thing this morning and found him sitting in his chair very upset, and when I asked 'What's up?' he just shook his head. Somehow, he'd got himself out of bed and into that chair beside the window and was very cold and stiff and as white as the snow outside. I called the nurse. Luckily, she'd stayed last night and she came down half dressed and looking oddly normal, like someone's mum. Usually, each morning, when she appears ready for work, she is plastered in God-awful orange make-up, for all the world like some old slapper. It's cruel of me, I know, thinking about her like this, but Christ, she is a horrible sight on a cold winter morning. Jason reckons she spends her days off plying for trade on the road up to the factories.

'Oh yes?' I said. 'You'd know all about that, would you?'

All he does is laugh. I like that about him. He knows when I'm joking. Andrew takes life so seriously. If I'd said that to him, he would have considered the implications for ages. He likes to pretend he's relaxed, but he isn't really.

Anyway, back to the nurse and Richard. Normally I've little respect for her, but this morning I was glad when she immediately took charge.

'Good heavens!' She took one look at him and

started clucking like one of the Hydes' chickens. 'Mr Wilde,' she squawked, 'getting out of bed by yourself is absolutely against doctor's orders.'

I knew he didn't feel well because he let it go and didn't tell her to bugger off as he usually does. She puts up with a lot from him without taking offence, which is pretty impressive, but at the same time she can be a pain in the neck and her voice doesn't help either. It's too high and screechy; she sounds like a bloody parrot. I guess I should be grateful and I am. I can do her job when I have to, but I don't like it much and he doesn't like me doing it. He is conscious of his dignity.

I went to make him a cup of tea while she gave him his bottle and saw to him below. By the time I came back, she had gone upstairs to get dressed.

'Drink this,' I said, leaning over him to put the cup to his lips. He sipped weakly, all the time gazing up at me with an expression of such sadness that I felt like gathering his old body in my arms and kissing him better. I noticed dry crusts of tears on his cheeks. Poor Richard. Some memory had really upset him.

Nurse saw me dabbing at his face when she came back and pushed me away. 'Move over, Sharon,' she said. 'I'll give him a top and tail and then it's bed for you, my lad.'

I looked at him and grinned to show him what I thought of her, but for once he didn't smile back. His old blue eyes just stared back at me for a moment before he turned away, back to gazing out of the window.

Later, after we'd got him into bed and settled him comfortably, he slept for a couple of hours

414

and it gave me time to listen to the tape and start to get it on to the computer. Now I know why he was so sad. It took me all my time not to cry too, when I listened to his voice describing how his son had died. At times it was almost impossible to hear it, because he must have been choking back tears, but I think I've got it down.

Thomas came in when I was typing and asked why I looked so unhappy. I didn't want to tell him, so I laughed. 'I'm not unhappy,' I said. 'It's just my face.'

'Well you've got a very funny face, then.'

'Not as funny as yours, cheeky.'

After we'd stopped laughing I told him that we mustn't make much noise today because Richard wasn't very well. His face fell. 'Is he going to die?' he asked.

I nodded. 'He's very old, love, and has a bad illness. I don't think he'll live much longer.'

He started kicking that damn football round the kitchen, even though I've told him a hundred times not to do it 'It's not fair,' he said when I told him to take it outside.

'I don't care. You're not to kick that ball indoors. Do you hear me?'

'I'm not talking about that, silly,' he shouted, picking up the ball and going to the hall door. 'Mr Richard going to die. *That's* not fair!'

He's right, it isn't fair. Richard doesn't want to die and I don't want to lose him, or leave here. This is the first time in my life that I've had a secure home and I'm going to hate to leave it. I love this house. I love the space and the light and more than that I love the fact that Thomas is safe and happy.

I know I'm clutching at straws. We can't stay here and I'll have to make a decision soon.

When he woke up I went to sit with him and we watched the snow swirling around the garden. It won't lie, at least that's what the forecast on the telly said. It'll all be gone by morning. But it was pretty.

'Did you listen?' he asked.

'Yes.'

He was quiet for a bit and then said, 'It hurt me getting all that out. I've never liked to think about that time.'

'It must have been terrible,' I said. 'I think you're very brave talking about it.'

'War is terrible. All of it. There's nothing good in it for anyone.'

'Oh, well,' I said, 'don't think about it again. Have a rest from your story for a few days.'

You'd have thought I'd told him to stop breathing, the way he looked at me. 'Don't be so stupid,' he snapped, and his voice was nasty. 'I'll be dead in a few days.'

I hate him talking like that. Even though he's so ill, I almost gave him an earful back, the old bastard, yelling at me. But just as I was taking a breath he stopped me. With surprising strength, considering how feeble he'd been this morning, he put out his hand and touched my arm.

'I'm sorry, my dear. I didn't mean to lose my temper. Not with you, of all people.'

I swallowed my sudden anger. 'It's OK. I don't mind.' I took his hand in mine and we sat in silence for a while.

'Is your story finished now?' I asked eventually. I am stupid, because after what he'd said just before, it's obvious that it isn't.

'No,' he said, sitting forward on his pillows, his chest heaving. 'I must get down some more. I have to tell it. It's got to be straight. The record has to be put straight.' His cheeks were burning hot now and the hand in mine was shaking quite badly.

I got worried and wondered about getting the nurse down again, but then I remembered that she had gone into town for some shopping.

'OK,' I said, 'calm down. I only wondered. We can do some more whenever you're ready.' What the hell, I thought. What difference can it make? I want him to be happy and if this is what does it for him, then so be it. Never mind what the nurse or even that creepy Donald Clewes thinks. Richard is the person who matters most.

He lay back on the pillows and for a moment I thought he was dropping off again, but he turned his head and looked at me. 'Get the microphone,' he said. 'I'll tell you about the jungle.'

I fastened the mike to his collar and sat beside him again with my notebook. I'm so glad now that I did that shorthand course. But he waved me away.

'Leave me now, Sharon. I want to be alone for this.'

I left and went into the kitchen to make some soup. When I walked by his room later I could hear him still talking and had to persuade the nurse not to go in. 'He's busy,' I said, and she gave me one of her looks but left him undisturbed for another hour.

It was when he was sleeping that I listened to the tape. His voice is getting weaker, but I know what he's saying, so when he started with 'I hated it', and then took a deep breath followed by a short silence, I waited and listened for the rest.

I hated it. Hated the dripping undergrowth that slowed us down so much that our patrols were often late reaching the rendezvous and the officer waiting for us would be nervously pointing to his watch and giving forth with a stream of curses. It steamed and stank. Horrible, sour, rotting smells of dead animals and people, but then sometimes it was disgustingly sweetened by the exotic ripening fruits growing around the edges of the dense wet forest. You could feel sick merely taking in a breath, but that could have been fear as well.

We were all frightened, and any man who says he wasn't is a liar, or mad. Nobody admitted it at the time, of course; banter was the order of the day, banter, filthy jokes and foul language. How else do men keep their courage up? Not the Bible, I can tell you. Even the padre, who was part of our company, kept his religion to himself, turning away and pretending to adjust his pack whenever we had a prisoner to dispatch. God was on our side, you see. The Japs were heathens.

Seeing Japs burst out of the jungle in front of us, yelling and screaming, firing wildly, with their little officers waving swords and the sun glinting off their glasses, was a sight that made my guts turn to water. It took all my training and nerve to stay calm and keep my finger on the trigger of my Lee-Enfield.

418

'Wait,' I would hiss to my squad, 'and keep your fucking heads down.'

I wonder if I could have been so steady if I had been just an ordinary squaddy. Being in charge makes you think more clearly, and having to care for frightened young men is a great boost towards behaving well. They liked me, I think, and trusted my judgement. Lewis's cheerfulness and good sense in battle helped too. Before he was killed, I managed to get him his stripes back. He deserved them.

That bastard Captain Parker came with us on one mission. Why? Well, I don't think it was his idea. All his career he had stayed out of direct trouble, hiding in an office and criticising those who did the real soldiering. I couldn't stomach him. Trying to play the big I Am when he barely knew what the hell he was doing. Jack Barnes took him aside and gave him a mouthful, which we weren't supposed to hear, but we did.

'You'll answer to a court martial for that, Lieutenant Barnes,' said Parker.

'Do what you fucking like when we get back to base, but here, keep your mouth shut. You haven't a clue what's going on and will get us all killed if you carry on.'

We fell into an ambush on the last night of our patrol. Our objective was to cut the railway line between Rangoon and Mandalay and cause havoc to the Jap supply system. We'd done it and were on our way out when we came upon a nest of Japs. Walked straight into them, surprising them eating their supper. Normally we would have smelt them first before stumbling into their clearing; you always could. It was their food you could pick out above the smell of the jungle, but that night the monsoon rains were teeming down, deadening everything for miles around, and we strolled into their camp.

'Surrender,' screamed Parker, before anyone had moved.

'Fuck that,' I lifted the Bren I'd been carrying that day, a useless weapon most of the time, and sprayed a round into the group sitting round the campfire. The rest of the squad followed my lead and Jack Barnes threw a couple of grenades into the clearing, but Parker ran around, hands up, begging the Japs to take him prisoner. To my alarm, more of them suddenly appeared out of the trees, firing like crazy and screaming the way they always did.

I'm not sure who killed Parker, but one of us did. He suddenly tipped over sideways, hands still in the air and lunatic eyes wide open. I know that I fired a volley of shots in his direction and out of the side of my eye I saw Jack Barnes raise his pistol and take careful aim. But then the Japs were after Parker too. Maybe they got him.

After it was over, we looked down at him, the only one of us killed, though a couple of men had wounds and one died of his later, in the hospital after we got back.

'What about him?' asked Jack.

'We'll bury, him here. Killed in action. Very honourable,' I said. I never looked him in the eye and he was the same. Nothing more was said, but I was secretly glad. All those years of snide remarks, ignorant comments and put-downs. Captain Parker was one man who needed killing, in my book.

Oh, it makes me tired even thinking about those years of fighting. It wasn't only the combat, it was the waiting. If I close my eyes, I'm in a little clearing, back against a tree, eyes peeled wide open for the slightest movement in the green dripping mass in front of me. And Lewis, beside me, sucking his teeth as he always did when all the world was still, and I can see the knuckles of his hand whitening as he gripped the barrel of his Lee-Enfield.

At night he would hum very softly, always the same tune: 'Bobbie Shaftoe'. I learned that as a child and didn't realise that it was a Geordie song until I heard him. Lewis didn't even know the words, only the tune, over and over again. It didn't matter how many times I told him to shut up: after a quick 'sorry' he would start up again.

'I been told that the little yellow bastards are probably deaf, man,' he would whisper, and then grin at me with brown teeth.

Bloody nuisance he was and I swear he once gave our position away with that damn song, but none the less I always felt safe when he was around. He would watch my back, see.

It was hard staying awake sometimes, especially when you'd been tracking through the jungle all day and crossing rivers on to higher ground. My legs would be like jelly when we stopped and I was almost afraid to sit down for fear of never getting up. And then when I did I could feel my eyes closing, sitting on the ground knowing that the forest around us and the rocks above could be swarming with the enemy, ready and eager to kill me.

This is Sharon again. Richard drifted off when I went in to him so I brought the tape back here into the kitchen to listen to while I made supper. Jason came round to join us. I told him about Richard's army service and how horrible he had made it sound.

'I knew about that,' he said. 'Everyone in the village does. He was in the thick of the action in the Far East until he was invalided out. I think he was what they called a Chindit, sort of special forces. They went behind enemy lines to blow up bridges and railways. You should see his medals. He pins them on for Poppy Day and my dad says that they would outdo every man in the district. He won the Military Cross, amongst other things.'

The medals are in the drawer of his desk. He got them out once to show Thomas, holding the double row out in his old shaking hand so that my little boy could take them.

'When did you get this one, Mr Richard?' he asked, pointing to a medal with a red, white and blue ribbon.

Richard touched the metal cross. 'I can't remember,' he said, and stared at the silver medal and ribbon as though it would tell him the story he had forgotten. 'I can't remember,' he said again, and he looked so distressed that I took the medals out of Thomas's hands and put them on the table.

'Enough now, love,' I said. 'It's time for bed.'

He went up and I stayed with Richard, who was looking at the row of medals as though they were something he had never seen before.

'This is the Military Cross,' he said, pointing to the one that Thomas had been waving about. 'And do you know, I can't remember what I did to get it.'

'It doesn't matter,' I said. 'Whatever you got it for, it means that you were a very brave man.'

'Maybe,' he said, sitting back in his chair to stare again out of the window. He is getting vague now and almost far away.

I came back to him this evening after Nurse had finished and he was more awake.

'I want to talk some more,' he said. 'I have to get it recorded.'

'OK,' I said. 'I'm all yours.'

For some reason that tickled him and he started to laugh; so much that it brought on a bout of coughing and he had to have a few whiffs from the oxygen machine before he was ready to speak again.

'I used to say that to Elizabeth, when she telephoned to ask me about a problem on the farm in Ireland. It was a joke between us, don't you see? I was always "all hers" in every way. She wasn't the same. She didn't want me as a permanent fixture after John was killed. "I can't be hurt again," she'd say. "You could be killed too." But I didn't give up.

'That's what I spent the money on, the money that Billy had given me and the extra that I'd saved. I bought her a farm in the west of Ireland. It was nothing much when we took it, a hundred acres or so, which sounds a lot, but land was dirt cheap then and that particular lot wasn't the best grazing. Later on she added to it bit by bit. She was a good businesswoman and I helped her with money, so by the end she had bought up the whole estate. Estate, ha! Six farms that brought in a few quid and a big grey stone house set in five acres of overgrown parkland that needed all of that few quid and more spending on it. It must have been wonderful once, but the last owner lived in it like a pig. Fair play, the old boy was well into his nineties when he passed on and had been taken for a ride by all his tenants, save Elizabeth.

'"My God," I said when I went over in the sixties and she had moved into the big house, "you're quite the lady of the manor. All this parkland, and a lake, for Christ's sake."

'All she did was laugh. "Nice, isn't it? Or at least it will be," she said, and rang the bell for the maid to bring us tea.

'From the drawing room, you could see across the park to the village church and the cemetery where my son was buried. As I stood looking out on the view Elizabeth brought me a cup of tea and lingered beside me.

'"We're all together now," she said. "That's what I always wanted."

'That night in her grand bedroom, she asked me to leave home and come and live with her in Ireland.

'"D'you mean that? Do you mean marriage?" I was flabbergasted. For all those long years after John died, she had kept me at arm's length, welcoming my regular visits but never wanting our old closeness to be resurrected. We'd been together often; I went to see her four or five times a year and we were as loving as ever. There was never a problem about our loving each other, that side of us never faded, but she wouldn't make the commitment and I had to be grateful for the part

424

of our lives that we did have. It wasn't so bad, you know. Not many people are lucky enough to have a love affair that lasts for nearly forty years.

'I lay on that huge four-poster bed beside her and gazed at the Chinese patterned wallpaper that she had left on the walls. It was torn in places and faded in others but most of it was fine. It was lovely: turquoise blue, with peacocks and pagodas and little bridges perched over running streams. You could stare at it for ever.

'"You want to marry me after all this time?" I said again, turning to face her and uncertain that I had heard her correctly.

'"Yes, I do."

'Oh, what a facer. I had wanted this for all of my adult life and now she was finally offering us the chance to live out the rest of our lives together. My Elizabeth, still beautiful at sixty with her white hair and brilliant blue eyes. She turned heads even then, when we went for a meal or now and then to the races, which I had grown to enjoy. My family had never gone racing. It was a bit too rich for our plain Protestant blood, but when I was with her in Ireland all that nonsense was put aside. A day on a muddy racecourse, with a roll of notes in one mackintosh pocket and a flask of whisky in the other, and I was a happy man. It didn't matter that I was getting on in years. I was grizzled now, my red hair so peppered with grey that I looked like an old dog fox who would be better off put out of his misery. But Elizabeth still liked me, still thought I was smart, and linked my arm when we were out, as though she was proud to be seen with me.

'"Will you, Richard?" She sat up in bed and pushed her hair out of her eyes. She was wearing a white cotton nightdress with a lace pattern on the front. It looked too big for her and I noticed how thin her wrists were as they poked through the frilled cuffs. "Will you marry me and come to live here with me?"

'Do you know what I did then? I burst into tears just like that stupid lad I'd been all those years ago when I couldn't have the thing I wanted. Now I had it and it was almost too much.

'She held me, soothing my face and whispering loving words in my ear until I had got over my tears and was able to kiss her and whisper my reply.

'"Yes, Elizabeth. Of course I'll marry you."

'That night I didn't sleep, but lay awake thinking about practicalities. I would have to sell Manor Farm and give up all my other bits of business. In the years after the war I did quite well in business, first in contracting, then building, and finally buying a garage and selling motor cars. It was being on my own that made it possible. Men with families don't have the time, but after Mother died I was completely alone at the farm. In the daytime, of course, there were men about, one of the old farm workers from Billy's time who had come home safe from the war and Ernie, who would stay with me until the day he died. I had another two men as well. I needed them because I was spending more and more time away on business and on my frequent trips to Ireland.

'I made money, a lot really, but apart from presents for Elizabeth and a succession of newer and bigger cars, I spent very little. The house was nicely furnished and well maintained and I would take myself off for a holiday in the mountains every year. Because of my war injuries, climbing was no longer possible, but I could walk, and I've explored the lower slopes of many of the great mountain ranges. I even went back to the North West Frontier one springtime.

'That market place in Peshawar hadn't changed one jot since my last posting there in the thirties, and as I walked through the busy dusty streets, breathing in the cold clean air scented with spice from the roadside cook-shops, I could almost believe that I'd never been away. But it was different, when you took a longer look. The British army had gone and although a few Europeans had stayed on, they were strangers now in a land in which they had no standing and little respect. I felt sorry for them and glad for the Pakistanis at the same time.

'Oh, I'm wandering again, and there's so little time to tell you the whole story. Give me a drink of that tea and I'll carry on. No, don't fuss, girl, I'm all right. Put that microphone closer to my mouth.'

I came home a couple of days later, to set in motion the sale of Manor Farm.

'What the hell has got into you?' said Fred Darlington when I went to tell him about putting the house and land on the market. He was retired from the police now but still living in the village, in one of the new houses.

'You know I've always wanted to be with her,' I

427

said, 'and this is my chance.'

'But you can't sell the farm. The Wildes have been there all this century.' He snorted. 'You know what'll happen. Another housing estate will go up.'

I thought that was rich coming from him, living in the estate that had laid waste to the beautiful grounds of Cleeton Hall. 'You're a fine one to talk,' I growled. 'And anyway, the place will have to be sold sometime. I've no one to carry on.'

That was the truth. I had no one and I longed to spend my last years with Elizabeth, so I went ahead with my plans.

I bought a diamond-and-sapphire engagement ring and a gold-and-diamond watch for her and put them in the top drawer of my dressing table. Every night while I was waiting for the sale to go through, I would telephone her and we would plan what we were going to do with the money. Doing up that ruin of a house was the priority, and then improving the land. Drainage was necessary and clearing the scrub. Oh, I had great plans. And all the time I would look at the ring and the watch and imagine her face when I gave them to her. Did I remember the watch that Johnny Lowe had given her and was I trying after all these many years to match it? I don't know. I expect somewhere deep in my heart I was, but I didn't recognise my foolishness. When had I ever? All I knew was that I was happy. Happier than I had been for years, with so much to look forward to.

One night, when I phoned, she sounded strange. 'What's up?' I said, nervous.

'Nothing, really. I've just got a bit of indigestion. Stop fussing.'

After that we carried on with our conversation as normal, but I could hear that she was breathless every now and then and I went to bed worried. I couldn't sleep and several times nearly picked up the telephone and dialled her number. But I never did. I knew that I would be doing it more for my peace of mind than hers.

The next morning I was tired and bad-tempered with the men when they came to work, shouting that the farm might be for sale but it still had to be worked properly.

'OK, boss,' said one of the youngsters, 'keep your hair on.'

That remark sent me into such a rage that I sacked him on the spot and turned to the others offering to do the same for them. Sensibly, they kept their heads down, and for the rest of the day only Ernie, who hadn't the brains to stay quiet, spoke to me.

'Two of the calves is scouring, master,' he said. 'Will you drench them?'

I was ready to go for him, boiling up again because something had gone wrong and my control of events was slipping away. I could feel my fist curling up and if he'd said another word I'd have hit him and enjoyed the satisfaction of taking out my frustration on him. But then I saw the fear in his face and sickeningly remembered that that was how he often looked in Billy's time. That brought me to my senses and I calmed down.

I went inside and telephoned the airport. There was a flight from Liverpool to Dublin that evening and I could hire a car and be with her before ten. That was the best thing to do, and before the men went I organised them to cover the farm.

A doctor was at the great house when I got there, his hat and overcoat lying across a chair in the bare and echoing hall.

''Tis the doctor,' said the little maid, 'the mistress has taken a turn,' and she showed me up to Elizabeth's room.

My heart was pounding as we climbed the stairs. How would I find her? What did 'taken a turn' mean? Was it only a silly little faint or something worse, and if worse why hadn't she told me? I was frightened and angry at the same time. It was so typical of her, always getting me in a state of confusion. I was ready to have a row with her and entered her room with a scowl on my face.

She was sitting up in the bed, supported by numerous pillows and a folded-up eiderdown. Her white hair flowed around her head in its usual wild way, and from where I was standing she looked no different from how she had when I'd left her only two weeks before.

'Is it himself?' asked the doctor, who was standing beside the bed.

'Yes,' she said, and grinned. 'See, I told you he would come.'

I hurried across the big room to sit down on the bed beside Elizabeth. 'What is it? What has happened?'

'I told you not to fuss,' she said, but I knew she was glad I'd come. Her hands held mine in a surprisingly strong grip and she leant forward to give me a kiss.

'It's the heart, this time,' said the doctor.

430

'Haven't I been telling her these last months not to do so much. But will she listen? Not a chance.'

'Away with you, you're nothing but an old woman,' Elizabeth whispered, resting her head on my shoulder. I took her in my arms then and held her, glad that she seemed to be her usual self.

'She should go to the hospital in Galway town.' The doctor gently pulled me away. 'I'm going to get the ambulance.'

'No!' She was determined, and when I looked up at the doctor he shrugged.

'I've been trying all afternoon to send her away. She said she was waiting for you.'

I turned back to Elizabeth. 'You must do what he says.' I spoke gently and sat down beside her again. 'He knows what he's talking about.'

But she shook her head. 'There's no point,' she said. 'And he knows that fine. It isn't only my heart. I've got cancer in my stomach. Haven't I?' She stared fiercely at the man who was even now unwinding his stethoscope to listen again to her chest.

'You have,' he said, 'and didn't you refuse an operation last month?'

'Right. So I'm staying here and Richard will stay with me. He promised.' She put her hand on my face and weakly stroked my cheek. 'You will, my love, won't you?' Her voice dropped then and she leant wearily against my chest. 'I don't want to die alone,' she whispered. 'Stay with me.'

I stayed. For only the three weeks that it took, for her decline was rapid. I got a couple of nurses in for her and the doctor called every day. He was a good man and never allowed her to be in pain,

431

so that in those three weeks we were able to talk and laugh over the good memories from our childhood and remember our happy times in the years after.

'I wanted you here after I'd gone,' she whispered one afternoon. We were in the great drawing room, she wrapped in a tartan rug sitting in one of the leather armchairs and me beside her in another. She had been quieter today and I could see that the pain medicine wasn't having its usual effect. In a minute, I thought, I'll go and telephone the doctor, but she was looking at me and compelling me to stay. Speaking had been an effort for her all day but she was still her determined self and forced the words out. 'So that we'd still all be together. That's why I didn't tell you.'

'I know,' I said.

'Will you forgive me?'

I nodded. I would always forgive her, whatever she did.

'Good.' Her head drooped back against the buttoned back of the chair and she closed her eyes. This was my opportunity to telephone the doctor and I started to get up

'Richard!' Her voice was as clear and sweet as it had been all those years ago when we'd raced across the hill above the farm and thrown ourselves breathless on to the heather. I leant over her and she opened her eyes and I saw for the last time that brilliant blue that matched the blue of the glass beads in the silver necklace. It glinted now above the collar of her nightdress, silver and blue lying heavy on her wasted neck.

'I love you,' she said.

'And I you.'

She closed her eyes again and lay back against the chair and when I came back from the telephone she had gone. I hope she hadn't known that I'd left the room and I hope that her last words and mine were echoing in her brain as she passed away. I think they were.

Of course, I let her down by not staying at her great house and being close to her and John. But I couldn't. It wasn't the same with her not there and I needed to be at home for my own comfort. It was at the farm that I could feel her presence. I could walk across the fields and remember her laughing as she drove the cattle in and I could lie in the little bedroom above the front door and imagine that she was beside me and that we were young again.

After the first couple of years I didn't even go back to tend the graves. It was too painful. But I'm going there soon and we'll be together, as she wanted.

Chapter Twenty-Six

I copied all the last recording even though I thought my heart might break. Poor, poor Richard. All those people that he loved, dying before him, and he living on for so many years.

He is so tired now, and thin. I can barely get any food into him even though I prepare the things he likes: little squares of cheese on toast, egg sandwiches and soup. The other day he said he could fancy a junket. For a moment I thought he meant a trip out and I must have shown my astonishment, for his face cracked into a smile and his shoulders started to shake.

'Not that sort of junket, you soft thing,' he growled, but he was laughing really. 'The milk pudding sort. You must know how to make that. God knows, it's easy enough. Mother made them all the time.'

I looked in one of the old recipe books on the shelf beside the Aga. It has a well-thumbed blue cover and 'The Women's Institute' on the front, and the name Mary C. Wilde in small neat writing on the frontispiece. I found a junket recipe and it seemed simple enough, if I could get the rennet. I'd never heard of it before but they had some at the health-food shop. When I came home I put it all together and let the pudding set. I'm sure I did it as per recipe, but he didn't want it.

'Sorry, my dear,' he said. 'I'm too tired just now. Maybe later.'

Thomas tried some after tea but made a terrible face after one spoonful. 'This pudding is absolutely yucky,' he announced in disgust.

Funny thing is that I quite liked it. It slips down easily and I liked the coffee flavouring that the recipe called for. I'll try him with it again later when he's in a better mood but God knows when that will be. All this last week he has been sitting in his chair looking at the garden and not wanting to continue his story. I know there's more because he told me yesterday that he was thinking about it. 'My mind is so full,' he said. 'Everything is swirling around and getting mixed up.'

'Talking about losing Elizabeth is bound to have an effect,' I said sympathetically, but he shook his head.

'It's not that,' he called after me as I went out of his room. His old voice shook with anger. 'It's what I haven't said yet, you silly girl. I have to make sure I tell it right. It matters.'

He sounded a bit like Thomas does when he's upset and I don't like it. It reminds me too much of my old life at home. Shouting and bawling was regular there. But at least Richard does have the excuse of age and infirmity, so I'm prepared to forgive him and carry on writing his story.

Actually, I'm beginning to enjoy it. At college, one of our tutors said we all should keep a diary, because even random thoughts were worth recording. 'It will improve your reasoning skills,' she said. And I do find a certain relaxation in a meandering account of day-to-day events. The only time I kept a diary Mum took it out of my bedside table one day and read it. She even showed it to Dad and Mrs Lane next door when they were all out at the pub. I swore then that I would never allow anyone to know me that well again. And they haven't. Even James didn't know me.

I hardly knew him either, and if he walked into this house tomorrow I'd have a job recognising him. He was a useless piece of humanity. His contribution to the world was Thomas and he didn't even know it. And never will.

Richard only asked about Thomas once, in a roundabout way, and I didn't tell him much and probably lied.

I have been into Richard's room to help the nurse, although reluctantly. I hate those nursing jobs, but I wouldn't tell him. That would be too cruel.

'Mr Wilde is getting weaker,' she said, 'and can't hold himself up when I want to change his pyjamas. Do you mind coming in?'

These days, she's nicer. Not so bossy. Even Thomas will run a message for her if she asks and he's very choosy about his friends. He can't bear Donald Clewes and makes a face whenever he calls to see Richard. Donald has asked me out twice, both times to a meal at the new Italian restaurant. I couldn't go out with him; he has fat hands and clean polished nails. It makes me shiver, just imagining those hands touching me. Stupid of me, I know, for the man is quite harmless.

Jason has dirty hands most of the time but he does try to get them clean. He's for ever got them plunged in that special cleaning jelly when I go round to his house for a meal. As though I cared. I love him as he is.

God! I've said it. I love him.

Richard was sitting up in bed when I went in with the nurse. He looks a bit brighter today and gave me one of our special looks when Nurse started speaking.

'Just going to get you all tidy,' she sang in her most irritating nursery voice. 'All shipshape and Bristol fashion.'

'God give me strength,' muttered Richard.

'What's that, dearie?'

He looked over her shoulder at me and grimaced, and when I moved forward at her beckon his eyes followed mine. He was trying to tell me something, I know, but I couldn't pick up what it was.

'Jim-jams off,' Nurse said, and slipped his wasted arms out of the baggy sleeves. I haven't seen him undressed before so the livid puckered scars on his left shoulder and the crescent-shaped one along his ribcage came as a shock.

'Oh!' I said before I could stop myself and the nurse looked round from where she was re-arranging the pillows.

'War wounds,' she stage whispered as though Richard was deaf and couldn't hear or see what we were looking at.

'Courtesy of a couple of bastard Japs,' he said with a grin and lifted his arm painfully to point at the scars. 'Soldier with machine gun here,' he touched his shoulder and then let his hand trail down to his ribs, 'officer with sword there.'

'Is that when you got your medals?'

He nodded. 'Bring me a drink when this bloody woman has finished because I'm ready to tell you about it.'

'Cup of tea?'

'Whisky!' He looked defiantly at the nurse, waiting for her to object, but she said nothing. All three of us know that it makes no difference.

'Is the microphone in place?' he asked after I'd put the glass in his hand and arranged the tape recorder beside him. I pinned the mike to his collar because sometimes he gets breathless and his voice drops to a whisper so I can't understand what he's saying. When I stay with him, I can remember what he says, but he doesn't always want me about. It's as though he thinks that some of the stories are too private for my ears, even though he knows I'll be listening to the recording and writing it all down. Maybe it's a pretence he's keeping up. He was like that today. First he said he was going to tell me how he won his medals and then he wanted me to leave him alone.

'Just leave me awhile,' he said. 'Let me collect my thoughts.'

'OK,' I said and I left him, wondering what he would remember. His memories are getting mixed up because he jumps around in time. But he is desperate to tell them so I went into the kitchen then and fetched Thomas. He has grown out of his school clothes, and as Nurse is here I can go into town. Besides, I need to get out of the house for a few hours. The waiting is getting me down.

I don't want to talk about the war or how I won my medals. It was a long time ago when I was young and full of life, and although the Japs and the jungle did their combined best to rob me of it, I managed to survive. Shot and knifed, I was, but I managed to walk out of the jungle. Being shot isn't immediately that painful. It's like someone punched you and it comes as a surprise, even though you are in the midst of bullets and grenades and people screaming.

Poor Jack Barnes got caught in crossfire one early evening when we walked into a Jap patrol.

'Scatter!' came the order, and as we ran into the sparse shelter they started up firing and we responded. Jack got it from both sides and when I reached him he'd a groove of flesh taken out of his

438

left cheek and several bullet wounds in his left leg.

'Christ!' I said as I made a tourniquet out of a piece of webbing and tightened it round his thigh. 'You should have been more bloody careful.'

He grinned, but his face was suddenly white and his eyes were beginning to roll back. 'Take charge,' he muttered. 'Leave me.'

'No.'

This was the first time I'd disobeyed orders, but I couldn't leave him: I had too many fond memories of his parents. So, as soon as it was safe to do so, I hoisted him on my shoulder and with him hanging limply across my back led my patrol back to base.

We were two days away from base when we were caught by another Jap patrol. That's when I was shot, standing up after lowering Jack Barnes to the ground. A bullet exploded into my shoulder and sent me spinning round to fall over the prostrate form of my officer.

I gasped and reached out to grab my rifle. Then the Jap officer burst out of the trees and slashed down at my chest with his sword.

It was his last effort on this earth, for with a contemptuous 'fuck off' Lewis shot him in the face and he toppled over into the scrubby undergrowth and died.

'Thanks,' I panted, grabbing my chest. When I looked down I could see a dark stain spreading over my breast pocket and beginning to travel in every direction. I struggled to my feet. Lying down wouldn't do me any good.

'You saved my life,' I said.

'My pleasure,' Lewis laughed. These encounters

with the Japs made him manic sometimes. It was just like the old days when he would fight all the civilians in the pubs. He was a cocky little bugger and I loved him.

He got his the next day. I was leading the patrol now while two men carried Lieutenant Barnes on a makeshift stretcher. My wounds, although not serious, kept breaking open and bleeding, so Potter and McLean were managing him. In truth, we shouldn't have carried him; it was against general orders and was slowing us up, but nobody was prepared to abandon him to the jungle and the enemy that was even now on our trail. We all thought the world of him; even the lads who were new to soldiering and hadn't known him as well as I had.

Fever had set in on him too and he was becoming delirious. I think that it was his shouting that gave us away. That bloody jungle was crawling with Japs, and out of the blue a burst of gunfire raked through us as we walked Indian file through the trees.

It didn't take long to finish off the two snipers but we lost three men and two were wounded, including Lewis. I had lost him in the melee and had to call his name.

'Here,' he replied in a halting voice and I turned towards the sound. 'What's it look like?' he said, raising his hand weakly and indicating his wound.

It looked terrible. He lay splayed out with his belly open, his guts scrambling out over his shaking body. The mixture of blood and shit dribbling over his trousers and shirt gave off a terrible stench.

'Not too good,' I said, as I grabbed the morphine shot out of my kit bag and stuck it in his arm.

'Lift me up, for God's sake; put me against that tree,' he whispered. He had tears in his eyes and a thin stream of blood trickled from the side of his mouth.

It was a struggle to lift him, for my left arm and shoulder were very painful, but I dragged him to the tree and propped him upright. He looked down at the mess that protruded out of his uniform.

'Oh, Jesus!' he gasped.

What could I say? His face was already going grey and I knew that he would die within the hour, but I kept up the pretence.

'Chin up, mate,' I said, and got out the first aid pack to stick a dressing over the worst explosion of guts. I reached into his kit bag and took his morphine syringe. 'What the hell,' I said. 'A double dose – can't do that much harm.'

'Go,' he gasped. 'There'll be more of them coming. Leave me.'

'I can't.'

'Fuck off. Take the others and get out. I'm finished anyway.'

He was my friend, you see. My mate. The one I grew to manhood with. Leaving him was the hardest thing I ever did. And I mean that, even considering the things that came after.

'Give me my gun.' He wouldn't look at me, didn't want to see what I know was showing in my face. 'And Richard...' He coughed and the flecks of blood that were bubbling into his mouth spewed into the air and smeared on to his face.

'Yes. What?'

'You'll see Sarah?'

That was when I bent and kissed him goodbye. My friend. My best mate.

It took us twelve hours to get back to our base camp and even though I worried about it for weeks afterwards I know that Lewis wouldn't have lived that long. Besides, there weren't enough men left to carry him. Not him as well as Jack Barnes. McLean had been killed so I shouldered Jack again, determined now that at least one of my friends would get out alive, but it did me no good. My wounds tore open and by the time we got him to the field hospital I was delirious with infection too.

And that was the end of my army career. I was sent back to India on the Red Cross plane and spent many months regaining my strength. In the end I was invalided out and came home.

It was September 1945 when I got back to the farm. The war in Europe had been over for nearly five months but the country was depressed. I was still in uniform then, although I was discharged from the army. My civilian clothes had been sent on home so I travelled all those miles still as a sergeant and proud of my service, but the uniform didn't seem to carry the same cachet as it had three years previously. I think people were sick of soldiers and anything to do with the war. All their excitement and sympathy had been used up on VE Day so none was left for us coming back from the

Far East.

I took the train out of London and settled into a damp and sour-smelling compartment where my only companion was a slumbering clergyman. It was a rotten day with heavy rain which trickled down the windows. For a while, I amused myself by tracing circles and squares in the steamy glass, but then my eye was increasingly drawn to the scenes outside. Bomb damage was rife: factories, docks and residential housing all blackened and desolate with lost roofs and disconnected walls of crumbling brick. How would it ever be repaired, I wondered, all that destruction and hopelessness, because it looked to me just like something from another planet or out of an H. G. Wells book. But when the train slowed down, my mood changed. I could see lads playing in the ruined buildings, shouting and laughing as though it was the most natural thing possible, and in a way that cheered me. Life did go on, after all.

I stood up as we approached my stop and painfully reached up to the luggage rack for my bag. Raising my left arm was still a struggle after my injury and an involuntary groan came to my lips. The clergyman, who had woken and chatted to me on the journey, offered to help.

'Let me reach that for you, sergeant,' he said kindly, but he was old and stooped and barely looked capable of getting his own small attaché case from the netting above the seats.

'No thank you, sir,' I said. 'I can manage.'

I put it on the floor beneath my feet and waited for the train to get into the station.

'Home is it, son?'

I nodded.

'Well, I'm sure it's a blessing for your wife and young ones that you've come safely through. And not only them. The country needs brave men like you to build it up again.'

It would have been the right thing to say, I suppose, for most people. But my son was dead and Elizabeth was far away in Ireland, refusing to come home. In her last letter, which I received just before leaving Calcutta, she had talked about her little holding and the cattle she'd bought and how she was selling produce to the local hotel.

'The place is popular with anglers,' she wrote. 'We get all sorts, Americans mostly. My butter and cream have become quite a hit.' Her last sentence was the most telling and gave me much pause for thought. 'I feel very peaceful here,' she had written.

How could I spoil that for her? It'd be too selfish. Nevertheless, I had made up my mind that as soon as I'd seen Mother and Billy I'd take myself off for a holiday at that hotel and see if I could do anything that would get us together again.

I got out at our little country station and noted with dismay that even that had been affected by the war. The waiting room and the fence were shabby and the wood showed through for want of painting. Weeds were growing up between the flagstones at the far end of the platform and the station master's little garden, which I remembered being a gem of colour and careful manicure, was neglected and overgrown. I wondered where he had gone, for he was nowhere in sight and no replacement was obvious. Only a feeble youth was on the platform, dressed as a porter, and all I got from him was a brief uninterested glance before he turned back to his newspaper, where I could see he was studying the football pages.

For a moment, I was angry. I thought of all the lads I'd known, some even younger than he was, who had suffered and died in the past conflict. They hadn't baulked at doing their duty; they'd been driven by an ideal that this young man patently knew nothing about. I felt like saying something, challenging his indifference, but then I turned away. Why should I care? Life had changed for everyone. The war had made different people of all of us.

'Oh, Richard, love,' said Mother, flustered from baking, when I walked into the kitchen. 'I've been sorely worried about you, but thank God you're back with us now.'

My arm and shoulder hurt as she gave me a hug, but I didn't let on. I wouldn't have upset her for anything. She seemed to have shrunk and her hair had gone entirely white in the years that I'd been away, but she still bustled about the kitchen with her old vigour, chatting as she laid the tea things in front of me on the smooth old table.

'Where's everyone?' I asked. The kitchen was gloomy from the rain outside and the house seemed quiet. I could hear the grandfather clock ticking steadily in the hall but the normal sounds of hens and cattle were muffled.

'About the place, working,' she replied. 'We've got a new Land Girl. Ida left; got into trouble by some German prisoner of war who was working on Felstead's farm. She's gone home to her family to have the child, and the fellow says he'll stand by her when he gets his release. The family isn't happy, though. It's bad enough him being a German, but they blame us for letting her out.' She shook her head and brought out a seed cake from the tin. 'What could I do? She's a grown woman. Here.' She placed a large slice of cake on a plate and pushed it across the table to me. 'The new girl is called Dorothy. Quite a nice type, but dreamy like.'

'I'm surprised you're still getting the girls,' I said, pouring another cup of tea into the familiar blue-and-white cup. 'I would have thought the men would be coming out of uniform and want their old jobs back.'

She raised her arms in a gesture of despair. 'Richard, believe me, we've tried. It was difficult enough getting them to work here before the war, but now they've gone into the factories in the town. Better pay, they say.'

I watched as she quickly cleared the table and put the plates into the sink ready for another round of washing up. Everything that Mother did was efficient and without fuss. She'd been looking after the house for so many years that her tasks were done so automatically that she barely noticed them.

'You know what the real trouble is,' she added when her back was towards me and her hands plunged into the sink.

I did. 'How is he?'

Her sigh was audible. 'The same.'

I went out then to find my brother and greet

446

him. The rain was clearing away to the east and bright shafts of late afternoon sun brightened up the yard. I was pleased to see how clean and tidy it was and, looking round, noticed with approval that the barns and sheds were all in good repair. I put my head round the door of the milking parlour and found it scrubbed and sweet-smelling. Those Land Army girls had worked well. When I went back into the yard, I met one of them opening the field gate and driving in the cattle.

'Can I help you?' she said, giving me a look which hinted that I was an interloper on this farm. She wore a broad-brimmed hat pulled well down over her face and a brown belted mackintosh over jodhpurs and rubber boots.

'I'm looking for Farmer Wilde,' I said, and then, looking at her closely, I recognised her as the girl called Gloria whom I'd brought out from the town that day, three years previously.

'I'm his brother, Richard. Don't you remember me?'

'Yes,' she said, fixing a probing stare on me through her bottle-bottom glasses, 'I remember you now, but you've changed. Been out East, I heard.'

'That's right.'

'Well, I have to say, you do look bad,' she said. 'Thin as a yard of pump water. I expect that foreign food wasn't to your taste.'

I smiled. Folks back home were ignorant of how we'd had to live and how some of us had had to die. And it was no good getting angry with them. It did no good.

'Mr Wilde is in the top field,' she said and

pointed back the way she'd come, as though I wouldn't know where it was.

I found Billy standing against the gate, rubbing some ears of wheat between his fingers. He didn't hear me approach, so intent was he on something in the field, and when I came up behind him and touched his shoulder, he jumped in fright.

'What? Who?' He turned with a terrifying expression on his face and his fists came up, ready to strike.

'It's me,' I said, 'home from the war.'

For the longest moment, I swear he didn't know me. His eyes narrowed and then opened and a puzzled expression was quickly followed by one of distaste. I was taken aback and gave a nervous laugh.

'Billy, it's me. Dick.' I put out my hand to him.

Recognition dawned then and his face cleared. 'Our Dick!' he said joyfully. 'For a moment I could have sworn it was the Maj...' He stopped in mid-sentence and shook his head as though to come to his senses. 'Where have you been all this time? I have missed you so.'

His arms wrapped themselves around me in a loving but most painful grasp. I could feel his shoulders beginning to shake as the tears started and soon he was sobbing like a huge baby.

'Come on, brother,' I said. 'No need for all that.'

'Every need,' he cried. 'You're the one person in the whole world I've been longing to see.'

I can tell you, it was most touching and I was extremely moved. My emotions, normally quite stable, had been battered by months of injury and illness and I was unable to keep the tears from springing to my own eyes. At that moment, I loved him as much as I had ever done. All the bad things that had happened were nothing; they could be put down to petty disturbances, expressions of individuality, or mere high spirits. Whatever other people thought about him didn't matter. Nothing compared to this deep family friendship we shared.

Of course, once I thought about Elizabeth, then the doubts crept in. I loved her more than life itself and I had believed her when she told me about my brother's brutality. But there, in the wheat field on a late September afternoon, I was prepared to take my brother's love and affection for the wonderfully comforting thing that it was.

'It looks ready for harvest,' I said, breaking away from the embrace and nodding towards the field.

Billy stepped back and took a deep shuddering breath. 'Yes, it does,' he said, 'and I'm starting tomorrow. Forecast's better,' he added, cocking an eye towards the sky and sniffing the air.

I caught a movement in the field behind him so I looked over his shoulder to see what it was. Billy saw my eyes and turned his head, straightening up as he did so and giving his tearful face a quick wipe with the sleeve of his thorn-proof jacket.

At first I couldn't see what had rustled the wheat or caused the bullfinches to fly suddenly out of the blackthorn bushes which hedged the top field. Then I made it out.

A girl was walking alongside the hedge, carefully keeping away from the growing crop. She walked with an easy gait, a short slight figure in beige breeches and a green jumper. Blonde curly hair bounced carelessly on her shoulders. In her hand was a sprig of new heather and I knew instantly that she had been walking on the hill.

'Who's that?' I asked.

'Dorothy.' The name came out throatily, and when I looked at him my heart sank. That old glitter was in his eye and his tongue had flicked out to lick at a dribble of saliva at the corner of his mouth. 'She's a tart,' he added, his voice cold and contemptuous.

'Oh, God,' I groaned, 'don't start all that again.'

Before he could answer, the girl had come right up to the gate and was standing beside us. She was pretty, not common-looking in any way, and modest, too, judging by the way she blushed when we looked at her.

I waited for Billy to introduce me, but he said nothing. Now he was turning to go, his eyes fixed on the ground and his breath heavy and disjointed. I felt angry and anxious at the same time. If he thought I was going to let him get away with this display of bad manners, and if he had it in mind to start abusing the girl, then I reckoned I'd better knock that idea on the head straight away.

'Hold up, our Billy,' I said, grabbing his arm and pulling him round. 'Aren't you going to introduce me to this young lady?'

I could feel the muscles in his forearm bunching up as he prepared himself to pull away or, God forbid, turn round and clock me one for my cheek. But then they subsided. Maybe he remembered the way I'd grabbed him by the front of his shirt that time before and threatened him. I don't know. Perhaps I was making too much of his disregard

450

for someone who, after all, was only one of his farm workers. Whatever it was he changed his mind and stayed beside us.

'This is my brother, Richard Wilde, home from overseas,' he muttered. 'She's Dorothy Painter, come to help.'

We walked back to the house together, the three of us, she and I chatting pleasantly and Billy silent but not as brooding as I'd feared. By suppertime he had become quite animated, talking about the farm and the village then asking me questions about the war.

'Do your injuries hurt much, Richard?' asked Mother.

'Just now and then.'

'My brother Percy was wounded in North Africa,' said Dorothy. 'His leg was blown off.'

That shut Billy up. He always hated the thought of people being physically impaired. But Mother persisted in questioning the girl. 'That's awful,' she said. 'Has he managed to get a job since he came home?'

'Oh, no.' Dorothy shook her head. 'He didn't come home. He died later out there. Gangrene, they said. His mate came to see us and said that it was a blessing he'd been taken. The smell in the hospital tent was dreadful.'

Crash! Billy's fist came down with a thump on the table. 'Shut up!' he roared. 'We're trying to eat our meal here. We don't want that sort of disgusting talk.'

Tears came into Dorothy's eyes. 'Sorry,' she muttered, and silence reigned in the kitchen.

Gloria had munched steadily through her meat

451

and vegetables without speaking. She was as plain and uncommunicative as ever and I think these attributes, if you could call them that, suited Billy. I did see her give a sly look towards the tearful girl and her mouth curled up in a little sneer. Rotten cow, I thought.

Dorothy ventured to speak again, this time to Mother. 'Mrs Wilde,' she said, 'do you mind if I go out tonight? They're doing a play at the church hall for Christmas and I'm going to have a part. Rehearsals every Tuesday and Thursday. I'll do the dishes first.'

'No, love, I don't mind. And don't bother with the plates. I'll do those. I want a good chat with our Richard anyway, so I wouldn't be any company for you this evening.'

It was like the old days: Mother and me by the kitchen range talking together on our own. Dorothy had gone out and Gloria had disappeared up to her room. I don't know where Billy went but he'd been quiet and huffy again since supper, so I was glad that his glowering presence was elsewhere. I mentioned my fears for Dorothy's safety to Mother. 'He's taken against her,' I said. 'Have you noticed?'

'Yes.' She sighed and shook her head. 'She should never have come here, and I'm keeping a close eye on her and on Billy. Fred Darlington's been round a couple of times too. He always says it's a social call, but I know better and I'm grateful.' A fox barked somewhere in the fields and I could hear the wind in the chimney. 'Billy doesn't like him, you know. He says that Fred minds everyone else's business and doesn't care what

Miranda gets up to,' she added.

'What does she get up to?' I asked, intrigued and saddened that some scandal should be attached to Miranda Darlington. I liked her.

'Nothing, of course,' said Mother wearily. 'She's got herself a part-time job in the village shop. Our William doesn't approve of married women working outside the house.'

We left it at that and then Mother asked me about Elizabeth and I told her of my plans to visit her in Ireland.

'You can't bring her back,' she said. 'It wouldn't do now. Too many years have passed.'

'I'm not planning to.'

She was quiet for a moment and then said, 'You won't stay there with her, will you?'

Her voice was low and plaintive. She'd had a hard life and things hadn't turned out the way she'd hoped, so it was unkind of me to answer the way I did.

'I don't know, Mother,' I said. 'But if she wants me there, with her, then I'll stay in Ireland for the rest of my life.'

Chapter Twenty-Seven

I went to Ireland the following month, sailing from Liverpool to Dublin and then travelling by train and ancient bus all across the island until I reached the village where Elizabeth lived.

She was bashing at a patch of stony ground with

a mattock when I walked up the narrow, fuchsia-lined lane and found her. Over forty now, she was as slim and strong as ever and her hair still thick and curly, although those silver streaks I'd seen last time had spread further and glistened brightly in the lunchtime sun. I didn't speak for a moment, for she hadn't seen me, so concentrated was she on the hard task she'd set herself, and I wanted to take in her face and body and all that whole aura of her that I loved so much.

It was she who spoke first. 'Hello, Richard,' she said, and then looked up with her old grin and laughed out loud.

Throwing down my bag I leapt over the low stone wall and ran to her. 'How did you know it was me?' I gasped, amazed by her as always.

'I always know.' She smiled and lifted her face for my kiss.

I stayed with her for a month, loving her as much as ever and needing her comforting desperately. She was kind and patient with me, letting me cry when I described what had happened in the jungle and holding me at night when the terrible dreams left me sweating and yelling out loud. It was she who allowed me to come to terms with the hatefulness of war.

I told her about my visit to Sarah Wilton and how I'd had to lie about Lewis's death.

'She believed me, I think,' I said. 'I hope so, anyway, for she's taken his death very hard.'

'Maybe she'll remarry.'

I wonder if she did. She was only young and that little girl needed a father. I lost touch with her after that: my fault, of course. I was not good at keeping up with acquaintances.

Elizabeth's farm was poor and I could see that, apart from the few acres of decent pasture where she ran her small dairy herd, the land was thin and stony and hopeless for anything other than some sort of hardy breed of sheep.

'I manage,' she shrugged when I questioned her about how she could live on the low returns she was getting. 'The rent is barely anything and I don't need many clothes, or fancy things.'

I remembered how smart she'd been in the thirties when we used to stay in the Northern Hotel in our garrison town and how people had stared in appreciation at her expensive clothes and coiffured hair. Now here she was, sitting opposite me in her tiny smoky kitchen, dressed in a plain blue jumper and an old grey checked skirt.

'Let's go into Galway town tomorrow,' I said. 'We'll have a bite of dinner, and I've some business to do.'

'Good,' she said. 'That'll be grand. I've got to pick up some worming stuff from the vet as well.'

I nodded and stared at her while the new thoughts I'd had whirled round my head.

'What?' she said. 'What are you looking at?'

'Nothing. Just thinking, that's all.'

She giggled. 'Don't worry; I've still got some decent clothes. I won't show you up.'

I found a lawyer in the town and with him and the help of the bank manager, who just happened to be his uncle, arranged the transfer of the money that Billy had given me that time before the war. With the extra money that I had added over the years, it came to quite a tidy sum, enough to

455

enable me to buy Elizabeth's farm and another hundred acres from the same estate.

The following week we went for lunch again and I picked up the deeds while she was shopping for our supper.

'Here,' I said, holding out the large brown envelope as we sat over a couple of whiskeys beside a roaring fire in the best hotel. 'This is for you.'

Slowly, she put down her drink and carefully opened the envelope. 'What's this?' she whispered. 'What have you done?'

'I've bought the farm for you. It's yours, and the land in the valley.'

If I'd thought she would be grateful and fall upon me with effusive thanks I was in for an unpleasant surprise. 'No!' she cried, slamming the envelope back on the table. 'I can't take this. I don't want anything from the Wildes.'

That girl. She was without doubt the most stubborn, difficult person in the whole world. For once I was really angry with her and the whole room of quiet, genteel visitors knew it.

'Elizabeth Nugent,' I shouted, getting to my feet, 'you will take it. You'll take it because I have given it, not the Wildes, because you are me and I am you, so in fact, I am buying it for myself. And,' I stopped shouting then and sat down again facing her, 'for our son.'

That hushed her quiet and she sat staring at the fire while the rain poured down outside and our fellow diners, seeing that the excitement was over, turned back to their plates.

'If John had lived,' I said in a quiet voice, 'I would have wanted to support him, you know that.' She nodded and I took another deep breath. 'He's here, all around us, isn't he? I can feel his presence when I'm with you, not only in the churchyard but in your house and in the fields and everywhere. By making you comfortable in this place, it's as though I'm doing it for him.' I took her hand. 'Can you understand what I'm saying?'

Well, she agreed in the end, and by the time I left was already looking to buy more dairy cows and to take on a farm labourer. I went with her to the cattle market one morning, sitting nervously beside her in the old van as she drove wildly through the country lanes. For the first time she asked me about Billy.

'I dreamed about him a lot when I first came here,' she said. 'I thought that he would come and get me.' She shuddered and put out her gloved hand to wipe the mist from the inside of the windscreen. It had rained now continuously for a week and I wondered if the sun would ever come out again. I was cold, as I had been ever since I came home from India. Elizabeth had taken me to a shop in Galway town where I bought a thick tweed suit of clothes and some stout boots and those helped, but I did miss the hot sun of the East. So when she shuddered, I shuddered too.

I grunted. 'He's just the same. Still got fixed ideas about women and is upset about the new Land Girl. She's pretty, see, but modest and quiet.' I thought about him looking at the girl in the field and my stomach lurched when I remembered the strange glittery look in his eyes as he watched her.

'I think I'll telephone Mother when we get to

town,' I said, suddenly feeling uneasy about the situation I'd left behind. 'See how she is.'

I was right to be uneasy. Things were bad at home and Mother was close to tears when I finally got through to her. Dorothy had disappeared and her parents had called in the police. 'They took Billy for questioning,' Mother cried, 'kept him for two nights.'

'What happened?' I was shocked and stared desperately through the telephone kiosk window to Elizabeth, who was standing outside looking anxiously at my troubled face.

'They let him go. He says it's all a mistake and that her disappearance is nothing to do with him, but the folk in the village are saying...' The line crackled and I couldn't hear what it was that they were saying, but I could guess. Her next words were quite clear, however. 'Please come home, Richard. I need you.'

Elizabeth looked miserable when I told her. 'You'll have to go, I suppose,' she sighed. 'Just when I was getting used to having you around.'

I think that if I hadn't gone then, but stayed, we would have lived there for the rest of our lives together. That barrier she had put up after John died had suddenly melted away and we had become close again. We talked about her plans for the farm as though the two of us were going to carry them out and I had already thought about bringing the telephone and, more important, electricity to the place.

'I'll only be away a week or so,' I assured her. 'In the meantime, get help in and I'll be back in two ticks.'

There was a strange atmosphere at Manor Farm when the taxi dropped me at the back door. A raw, squally wind was blowing across the fields, pulling at the bare thorny branches of Mother's favourite climbing rose, which normally clung snugly to the outside scullery wall. Now the wind had dragged it from its moorings and it was waving about trying to catch the threads of my coat as I stood by the door looking across the yard. Flecks of snow were dancing in from the mountain, not enough to lie but enough to drive the poultry into their shed where they perched miserably, waiting to be closed up for the night.

I could hear the cattle restlessly stamping in the shippon and I wondered if they'd been milked, for it was late afternoon and no one was about. Even the kitchen, Mother's domain, was empty when I went inside and called for her. My shout of 'Mother' echoed hollowly through the gloomy rooms and the only reply I got was fierce rattling from the windows as another gust hit the side of the house. To add to my misery, I could hear the wind howling in the chimney, something that I'd never liked, even as a boy, and I wished desperately that Mother, or someone, would come.

Slowly I walked up the stairs and went into my bedroom. The bed was turned down, ready for me, and someone, Mother I suppose, had put a carafe of water and a glass on the bedside table. Beside it was the little biscuit tin that I knew would hold four plain crackers, Mother's treat for visitors. My room had remained unchanged since

459

my boyhood. The two narrow single beds and the two bedside tables remained at right angles to the window. For a moment, I was a youngster again, running in after school and throwing myself on the bed ready for a guilty read before I was called down to do my chores. I looked over at the bed that had been Billy's. He had long since moved into the big room that had been Father and Mother's, and although on my visits home I had heard him snoring away in there I was sure he was lonely. Our Billy didn't like the night. He didn't like waking up and finding himself alone. I suppose I should have felt sorry for him, but I was remembering that he was the reason I'd had to leave Elizabeth, yet again, and I muttered an oath to the silent room. My damned brother was like a millstone round my neck.

Dusk was falling in the yard when I went outside again but now I could see movement from the barns. The cows were going into the milking parlour and I followed them in, hoping to find Billy and vent the anger which was growing with every second.

He wasn't there. All I found was Ernie, cooing and cushing at the beasts as he tied them into the stalls and began the long round of milking.

'Mr Richard,' he said in his dull, unsurprised voice. 'You're back again.'

He looked older and pinched in the face, and when I drew closer I saw that he had a cut lip and a yellowing bruise on his cheek.

'How did you get that?' I asked, pointing to the injury.

He shrugged. 'Master.'

'Where is he?'

He shrugged again. 'I don't know. He's gone out in the car.'

'Well,' I sighed, my heart thoroughly sunk with the situation I'd found, 'we'd better get these beasts done.'

We'd finished the milking when I heard the sound of a car drawing up and I rushed outside, ready to confront our Billy, but it wasn't him. Marian and Mother had driven up and, spotting me, Mother hurried out of the Bentley and came over to give me a welcome hug.

'Oh, Richard, love,' she crooned. 'I thought you'd never come.'

'I said I would.' I knew I sounded impatient but it was hard to keep the annoyance out of my voice. I'd been the rejected one and now all she seemed to want was me there to pick up the pieces.

'I know,' she said, brushing aside my irritation as though she hadn't heard it. She had; she could always tell what I was thinking. 'But we weren't sure; we thought that you might not want to be bothered.'

Behind her, Marian shook her head and gave me a warning look. 'Hello, Richard,' she said. 'You find us in difficult times again.'

My sister looked almost as old as Mother. She wore a brown wool coat and a mannish trilby hat that completely covered her hair. All the prettiness that she'd had as a girl had vanished and on that cold November evening, in the wavering yellow light that shone out from the shippon, all I could see was Granny. The dull brown eyes and the sharp witch's face were an exact likeness and even

461

her hand, when it reached out to take mine, was wrinkled and claw-like, just as Granny's had been. Why hadn't I noticed it before, I wondered. After all, I'd seen her only a few weeks previously before I'd gone to Ireland.

'Where is he?' I asked, sighing as I sat down in the chair beside the range and pulled off my boots. They were Billy's boots really; I'd taken mine with me to Ireland and left them there. Had I done that deliberately? I think I must have. Something of me should be on that farm; after all I was going back soon.

I'd looked for Billy's boots in the scullery before I'd gone into the yard and found them placed neatly side by side under the window. They were cleaned and hosed down as was his usual practice. Whatever else had been going on, he was still careful about his apparel.

'He was here before I went out,' Mother said, busy now with the kettle and teacups. 'He knew you were coming; I told him this morning. He's looking forward to seeing you.'

Marian sat at the table and took off her hat. Her hair was a mixture of brown and grey, parted in the centre and dragged into a bun at the back of her neck. It was a big bun for she'd always had thick, coarse hair, and at the sides of her head, above her ears, two rows of kirby grips held every last strand in place. The grips glinted in the lamplight and that was the only thing about her that shone, for her face was pale and dusted against any possible glimmer and her coat, dress and lisle stockings were uniformly dull.

'Mother and I have been having a spot of tea in

town,' she said. 'It's been hard for her these last few days, what with being short-handed here and ... other things.'

I shook my head in weary irritation. She and Mother were amazing. A girl who lived in our house had disappeared, my brother had been taken in for questioning and they still couldn't bring themselves to talk about it. It was ridiculous. If they wanted me at home to sort it out then I wanted everything out in the open. They damn well had to talk about it. I thought about the blonde curly-haired girl who'd sat opposite me at the kitchen table only a few weeks before. She had seemed harmless, naïve almost, and not the type of girl that our Billy would take against. Mind you, he had called her a tart on the first occasion I'd seen her. Something about her had obviously struck the wrong chord with him. But what had happened to her, and why were the police suspecting my brother? No one was prepared to tell me that.

'Tell me about Dorothy,' I said. I watched my mother and sister's faces cloud over but I was too weary and fed up to feel sorry for them. 'Come on,' I said, 'speak up. Let's hear what happened.'

They were saved from answering immediately, for another thought, which had been vaguely swimming about in the back of my mind, struck me and I got up to look out of the window. It was dark now but the wind was up and bits of paper and twigs were blowing about the cobbled yard. Ernie had gone home to his old mother and the lights in the barns and shippon had been turned off. Only the storm lantern that we always left on at night was lit. It threw an eerie glow over the corner next to the house, but beyond it all was dark. No one was out there.

I turned back to Mother. 'Where's the other girl? Where's Gloria?'

She gave a little moan. 'Gone,' she cried. 'Went the night that the police let Billy come home. She said it wasn't safe here any longer.' Mother's voice choked. 'I was very disappointed in her. I thought she had more sense. After all, she's been here for nearly five years and knew us as well as anyone.'

I sat down again and dragged my hand through my hair. What a mess. How shaming for the family. 'And I suppose there hasn't been any sign of Dorothy yet?'

Marian shook her head. 'No. They're not really looking any more. They searched the farm and the fields. I think they went through the village too because she was last seen at that play rehearsal at the school. She left there at about ten o'clock and was never seen again.'

I hated saying it, but I had to. 'Was Billy out that night?'

Mother said nothing and I looked at Marian. 'Well?'

'Mother says he was about the yard, she thinks.'

'Was he?'

Mother's round face crumpled and the handkerchief she'd been twisting between her fingers went swiftly up to her eyes. 'I don't know,' she cried. 'I didn't see him after supper, but he always takes a turn about the yard. He's a hard worker. You know that.'

'And he goes to town sometimes,' I said, my

wife of an important businessman and former mayor. He lived on years after Marian died and he and I remained good friends. He didn't marry again, but I do know that on the evening he passed on it was a young woman who reported it to the police and the doctor.

He wasn't with us that night, though, and I could have done with him, another man, to help me tackle our Billy. I had the feeling that I was in for a difficult time.

'Where's your Albert?' I asked.

'In Toronto, on business,' she said. 'He's been away for over a month. Coming home next week. Why?'

'Why d'you think?' I was annoyed. 'He could be helping us with this problem. He knows all the authorities. They're all in the same organisations.'

Marian frowned and pursed her lips together. 'Don't be silly, Richard,' she said. 'There's nothing that Albert could do. Anyway, we don't want outsiders interfering with our business.'

You see, that was their attitude. In this instance, even Marian's husband was an outsider, and when I looked round at Mother I saw that she was nodding her head in agreement. It was hopeless.

We spoke little through supper but we were all straining our ears for the least sound from the yard. Who would be the first to hear Billy's car crunching over the cobbles and look up nervously? I had decided that it must be me and that I would go outside and confront him straight away, before Mother had any chance of softening the blow. But

467

it was a waste of time, for the wind was still crashing down from the mountain and all other sound from the yard was muffled. 'I'll go and check on the animals after this,' I said, and was just taking my last gulp of tea when the kitchen door was thrown open and Billy walked in.

'You've come!' he shouted, so cheerfully that all thoughts of an immediate fight with him were driven from my mind. He turned towards the sink. 'Just wait a minute while I wash my hands.'

Confused, I half rose from my chair, cautious and ready for anything but certainly not expecting him to be so normal. Although I had no real reason to expect him to be different. It wasn't as if the police had charged him with anything or his supposed involvement was anything more than rumour.

But I pushed back my chair and went over to greet him. He was busy with the Vim and the dishcloth, scrubbing away at his hands, doing each finger individually. I waited while he rinsed and then dried them vigorously on the roller towel.

'Now then,' I said, holding out my hand, 'how have you been?'

'Very well.' He grinned and straightened his cuffs before taking my proffered hand. He was dressed in his market clothes, tweed suit and yellow waistcoat, Father's watch chain stretched across his flat stomach, the timepiece safely in the deep pocket. I have that watch now and it is still as accurate as ever.

'Oh, are you?' I said. 'I heard there'd been some trouble.'

The grin disappeared like snow off the yard and

was replaced by a lowering of brow and that cruel indifferent look I used to fear. These days I was too old to care about it. I knew that even with my injured shoulder he would have a hard task to physically beat me and I could easily cope with any rough language or remarks.

'Nothing that matters,' he said, and turned to Mother who was standing aimlessly beside Marian. 'I suppose there's some supper somewhere for a hungry man?'

His words galvanised her into action and without further ado he sat down at his place and fixed his napkin into the top buttonhole of his waistcoat. His face cleared and he looked at me with the indulgent expression I remembered Father using on the rare occasions when he was pleased with me.

'Well, Dick,' he said, 'have you had a good rest?'

He was behaving so naturally, concerned for my welfare and patently not bothered that I had come home solely because he was in trouble with the police. My opportunity to question him about Dorothy had gone and I had little stomach for asking him what he'd been up to in town. I gritted my teeth.

'Good!' he said when Mother put his food in front of him. 'I've been right hungry. The wind is bitter this evening.'

'Where've you been?' I asked. 'I thought you might come to the station to meet me. Mother said she told you I was coming.'

'I had a bit of business to do in town,' he said. 'Couldn't wait.' He shovelled a great forkful into his mouth and didn't notice the darting looks that Marian and Mother were passing to each other. My stomach was in turmoil.

I got up. 'I'll go and check on the animals,' I said, my desire to be out of this kitchen and away from my brother now overwhelming. 'I've finished my supper.'

'Wait!' He picked up the last piece of bread and butter and stuffed it into his mouth. 'Wait, our Dick. I'll come with you.'

'No!' It came out so forcibly that even he was stopped in his tracks, and his animated face fell into almost a child's puzzlement.

'No.' I softened my words. 'You've been out all day. Just finish your food first. Mother's got sponge pudding.'

But there I stopped, because suddenly, above the diminishing sound of the wind, I heard a long high-pitched howl. Mother, who was dishing up a large portion of the treacle pudding, jumped in alarm and the spoon fell out of her hand and dropped with a noisy clatter on the stone flags beneath our feet.

'Oh!' said Marian, putting her hand up to her face. 'What on earth was that?'

The howl was repeated, lower this time, animal-like and frightened, and then the wind got up again and copied the sound in the chimney and the windows rattled. The atmosphere in that kitchen was one that would have scared the bravest of men and, that night, I was as close to believing in ghosts as I ever have been.

Why did we all look at Billy? Why did we think that he had something to do with it? I don't know, but of course we did and he stared back at us, his boot-button eyes screwed up in concentration and his lips quivering slightly.

'What's that bloody racket?' he said, putting his hands on either side of his plate ready to lever himself out of his chair. His jolly face had disappeared and was replaced by a cold still one that boded no one any good.

Dear God, I thought. What's he gone and done now? And I readied myself for whatever it'd be.

Imagine my surprise then when he suddenly leapt from his chair and burst into extravagant laughter.

'I forgot!' he cried, and turning on his heel he ran to the back door.

Crash! It was thrown open, there was a breathless pause and then we heard another crash as it slammed shut. Billy was back in the kitchen holding a shivering young terrier in his arms.

'It's for our Dick.' He laughed. 'Here.' And walking swiftly across the kitchen until he was in front of me, he thrust the little dog into my arms. 'It's a welcome home present,' he said, laughter gone now and a more formal tone adopted, 'for my dear brother who has been overseas.'

I was flabbergasted and stood there like an idiot, hugging the little brown-and-white dog close to me and feeling the muscles beneath her smooth coat begin to relax. Soon she lay comfortably in my arms, and when I looked down at her she reached up gently and licked my nose. I was smitten. How could I be angry now? Billy was looking at me with tears once again in his eyes, and between gulps and blubs he drew out papers from his inside pocket.

'She's a good 'un, mind,' he snivelled. 'Full pedigree and all that. I know you like dogs.'

'I do,' I said, and put out my hand to grip his arm. 'Thank you.'

There was no more time for thanks, for we were interrupted by the jangling of the front-door bell.

'Who the hell is that?' said Billy, snapping his head round, the pleased grin fading. 'Are you expecting company, Mother? Or is it the...'

The word 'police' was left unspoken but from the sudden look of fear that came into his face, I knew what he was thinking.

'It's the doctor, I think,' said Marian, joining in at last. 'I asked him to call. I thought you've been looking peaky lately and Mother said she didn't think you'd been sleeping too well. I went to see him this morning.'

Mother went to open the door but Billy turned towards the scullery and reached for his coat, all laughter flown away. 'I don't need the doctor,' he spat. 'Tell him to go to hell.'

'Billy,' I said, not loud, but determined. 'See him. I want you to.'

He stood with his hand on the peg, not looking at me, but muttering another conversation with himself. I looked round the kitchen, wondering where to put the dog because, if necessary, I was going to physically stop him from going out. I didn't have to, because his muttered conversation came to an end, and letting his hand drop he edged back into the room and leant casually against the sideboard.

'I'll stay,' he said, his eyes cold and suddenly weary. 'But it's a waste of time.'

Chapter Twenty-Eight

'Did the doctor help?' I asked him, because now I'm fascinated with the horribly strange brother. All these months that he's been writing and recording this story, he keeps coming back to Billy and their relationship. Why can't he see how awful Billy was to him, so cruel when they were children and plainly mad when he was an adult? Why did Richard feel that he had to care for him?

They were all monsters in that family: Marian cold and nasty, father distant and unloving, and as for his mother? I can't understand that relationship at all. She must have been the most selfish person in his life. She was always trying to make him do things that would make life easier for her. That isn't love as I would reckon it.

Take that back about the mother being the most selfish. What about Elizabeth?

Poor Richard.

'What?'

He seems to be deafer than ever today, although Donald Clewes says it isn't so much deafness as lack of concentration. Richard is reliving a life in his head. Everyone he cared about is dead, most of them gone years ago when he was still young enough to find another life for himself. I've looked at the photographs in the album and he was a handsome man any woman would have been proud to have for a husband. I'm sure he was good, kind and generous with his money. I do wonder about those years after the war when he was running the farm and living here with only his mother. Surely he had someone who he could go to, simply to talk? Surely he had a woman, somewhere, whom he called on, for comfort.

Oh, I know he went to see Elizabeth in Ireland, but the trips were very infrequent, and reading between the lines I think they were pretty stressful. She sounds like a difficult person.

'I said, did the doctor help Billy?'

Richard nodded slowly. The collar of his pyjama jacket keeps slipping to the side because he's so thin. I got up to straighten it and to make him more comfortable against his pillows. He leant on my chest as I pulled him forward and sighed deeply. He weighs next to nothing and, as Nurse says, managing would be easy if he weren't so tall. 'I like them small and compact,' she says. 'They fit in the bed better.'

'You smell nice,' he said. 'Clean.'

'Well, I hope so.' That made me smile, but I knew what he meant. Clean is the best scent.

'Mother always used Attar of Roses. It was her favourite, and she would dab a little on every afternoon when she changed out of her house dress. Granny said she was vain and that there was no place in a farmhouse for perfume.

'"And you'd know all about that, wouldn't you, Mother Wilde," said Mother sharply, when Granny had mentioned it for the umpteenth time.

'That gave Granny a start and she sat up straight, gripping her teacup. "No need for that, Mary Constance."

'Aunty Fanny and Aunty May pursed their mouths into little buttons and looked at their shoes. They were shocked and a little envious of Mother, for they didn't dare answer Granny back.

'"Every need," said Mother, very brisk. "I won't be reproved in my own parlour. Now, who's for another cup of tea?"'

Richard laughed, his old shoulders shaking against my chest, and I put my arms round him and hugged him. Oh, I do feel so close to him. His humour is mine and his feelings for things are the same as mine. It's because we come from the same stock. I know that, and I think he does too although it's never mentioned. What would we be? Cousins?

'Tell me about your brother and the doctor. Did he help him?'

'He did. As far as he was able, but Billy was a reluctant patient. Didn't realise, you see, that he was ill. And he was, you know.'

I liked the new doctor, Dr Trevor he was called, and he was young, younger than me, which I found strange.

'Good evening, Mr Wilde,' he said when Mother showed him into the kitchen. 'I hear you've been feeling poorly.' He had a grey felt hat in his hand, and his medical bag, which he set down heavily on the table. As he leant forward, his mackintosh fell open and underneath I recognised a brown striped demob suit. Not long out of the army, he was, and I warmed to that.

At first, Billy wouldn't speak to him. He stayed leaning against the sideboard for a minute, giving the doctor the once-over before going back to sit at his place at the table. He lifted up the teapot and poured himself a cup of tea.

'I'm all right,' he said. 'My family fuss too much.'

Dr Trevor gazed at each one of us in confusion and then turned to look at Mother. 'Mrs Wilde?' he said. 'Are you sure you need me?'

She didn't know what to say, I could see, and her cheeks burned red with embarrassment. Marian was her usual silent self so it was left to me to speak.

'Excuse me, doctor,' I said, 'I'm Richard Wilde, Mr Wilde's brother. Perhaps I can explain.' I led him out of the kitchen and into the hall.

'That's a fine dog you've got there,' he said as we stood beside the polished dresser.

I looked down at the pup, who had gone to sleep in my arms. She had felt so immediately a natural extension of my life that I'd almost forgotten I was still carrying her. Now I put her down on the floor beside my feet where she sat, most obediently, one small paw resting on my shoe.

'Doctor,' I began, 'I think my brother is having another nervous breakdown. It's happened before and Dr Guthrie prescribed pills to help him. He doesn't realise he's ill, but the family can see that he's getting worse. I've been away until today, but my mother and sister have told me. And, of course, there has been some trouble with the police.' I stumbled there, wondering how to put it, but the doctor held up his hand.

'You don't need to tell me about that, Mr Wilde. I know all about the Land Girl and I've read Dr Guthrie's notes. My feeling is that he needs help. Possibly in hospital, if he's willing.'

I shrugged. 'I can't see him agreeing to that, but he'll take the pills, I think. He did last time.'

The doctor frowned. 'I'm not sure about drugging him. It'll keep him quiet, but that's no help, is it?'

Yes! I longed to cry out. Just keep him quiet. Don't let him make trouble. But I said nothing as we walked back. The little dog trotted beside me and I had a moment's concern that she must need a bowl of water by now and that I'd been remiss in my duty of care for her. But she would have to wait. Getting Billy sorted out was paramount.

'The doctor wants to talk to you,' I said, going over to him and putting my hand on his arm. He shook it off and I could see his fists beginning to curl up. He was getting angry and the beginnings of a muttered conversation started.

'Billy!' I said again, sharper this time and with more meaning in my voice. 'On your feet!'

My voice sounded harsh in the silent kitchen. Outside, the wind had dropped and a steady drizzle was pattering gently against the windows. Mother and Marian held their breaths and watched as Billy slowly lumbered out of his chair. He could have done anything and I got myself ready for the head-down rush that he might make. When we were children that's how he always got me, winding me first by bashing his head into my solar plexus, and then when I was lying on the ground gasping for breath he would raise those huge fists and pummel my face bloody. I wondered if he thought he could do that now; if he

477

imagined I was that same weak boy, who hated fights and always let him win to save myself from further pain. I didn't think so and I was proved right.

He straightened up and let out a mirthless laugh. 'Yes, sergeant,' he cried and did a mock salute. 'Attention!' He stood, dull-faced and compliant, so that the doctor could examine him.

Mother and Marian went out of the room but I stayed, watching as Dr Trevor gently pushed Billy back in his seat and did a quick examination of his vital signs. I took the opportunity to fill a bowl with water and put it on the floor in the scullery for the pup. She drank gratefully and then whined and ran in a little circle.

'The dog needs a piss,' said Billy. He'd been watching her, his face turned away from the stethoscope and the probing looks he was getting.

'I know,' I said, and I took her outside, where she relieved herself against the back wall and then ran away further towards the field to do more. After a while, I whistled and she came running back, wagging her little tail and doing babyish jumps beside my leg. I could tell already that this dog and I were going to be fast friends. I'd call her Nell, I decided, same as the dog I'd had as a boy and loved very much.

'Come on, Nell,' I said. 'Time to go in.'

When we went inside, Dr Trevor was sitting next to Billy. 'Your brother wants your advice,' the doctor said. 'Should he stay here or go into hospital? He wants you to tell him.'

'He must stay here.' The words were out of my mouth before I had time to think properly. My

478

reaction was instinctive, the Wilde way of doing things, and all my years away and my anger with Mother and Marian for their secretiveness was as nothing. Faced with the choice of sending Billy to an asylum or looking after him at home, I behaved in exactly the same way as they had done.

The doctor frowned. He plainly thought that I was wrong, but he had left the choice up to me and had to go along with it.

'You'll have to be here to look after him,' he said quite sharply. 'No going away again.'

I nodded. 'How long will it take?'

He shrugged. 'Who knows? He'll probably need some type of tranquilliser for the rest of his life.'

Billy snorted and stood up. His fists were curling and uncurling and I saw him look across to his jacket hanging on the peg by the scullery door, as if longing to get out of the kitchen.

'Wait,' I growled and he sat back down and stared at the table.

The doctor got to his feet and picked up his hat and medical bag. 'Well?' he asked, looking at me. 'Are you sure?'

'I'll stay until he's better.'

Why did I behave so stupidly? If I'd had the guts then to send him away then maybe my life would have changed and I could have spent all the years after with Elizabeth. But I didn't. I had to act in our set way.

It was only later that I wondered. There were days when I longed to go to the doctor's surgery and say that Billy must go into hospital. That way I would be free to go to Elizabeth. But then all the doubts set in again. Who would manage the farm? How would Mother hold her head up in the village?

And there it was. Either I remained here and made sure that my brother behaved himself or I could chuck it all, turn my back on the family and return to Ireland.

O God, help me, I prayed. Me who had long since given up believing and was now, to all intents and purposes, an atheist. This was one burden too many and it wasn't fair. I wanted a life of my own. I deserved it.

Once again I'd been forced to make the choice between home and Elizabeth and I'd chosen to stay at home. I was such a coward. All those medals for bravery were nothing but a joke. When it came to the really important decision, I ducked it.

So I stayed. I fed the pills into Billy morning and evening, watched him trail around the place like a zombie, not caring about the stock, or the land. He spent a lot of time in his bed or sitting in his chair by the range, unshaven and smelling, waiting for Mother to put a mug of tea in his hands.

The farm was no problem. I could run it as well as he could. After my years in the army, organising men and handling difficult situations, the problems that I faced at home were as nothing. Labourers came back once they knew I was running things, good men who knew their jobs and even an ex-Land Girl who had become an expert in the dairy. Mother was able, at last, to retire from farm work. Not without a struggle, though.

'She's no idea,' said Mother, walking through

the dairy one evening and examining the cheeses put up to dry on the shelves above the sinks. It was spotlessly clean in there and the muslins wrapped round the cheeses almost glowed, they were so white.

'What's wrong with them?' I asked, disappointed that this new employee whom I had worked so hard to persuade to come to us might turn out to be useless.

'Too wet. No flavour.'

Well, if Mother was right, the people in the market didn't agree. Our cheese and butter sold as well as ever and after a few weeks Mother stopped complaining. I don't think she really meant it. It was a last effort at keeping control of one of her little empires. I kept the girl on for years, Thelma, she was called. She married one of the Rafferty boys.

Elizabeth was angry with me and that was the worst thing about the whole situation. I explained in a letter how things were, and then after she had the telephone connected I tried again to convince her that my absence was temporary.

'How can it possibly be?' she asked.

I despaired as I recognised that old, cold tone of rejection that had crept into her voice. The distance between us couldn't only be reckoned in miles. She had been rebuffed again and that was my fault. I knew she thought that if I had any guts I would turn my back on the family who had been nothing but trouble to me and go to her. The rest of my life could then be spent in the shelter of her love. And God, I needed that. It

481

had to be my turn some time.

'Once he's back on his feet, I'll be on that ferry,' I said, meaning it and trying to convey how much I wanted to be with her and not at the farm. 'You'll see. Nothing will stop me.'

'No,' she said bleakly. 'You'll find another excuse. You've never been able to untie the apron strings.'

It wasn't fair, of course. I'd been away for years, made the break as a boy. If it hadn't been for my injuries, I would have stayed on in the army after the war. But this was different and she didn't understand. Father had worked so hard to get Manor Farm and I can remember his words now on the day when he came back from the bank having signed the papers.

Listen to me, William, and you too, Richard. Manor Farm is now Wilde land and that's the way it's going to stay. When I'm dead and gone, you must keep the place always.

Father's words mattered to me, probably more than to our Billy even though he loved the land as any good farmer would. I could never imagine it going out of our hands, and in those cold, miserable days just after the war, I couldn't leave. I had my responsibilities.

'Wait,' I begged her, 'just a few weeks. Once he's settled down again, I'll come to you.'

I don't think she believed me right from the start, and as it turned out she was right. I never left the place after that. Not for good, that is. I went on holidays all right. I'd got a taste for travel after my years abroad, and I always spent six or eight weeks a year in Ireland too. But all those years in between that first visit after the war and the penultimate time, when she asked me to marry her, she didn't seem to want me as a permanent fixture.

Did it suit me? I think it must have. Perhaps I was better being alone. I've been a selfish man, loving my own company and the freedom solitariness gave me to live in my own way. And I've never been short of money either. I turned out to be a good farmer. Though not one like our Billy, who had such a feel for the land and could go out in the early morning and tell you just from the smell of the air what the weather would be like for the rest of the day.

'It'll clear up before midday,' he'd say on mornings when rain was driving in from the west and the hill behind the house was just a shadow in the mist. 'We'll be able to get some tractor work done this afternoon, so don't think you buggers are going to muck about in the barns all day.'

This last would be directed towards our farm hands, sheltering under the corrugated roof of the tractor shed, vainly hoping that he might send them home for the day. 'A day's work for a day's pay,' Billy would add with his customary rough tongue, 'so get that machinery oiled down instead of arsing about!'

No, I wasn't the farmer he was, but I was able to bring in innovations and find different markets. I set myself up as a contractor and then branched out into building work so that by the time I retired I barely did any actual farming. Geoff Rafferty, Thelma's brother-in-law, someone I'd known since infant school, managed the place for me and a right good job he made of it too. He didn't live here but came every morning before seven from his house in the village. I kept him on for years. He died on holiday one August. Keeled over on the prom at Eastbourne. A real shock that was. That was when I leased the land to the Hydes.

That all came later, of course, after Billy had died, because while he was still alive we did things his way, exactly as if he was on the spot, directing us. The only difference was that with him indoors and not glowering around the yard and the fields, the men were more cheerful. They would josh amongst themselves and make sure that I was included when they told men's jokes. I liked that. It was almost as good as being back in the army.

Mother loved me being at home. 'Sit down, Richard,' she'd say every morning after milking, and set before me a gigantic breakfast. Rationing never seemed to affect us, except for coal and getting enough points for clothes. Those winters were cold after the war. They seemed colder than they'd been before but perhaps that was because I'd been away in the East for so many years

The doctor called about ten days before Christmas. He was a different one this time, who explained at the door that young Dr Trevor was ill and that he was a locum, taking over for a few weeks. He was an older man, past retirement age, I thought, and judging by the state of his hands and the mud on his boots something of a countryman as well as a doctor. Indeed, as we walked through the hall, he talked about his herd of beef cattle and how he was breeding for muscle.

'Mark my words,' he said, 'lean tasty beef is what the customer wants and must have.'

I listened politely, but at the time I didn't believe him. The customers I knew simply wanted enough to eat during the long years of rationing.

I took him up to the bedroom where my brother spent most of his time. Billy looked terrible, pasty-faced and unshaven. His hair was wild, greyer now, and needed cutting. The smell of his sour unwashed body made me wrinkle my nose even on the landing outside his room.

'How are you today, Farmer Wilde?' the doctor asked, putting down his bag and sitting gingerly on the edge of the bed.

'I'll do.' Billy's words were muffled and accompanied by gaping yawns and much scratching.

'Getting up and about, are you?'

'I get up for me dinner.'

'But otherwise, here. Is that it?'

Billy nodded and turned away. He wasn't interested in the doctor. He wasn't interested in anything these days. The pills saw to that.

'Mm.' The doctor looked up at me. 'I think we might change the treatment now. He can't spend his time up here; it's not a proper life for a farmer. Let's see if we can make sure he has a jolly Christmas. I'm sure it would be more pleasant for you and your mother.'

He brought out his prescription pad and I watched as he wrote a couple of lines. His handwriting was beautiful, nothing like a doctor's traditional illegible scrawl, and when he handed it to me I could read every word although I didn't know what the medicines were.

'No more sedatives,' said the doctor. 'I want him built up now, so I've prescribed a tonic and some penicillin for those cuts on his arms. They're going septic, hadn't you noticed?'

Of course I'd noticed. Billy's new habit of picking bits of skin off his hands and arms had irritated me and Mother for the past few weeks.

'Stop that, William!' Mother would say sharply at dinnertime as Billy dug the tines of his fork into his arm. He'd take no notice and scrape away at an imaginary itch until a hole had been made in his skin and blood started to flow.

I couldn't bear to watch and turned away to try to savour my own food as Billy took his fork from the septic cuts on his arm straight to his plate. Everything in front of him would be shovelled into his mouth and then he would look at me, waiting for me to give him his pills. I found it quite disgusting, so despite my concerns about his possible behaviour I was glad when the doctor decided to try to bring our Billy back to normal. In a way, we could cope with his unstable personality better than that of this unkempt stranger in our midst.

I withheld the sedatives that evening and again the next morning, so by midday our Billy was out of bed and in the kitchen.

'Go and have a wash and a shave,' I told him when I came in for my dinner, 'and then you can help me with the pigs.'

'All right,' he said. Tears were in his eyes, which I didn't like to see, and I got up to help myself to more potatoes from the pan on the stove. Mother had gone to Marian's for the day and had left me in charge of the meal. I looked at his plate, cleared of food but with the knife and fork thrown untidily on the table beside it. That was all against the way we'd been brought up. Mother and Father had been most concerned about our table manners. He watched me as I piled the spuds on and I felt suddenly guilty that I wasn't being kind enough.

'Have you had enough?' I asked.

'Yes. Very good.' He looked stupid and confused. 'What did you say I must do?'

'Have a wash!'

Three days later he was almost back to his old self, striding about the farm and grumbling at the way he said I'd let it go. I didn't mind. I was simply glad to see him looking clean and composed and beginning to regain his strength.

'Just like the old days, eh, our Dick?' he said as we got up together in the morning to take the cattle into the milking parlour. 'D'you remember when we were little lads and sent the dog across the meadow to bring them in?'

He shook his head, smiling at the memory. 'Those were the best times, I reckon,' he said.

Were they? Maybe for him, but not for me. Not the best times. I could think of many better times, in India, for example, riding through the high passes where the air was bright and cold and the hawks circled above us, mewing a warning. And what about those stolen, breathtaking moments with Elizabeth when we were first able to express our love? I thought of the afternoon sun chinking through the thin curtains of the bedroom at the Gate House, lighting up Elizabeth's naked body so that her skin glowed warm and creamy and made me ache with desire. Those were the sorts of good times that I remembered.

'Maybe,' was all I said. I wasn't going to upset him by pointing out that I'd had more of a life than he had. Besides, when you looked at it coldly, neither of us now had much to boast about.

So in the few days before Christmas my brother came back to life and the atmosphere at Manor Farm improved no end. Mother was happy again, humming little tunes as she bustled about the kitchen, baking mince pies and taking trips into the town with Marian, to make sure that all the preparations for Christmas Day were well in hand. We were going to have the day at home as usual, just the three of us, and quietly, because Billy had been ill and it was thought reckless to expose him to all the family and friends who might drop in.

On Boxing Day we had been invited to Marian's. I didn't know if we were going; that was still on hold, depending on Billy. Albert had been round to see him, checking him out, I supposed. It was difficult for my brother-in-law, being such an important person in town and having a suspected murderer in the family, but, fair play to him, he remained faithful to us.

'How are you doing, Richard, old man?' he said, shaking my hand warmly as I met him at the back door and brought him into the kitchen. Billy was walking the fields and Mother had taken Marian into the drawing room to look at the Christmas tree I'd brought in from Cleeton's wood.

'I'm all right,' I said.

'Injuries healing up?'

I nodded. My shoulder was still stiff and some-times I would get a piercing pain deep within the flesh. I wondered if I had a bit of shrapnel still in there, lurking about, but I did nothing about it. I'd had enough of doctors and hospitals. The night-mares that had bothered me in the first few months after my discharge were beginning to lessen. Elizabeth had helped with that, so those horrible nights when I would wake up screaming and terrified, waiting for the bastard Jap officer to plunge his sword in my squirming guts, now only came occasionally.

'How's Elizabeth?'

I was startled. No one in the family ever men-tioned her these days, even Mother, and she had been very fond of her. But Albert brought her name up as though it was the normal thing to do. I decided to respond in kind.

'She's fine,' I said. 'I'm going back to Ireland as soon as Billy's better.'

'Good,' he said, lighting up one of his large cigars and blowing a gale of blue smoke into the room. 'She's a lovely girl and you're best out of here. Do what makes you happy.'

We said no more because Mother and Marian joined us, but I was glad to have Albert's bless-ing, at least.

In the days leading up to Christmas, work on the farm continued as normal. On the actual day, the men would get a holiday and Billy and I would have to manage on our own as well as take extra time out for sitting down to our Christmas goose. If we went to Marian's on Boxing Day, Ernie would be left in charge for a few hours. It didn't bother me, but Billy was already grumbling.

'He's bloody useless at the best of times,' he

said to me one morning as we stood together in the yard 'Look at him, leaning on that shovel. Lazy bugger!'

This was the old Billy, and despite this sign of his returning temper I was glad to see him interested and involved. It meant he was recovering and I would soon be able to get away to Ireland.

'Move your bloody arse a bit quicker,' he yelled to Ernie and I watched him stride angrily across the yard. The poor fellow was struggling to clean out the bull pen while keeping an eye on Conqueror, our Friesian bull. Ernie was scared of him and rightly so in my opinion. He was a wicked devil, best pedigree or not. But our Billy didn't fear any animal, and he climbed over the gate into the pen and snatched the pitchfork from Ernie's hand and shoved him against the wall.

'Put your back into it, like this,' and Billy demonstrated how to clean away the foul straw into the corner before gathering it into the barrow. Conqueror watched him with a nasty gleam in his eye, and even though he was tethered by a chain attached to the ring through his nose and to another ring mortared into the wall he was pawing at the ground, the bunched muscles beneath his fine black-and-white hide shivering in anticipation.

'Boss,' muttered Ernie urgently as both he and I saw the bull strain on his chain and bits of mortar start to flake away from the wall as the ring began to move.

'Billy,' I called, 'watch out. He's getting loose!'

In the old days, my brother would have sized up the situation in a flash and either given the bull a warning poke with the pitchfork or vaulted easily over the gate to get out of danger, but today he wasn't so fast.

He looked up slowly, his mind still apparently occupied with the tongue-lashing he was meting out to Ernie, and turned his head just in time to see the ring burst out of the stone wall. I watched, horrified, as the length of chain whipped an arc through the air and landed with a sickening crack on our Billy's broad shoulders.

'Agh!' he cried and fell gasping to his knees in the muck before rolling heavily on to his side. He was winded as well as thrashed by the chain. The bull swung his head dangerously from side to side and snorted. I saw the red hot gleam in his eyes and my heart lurched.

'Get out!' I yelled. 'He'll have you!' But Billy was dazed and only slowly started to climb to his feet. There was nothing for it; I had to get in there to save him. I dashed to the gate, grabbing a hay rake as I went, but to my astonishment I was beaten to it. Ernie, who had been standing by the back wall where Billy had pushed him, ran forward and with great presence of mind grabbed the end of the chain. He yanked on it, using all his poor strength, so that it pulled at the ring that pierced the bull's nose. That brought Conqueror's pawing and head-shaking to an abrupt halt and he bellowed in pain as Ernie's chilblained fingers wound the chain round his wrist to make sure it didn't slip away.

'Jesus!' I cried, getting over the gate and helping Billy up. 'Are you hurt?'

He didn't answer. Blood was beginning to seep through his overalls from the cuts on his shoulders, and when he stood up his eyes were wandering all over the place. He was still dazed.

'Come on, our Billy,' I said, and led him to the gate. He was in no state to climb over, so I pulled back the latch and led him through.

'Good work, Ernie,' I called over my shoulder, and then shouted to one of the other men who was just driving into the yard on the tractor and looking out of the Perspex window wondering what was going on, 'Get in the pen and help Ernie with the bull. Fasten the bugger to something heavy.'

The wind was bitterly cold off the mountain that day as I helped my brother inside, but I don't think that was the only thing that was making him shiver. He'd been frightened. Maybe for the first time in his life.

Chapter Twenty-Nine

He's so tired now. I pleaded with him last night to stop and rest for a few days but he shook his head.

'It has to be told,' he whispered. 'All the things that happened. I want to say it while I can.'

He looked over at me then and must have seen something in my face because he spoke again, stronger now and more forcefully. 'You needn't look like that, girl,' he said. 'I haven't got much longer and well you know it. That idiot Clewes has told you, hasn't he?'

492

He did when he came round the other day. He put his stethoscope against Richard's thin chest and listened for a moment before replacing the pyjama top.

'Constitution of an ox, Mr Wilde,' he said heartily.

All Richard did was snort. 'You're a lying little bastard,' he grunted, 'and I'm a fool for letting you come to the house.'

Nurse did her tut-tutting thing. She is respectful of medical men and hates it when Richard treats the doctors like ordinary mortals, but all Donald Clewes did was grin. I was standing by the door, but Richard called to me, his voice breathless and wavering with the effort.

'You don't want him in the house, do you, Sharon?' Without waiting for my reply he turned back to Clewes. 'No. See? She doesn't, so you can bugger off.'

Afterwards, in the kitchen, while he was writing another morphine prescription, Donald got his own back.

'The old boy is losing it. He's throwing little strokes, I think. It's making him confused and inclined to say odd things.'

'I haven't heard any,' I said. 'As far as I'm concerned, he sounds perfectly rational.'

That shut him up and I'm glad. Richard was right; I don't want Donald Clewes in the house. Life's complicated enough.

I'm writing this at one o'clock in the morning. Thomas has been fast asleep for hours and I think Richard is dozing. I'll look in on him before I go up. He'd like that. I've copied the last recording: all

493

that stuff about his brother and the way Elizabeth was so mad at him for staying on at home. She never understood him. If I can see that he had responsibilities to the farm, why couldn't she? Why would she never cut him any slack? I don't know how he put up with her. He never blames her, in fact; in the entire story that I've written on this computer he hardly blames her at all. Only once, or twice, maybe. When she married for the money and the farm and then, later, when he thought she had got pregnant by Billy.

After recording that last piece, he lay back on the pillows and gestured to me to give him that photograph of the three of them as youngsters. It was lying across his chest when he went to sleep and the frame was sticking into him. I took it away because the slightest bump brings him out in a huge bruise. I've glanced at it before from time to time but now I studied it carefully and, no doubt, Elizabeth was beautiful, all that hair blowing around her face and those eyes that look straight into the camera. It's almost as if she knew then that people years later would be looking at her and she is trying to tell them something.

The brother, on the other hand, is nothing much. He isn't even smiling, only looking out with dull eyes and a sort of exasperated expression. It's as though he thinks that having his photograph taken is a waste of time. I expect he did; from what Richard has told in his story, Billy had no patience with frippery. And there is Richard, at seventeen. Tall and gawky, in an open-neck shirt, with his eyes turned away from the camera, towards Elizabeth. I wonder if he knew he loved her then?

I'm finishing now; too tired.

I had to get Donald Clewes back this morning. Richard had some sort of attack in the night. He couldn't catch his breath, and for a while his left arm dangled out of the bed and he couldn't lift it up.

Nurse said he'd had a proper stroke and that he would be crippled now for the last few days of his life, but when I went to him after breakfast that arm was tucked up beside him and to my astonishment he managed to wiggle the fingers at me in a little gesture of 'hello'.

'I wish you'd stop frightening me like this,' I said, pretending to be cross.

'It'll be soon enough, girl,' he muttered, and then gave me a little grin.

It broke my heart. 'You old fool,' was all I could manage as I wrapped my arms around him.

'I want to get on with the story,' he said when I drew away.

I nodded. I don't care what Clewes and the nurse have said about him resting. This matters more to him than anything. 'OK. Let me get my notebook and the recorder,' I said, and went out of his room. Thomas met me in the hall.

'Can I go in and see Mr Richard?' he said. He seems to be growing up so quickly. His legs look knobbly at the knees like a young colt's and the sleeves of his sweatshirt never reach his wrists.

Richard watches Thomas all the time, seeing himself, I suppose, because I have no doubt that we are related in some way. I don't think Mum knew much about my father's family. He was a boy

495

from the village and Mum is a townie, as she likes to tell everyone. But she did know about his aristocratic background. Perhaps she hoped that there would be some money to go with it. Sadly disappointed, she was. My dad never had a penny to spare; it all went on the horses. And then she got in with my stepfather, whose money went straight from his pay packet into the pub. What a pair they were, she and Barry; how I hated them. They shamed me.

My father's name was Thomas.

'Mum,' said Thomas again, when I didn't answer.

'What?'

'Can I go in to Mr Richard? Nurse said no, he's not well. But he expects me, every morning. I have to tell him about the weather and what's coming up in the garden. Anyway, I haven't told him about the fox cubs Jason and I saw. Jason says he'll have to shoot them.'

'Oh!' I said, wondering how to soften this new blow. 'How awful.'

'Don't be silly, Mum. They'll grow up and get the chickens and maybe the young lambs next year. They're no bloody use to man nor beast. Shooting's too good for them!'

He saw the frown on my face. 'That's what Jason says,' he said defensively, beginning to blush when he realized that he'd used the sort of bad language that I complain about.

'Go in now. Tell him about the foxes,' I said, 'while I get my notebook.'

Nurse was in the kitchen with the cleaning woman. They were sitting at the table over the teapot, both gloomily shaking their heads, and I heard Nurse say that Richard was on his last legs.

'This extra dose of morphine will finish him,' she said, leaning closer to the cleaner and lowering her voice, 'but it will be a happy release. Life has nothing for him now.'

She spoke with that sort of almost gleeful anticipation that comes over people when they are awaiting a death. I hated her at that moment. It's early March now and another rainy day outside so the kitchen was steamy and close, with the smell of last night's dinner still clinging to the air. I went straight to the window and opened the half-light.

'Oo.' Nurse shivered. 'I'm not sure we need the window opened.'

'I am,' I said and pretended not to see the look that passed between them. They think I'm getting above myself. After all, officially, I'm still only a lodger here and, even worse in Nurse's eyes, someone who arrived here, courtesy of the council, as a carer. Not qualified like her. I have no real status as mistress of this house. It's just that Richard trusts me, and loves me. He does, I know that. And he loves my Thomas.

Andrew Jones turned up then. I saw him through the window, sloshing across the garden from his car, and he gave me a wave. I waved back and went to the kitchen door to let him in.

'Hello, Sharon,' he said, giving me a kiss on the cheek. I could feel another look passing between Nurse and the cleaner.

'I wasn't expecting you,' I said. 'Did you get a call from someone?'

He shook his head. 'I met Dr Clewes in the

village just now. He said Mr Wilde had taken a turn for the worse. I thought I'd call and see how he was.'

'So much for professional discretion,' I said and didn't bother to keep the contempt from my voice.

'It was kind of you to enquire,' said Nurse from behind me, putting on her caring, confidential voice. She thinks I'm rude to these professional men and that anyway she has the only right in the house to talk about medical matters. 'Mr Wilde has indeed taken a turn for the worse and we fear that he has only days left.'

I wanted to kill her, the old bitch. How dare she measure out Richard's life like that? My face must have gone red, for Andrew put a warning hand on my shoulder. 'Get your mac,' he said, 'and come for a walk round the yard. I want to talk to you.'

I hesitated. I'd promised Richard to go back with my notebook and the tape recorder and I didn't particularly want to talk to Andrew, but I needed a breath of fresh air. The atmosphere in the house was stifling.

The rain had eased a little as we walked across the yard towards the home field. I could see blue sky over the mountain and the clouds were scudding furiously away to the east. Somehow, this year I have missed the season changing from winter into spring. My mind has been entirely taken up with Richard, even to the extent that I have ignored my set work from college and am behind in handing in my essays. I haven't even been taking flowers in to Richard and I know he loves them.

Why hasn't he asked me? He always used to. Poor Richard, his mind is taken up top. This blessed story is obsessing him and he is desperate to put the record straight before he goes. I've guessed what happened, and to me it doesn't seem to be such a dreadful thing. What does it matter that Billy did away with himself? People commit suicide every day and as he was mentally ill, well, it would not be unexpected. In those days they didn't talk about it, did they? They were so concerned about family pride. I'm sure that is why Richard is so ashamed. He thinks he didn't do enough to save him.

Perhaps it was for the best. What if Billy had really been a murderer and been caught? They hanged people then.

'Did you know that Richard had an older brother?' I asked Andrew as we leant against the field gate.

'Yes.' He nodded. 'I've seen all the deeds and wills of the Wilde family. William wrote a will in favour of his brother in 1944. It superseded one he'd written earlier in favour of his son. It wasn't legal, of course. The wife would have had first call. But we have a notarised letter from her a few years later, removing herself entirely from the inheritance. I have presumed that the child was dead.'

'He was killed in the Blitz,' I said. 'In Liverpool.'

He nodded slowly. 'I didn't know that,' he said. 'It must have been a dreadful blow for the family.'

I had another thought then. 'When did Richard inherit?'

'I think it was in the early fifties,' Andrew said. 'The brother was assumed dead because he disappeared and he was never found, dead or alive. They wait seven years, you know. There's a copy of a police report, saying that they thought he'd killed himself because he was suspected of committing a murder. The local bobby, Sergeant Darlington, had a theory that he'd gone to Llandudno and drowned himself. Apparently that's where they went on holiday as kids and he was fond of the place. There're earlier reports, too, from when he was taken in for questioning.' He laughed lightly. 'It's hard to believe, isn't it? When you know *this* Mr Wilde and know what a decent chap he is.'

I didn't say anything. Richard had believed it, although he never actually said it.

'Sharon.' Andrew took off his cap and gave it a shake. It had stopped raining now and the sun was shining on the mountain. Everything was fresh and I could smell the wind blowing across the young grass in the hay meadows.

'What?'

'I want to ask you something.'

'What?'

'Will you marry me?'

This is the third time he's asked me. Once when we were away last year and then again after Christmas. You have to give him points for persistence, and when all's said and done he's not a bad person. In fact, I like him. You don't find many as honest and hardworking as he is. But I don't want to marry him; I don't love him.

You see, Andrew would take me away from here, to town, where I would have to become part of his set. All those things he goes to, like the Rotary and the Chamber of Commerce – all those functions where I would have to dress up and pretend to be having a good time. And if I married him, I would

500

have to pretend about loving him too, otherwise it wouldn't be fair. You can't play fast and loose with that sort of thing.

I looked round at him. He's heading for forty now and I noticed for the first time that his hair is going grey. In a year or two he'll look distinguished and will be a catch for anyone.

'Why haven't you married before?' I said, putting off the inevitable answer.

'I never found anyone I truly loved.'

He said it quite simply, almost as a child might, the way Thomas tells me things, straight, without any nonsense. And there it was: the whole difference between us. In a way, it was the nicest thing he's ever said to me and I couldn't resist putting my hand up to his face.

'You are a really good person,' I said, 'but I can't marry you. You could be my best friend, Andrew. The person I could turn to, someone I trust absolutely, but not my husband. I don't love you like that.'

He looked away then and over the fields towards the river and my eyes followed his. I could see the tractor in the water meadow. Jason was there driving backwards and forwards, dressing the field so that the pasture would be ready for when he turned the cattle out.

'Is it him?'

I nodded. 'I think so. He wants us to marry after...' I left the end of the sentence. He knew what I meant.

We were silent for a minute and I waited, praying that he wouldn't persist this time. He didn't. When he turned round, he bent his face down and gave me a kiss on the cheek.

'Friends will have to do then,' he said, and casually linked his arm in mine as we walked back to the house. I pretended not to notice the damp patches on his cheeks.

'I thought you'd forgotten me,' said Richard when I went into his room carrying a bunch of paper-white narcissi. His voice was weak, and every now and then he would stop to catch his breath. He watched as I put the flowers into a vase, arranging them so that the light from the window shone through the fragile petals. They brought a sharp fresh scent of the spring garden into the room.

'No. I haven't forgotten you,' I said and, leaning over him, fastened the microphone to his pyjamas. His body was shaking slightly and he felt hot. 'I was talking to Andrew Jones.'

'Offering again?'

'Yes.'

'You'd have a good life with him. Big house in town. Holidays in Spain.'

'I don't love him,' I said.

He was quiet then and I waited for a few seconds before asking, 'Are you up to this now, Richard? Maybe you should rest.'

He ignored me. 'I loved Elizabeth all my life. Even when I knew she'd rejected me and after, when she wouldn't have me. When Billy was declared legally dead and we could have married and been together, she said no. Wouldn't come back to the farm, you see, and I, like a fool, wouldn't leave it.'

Fred Darlington asked me about her after I came back from the lawyer in town. We'd been to hear the reading of Billy's will, Mother and Marian and me. I left the women at Marian's house and came on home alone. I wasn't sorry that they'd decided to stay; I needed the time alone in the car to think about what I'd just heard.

It was as I was driving through the village that I saw Fred. Over the past few years, our friendship had waned; too many difficult memories, both of us feeling guilty. But today I suddenly felt that it was all behind me and I stopped beside him, just past the school, and got out of the car.

'Hello, Dick,' he said, taking my hand in his firm shake. That was something in itself. We weren't like that in those days. You only shook hands with people you didn't know well, or on special occasions. But I think he was glad I'd stopped and wanted to show me that he had no hard feelings.

'Fred. Nice to see you.' He had grown heavy over the years, in both fat and muscle, which stretched his uniform jacket to bursting. I suppose it was Miranda's cooking and the contentment that his three daughters brought to them. The eldest, Jackie, had done very well in school and surprised the whole village by going on to university. I remembered that little girl with her black ringlets, always holding on to her daddy's hand in the garden. How she loved him. I was envious of him, I won't deny that.

'How are things?'

'Pretty good. I've just been to the solicitors to hear Billy's will. He'd left me everything.'

Fred nodded slowly. It was now nearly eight

503

years since Billy went and nobody mentioned him any more. It was as if the people in the village had forgotten that he ever existed. Mother only talked about him occasionally, when she was remembering something that happened when we were children or perhaps when she talked about the horses. The adult Billy was beginning to be wiped from everyone's memory. Not mine, though. In those first years I thought about him every day.

'What about Elizabeth?'

I shrugged. 'She said she wanted nothing. Refused to fight the will even though I went to Ireland and begged her. I've arranged that she'll have an allowance. She's accepted that.'

He grinned, allowing something of the old schoolboy Fred to show through. 'She always had a mind of her own, that girl.' His face got serious again. 'So it's official then. Billy is dead.'

I nodded and we didn't look at each other for a while. I studied the wing of my car, noticing that it had yet another dent in it. I would be able to afford a new motor now. Billy had left a substantial legacy, far more than I could have imagined. He must have been squirrelling it away since Father died and I wondered how he'd managed it. Selling high and buying cheap, I expect. That had been his way.

'Come and have supper tonight,' Fred said suddenly. 'Miranda was only saying the other day that we hadn't seen you for ages.'

'Thanks, I will,' I said, and got back in my car. It was strange. After all these years of uncertainty, Fred and I were back as friends.

You know, I was the beneficiary of three legacies.

Billy's, making me master of Manor Farm, the sole owner of nearly five hundred acres of land and all the buildings and stock upon it. That was as well as the money in the bank and, to my great surprise, a parade of shops in town. How had Billy come to buy those? And why? I didn't know for ages until one winter day, some years after, a woman came to the house asking to see me.

'Mr Wilde,' she said, after I'd shown her in and sat her on a chair in the drawing room. 'Mr Wilde, can I talk to you about my rent?'

She was a woman slightly older than me and, from her appearance, the world hadn't dealt kindly with her. Her face was lined and over made up and her thin bare legs looked too obvious in a girlishly short skirt. This was not a woman who had lived what Mother would have called a respectable life.

'My agent handles all the rents,' I said. 'I know nothing about them.'

We let out the shops and the flats above them and they brought in a good few bob. It was those and the rents from the couple of cottages on our land and the Gate House that made up the income that I gave to Elizabeth.

'I know that,' said the woman, 'and I wouldn't bother you normally, but he's put them up and I can't afford to pay. I've nowhere else to go.'

Her face crumpled up then and I watched in horror as tears started to drip down her face. They made white channels in the bronzed make-up and it was such an unpleasant sight that I looked away and picked up the poker to jab at the coals on the fire. I hated women crying.

She started rooting through her white plastic handbag and to my relief took out a handkerchief, but that wasn't all. A piece of paper was produced and waved before my eyes.

'Read that,' she sniffed.

My heart sank when I took the paper and scanned it. I recognised the writing instantly. It was Billy's. 'This is to confirm,' he had scrawled, 'that Edna Knox can stay in the flat, No. 2, The Parade, for as long as she likes, at the same rent.' It was dated during the war, but not witnessed nor even signed. In law it had no value. But I knew it as Billy's promise.

'How much do you pay?' I asked.

'Ten and six a week.'

'And what are they putting it up to?'

'Three pounds.'

I didn't know, but I guessed that that was about right. Ten shillings and sixpence was nothing really. But why had Billy made the promise?

'Why did he promise you this?'

I knew. In that moment I knew who she was and why she had this crumpled piece of paper. But it took her a while before she could bring herself to tell me.

'I promised to drop a case against him,' she muttered finally. 'In exchange for that.'

This was the prostitute that our Billy had beaten up – nearly killed, according to Fred – and this was why she hadn't taken him to the law. I wondered what she'd looked like then. Younger, certainly, but no looker. And he had preferred her to Elizabeth. He must truly have been mad.

I felt angry with her. How dare she come to this

house, bringing back old unpleasant memories? I shuddered when I thought of what he had done to her and how everyone had known it was him. Such a dreadful exposure of our family in public. I was inclined to throw her out on her ear and let her manage as best she might. After all, women like her know what the consequences might be when they take up that style of life. But I looked down again at the paper and saw Billy's badly written and untidy promise. I owed that to him.

'Very well, Miss Knox,' I said, standing up. 'I'll contact my agent and we'll leave the rent as it is. But remember, this is a legal document and you are never to mention it in public.'

I was lying, but she didn't know that; she was simply grateful, and tried to take my hand to thank me.

'He loved this house,' she said as I showed her to the front door. 'And he spoke about you too. Very proud he was. Of your medals and all.'

That ten and six rent didn't last for long. She died the following year in hospital. Cancer, I think.

Marian had cancer. In the womb. That place of hers that had barely been used and had only been a nuisance to her. Albert told me that she was going die; the doctor had told him, but not Marian.

'I'll miss the old girl,' he said, and surprised me by taking out a large hankie to wipe away copious tears. 'Even though, you know ... we haven't been that close, in that way. We've been friends.'

She was quiet about her illness. We never mentioned it when she came here or I went to hers, but it was like an aura hovering over every conversation. And that last week, when she was in bed in her large house in town, the atmosphere of death was so thick that you could have cut it with a knife.

'You've been lucky, Dick,' she said. Her face was as white as the pile of pillows she rested against and her hands had become like claws. A black, leather-bound Bible lay on the bed beside her and she stroked it every now and then, as though it was offering some measure of pain control. Who knows? Maybe it was.

'Lucky?'

'Yes,' she said. 'You had Elizabeth. Someone you loved very much.'

'Well, you had that too. Albert is a grand chap.'

She smiled. Her teeth were sticky and strings of saliva clung to her lips. I could see and smell where previous saliva had dried in yellowing crusts at the corners of her mouth.

'No,' she whispered, 'it wasn't the same. I couldn't be like that, it's not in my nature. Any more than it was in our Billy's. You're different, you know that. But I always loved you like a brother.'

It was meant kindly, I supposed. She was letting me know that she understood the circumstances of my birth. I wasn't really a Wilde. But she didn't mind.

There was something I'd always wanted to know and this was my last chance to find out.

'Marian.' I leant forward and took her hand. 'Did Billy know?'

'No,' she whispered. 'It never occurred to him.

508

You were Dick, his little brother, and that was it.'

I sat back and thought about Mother and the Major. Could it be that I was conceived in that same bare bedroom where Elizabeth and I had our young days and nights of passion?

'Father was just as bad.' Marian's whispered croak broke through my happy memories.

'What?'

'Think about Mabel Parry,' she said.

We were quiet then and later she died, holding Albert's hand while I stood by the window looking down at townspeople strolling casually along the avenue, enjoying the scented air of an early summer evening. I wept for my little sister, who was my big sister, really.

She left me money. Her money, as opposed to hers and Albert's. I was embarrassed to receive it but Albert told me not to be so silly.

'I've got plenty, Richard, lad. Anyway, she wanted you to have it. "It should go to the farm," she told me. "Father said that we always had to keep the place in the family."' He drew on his cigar and gazed thoughtfully at the ceiling. 'That father of yours has had a lasting effect on all his children.'

I bought the Oaks farm with Marian's money, the one that had been Sammy Philips's place in the old days. Only a couple of hundred acres, but good land and good tenants. I sold it back to their son only a few years ago, but he went under. Didn't bother to work it properly, and he drank. Houses have been built there now.

Of course Mother had gone before Marian died. I told you that, didn't I? Heart attack it was. I was left alone in this house. Time passed slowly, at first. I did business, I travelled and I spent several weeks every year with Elizabeth in Ireland. But in the evenings, here in the quiet, I did dwell on the past, and some nights the dreams came back. The Jap officer with his sword, and then, sometimes, Billy got into the dream. That was later, after Elizabeth died and I had a sort of breakdown. The doctors wanted to dose me up but I wasn't having that. I went to India. Oh, it was wonderful. It saved me.

He dropped off to sleep and I came into the kitchen leaving him to dream of India, of spice-laden air and bright saris and dusty roads. One day I'll go there too. He's made it sound so wonderful.

The cleaner has gone and Nurse has driven into town. She is going to do the supermarket shopping today. Her offer. I wonder if she is trying to get back into my good books. There's no reason why she should. In a few weeks we'll never have to see each other again and life will be completely different.

Thomas has gone over to Jason's place this afternoon. He likes Jason and it's good for him to have a father figure. He asked me the other day if I was going to marry him.

'I might,' I said, 'in a few months. Would you mind?'

'No. I like him and I like his house, although not as much as here. This has been the best time in my life.' Poor kid. Nearly ten years old and only in the last year has he had the best time.

'You know we'll be leaving here when Mr

Richard dies? You understand that?'

His face fell. I shouldn't keep telling him about Richard dying but I don't want it to come as a shock.

'I know,' he said.

Now he has run across the fields, careless as a child should be, and will have a lovely time while I sit here and write up these latest notes.

Chapter Thirty

'Are you there? Is the microphone attached? I want to tell you now. Now!'

'Yes! I'm here, I'm listening. Just speak, Richard. Don't worry, I'll hear you.'

'Oh, Elizabeth, why are you so cruel? I love you. You know that, and what I did was for you. Not me.'

'Richard! Listen! It's Sharon, not Elizabeth. Tell me, just tell me. There's no one else here. Carry on from where Billy was frightened by the bull. Ernie saved him. Remember?'

He started to speak then, and his voice was so quiet and weak that I had to sit on the bed beside him and hold the microphone close to his mouth.

'Oh, I do,' he whispered, 'I remember everything. Ernie. Poor old chap. He lived a long time considering that he had no sense. Even after his mother died and I found him in that hovel of a house, living on bread and pissing against the wall because the septic was blocked up. He should have starved to death then, and would have if I hadn't taken him in hand.

'"Are you managing, lad?" I asked a couple of weeks after the old lady passed on and all he did was nod, so I took no notice. I went away, to Ireland to be with Elizabeth, but when I came back I saw little Ernie gnawing at a bloody turnip in the top field and I knew. I went straight to his cottage that evening and the poor sod was standing in his kitchen looking at the gas cooker as though it was a space rocket. He hadn't a clue. Didn't even know how to feed himself. The place stank and the poor bugger hadn't had a change of clothes since his mam died.

'"Come on," I said, "you're living with me."

'Mrs Kirby, who did for me then, wasn't pleased, but I made sure that she knew it was either Ernie or her job. She soon came round. He died only a few years back, in a nursing home. I put him there when he got really bad, not knowing who I was and not able to get about, but I missed him sitting by the fire, keeping me company.'

'Richard!' I interrupted, 'tell me about Billy and that Christmas week. What happened?'

'I don't know.'

'You do. Just tell me and get it off your chest. Then you can sleep easier.'

'...will I, girl? Are you sure?'

And then, trust Nurse to come in at exactly the wrong moment.

'I think you'd better leave him now, Sharon. He needs to rest. Look. He can barely keep his eyes open. Anyway, it's time for his injection.'

'No! You mustn't, not now. Go away, Nurse.

Please. Richard wants to finish his story. Let us have just another little while together and then I'll call you. Please.'

'This is ridiculous. You can't interfere with my treatment like this. If you don't let me near him, I'm going to call Dr Clewes.'

'Get out! Get out, now... She's gone, Richard. We've got a little time before she comes back.'

'...You've been a good girl, Sharon. I've loved having you here. So good, so kind. Helping us...'

She's been good, hasn't she, Mother? She can make the cheese and butter almost as well as you, can't she, and she's better than the men with the cattle. It was a good day when she came to us. Do you remember the day she arrived? You and I were in the bedroom sorting out Father's clothes and we saw her from the window, walking down the drive. That hat! Those curls, flying crazily about in the spring breeze. And when she came into the kitchen I watched as she ate your fruit cake. Two pieces, wolfed down. But so dainty she was in her eating. And her eyes laughing at me over the plate. I was almost too shy to laugh back.

You looked at her ragged cuffs and I saw your mouth curl. Not our sort, was she? Oh, I hoped so much that you wouldn't send her away. I loved her even then.

I tried to tell her about Billy, you know, but she wouldn't listen.

'Tell me nothing,' she said. 'I don't want to know. Whatever has happened is for you and your family to think about. I'm well out of it.'

She was lucky. I had it on my mind for years.

513

Dear God, I was never free of it. If I got up in the morning and it was frosty, with the mist lying low on the mountain, then I was back to that Christmas Day, reeling with the horror of what I'd found. And if Nell went scrabbling for rabbits in some place that I didn't know, then I would feel the bile rising in my throat and have to scream at her to come away.

Billy changed after that business with the bull. He was someone entirely different and we didn't know how to cope with him. It wasn't as if he had gone back to being violent. We could have almost managed that, because I was well able to look after myself and Mother and now the men took their orders from me.

But then neither was he the dirty, drugged man who had spent his time lying in a stinking bed. Would that have been better? I don't know. All I do know is that after that day in the bull pen, he barely moved from the chair in the kitchen or slept more than a few hours at a time. My brother had turned into a pathetic frightened wreck, silently refusing food and almost incapable of holding a conversation.

Christmas Day dawned milder than the previous days. But it was dull and misty and the cloud was low on the mountain. Mother and I exchanged small presents, a scarf for her and a heavy gold signet ring for me. I thought it must have been Father's and was surprised that it hadn't been given to Billy, as the elder son. But when I examined it, the initials EC were part of the design and I knew who it had belonged to. It was the only hint Mother ever gave and even then she pretended that the fancy scroll was some sort of Celtic design. I was pleased to have it and even more pleased when I found that it fitted my left little finger perfectly. Elizabeth gave me a ribbing about it when she noticed it.

'One of the quality now, are you?' she laughed, but then agreed that it was very fine and that I should be happy to wear it. That was later, though.

That Christmas dinner was hellish. Only the three of us: Mother, Billy and me sitting at the dining-room table, the forced jollity of the occasion soon giving way to an anguished silence and the dinner eaten without any enjoyment. Mother had laid the table with her customary care, bringing out all the best china and silver, and decorated the room with branches of holly and tinsel. But somehow the decorations only made the whole day more painful. They were a terrible reminder of happier days when we had all had such fun.

We ate at midday, as usual. Even on Christmas Day, we farmers got up early to see to the stock, so we couldn't wait for a later dinner. For all that we ate, though, we might just as well have gone without. The slices of goose, so lovingly prepared by Mother, that lay on my plate were only picked at so that the fat congealed white and thick and the vegetables grew cold. Her plate was the same. All we thought about was the still figure at the head of the table who gazed hopelessly into space and didn't even attempt to pick up his knife and fork.

'Bring in the pudding, Richard,' said Mother quietly, gathering the dinner plates and spooning the leftover vegetables into one dish, but I shook

515

my head. I didn't want it and I knew that she would only push her helping around her bowl.

'Let's have it later,' I suggested, 'when we feel more like it.'

At my feet, Nell whined and scratched gently at my leg. She needed to go out.

'I'll take the dog for a bit of a walk,' I said, pushing my chair back and standing up.

'All right,' said Mother. 'You can have tea and Christmas cake when you come back.'

I looked at Billy. 'Fancy a walk?' I said. 'Fresh air will do you good.'

He shook his head slowly as he heaved himself upright and wandered aimlessly out of the room. In the kitchen he sank heavily into the chair beside the range.

'How about a little drink?' I said. 'Mother's got a bottle of port here.'

He shook his head. 'No,' he said, and his voice was more gentlemanly than of late. 'No thank you, Dick. Not right now.'

'Sure you won't come with me?'

'I'll just sit a while.'

Despite the unseasonable mildness of the air, I felt cold up on the hillside. The mist hadn't lifted all day and the air was heavy with moisture, the heather wet beneath my feet. Once or twice my boot slipped on a partially buried rock and I was pitched forward on to my outstretched hands. I wanted to cry. I was without human company. I was alone, and the earth smelt mouldy.

Nell was in heaven. She ran ahead of me, sniffing out rabbit trails and following them for a while before being tempted by a different scent and changing direction. I walked along behind her, hardly caring where she led me, for my mind was too full. My problems would never be solved; I was destined to be away from Elizabeth for ever. I knew that now. This was my punishment for stealing her.

I was angry, angrier than I had been since I was a young man and left home. The farm had dragged me back, taken my independence and promised me nothing except a form of living that I had already rejected. 'No!' I shouted to the blank air ahead of me. 'Oh, God, no!' But only the squeals and cries of Nell answered me and hot tears spurted into my eyes. I stood bereft of hope on the damp heather hillside and wept.

After a while I gave up. It was pointless, infantile and only compounded my desperate misery. Then something that I had heard, but hadn't registered, forced itself into my consciousness. It was my dog. She was yelping, and the sound was muffled, high pitched and frightened.

'Nell!' I called. 'Nell, come here!' But she didn't appear. Only the frightened barking continued and my stomach twisted in a spasm of fear. Had she fallen? Was she caught? Had she come across a fox and been bitten? All these thoughts tumbled through my head as I pushed forward up the hill towards the muffled sound of her cries.

'Where are you, girl?' I called, looking to right and left through the mist and trying to follow the sound.

I was by the caves now, where we used to play as children, and the yelping was closer but I couldn't

517

see her or the old entrance to the caverns that had once frightened us so much. The rock face looked different; the arrangement of stones had changed and I was bewildered. This was where the cave should be and she was close – I could hear her – but where was that dark hole that Billy used to dare us to enter? Then, as I looked more clearly, I could see that it was the same place. Large stones had fallen into the gap, leaving only a little rabbit hole. Nell must have wriggled through.

'Come on,' I called encouragingly, kneeling on the wet scrub of grass and heather beside the closed-off entrance. 'I'm here. Come out.' But though I waited several minutes and kept up my urgings, even to the extent of lying down and putting my face close to the little gap and whistling, it was in vain. Nell didn't appear.

There was nothing for it, I decided eventually: I would have to pull away the rocks and get her. I grabbed at the first big stone and heaved it towards me. To my surprise, it came away easily, tumbling out of my hands and rolling heavily down the hillside. I had imagined that these rocks were the result of some sort of fall from the roof of the cave and would be earthed in and stabilised with several years' growth of weeds. Not so. With increasing ease, I pulled at the stones, throwing them aside and allowing them to fall away behind me until soon a large dark hole that was the entrance to the cave was exposed.

'Nell!' I called. A man could easily have got through the gap that I'd made, but she didn't come. Her barking continued, furious and frightened, so I worked on until, peering inside, into a dark made denser by the misty afternoon, I saw her. She was held fast by one leg, caught by a band of what looked like a root, a white root. Nettle, maybe, I thought.

'All right, girl. I'll get you.' I was calm, glad I'd found this little dog who had so quickly made a place in my heart.

I squeezed in, putting aside my fears of years ago, and crawled forward until I was lying beside her and could pull at the band round her leg until it gave way. It was when she hopped out, with a grateful lick at my hand, that I realised it was cloth I was tugging, so I looked more closely at the ground

I cannot explain to you the horror I experienced then. I had crawled in on top of a rotting body, a body in beige jodhpurs and a green jumper.

'God!' I screamed, flailing my hands away from what I'd previously carelessly touched, and wriggled my quaking body backwards out of the cave. On that hillside, I vomited up the meagre remains of my Christmas dinner, greasy pieces of meat and cubes of vegetable spewing out onto the rocks, leaving me choking and gasping in utter revulsion. Even when nothing was left, I heaved trickles of burning yellow bile until finally I could only dry-retch and I lay face down, exhausted, in the heather.

When I raised my head, the mist was beginning to lift. A weak shaft of winter sunshine pierced a hole in the clouds and shone feebly on the ground around me. It warmed my back and helped soothe the shaking and tremors that racked my body. In my head, I was back in the jungle, waiting for the Japs, knowing that soon one of them would burst, screaming, from behind a tangle of bamboo and liana and stick his sword into my squirming guts. I reached instinctively for my rifle, but of course it wasn't there. Nor was the service revolver that I had taken to wearing at my belt in those last months. I was alone and exposed to all that the world might throw at me.

Nell whined and nuzzled at my face, which brought me partially back to my senses, and after a moment I got up. Had I imagined what I saw? Was this only another manifestation of those nightmares that had troubled me so much in the months since I had left India? The dog wasn't bothered. She frisked about my feet, eager for the return journey down the hill, wondering no doubt why I was lingering so.

I could have done what she wanted and maybe I should have. If I had, then what happened after could have been avoided and I would have lived my life, this long endless life, without those new pictures which would rest in that compartment in the brain reserved for the worst things of all. More important than that, I wouldn't have had to live with the guilt. But I didn't walk away. I had to look again, even though every fibre of my body willed me not to. Bracing myself, I walked back into the cave.

It was the Land Girl, Dorothy. The face wasn't recognisable, but the hair was, baby blonde curls lying stiffly about the detritus that her head had become. I could recognise the remains of her uni-form and see the tatters of her jumper where it had been ripped away from her chest. Underclothes, stained and torn, were exposed, and I could see that it had been a small strap lying loose on a wasted shoulder that had caught my Nell and caused me to witness this utter devastation.

The poor young woman lay where she had been placed, after death, I guessed. She must have been killed by my brother somewhere on our farm and dragged up here to be hidden from her grieving parents and the rest of the world.

'Oh, Jesus,' I groaned, imagining what awful viciousness she had known before she died, what terror and despair. I thought of how pretty she'd looked walking through the top field, with the sprig of heather in her hand, and I felt the nausea rising again. What a terrible end to a young life.

My blood was boiling with disgust and rage and I knew this time I had to confront my brother and make him confess to his dreadful crime. I turned to go but just then a ray of light from the watery sun pierced the gloom. It shone upon what I first took to be a bundle of sticks further back in the cave but then, as I narrowed my eyes and forced them to focus, I saw what it really was. Not sticks, but bones. A skeleton – maybe even two or three – lay back there, a few scraps of cloth still clinging to the bones and a jumble of shoes kicked carelessly about the dry dusty floor of the cave.

I don't know how I kept my mind on that walk down the hill. The sights I'd just seen were as horrible as any I'd witnessed in the war and I felt that I was right back in the conflict and should ready myself for whatever might come next. There was no peacetime for me here, no relief possible, not with how things were. I couldn't live with it.

The studs in my boots rang harshly against the cobbles in the yard as I marched swiftly across to the back door and fumbled impatiently at the latch. When I strode into the kitchen, fists clenched and face set, I was ready for what I was about to do.

'Billy,' I said, my voice cutting the gloomy silence of the afternoon, 'get up!'

But when I looked towards the chair beside the range where I had left him only an hour earlier, it was empty. The entire room was empty, so I ran into the hall and looked through the open doors of the downstairs rooms. All were silent, neat and unoccupied. In the drawing room a bright fire burned in the grate and Mother had prepared the tea trolley for her promised Christmas cake and tea. But she wasn't there and neither was Billy.

I began to have the most dreadful feelings of foreboding and climbed the stairs quietly, petrified that I might find something to give me even more pain. Had he guessed what I would find, knowing by some brotherly instinct that I would be coming home ready for the final confrontation, and prepared in advance? He wasn't in his bedroom, or in any of the upstairs rooms. I even searched the attics but they were still and quiet, my presence merely disturbing the dust and causing a bundle of photographs, left piled on top of an old velvet-covered piano stool, to slither gently to the ground and scatter across the bare floorboards.

I ran quickly down the stairs again and on the landing I paused outside Mother's room. To my relief I could hear the faint sound of her breathing and that little popping snore she made. Mother was having her afternoon sleep. She was safe, and relieved but still sickened I went to my room and pulled my army kit bag from under the bed.

The service revolver that I'd brought home only weeks before was there, snug in its brown leather holster. I sat on the bed and put the gun down beside me. My head was buzzing and I needed a moment of calm before what came next, so for a moment I lay back on the pillow and turned my head towards the table where my boyhood possessions were still laid out. My Chinese box with the Roman coin, the dagger with the carved handle and some of my old books, all old friends and comforters. Memories of a happy childhood, and they still gave me a measure of peace.

I swung my legs off the bed and picked up the gun. It felt comfortably heavy in my hand, a familiar weight and something I realised I had missed in the months since my discharge. Now it needed to be checked, so carefully I wiped away the oily dust that clung to the barrel and looked down the sight. Putting it close to my face, I could smell the oil and breathed it in slowly, trying not to get excited. How many times had I told my men that?

And now I loaded the bullets into the chamber one by one, remembering all the times I had done this before going into battle. Was there pleasure in the routine? Maybe.

'Bed,' I ordered Nell when I went down to the kitchen, and like the good dog she was she ran to her basket in the corner and curled up. I didn't want her with me now. Whatever happened,

Mother would take care of her.

So I went out again into the afternoon of a Christmas Day that I would never forget. Out to a quiet farm, where the cattle in the enclosure methodically chewed their cud and the hens pecked for worms in the orchard. The bull watched me as I searched the buildings one by one. There was no need to disturb him. I knew that would be one place Billy wouldn't go.

I found him. He was in the old barn, standing with his back against the far wall, almost hidden by a stack of hay bales.

'I want you, Billy,' I said, moving towards him and pushing over the top couple of bales so that he flinched and stepped to one side. He knocked over the saw horse the men had been using the day before and the big saw and an axe clattered dully to the dusty floor. He didn't even look down at them but kept his eyes on mine.

'I know what you did and where you put her,' I said, keeping my voice even and cold.

At first he didn't speak but then, in an attempt at his old bravado, he gave a wild laugh. 'I don't know what you're talking about, our Dick.'

'Yes you bloody do, you wicked bastard. Dorothy. I've found her.'

His face was yellow. Maybe it was the poor light glancing off the hay, but whatever it was, he looked evil. His lips moved as though he was talking but no noise came out, and his eyes moved up in their sockets so that the whites showed up bright like a spooked nag.

He didn't look at me but kept gazing at the oak rafters. When he finally answered, his voice was sneering and contemptuous. 'Who's Dorothy, then? Some slut that you've lost?'

This made my cold anger return to boiling point and I stepped forward and grabbed him by the collar. 'I'll show you who she is,' I snarled, and pulled him forward.

My brother was always stronger than me when he wanted to be and this was one of those times. With a sudden heave of his thick forearm, he shook me off, and bringing up his other hand he gave me a punch on the jaw that sent me tumbling head over heels on to the floor.

Blood from a split lip seeped into my mouth and I saw stars sparkling in and out as I worked desperately to clear my head. Bits of straw and hay floated in the dust which my fall had raised and as my eyes began to focus properly again a much more frightening sight lurched into view. It was Billy, holding aloft the axe that he'd knocked over earlier, which was now only a couple of feet from my head.

I suppose it was my military training combined with some sort of native self-preservation that forced me to my feet. Before he could take another step, I was upright and facing him, with my service revolver pointing at him.

'Stay back!' I said shakily, for I still felt groggy. 'Or, by Christ, I'll fucking shoot you.'

He wasn't that demented. He knew I meant it and he stopped still in his tracks and gave a stupid laugh. 'Sergeant Wilde, is it, now. Back in the war.'

It was a war, you know. Good against bad, decency against absolute wickedness, and I wanted him to know once and for all that he was a truly evil man. I gestured with my revolver and pointed towards the door.

'We're going for a walk,' I said. 'Move!'

I'll never know why he obeyed me. Was it the gun? I don't think so. Perhaps he thought that he would have plenty of opportunity on the hillside to get away from me or even to catch me unawares and attack. Whatever it was, he shrugged and, turning, headed off across the yard towards the fields.

The winter light was fading fast now as we climbed the mountain. I never told him once where we were going. I didn't need to: he knew better than me and he strode out, climbing steadily towards the caves on a journey that he had made many times before. I walked behind him, holding the revolver, but it was only a gesture. If he'd turned and struck out at me, I'd have been caught. For my mind had slipped back to years before when we had run and climbed on this hillside, laughing with the pleasure of being young and innocent. This was the place where I found a coin. Just over there was where Elizabeth had flopped down on to the heather, her hair escaped from its ribbons and falling gloriously awry over her shoulders. Even Billy had paused in his search for wheel tracks to admire her. Oh, we had such fun when we were children.

Now on this winter day we were here again. Not a glorious winter day like those in our youth when we'd screamed with excitement as we clung to the sledge rope, flying on greased runners down this very hillside, but a sour, misty, adult day. We were two middle-aged men now, on a journey that would never have an end.

Billy stopped a few yards away from the entrance to the cave. I hadn't replaced the rocks, and if he hadn't guessed before he could be in no doubt now of what I had seen. A light rain had started to fall, adding further misery to the afternoon, and I watched as it plastered his greying hair to the back of his neck and dripped from his reddened ears. Seagulls, blown inland on the west wind, moaned above us and little movements registering at the sides of my eyes told me that rabbits were hurrying into their burrows to be safe before nightfall. It was the beginning of twilight like every other evening, yet not like any other. We might have been the only two people in the world.

'I'm glad it was you,' Billy said, his back still towards me. His voice, though quiet and amazingly conversational, echoed bleakly off the surrounding rocks. 'Not someone outside the family.'

'How could you be glad?' I cried, sick at heart and despairing. 'How could you want me to see it? Just look at what you've done.'

He glanced towards the cave but made no movement towards it. 'I only did what was necessary. They had to be killed.'

'Why?' I cried. 'Why?'

He shrugged and then slowly turned round to face me. 'You know as well as I do. They were bad women, sluts. Asking for it. Talking dirty. Doing dirty things. I couldn't let them be like that, could I? Somebody had to stop them.' He paused and, bringing a shaking hand up towards his face, slowly rubbed at an invisible mark. 'They tried to make me different. Like them.' His voice was low and breaking and I saw his face screwing up in a kind of agony. 'I had to be respectable. Like Father.'

There it was, in a nutshell. He wanted to be like our father, that perfect stern man who lived by a set of standards that anyone'd want to achieve. In his naivety, how had Billy managed to twist that perfect code? Mother was right. He was ill.

I swallowed. 'Is Mary Phoenix in there?'

He nodded.

'Who else?'

'I don't know. I can't remember.' He had started to cry now, standing in the rain, his tears mingling with the drizzle, and I wanted to go over and take him in my arms. We were brothers who had grown up sticking up for each other. Why, this was the person who had saved me from drowning. The surrogate father, generous and always loving.

The gun felt heavy and I let it dangle from my hand. I could stop now and pretend that I'd never seen what was in the cave. What would it matter if I took stones and stuffed them into the hole and covered up the crimes that my poor mad brother had committed? Would it bring any one of them back to life? No, it wouldn't.

But I looked again towards the cave and thought about the sad disintegrating mess that had once been a beautiful young girl. I thought of the pile of bones that spoke of other murdered women, lost for ever to their families. I knew that I couldn't ignore it. He would never stop, couldn't, and what he had done was wicked. Nothing he said, or I thought, could get away from that.

'I have to tell the police,' I said.

'No.' His weeping had stopped but he put up his hands to cover his face. When he spoke again, his words were muffled but colder and more calculating. 'Think about Mother,' he said, carefully. 'It will kill her.'

It would. I knew that. Her pride in the family was fierce and Billy's arrest and subsequent trial would be more than she could bear. Nevertheless, I had made up my mind. I would lead him down the hillside and phone Fred Darlington. Let someone else take over the responsibility.

'I can't help that,' I said. 'I'm turning you in. You deserve nothing from anyone.' I thought again of that poor girl, and the others. 'You deserve to hang.'

He nodded at that and lowered his hands. He looked submissive for the first time and I felt desperately sorry for him once more. When I spoke again it was to soften the blow.

'But it won't come to that. You'll be sent to an asylum. We'll visit you, Mother and I.'

But suddenly he looked bigger and a low growl rumbled as he took in a deep shuddering breath. His chest expanded, and as those huge shoulders straightened he was the Billy of old: broad, strong and fit for the hardest task. I looked down at his hands curling into huge fists and I tightened my hold on the gun, trying to keep it steady. How on earth was I going to get him down the mountain?

I jerked the gun towards the rabbit trail. 'Get moving!' I ordered.

He remained still, staring at me with a face so twisted and horrible that I hardly recognised him.

529

'I should have done for Elizabeth,' he said, his voice so cold and full of menace that my guts squirmed and turned to water. 'She was the biggest tart of them all.' He moved his shoulders, flexing the muscles in his upper arms and balancing restlessly on the balls of his feet. He was getting ready to rush me.

'I might yet.' He gave a short mirthless laugh. 'I know where she lives in Ireland. I've always known. One of these days I'll go over there and get her. I'll make her suffer for her filthy ways.'

His eyes glittered in the fading light and his body loomed large in the mist swirling up from the heather. All I could think of was the ogre he had promised would rush out of the cave and get me.

'I can shut her up,' he was saying, his voice getting higher and more excited. 'I'll teach her to lie there, showing me her naked disgusting body. I'll take her by the neck and...'

I shot him then. The revolver pointed at his chest almost without my knowing and my finger squeezed the trigger as easily as if I was back in the jungle and a bastard Jap had suddenly appeared out of the trees.

The noise echoed all round the mountain and then died away while I stood there, shaking, looking down at my brother, who lay on the ground a few yards away from me. He wasn't dead. I'd missed his heart, shot him high in the chest, but it was bad and blood was seeping quickly through his shirt and jacket.

He stared up at me. His face had returned to normal, the twisted sneering mouth straight and that mad glittering look gone. He didn't even seem to be shocked or in pain, and as I gazed down all I saw was my father's eyes, praising me for collecting the laburnum blossoms. And my heart broke.

'Oh, God,' I cried, kneeling down beside him and pulling aside his shirt to look at the neat bullet hole from where a bright red stream trickled. 'Oh, God. What have I done?'

He coughed and a froth of blood bubbled out of his mouth. 'Dick,' he gasped, his eyes fixed full into my face.

'What, Billy? What is it?' I cried, and put my head close to his lips to catch the faint words.

'You are the best brother a man ever had, our Dick,' he whispered through the bubbles, and tiny flecks of his blood spattered on to my face. 'I've been right proud of you.'

I took him in my arms then and held him. My brother, the person who had loved me all my life and cared for me better than any father, was bleeding to death on this bitter mountainside and I was responsible. And no matter how tight and close I wrapped him in my arms, his body was leaden and cold and I could smell the life draining out of him.

He whispered again. 'Finish it, lad. You wouldn't leave an animal like this.'

It was the right thing to do, but I wept as I shot his brains out.

Mother was waiting for me in the yard, anxious and flustered, her fat little hands winding in and out of her apron.

'Where have you been?' she cried. 'I can't find Billy.'

'I know,' I said. 'I'm going out.'

'To look for him?'

I didn't answer but left immediately, jumping into the car and driving along dark and deserted roads until I reached the village. No one was about; it was Christmas night and people were together in their homes enjoying the festivities. Happy respectable families who lived normal, contented lives and would never know the horror I had just experienced.

The police house was full of light and through the undrawn curtains I could see Fred, Miranda and their daughters sitting round their dining-room table; Fred was wearing a paper hat and laughing as he held up a sparkling glass towards his smiling womenfolk. Firelight danced in the grate, throwing a warm and rosy glow over the scene, and as I watched the youngest daughter got up from her chair and ran round to give her father a hug. It was a glorious tableau of peaceful family life and here was I about to spoil it.

But I had to.

'What is it?' said Fred when he came to the door and saw my dishevelled and bloodied state. 'Come inside.'

'No!' I said, terrified that the women might see. 'You must come with me.'

Thank God for Fred. He was a man who understood the meaning of urgency. Without a word he turned and went back inside his house. I heard him exchange some words with Miranda and the girls and moments later he reappeared, paper hat gone, sensibly dressed in mackintosh and cap. He was carrying a large torch. He nodded his head

532

towards the torch. 'I'll expect we'll need this.'

'Yes.' I didn't stop to wonder how he knew that but got into the driving seat of my car and tapped my fingers anxiously on the steering wheel as I waited for him to get in beside me.

The torch wasn't necessary on the mountain. The cloud and mist had blown away to the east and a penny moon eagerly lit our way up the track. No words were spoken between us, and when I stopped Fred stopped behind me and waited patiently until I stepped aside and indicated Billy's body.

He lay where I'd left him. His one remaining eye was open and staring up at the moon. I knew it was my brother, but I didn't feel that the Billy I had known was this sad remnant of humanity. This was a body, not a person.

'I shot him,' I said abruptly. I had to say it. It had been bursting out of my lips since the moment I knocked at Fred's door and couldn't be kept to myself any longer. And then, in case he didn't recognise the corpse of my brother, I added, 'It's our Billy.'

'Yes,' said Fred, kneeling down beside him. 'I know.'

'I had to do it. You go in that cave and see what's in there. It was me or the hangman.'

He got up then and, switching on the torch, went into the cave. This was the brave Fred of old, the one who bested our Billy and showed him that he wasn't afraid, but I was still the scared little brother and hung around outside, watching new clouds flit across the moon.

'Answers a lot of questions,' was all Fred said when he emerged from the darkness, but I realised it wasn't only the ghostly light of the moon that made his face look stark and white. He handed me the torch while he brought out his handkerchief to wipe his face.

'Mary Phoenix is one of them,' I muttered. 'He told me that. He couldn't remember the others.'

'Jesus God,' Fred groaned. 'He was mad. I told you years ago.'

'I know that, now.'

We stood together beside my brother's body, facing the dank cave that contained the bodies of women he had murdered. Could it be that there were other sad corpses in undiscovered places? I thought back over the long years and wondered.

Fred got out a packet of cigarettes, handed one to me and then walked a little distance away from me to smoke his. I watched him as he sat down on a rock in front of the cave and I conjectured what the next steps would be. Would he produce hand-cuffs from his coat pocket and secure me before leading me down the hillside? Or would he read me my rights, as I'd seen at the picture houses? I waited, submissive. I knew what I deserved.

'Right.' Fred ground out his cigarette on to the rock and tossed the stub into the heather. He stood up and took off his mackintosh and jacket. And as I watched on that Christmas evening I was astonished to see him pull down his braces and unbutton his trousers. He stood on that cold hillside in his shirt and underdrawers and looked angrily at me.

'Don't just stand there. Pick up his shoulders,

Dick, and I'll get his legs.'

'What?'

'You heard me. Get on with it.'

I bent and took my brother under the arms while Fred lifted his legs and, between us, we carried him to the cave. It was hard getting in, squeezing past the big rock, but we did it, and laid my brother on the ground beside the other bodies. He lay on his side, so the last vision I had of him was a bloody mess of bone and brain, and that has lingered with me always.

It took Fred and me hours to block up the hole, stumbling about on that hill to find stones of a suitable size. We did it better, I think, than Billy had done, first arranging the rocks and then packing them tight with earth and pebbles. Finally, I tore small branches of rowan off the few trees that grew up there and laid them over our work. One of those branches took root, because I saw it green the next year when I was there. I could never stay away for long. I had to keep reminding myself of what I'd done.

I stopped outside his house after I'd driven back into the village. He sat quiet in his seat for a while, not saying anything, and I sat too. I was drained and sick.

'We'll never speak of this, do you hear me?' His voice was full of authority.

I nodded.

'I mean it,' he said. 'Not to your mother, nor your sister nor me to Miranda or the girls. And we'll never speak of it to each other. Do you understand?'

'Yes,' I said, and I found myself weeping.

I never have until now, Sharon. I told Mother that Billy had gone away and that is what the whole village believed. But she knew. She washed my clothes and comforted me in the nights that followed when tears came unbidden as we sat beside the fire. But I never did tell her.

God forgive me, I had to do it. It would have brought such shame on the family and Mother couldn't have borne it. I couldn't have borne it. But he was my brother and I loved him.

'Richard. Listen to me. It's all right. I understand. I think you are the bravest man I ever knew. Rest now. It's over. You've told me and we won't speak of it again. Nothing you've said changes what I feel for you. I love you, do you hear me? Just as always.'

'Do you, Elizabeth? Do you? Oh, I hoped you would. Let's go out now. Come for a walk on the hill. Come on, Mother doesn't need you in the dairy just yet. Billy knows where the buzzards are nesting; let's go and see. Come on...'

Epilogue

Richard died six weeks ago, on the day after he told me the ending of his story. I was with him, holding his hand, and Thomas wandered in and out all morning, bringing bits and pieces from the garden to try to make Richard smile. It worked once, when Thomas brought in a couple

536

of bits of greenish-blue eggshell that he'd found beneath the plum tree.

'That's a bullfinch egg, son,' Richard whispered as Thomas held the shells up to show him. He gave one of his grins but then he closed his eyes and drifted off to sleep.

He died in the afternoon, soon after Nurse had given him his injection. I didn't stop her because I knew that he was ready. As she rolled up his pyjama sleeve he turned his face towards me and stared into my eyes. There were no words. We didn't need any. I nodded, because I knew what he was saying, and smiled my own goodbye. I think that my face was the last thing he saw before his eyes closed and he went to sleep. I hope that made him happy.

Afterwards, Donald Clewes came to the house to certify the death.

'They only gave him six months, at the hospital, when he was diagnosed,' he said when I took him into the kitchen for a cup of tea. 'He managed fourteen. That was you. You kept him going.'

I shrugged. Maybe. I don't know. It was more likely wanting to get to the end of his story that spurred him on. 'What now? Where will you go?'

That was when I cried. I felt as though my world had crashed down all around me and I had no idea how to escape from the wreckage.

'Come on, Sharon,' said Donald, and clumsily put his arm round my shoulder. 'After all, you can't say that you weren't expecting it. I was.'

The idiot. If he thought that would make me feel better then he couldn't have been more wrong. It only confirmed what a second-class person he was.

'Go away,' I said through my tears. 'Leave me alone.'

It was Thomas who coped with me best. He understood that I was overcome with grief, for he felt it too. He dropped his little carroty head on to my shoulder and sobbed. So we held each other and that was a comfort. After a bit he asked if he could go and tell Jason.

'He should know,' he said, wiping his eyes with the back of his sleeve, looking so serious and grown up.

'Yes,' I said, calming myself for his sake. 'And I'll phone Andrew Jones.'

The following week, Andrew and I flew to Ireland with Richard's body. When we arrived at the little white church in the corner of a small village, the minister was waiting for us with two or three of his parishioners. I don't know why they came, maybe they went to every funeral, but in a way I was glad they were there. It made Richard's burial less of a hurried, impersonal business than it might have been.

The grave containing Elizabeth and John had been opened and Richard was finally laid to rest beside the two people he loved more than anyone else in the world. Andrew gave my hand a squeeze as the minister intoned the words 'earth to earth, ashes to ashes, dust to dust', but I was fine. My crying was all done. Now I was happy that we had carried out Richard's request.

I read the stone above the grave. *Elizabeth Nugent Wilde born July 30 1904, died March 10*

1966. Devoted Mother of John Edward born March 30 1932 who departed this world March 23 1942. May they rest in everlasting peace.

Richard has arranged for his epigram on the stone. It will read *Richard Colenso Wilde born December 20 1905, died April 29 2001. Loving Father of John Edward and faithful until death to Elizabeth.*

I like those words. They're simple but they have meaning. For me, knowing the whole story, they are perfect.

'You loved him, didn't you?' asked Andrew as we walked away from the cemetery down the quiet village road. In front of us were the iron railings and the fancy gates of Ballinbar House, Elizabeth's home, which I have recently been told is now mine. It is grand in every sense of the word. No wonder Richard teased Elizabeth about it. I have no idea yet what I'll do with it. But then all the consequences of Richard's death have left me stunned and almost unable to take them in.

'Sharon.' Andrew's voice broke into my thoughts again.

'Yes? What?'

'You loved him?'

'Yes.'

I did. Not like a father or a grandfather; I loved him like a lover. I could never tell anyone, they wouldn't understand, but what I felt for that old man was closer to true love than I have ever felt for any man. Being with him was heaven. Oh, I know he was old and sick and I was aware of how frail he was as well as anyone else, but listening to his story and writing down all his adventures, I could see beyond the shell of a man he had become. I loved the person inside. The kind, faithful and passionate man that he was.

'Yes, I loved him,' I repeated to Andrew, and took his arm as we strolled up the long drive towards the fine Georgian mansion ahead.

That last tape hasn't been transcribed. I let Andrew listen to it and he sat with his hands steepled under his chin until the end.

'Poor Richard,' he said. 'That explains a lot.'

'Should I write it down?'

He was quiet while he thought about it. 'It's up to you,' he said finally. 'If you transcribe it, then it could be open to the world and Richard's reputation would be destroyed. But if you keep it to yourself, then you will have to live with the knowledge for the rest of your life. As he did. Not the same, of course, but perhaps a heavy burden to bear, considering that he's your benefactor.'

'What would you do?'

No long consideration this time. 'I would get rid of it,' he said. 'The man was a hero. He doesn't deserve to be thought of as a murderer. Besides, what good would it do to anyone? Sergeant Darlington had the right idea.'

That was over a month ago now and I still haven't made up my mind.

Richard left me and Thomas so much. This house and the farm. The properties that are rented and the house and land in Ireland. According to Andrew, all that's left of the original will is an amount to the Phoenix family and a considerable sum of money to his old regimental charity. Before, he had made a list of bequests to lots of charities both here and abroad. They have lost out and I feel guilty about it. Andrew says I shouldn't.

I gave Andrew the duelling pistols. Maybe I should have saved them for Thomas, but I don't think he will ever appreciate them. He's a born farmer, my son. He'd see the pistols as nothing more than toys. Andrew was quite moved, I think, but he pretended to be casual. 'Nice to have something from the old boy, but you shouldn't have done it,' he said.

'I want to. I couldn't have managed without you.'

He nodded then and gave me a kiss on the cheek. He has been a brick.

I have the jewellery too. It was in a box in the bank and we went one morning to collect it. The rings, some of which I think were Mother's, are too small for me, but there are brooches and two diamond watches and of course the blue and silver necklace. I'm wearing it now. It lies flat and heavy round my neck and I touch it and remember how Richard bought it from the gypsy woman. I'll always wear it.

Jason has asked me to 'name the day' and Thomas keeps wondering when we're going to move into Jason's house. My son is spending more and more time over there and I don't mind that. Jason has been so good for him. But I can't, not yet. I had promised to marry him when I was free from looking after Richard and I am free now. The thing is that I am free, but different. I'm not sure what I want now.

Perhaps I'll go away for a while. Get my head together. What I would really like is a sea trip. On a big white boat where I could have a cabin to myself and only talk to my fellow passengers if I felt like it. It would stop at Gibraltar, for perhaps a day, and then on through the Mediterranean. I'd make sure I was on deck to see the Suez Canal and watch men walking beside camels and not thinking that there is anything strange in what they're doing.

And then we'll sail out into the hot brown Arabian Sea and I'll lean over the rails, letting the heavy spice-laden air waft over me. There'll be a blue haze on the horizon and if I screw up my eyes I'll just be able to make out a line of land.

India.

We'd like that, wouldn't we, Richard?

The publishers hope that this book has given you enjoyable reading. Large Print Books are especially designed to be as easy to see and hold as possible. If you wish a complete list of our books please ask at your local library or write directly to:

Magna Large Print Books
Magna House, Long Preston,
Skipton, North Yorkshire.
BD23 4ND

This Large Print Book for the partially sighted, who cannot read normal print, is published under the auspices of

THE ULVERSCROFT FOUNDATION